Jasper Mountain

Kathy Steffen

Enjoy the trip up Jasper Mountain

Kathy Steffen

Medallion Press, Inc.
Printed in USA

DEDICATION:

To Ted Groft, my father, who taught me to forge ahead and jump right into deep water without fear. He was always there to catch me in case I sank. He's been with me for every book's research and manages to keep his sense of humor, even when plunging down the shaft of a mile-deep mine or staying overnight in a haunted mining hospital.

Published 2008 by Medallion Press, Inc.

The MEDALLION PRESS LOGO
is a registered trademark of Medallion Press, Inc.

If you purchased this book without a cover, you should be aware that this book is stolen property. It was reported as "unsold and destroyed" to the publisher, and neither the author nor the publisher has received any payment from this "stripped book."

Copyright © 2008 by Kathy Steffen
Cover Illustration by Adam Mock

All rights reserved. No part of this book may be reproduced or transmitted in any form or by any electronic or mechanical means, including photocopying, recording, or by any information storage and retrieval system, without written permission of the publisher, except where permitted by law.

Names, characters, places, and incidents are the products of the author's imagination or are used fictionally. Any resemblance to actual events, locales, or persons, living or dead, is entirely coincidental.

Typeset in Baskerville
Printed in the United States of America

ISBN# 978-193383658-4

10 9 8 7 6 5 4 3 2 1
First Edition

ACKNOWLEDGMENTS:

I owe everything to my family for their continued enthusiasm, support, and belief in me and my writing: my husband, Rob; my mom and dad, Eva and Ted Groft; my sister Jane; and my dear friend Eddie.

I have visited wonderful places during the research and writing of this book. Special thanks to the museums in Cripple Creek and Colorado Springs, Colorado, in particular the Mollie Kathleen Gold Mine and the Western Museum of Mining and Industry.

My gratitude to my first reader and greatest supporter Jane Groft. Also many thanks to everyone who has critiqued and encouraged me along the way, especially Kevin Lamport and Lori Devoti. Thanks to the University of Wisconsin writing program: Marshall Cook, Christine DeSmet and special thanks to Laurel Yourke who inspired me to not give up on this story. Thanks to WisRWA Madison for their enthusiasm and wonderful, positive energy.

And a special thank you to everyone at Medallion Press for their talent, hard work, and dedication.

Previous accolades for *First, there is a River*:

"A supremely contemporary story in an authentically depicted historical setting. A novel that will ring true with women readers of all types."
—G. Miki Hayden, Edgar and Macavity winner, and author of *The Naked Writer*

8 ½ GRIFFINS
"Remarkable, haunting and utterly unforgettable. Emma captures the reader's heart; you desperately want her to find happiness and healing. You hope she'll find a way to love again even though she's suffered so much pain. Her inner strength is admirable, all she needed to escape her husband's cruelty was someone to lend his or her aid and support her during the healing process."
—Sharyn McGinty, www.inthelibraryreviews.net

"Set in 1900, Steffen's debut presents a captivating view of life aboard a riverboat a century ago . . ."
—*Publisher's Weekly*

★★★★½ STARS!
"The healing power of the river and the magic of love are explored in this emotionally fulfilling and beautifully written tale of good triumphing over evil. Readers will cheer for Emma."
—Barb Anderson, *Romantic Times Book Reviews*

"Kathy Steffen provides her audience with a powerful historical fiction that focuses on the lack of rights for women and the lack of protection for children. Emma is a fabulous as the only reason she remains with abuser Jared is their offspring, but once he sells them into child labor, she has no ties. The support cast including the river and the boat is strong as it brings out a bygone era. The romance is unnecessary though well written as *FIRST, THERE IS A RIVER* is foremost a character-driven deep historical tale."

—Harriet Klausner

Jasper Mountain

Kathy Steffen

Courage is resistance to fear and mastery of fear,
not the absence of fear.
—Mark Twain

Chapter 1

Tumbling Creek Ranch
Texas, 1872

It was amazing how fast hell descended on a man.

At first, the black puff in the sky didn't seem much of a threat. Surely, nothing to worry over, especially for a man used to living in the harsh conditions of the West. The next few days went by, and Jack thought the smudge looked to be a damned sight closer. As the week wore on, black and gray spread, growing to a cloud of threatening proportions. Jack's father, Jack "Buck" Buchanan Sr. ordered his people to dig trenches, haul water from the creek, soak buildings, and cut back brush. He convinced almost everyone at Tumbling Creek Ranch the fire heading their way was nothing more than a nuisance. They'd lived through brush fires before.

"Only fools and cowards run, and they'll get what they deserve." His gravelly voice thundered with his usual Buck-style certainty. The residents of the ranch looked up to Jack's father as if he were a god. Most chose to stay. So did Jack. For him there was no other possibility. Protecting the ranch and his family was his duty as a Buchanan.

On Saturday morning, Jack woke, rolled over, and blinked. He'd overslept, he could feel it. Grit filled his eyes, and they burned.

All his senses sharpened, and he bolted to his feet. Everything felt wrong. The air smelled like the remnants of a bonfire, and murky gloom filled his room instead of morning. Outside his window, a weak smear of light replaced the rising sun. He blinked. Again. His eyes felt as if someone had dumped sand in them.

Fighting panic, he threw on his clothes, crammed his feet into boots, and made his way down the hall to Buck's office. He tried not to run, but the ricochet of his heels against wood clacked faster and faster. Jack slammed through the door, skidded, and caught himself before he all-out fell. So much for not panicking.

His father stared out the window into murk, his arms crossed. Buck's calm made Jack feel a little silly for his entrance, but damn it, the fire was close. And coming closer.

Buck turned and glared at his son. "Decide to sleep in and miss morning chores? Your sister's already got half your work done."

"The fire's just about on us. Now will you give the order?" Jack asked.

Buck's weather-hardened face closed into a scowl, and his ice-blue eyes pierced, made even more intense by white eyebrows bushing over them. "What order? To run? That's what you suggest we oughta do, son? Run?"

"If we stay we'll die."

Buck stared a moment before he answered, and Jack watched his father take stock of him. By his expression, Jack knew he came up short. "Boy," Buck finally growled, "I thought I raised you better than this. Nothing makes a man run from his home. Nothing."

Frustration bloomed through Jack's panic, and he clamped onto it, grateful to feel something other than fear. "The ranch is as good as gone." He took a step closer. "These people trust you, Pa, they trust their lives to you, and that's probably the only thing we can salvage at this point. You owe them—"

"If I ran every time something threatened Tumbling Creek, we'd be living in a cave by now. We've faced fires before. We're ready."

"Not for this. This isn't just an inconvenient brush fire."

Buck returned to studying the murk outside his window. He stood, immovable, like one of the solitary boulders sitting in the desert, everyone wondering how such a huge and solid thing got there in the first place. No way to go around, because the stubborn old rock was not about to budge. Not now, not ever.

"Pa. Please."

His father's back expanded with a sigh. "I can't believe I've lived to see this." He whipped around to again look at his son, his expression stone. "Run, then, boy. If that's what you're made of. I'll stay and protect Tumbling Creek." He turned to stare out the window, and spoke to himself as if Jack wasn't even in the room. "My own son. A coward."

Jack stumbled back. If Buck pulled out his Colt and shot him through the chest, it wouldn't rip the way that word did, branding him with a deep, painful heat. Although he was an adult, Jack's father possessed the power to humiliate him as if he were a child. He'd grown up following in Buck's footsteps. Tall, strong, blond, with the same ice-blue eyes, folks said he was the image of Buck in his younger, row-kicking days. People constantly remarked they seemed like the same man, just two different generations.

Jack respected Buck and usually acquiesced to his father's knowledge and experience. It took a tough man to make the difficult decisions and successfully run a ranch. And with one word he had made it clear he didn't believe his son was that kind of man. Or any kind of man at all.

Coward.

"I hope to God you're right, and I'm the one misjudging." The tremor in Jack's voice only hinted at the burn spreading in his chest.

Warning still prickling over his skin, he left the main house and started his chores. The air thickened. His horse, Willow, fought against leaving the safety of her stall. He finally managed to saddle and coax her out, although along with smoke, her terror permeated the air. And that, Buck had reminded Jack over and over, was his biggest weakness. The way he allowed his empathy for others to get in the way of what he had to do. Maybe his foreboding about the fire was worry over the other residents. He sure hoped so.

Jack squinted and saw flames, now only a few miles away, leap over the first trench like a child playing hopscotch. The fire crackled with laughter, consuming everything in its path.

Never mind Buck. He'd face him later. If there was a later to face.

The ranch became a frantic mass of movement as every man, woman, and child at Tumbling Creek ignored Buck's earlier reassurance and piled the pieces of their lives onto wagons.

Jack rode to the house to get his sister and her two boys out, now.

Outside one of the smaller buildings on the homestead, Leno Santiago, a ranch hand, filled his wagon while his frightened family looked on.

"Leno, no! Leave everything! Just get the hell out of here!" Jack yelled and dismounted. But it was too late.

"Holy Mother of God." Leno dropped to his knees. His wife stood behind him, clutching her small daughter.

Jack spun around and felt a gentle shove of hot air. Then Satan blew his breath across the ranch. A howling rose, and despite the heat, ice spread through Jack.

Fire, moving faster than stampeding mustangs, engulfed the gate. Tumbling Creek's carved wood symbol—two horseshoes encircling a "TC"—had bridged the road proudly for decades. It burst into flame.

Jack grabbed a horse blanket from the wagon and threw it in the trough. "Get down! On the ground!" he shouted. Leno hesitated, grabbed his wife and daughter, and fell with them into the dirt. Every muscle strained as Jack lifted the weight of the soaked blanket and slung the shield over Leno and his family. He jumped into the trough.

Quiet wrapped around him, cradling him and cooling his skin. Then, a muffled roar. Light, brighter than a thousand suns.

I'm dead. It's not so bad.

Pain squeezed across his chest. Nope. Not dead. Alive. And running out of air.

Stay under.

He'd rather drown in a horse trough than breathe in fire. Jack didn't want his last moment on earth to be spent crying like a baby and praying for death. He would face death like a man. Well, as much of a man as he could be hiding in a trough.

Through the cool blanket of water, he thought he heard screaming. Livestock? Leno and his family? Buck or his sister, Jo? Jesus, her boys? Please, God, not the boys. If the drumming of his heart would calm a little, he might be able to tell.

Spots flashed in white light. The flashes gathered, darkened. Bees. Millions of bees. Buzzing.

Damn Buck, anyway. Stubborn old bastard. They'd seen the smoke days ago. Days wasted while Jack argued with his father to evacuate. Jack had been right. Not a coward. Right. Not that anyone would ever know. Charred corpses told no tales.

More bees. Buzzing. Louder. His chest was going to burst.

He gave up and shot out of the water, pulling in a searing gasp. And another. Breathing hurt, but much to Jack's surprise, it didn't kill him. Everything around him burned. Everything. Except it was snowing. Fire and snow?

Lord, have mercy, he'd gone insane.

Soaking, he pulled himself over the trough and rolled onto hot dirt. Flakes swirled around him in a meandering dance. He crawled through a blizzard of cinders, and lowering his head, he drew in air tangled with dirt, ash, and heat. The taste of death coated his mouth. Bitter. So goddamned bitter.

He raised his head and looked into Leno's face, peeking out from under the blanket. Thank you, God, Jack thought. Leno's eyes were riveted to the main house, now a crackling skeleton, and Jack followed his gaze to experience one final horror. A shadow lurched. Someone in the house.

"Jo!" he yelled, even though he thought his voice had burned clean out of his throat. Miraculously, he rose to his feet. His sister. He needed to get her, carry her out to safety. He ran to the porch, his arms over his face, shielding his eyes from heat and flames. The skin on his arms blistered and peeled back, raw muscle screaming. He'd never known such exquisite pain. Almost unbearable. Almost impossible. Almost beautiful in its purity.

The house gave a final crackling groan and collapsed. A fist of heat slammed into him, and Jack flew backward through the air.

Those bees. They finally stopped buzzing.

Tent City.

Except *city* was too good a name for this place. Flimsy cloth stretched over poles, rock, rubble, or whatever else was available. All that was left of Tumbling Creek Ranch, tents and people scuttling between them like desert bugs. They used any and everything remaining from the fire: horse blankets, curtains, sacks, clothing, sheets. Feed bags. The result, tattered rags among ruins, was no place for humans to live, but it was the only place they had.

The landscape seemed so strange to Jack, right out of a nightmare from which he was beginning to believe he'd never waken. Lumps of black rubble rotted where buildings had stood proudly for decades. Skeletal trees reached up, trying to touch the white scorching eye of the sun. The smoke was gone, but it had lingered for days, creeping along the ground, refusing to dissipate, hanging, clinging, and reminding them all at any moment hell might be unleashed again. However, here they stayed. There was nowhere else to go.

The schoolhouse was the only building the fire had left standing. Strangely, it went untouched. They used it to house the injured and anyone with young children. Jack and the other men buried the dead right away, at least what was left of the victims. Friends and family. His sister, Jo. Fourteen in all. Shallow graves were all they managed, so they piled rocks on top to insure scavengers wouldn't get their loved ones. The heap of stones sat just beyond Tent City, reminding them of exactly how much they'd lost.

Jack supposed he should count his blessings. Buck survived, too ornery and stubborn to die in a fire he insisted was not a problem. Jo's boys survived along with most of the ranch children. The schoolhouse. A miracle, most said. Jack figured the wind shifted, or something equally logical had happened. He didn't believe in miracles. Not anymore.

He clutched his book. *Tales* by Edgar Allan Poe. This book, a survivor as well, had been in Willow's saddlebag. In the aftermath of the fire, when he battled shock from pain and loss, when nothing seemed right, he looked up to see Willow cantering in his direction. The others were just as excited to see her. One of their loved ones, home, delivering the book Jo gave to Jack on his last birthday. Seeing Willow return and holding a precious piece of his previous life gave him all he'd needed to get going again, to step back into life and duty.

Except the burning in his chest wouldn't go away.

He flipped the book over in his hands. He couldn't open it. Although reading Poe's macabre tales would fit in this landscape, it didn't feel right, opening a book when his sister would never read another word. Together, they'd shared the love of stories. Other worlds. New ways of living and thinking.

Jo. His books. His life. The ranch. All ashes. All gone.

He shook his head. Pity was for the others, not him.

Jack slipped the book back in his bag, leaving it next to his lean-to, and his bandaged arm bumped the edge of its frame. Hurt reverberated up until his teeth rattled, but the pain throughout his arm was easier to bear than the smoldering lump of coal in his chest. No matter what he did, it just sat there, burning.

This whole mess, this disaster, was his fault. Not his father's. Buck acted, as always, like Buck. Stubborn and sure. Refusing to stand down to any threat. Jack had known it wasn't a typical brush fire. He'd sensed, down to his bones, the fire meant disaster coming their way. And still, he'd acquiesced.

The ranch destroyed, nothing left other than piles of rubble and ash, courtesy of Jack Buchanan, cowardly son.

Jesus, Mary, and Joseph, why hadn't he died with the others?

The weight in his chest expanded until breathing became a Herculean effort. He felt like one of the living dead he'd read about, bodies moving without heart, soul, or any semblance of a real life. But, there was such a huge, monstrous pain deep inside him. He supposed if he really were a body without a soul, he wouldn't feel anything. Even though he tried to do just that.

Damn it all, anyway.

"Jack, please, share our dinner?" Leno stirred a pot over a fire, which seemed to Jack to be sacrilege, starting a fire in such a place, but they all had to live, didn't they?

"No thanks, Leno."

Maria, Leno's wife, popped her head out of their tent. "Jack, please, come and eat with us. You haven't had a decent meal since the . . ." Her voice trailed off. Maria worried about him, Jack knew. For some reason she thought him a hero and told everyone about his bravery. She claimed he'd saved her family.

He was hiding in a trough when the house caught fire. Floating in tepid water when flames engulfed his sister. And thirteen others. Yep, hero. Bravery. That's what came to mind.

Well, hero or not, he needed to keep everyone's spirits whole. Almost a month had passed since the fire, and Jack spent all his time going from family to family, trying to put pieces of lives back together. Mostly he listened and reassured. To him, his words sounded empty. They all lost just about everything: possessions, clothing, and the ranch, every head of cattle, sheep, feed, storages, most of the buildings. They'd been able to salvage enough to erect Tent City, however their scant supply of food was almost gone. Right after the fire Buck headed to the nearest town for help. The once-powerful Buchanan family had next to nothing now, but he and Jack decided to spend what little they had left to help the survivors. Try to find them work, or passage out of this place.

A small puff of dust on the horizon grew, and Jack squinted. Buck? The puff solidified into a rider. No, two. They drew nearer, and Jack saw it was, indeed, his father with someone else. Despite everything, a touch of excitement flickered in him. Something was coming, and it had to be better than this mess.

The riders came closer. Jack recognized Buck's stature. The other man wore gray and rode on a gray mount. He blended in with the colorless landscape, and for a second Jack thought a ghost rode next to Buck. A portent of death. They neared, and Jack saw the man was solid. Sure. Not a creature of gray wisps but of tempered steel.

The riders slowed, and Jack experienced a bolt of recognition. Deep within, memory stirred. Aristocratic face, strong features. The gray at his temples and in his eyes reinforced the illusion of a man forged of metal. In the midst of all the colorless clothing and hair, his eyes pierced through Jack; intelligent, cold.

The riders stopped, dismounted. The gray man's eyes caught Jack's, and he found himself unable to look away.

Buck broke the connection. "Jack, this is my friend, Victor Creely."

The name resonated deep, under layers and layers of memory. Jack followed the tickle. Victor Creely. He and Buck grew up together, very poor, and were buddies and rivals both. The stories bubbled and surfaced from inside Jack's mind. Tales of impossibly plucky and brave boys, the most loyal of friends who, against all odds, would grow to become men of fortune. Victor Creely. His father's oldest and dearest friend. Victor went into mining to find his fortune. Buck into ranching.

Tough men. Men who fashioned the world to their will. Men who survived.

Victor stepped forward and extended his hand, his grip iron-solid, like his face, his gait. His eyes never left Jack's.

"Little Jack Buchanan Junior. I haven't seen you since you were a boy." The voice. Soft and quiet, and running beneath the velvet sound, something hard and unmovable. "Buck filled me in, told me all about you. I've been looking forward to meeting the man you've become."

Jack almost laughed. Some man. He wondered what Victor Creely was doing here, so far from his gold. "Don't you live in the Rockies?"

"When I wired, he came. Faster than I thought possible," Buck said.

"I heard your father needed me. I rode night and day. There are no limits when it comes to my oldest and dearest friend." Victor's words were warm, but a chill shuddered through Jack.

"Victor's the president of the mining operation at Jasper Mountain," Buck said. "Practically owns the whole goddamned town." A desperate hope edged into Buck's voice. "Jack, our lives, our ranch. It's not over, son."

Jack finally turned his attention to his father. Buck seemed so old and worn. Like a pair of spurs, dull and past the time of usefulness. Jack thought of everything the fire had destroyed—buildings, supplies, food, clothing, all the livestock. People.

"We've lost so much," Jack said, soft enough so as not to disturb the nearby dead.

"We can rebuild the ranch. Victor has a proposition for you."

"Actually, Jack, it appears you can help me as much as I can help you." Victor Creely smiled. "I hope you'll see our mutual benefit and accompany me to Jasper Mountain."

Despite the heat of the day, something in Victor's voice, or perhaps the cold calculation in the mining mogul's eyes, turned Jack's blood to ice.

Chapter 2

Nebraska, 1873
Eight Months Later

Milena Shabanov sank to her knees before the heap of rocks. She ran her hand along the surface. Rough texture scraped and bit at her palm.

This pile of rocks. Her father's grave.

Others in the settler party drew around to pay their last respects. The presence of these people did not comfort Milena. Sorrow grew, round and ever expanding. Pain settled heavy in her chest. Her heart hurt. "Baba," she whispered.

Dirt and sand blew across the barren land, pelting her like a thousand tiny cruelties. Her hair whipped about, helplessly caught in the wind. She was so very tired. Too young to carry the burden of such fatigue. Baba was all she'd had left of her life, her people. She wondered, should she follow him into the refuge of death? She'd followed him to this barbaric country, the two of them fleeing from Bukovyna, their homeland. She and her father had barely escaped from the *MoortYak*, the holocaust bringing about the End of All Things. They'd had no choice but to run, the last alive of their *kampania*—their people.

After a sea voyage that seemed to last a thousand years, Milena and Baba had landed in New York City. Forgotten children played in gutters and angry men roamed the streets. She found the crowded, violent endlessness of the city as monstrous as the ocean; still, she made the best of it. Watching her father go into the horrible factory, coming home every night with additional years of age etched into his face, had broken her heart. Yet she greeted him with a smile and a supper they shared, food enough for only one.

"You grow much too thin, *hoordo chiriklo*," Baba told her one night. "We must plump you up and find you a husband."

This, she did not want. Just as she did not want the nickname he'd begun using—tiny bird. He insisted she was, indeed, his *hoordo chiriklo*, one who brought joy and music into his drab existence. But Milena wanted to find a job, to work, to help her father. Baba refused to hear of it. He said he did not want her in the cruel grasp of the city. She wanted to answer back that she'd seen her family and friends murdered in their homes and fires lit to burn their memory to ashes, but she kept this reply within her. He did not need such a painful reminder.

Then her father heard a song of riches calling from the other side of this savage country. "In the West, gold tumbles down rivers and into the pockets of those brave enough to make the journey. And we are travelers." He spoke with hope for the first time since the *MoortYak*.

The two of them signed on to journey west with others. A party, the group called themselves, although Milena saw no dancing nor heard any laughing, not even when they stopped to camp at night. These people built bonfires to cook food and keep warm, yet they did not gather around the flames to make music, dance, or tell stories, like Romani would have done. She remembered her people traveling together in the old country, members of the same *kampania*, watching and caring for each other, making families for life. These American travelers stayed separate and looked out only for themselves.

The journey ended in this strange, foreign place. Now Baba's grave. Stones dug into her knees, yet she held tightly to the rocks of her father's final resting place. Tears slid down her cheeks. This barbaric country claimed those who were not strong enough, and Baba lay beneath stones, a sacrifice and testament to the harsh unforgiving nature of the land. Why should she think she would fare any better? Especially without him.

The party filed away, one by one, until she sat alone.

No. Not alone.

She glanced over her shoulder, and there he stood. The giant of a man whose wagon shadowed their own during the journey, sometimes far; too often, close. The man who'd been with Baba when he died. Claimed her father fell in the stream. Hit his head. Drowned.

To Milena the giant had no name; she thought of him as the Dim Swede. The blood of his ancestors was mixed, and as a result his Scandinavian appearance—light skin and hair—was muddied, with no color at all. He wore beige clothes and a brimmed brown hat. He was like a bedspread faded to a bland version of what it once was. Except for his eyes, a blue so bright it seemed a light burned behind them, reflecting everything and absorbing nothing.

He wore his need plainly. He wanted her.

He frightened her. The Dim Swede towered, the biggest man she'd ever seen. His hands were enormous. Before his scouting mission with her father he'd offered money, explaining he wanted to make Milena his wife. Baba disliked the Dim Swede, didn't trust him, and even though he wanted a husband for his daughter, he turned the Swede down gently and with great politeness. He did not want to make an enemy of this man, he whispered to Milena.

Looking up into the Dim Swede's cold, flat eyes, she knew her father had been right and perhaps his insight had cost him his life. The huge man smiled down on her with a hint of a smirk, holding his hat in his enormous hands. "My condolences, Laney." His voice rumbled deep from his mountainous body. The sky behind him blistered into sweeps of orange and yellow. She turned back and cast her eyes down to the rocks. The sun hovered at the horizon and finally dropped.

And still, he stayed.

Bonfires sprang into existence and speckled the dark silhouette of land.

And still, he stayed.

The heavy dark of night blanketed the desert, and Milena watched the moon, almost full, travel across the sky.

And still, he stayed.

Please, she prayed, make him leave. She closed her eyes, determined to keep on her knees, in this very spot, until she was alone. The heavy dark of night began to thin as morning approached.

She refused to turn to him. She would stay here forever if she must.

Chapter 3

Jasper Mountain Copper Mine
Territory of Colorado

"Come on, Jack. Ain't hardly no time for a trip to Fool's Paradise!" Digger's carefree voice ripped Jack from his gaze looking east. Dawn spilled pastel mists for miles over the flatland leading to the Front Range. Fingers of gold, pink, and lavender extended up Jasper Mountain, illuminating the town. A beautiful morning.

He'd been imagining himself and Willow thundering across the wide-open range. In actuality, his mud-crusted boots trudged along Gooseneck Road, leading him straight up the side of Jasper Mountain.

Digger sighed. "Jack! We's gonna be late if you don't get your sorry ass movin'!"

"Now, Dig," Tom Gallagher admonished in his good-natured Irish lilt, followed by a look to the sky and back again, "let Jackie be. He's smilin' and far away from here, which is a bit of a miracle in itself."

Jack hurried to catch up with his friends, the gravel road crunching beneath their boots.

"I got no hankerin' for Jory to plant his boot up my ass again," Digger replied.

"Spendin' a fair amount of time dwellin' on asses this mornin', lad."

"Can't help it." Digger shrugged and grinned. "I'm surrounded by 'em." He took off his hat, tossed it into the air, and wove around to get it to land on his head. It struck his shoulder and flipped into the dirt. He scooped it up, ran his hand through a mess of blond hair forever in need of a good haircut, and plopped the hat back on his head.

Jack blessed the good fortune that had brought him such friends, especially considering the circumstances under which their friendship had grown. The Jasper Mining Company. Hell on earth.

The headframe, a tower spearing up from the top of Jasper Mountain, marked the collar of the mine shaft. The structure looked for all the world like a gallows. Up there men didn't hang by the neck to meet their destiny; they were lowered to serve out a never-ending sentence deep within the mountain.

Victor claimed he had brought Jack to Jasper for help with the growing miner unrest. Trouble was, Jack suspected his position was supposed to be a way for Victor to find out what was going on with his workers. Trouble compounded, as trouble was in the habit of doing, because Jack agreed with the men and hated the mine more every day he worked it. Most of the miners couldn't leave, didn't possess the money or the way out of Jasper. Travel across the desert going one way, or over mountains going the other, most likely meant death.

The lure of gold held many here. Despite logic, men hoped to find a new, untapped vein of gold to make them rich beyond imagination. Rumors spread of a treasure in the mountain; the biggest gold strike of all hadn't yet been found.

In reality, Jasper meant backbreaking work and meager pay.

"Nothin' like lookin' forward to the day's work," Jack mumbled.

"Another day sunk in the muck of morosity, Jackie?" Tom asked.

Jack shrugged. Tom was obviously doing his best to cheer him up. With Tom's long nose, light mop of curls, and gentle disposition, he reminded Jack of a sheep. They'd lost the entire Tumbling Creek herd, five hundred head of sheep, in the fire. He sighed. There he was, thinking of the ranch again. Even eight months in Jasper's mine hadn't cured him of returning to that day, wishing he'd done everything differently.

Digger snorted. "I can't wait to git down in that mine. Best part of the whole damned day. Who needs sun and air? We got rock and mud."

Tom grinned. "And don't you be forgettin' all the copper and silver. And gold, boy-o. Never forget the gold."

"Yeah, I sure love to work my body to bleedin' so Victor Creely can line more gold in his pockets." Digger squinted and nodded to Jack. "No disrespect intended."

Jack wished he resented the president of Jasper Mining Company the way the other men did. He wanted to feel more a part of the brotherhood of miners; instead, he always peered in from the outside. He owed Victor everything. At the very least, after what Mr. Creely had done for his family, he owed the man his loyalty.

"You two ever think of dyin' down there?" Jack asked.

"Naw." Digger shook his head. "That'd be the easy way out. 'Sides, what would Death want with me? She's seen me work. I ain't worth the trouble."

Jack contemplated Digger. "So you think Death's a woman?"

Digger flashed his grin. "I sure hope so. A right purty one, too. Better be if she expects to git her arms around me."

Tom shook his head. "I can't afford to dance with Mistress Death, Jackie. Not with my girls in need of a proper dowry."

Jack shrugged. "No dowry's necessary in America. This is the new world, Tom; you aren't in Ireland anymore. Besides, you claim your daughters are beautiful. Beautiful women don't need money to get a husband."

Tom snorted and kicked at a pebble, and when he looked back up, Jack thought he saw a glimmer of moisture in Tom's eyes. "Beauties they are, Jackie, beauties all. The Gallagher girls. Lovely enough to bring a man to tears. Take after my Maggie. Oh boys, the dregs of men who come to call! I wouldn't offer my goats to them." He nodded. "Money's what I need to give me girls a decent future. Once I have enough, they can decide who is best suited to them." He paused and looked out over the Front Range. "The only thing worse than bein' a man with no money is a woman with no money. That, Jackie, is the most horrible fate of all."

"I'll take one-a them purty daughters off your hands!" Digger offered.

"And there's exactly what I mean." Tom gestured to Digger. "Dregs."

Digger frowned.

"But you're welcome to one of me goats, Dig. Any time."

Tom bolted up the road with Digger chasing close behind. Jack smiled to himself and continued his walk, glancing up at the headframe. His smile faded. The gallows waited.

Too soon they took their place in the cluster of miners waiting under the headframe for their turn on the platform.

"There she was, big as you please," came a mutter from behind. Jack didn't bother to turn around. He knew Jory's voice well enough.

Jack glanced over to Tom, who returned an irritated smirk.

Jory continued. "The Angel of Darkness. She passed us by, and her breath blew across my privates, cold as winter." Jory slurred in his thick Cornish accent and stumbled into Jack's back. "I do pardon myself; I should know better than to bump Creely's pup."

The man was a drunk. And an idiot. And Jack's boss. Jack ignored the insult. A fight with Jory would do no good, much as he'd like to pound some sober back into the man.

"Gobshite," Tom said under his breath. "He's the type what gives the Cornish a bad name." His voice rose. "Hey, quit shovin', boy-os!"

Jory's push had almost caused Jack to stumble over Mouse, the youngest miner in their crew. The boy, with his round face and huge eyes, might look like a dirty, sad little elf, but he wore adult clothes, work boots, and often smoked a pipe. He imitated a grown man's walk, so he swaggered. A kid like him should be playing pranks and pestering schoolgirls, not smoking a pipe and waiting in line to be lowered into the earth. Mouse was deaf and therefore immune to Jory's constant babbling about ghosts wandering in the mine, but the other men wore fear on their faces along with dirt and were resigned to both.

Jack thought it silly, to be afraid of ghosts. There were real enough problems to face. Sometimes, deep under the layers of the mine, a lantern blinked out. Every so often, several of the candles surrendered their struggle against the dark and flickered out, one, two, three. All in a row.

One. Two. Three.

The miners believed Death roamed the tunnels and searched for a man to take when the others weren't looking. The candles snuffed out when the Angel of Darkness brushed past. Most miners employed at the Jasper Mining Company were men carrying a mantle of superstition passed down through generations, from the old countries.

Jack didn't believe in the fantasy of such foolishness. He knew death intimately, and it wasn't some beautiful and mysterious ghost moving about in stealth, taking life in a gentle moment. No, death was fast and harsh. Cruel. And hot.

He took his place on the platform. Miners loaded on and wood trembled under their weight. They anticipated the drop into the earth, the only sound heard, the hollow shush of men shuffling. No one made eye contact. Even Tom and Digger kept quiet.

Men with no heart, no soul. No life. And Jack was slipping into their world. One of the walking dead.

The platform descended and life disappeared, replaced by a dropping sensation followed by rushing black. The weight of tons of rock and earth bore down, closing in on him.

This must be what it's like when you're dead.

When Jack first came to Jasper Mine, he didn't mind sinking down in the mountain. Cradled in dark, the rich smell of dirt surrounding him, clinging to the air like clods to a shovel. Just like a grave. No less than what he deserved. He reminded himself he worked in the mine for his family. The boys. Buck. The ranch. Remembering helped him face the moment when the waiting earth swallowed him into a netherworld of dark heat and torturous work that pushed a man to the edge of his soul.

When Victor Creely laid out his plan for Jack, he briefly touched upon the need for Jack to spend time with the miners, wearing their boots, working with their tools, digging in their world. Getting to understand them and win their trust. Victor presented Jack's role to him as a liaison, a bridge between the miners and officers.

Jack had been in Jasper long enough to see that the miners

languished in a pit, and the men needed much more than a bridge to nowhere to ease their complaints. He didn't blame them one bit. Pay was pitiful. The work, dangerous. Simply put, working in Jasper Mine was a living hell.

On the other hand, he owed an enormous debt to Victor. The man had swooped in and saved his ranch and the families. They were rebuilding, thanks to Victor Creely's money.

Victor assured Jack he'd only have to work down in the mine for a relatively small amount of time. Jack had worked in the mountain for about eight months now. Despite how much Jack hated working underground, he was in the right place. He belonged down here. He deserved every minute of Jasper Mine.

The platform jolted to a halt, the miners' bodies so packed together they held each other from falling. They stepped into their world of dark and rock, hanging their lunch pails on high nails to keep the rats from getting their food. Passing a flame, they lit the candles on their hats, or hardboils, as the miners called them. Dipped repeatedly in boiling glue, layer after layer, the hats dried rigid enough to protect a head against anything, even a rock. An ingenious process, Jack thought. One of many devised to keep the earth from exacting retribution on man for his invasion.

"See you boy-os up top." Tom waved and walked into the north end of the tunnel, whistling as he went. Happy, despite being underground. He had a family and love to return to someday. A thing so precious, yet Jack knew, so fragile.

Tom shrunk until he became no more than a flickering light, and then black swallowed that, too, as if Tom had never existed.

Digger sighed. "Come on, Jack. We got to get this rock blowed up by sundown."

Jack lifted a huge sledgehammer to his shoulder, hunched over like a troll, and scuttled to catch up with Digger. The two men stopped when they came to the end of the tunnel and faced the rock wall they would soon destroy. Good enough for the damn thing. Jack actually enjoyed blowing away bits of the place. He liked to see another chunk of this world crumble away and disintegrate.

"A man just doesn't belong under the ground, Dig. Leastways, not till he's dead."

Digger's face took on a serious expression. "What in blue blazes has got you thinkin' so much about death? Jesus, Jack, you need a drink worse than me this mornin'. You're in a awful poorly mood."

Jack shrugged the huge hammer from his shoulder and onto the ground, thinking about the night before. He'd finally opened his book, begun reading again. He'd missed it so much. He needed the chance to get away, go somewhere else, even to the dark places Poe took him. "I guess I'd better stop reading Edgar Allan Poe before I go to bed. Messin' with my good and kindly nature."

Digger's seriousness melted into confusion.

"He's an author. A writer," Jack explained. "He writes stories about ghosts and death and such."

"Ha!" Digger said. "I knew there was a good reason I never learnt to read. Who needs such a thing? Edgar Allan Pope. Jesus." He held a drill bit to the wall.

Silently saying a prayer his aim would hold true, Jack lifted the hammer. A shock ground down his neck and back, nothing to compare to the bolts about to reverberate through him once he started swinging the damn thing and it hit. He went home every day, his body rracked with a thousand blows, as if he'd wandered into a violent crowd and been beaten and trampled.

And that, he figured, was good enough for him.

The Dim Swede had a name after all. Rolf.

Three days after her father's death, and here she was, sitting beside the man. She'd been determined to stay at Baba's gravesite, but in the morning when the party left, Rolf lifted her and carried her back to the camp, tossing her into his wagon like she was a sack of feed. He claimed her then, for his own. When she protested, the men of the party informed her it was Rolf's right, the law of the land. The women of the party told her she was lucky to have so strong and able a man take her into his care.

She tried to run. Rolf came after her, tied her down inside the wagon while they traveled, then to its wheel for the night, explaining she'd die out in the middle of nowhere. She realized the uselessness of protest and calmed, planning her escape. They would not be in the middle of nowhere forever.

The next day she traveled obediently by his side during daylight and watched while he made camp at sunset. After he built a fire, he sat beside Milena and ran his hand up her back, clenching her neck with his huge fist. He sighed deep with contentment. She kept the shudder running through her trapped inside, and looked to the distant lights floating in the sky. What were they, she wondered as she watched the cluster of lights hovering in the air. Were they faeries or mountain spirits?

"Tonight's our night, Laney," Rolf said, chuckling. She did not like the sound of his announcement. "Sorry you forced me to keep you tied up to the wheel last night. You've come to your senses now, I guess."

"What are they, the lights?" she asked.

"Jasper Mountain. There's a town up there. Minin' town."

Hope raced through her. Had they arrived, finally? California? "This is the Land of Gold?"

Rolf smiled like she was a child who danced well and amused him. "Nope. Copper mine, some silver, too. Most of the gold loads been tapped out for a while, but folks think there's still treasure somewhere up there. We'll go through the town on our way over the mountains. That's where we'll get new supplies before the pass and you and I kin get hitched. I'll make an honest woman out of you right up there, in Jasper."

Milena's heart quickened. Finally, escape was possible. A town.

"Come on, Laney. Let's git inside." He practically dragged her into his tent.

"No, Rolf. This is not possible." Milena scrambled to the rear of his tent and raised her hand, desperate to stop the advances of the charging beast. The dark lust in his face sharpened to anger. She continued. "It is my time," she lied. "I am *marime*. You must not touch me."

His anger softened to confusion. "Stop all your foreign babblin'." He grabbed her arm. "You're so purty. I know we should wait, but I jest cain't. My intentions is honorable, Laney. We'll be married in a few days anyways."

How could she make him understand? "I bleed." Her face flushed with her lie and the shame of that which should never be mentioned, but this was the only idea she had to stop him. He dropped his hand from her arm and anger returned to his face. His eyes narrowed.

"Who hurt you? George? When I weren't lookin'?"

"No, no," she answered. "It is my, my . . ." She searched for words she did not possess. "I do not know your word for this. To my people I am *marime*. You must not touch me." Still, no understanding on his face. "It is my time with the phase of the moon." He still appeared confused. "Rolf, this comes when there is no child. My cycle."

Jasper Mountain

"Oh! Woman difficulties," he said, realization lighting his bland face. "Why didn't you jest say so?" He grabbed her, pulled her to him, and flopped down. Wrapped in his arms, she had no choice but to fall over with him. For one horrified moment, she thought he would take her anyway. He nuzzled her neck and wedged in close to her. She did not understand his barbaric ways. A Romani man would not touch a woman when she was *marime*, not even come near. This man, he always touched, always grabbed, as if brute force could hold her to him.

His body settled in along her back, and he threw a leg over her. He was a human vise, clamping her to him. He kissed her behind her ear, and she shuddered.

"You cold, Laney?" He pulled his blanket over them and tucked her into him. "I'd like to warm you up, good and proper. This'll have to do for now." His voice dropped, quieter with each word.

Milena listened to the even sound of his slumber and held to her vision of Jasper Mountain. Her only hope. Her salvation.

Veins of copper shot though rock and glittered in the lamplight. Soon, this wall would be blown to bits, courtesy of Jack Buchanan and his marvelous gunpowder tricks. He brushed powder from the front of his coveralls. Wouldn't do to be part of the light show.

After he and Digger spent their shift drilling small, tube-sized holes, Digger went up top with the rest of the team and Jack worked alone, packing the holes with gunpowder and wicks. Jory had led the men up and out to safety, and Jack figured the night-shift workers waited up top for the explosion to happen. Here, underground, the night never ended, and he had no idea what time it might be. Truth to tell, he really didn't care. He just needed to get this blast done before morning.

Now the final step. Jack trimmed the first wick. Then the second. He trimmed the next fuse.

Coward.

He considered cutting the final fuse a bit short, and he wondered if he'd beat the explosion out of the tunnel. Maybe he could. Maybe not.

"Ahhh, Christ Almighty, another day down in this mine and I won't be any fun at all. I got to stop feeling so damned sorry for myself," he said to the rock wall. "Look at you. You don't pity yourself at all, do you? And I'm about to blow you into tarnation. Damn it!" he said, realizing he needed to recheck the charges. He'd lost count of the lengths. "Jesus, look at me. Distracting myself by talkin' to a wall."

He concentrated on trimming the remaining fuses to the perfect lengths. A breeze tickled the back of Jack's neck. He whirled around and fell on his butt, but he recovered quickly, looking into the dark. No one was there.

He knew he was alone, yet he sensed someone watching. Jory had been coherent enough through the reek of whiskey to order all the men back to the surface before Jack started the final moments of the job. So, who else could possibly be down here?

"Jo?" he called out his sister's name and grimaced. "Now, what the hell made me say such a thing?" He was spooking himself was all. He returned his attention to the wall and fuses. Damn, this blast was going to be good. Victor Creely and his New York investors would get a payload from this one, he was sure.

As always, he did one final check. Once he was up top, he would listen and track the explosions as they shook the mountain. Even though it was the shift boss's job, Jory couldn't count sober, let alone during his current and most constant state. It wasn't unusual for miners to lose their lives, digging for ore with an unignited tube hiding in the rubble.

"No one'll die from my work," Jack vowed to the wall before him. Enough shadows already lurked deep inside. Enough people were dead because of him.

A hand grabbed his shoulder.

He jumped and banged his head on the cave ceiling.

"Sorry, Jack. I knew I'd scare you." Digger's voice, sheepish, broke through the dark.

"I'm not scared," he barked. "What the hell do you think you're doing?" Digger should know better than to disturb a man during the final check. His place was waiting up top with the rest of Jack's group.

"Good thing you're so persnickety about checking this stuff before you light it. We got to hold the blast."

Dread bubbled up. "Why?"

"Tom Gallagher's missing. He ain't up top; he ain't nowheres."

Jack and Digger's candles blinked out.

Chapter 4

Little by little Milena moved away, always one small move so not to wake the lumbering beast. First, she pulled her arm to her side, and waited until his breathing returned to even. Next, she pulled her hair out from under his head. Again, she waited.

Rolf snorted and rolled onto his back. She sat up. His mouth dropped open and a horrible rattling began. She crawled out of the tent on her hands and knees, each movement painstakingly cautious. Finally outside, fresh night air greeted her as she stood. She filled her lungs and tasted freedom.

The moon watched, full and close. Light spilled over the slumbering camp, painting the landscape in shades of gray. She dare not stop for any supplies or even a horse. She crept past the tents of the party, filled with those who did not help her but leeringly informed her of the law of the land. Informed her she was lucky.

Lucky.

Once she was sure they wouldn't hear, Milena broke into a run and her feet pounded the ground, beating a cadence to jolt up her legs and hammer through her chest. Or perhaps it was an echo of fear. She ran. Fast. Her heart thundered even faster.

When he woke to discover her missing, nothing would stop Rolf from coming after her. She yanked her skirts up and ran faster, gulping in air thick with grit. She ran endlessly, for hours it seemed. Her breath came with more difficulty. Her legs ached, but she refused to stop. She would have no other chance to escape him. Running was her only hope.

The mountain named Jasper rose ahead. A sacred place. The Ancient One called her now, the promise and magic of the mountain pulling her. What she left behind urged her forward. She ran, propelled by fear and anger at them all. The Dim Swede. The party. Perhaps, even Baba. And most certainly, at herself. She'd been as strong as she could, and still it wasn't enough to survive on her own terms. So now she ran, finally, on her own terms.

Her head hit the ground before she knew she fell. Her jaw stung with the impact. She stayed for a moment facedown in surrender. Despite her precautions, somehow, he'd still heard and followed. She rolled over to face him.

A full moon hung heavy in the sky, its glow softened by a veil of blowing earth. Nothing else. No one else. Relieved and confused, Milena sat up. Someone had stopped her. Yet, she was alone.

Perhaps not, she thought.

"*Shuv'hani?*" she whispered against the howl of the wind, calling upon the soul of her grandmother who in life was a mystic wise woman. The shroud between the realities did not hinder a *shuv'hani*, and Milena sensed her grandmother watching over her from the Otherworld. Or was her feeling just hope, longing?

"*Shuv'hani?*" Milena asked again. "Help me. Please. I am lost." She gasped in and heard her own sob. No. She brushed gritty tears from her face.

Milena.

She leapt to her feet and scanned the landscape. A vast, solid darkness loomed like a fortress before her, the start of the mountain range.

Milena.

She regarded the path behind her, the way back, where she'd left the small party of settlers, along with an endless land of dust and dead branches. Her father's grave. And the Dim Swede. There was nothing there for her.

She turned her back on her past for good. Moonlight poured over the mountains, rimming them in shades of silver. Sitting high above the range, Jasper Mountain towered over the land, a giant that broke through the ground to reach for the heavens. The Ancient One watched her. Called her.

Even at this late hour, lamps of the town glittered like jewels in the sky. A *maje*, a vision. Civilization. A place where she could survive. She closed her eyes and bent her head in prayer. *"Mi Duvvel opral, dik oprè mande."* My God above, look down upon me.

Milena opened her eyes and ran toward the range with her spoken prayer and a reminder of her strength.

After all, she had a mountain to climb.

Hours passed, and although she trembled with exhaustion, she did not stop. Finally, she met the start of the mountain range, and every step up meant one more away from him. She left the safety of the trail behind, determined he not have a chance to find her. She traveled on instinct. Faith. The higher she climbed, the cooler the night. Fresh air, finally devoid of sand and dust, blew around her. She filled her lungs. Freedom tasted sweet.

A boulder the size of a house thrust up from the land with no way around it. Milena felt around in the dark until she found places to hold, and she hoisted herself up. Once she crested the huge rock, she scrambled on her hands and knees.

A meadow stretched before her, silver grass and trees, all still.

All silent. A small lake reflected moonlight. Ancient ones from the Otherworld walked here. They swirled, watching her, curious to be interrupted. She bowed her head and whispered a request for permission to touch such sacred ground. The moonlight brushed across the land, claiming it for her own. The Pass of the Moon. Milena felt the magic of almost touching the heavens from this great height. The Moon comforted her, a faithful and constant friend who kept watch over her on this journey.

She rose to her feet, lifted her shawl above her head, and spun around, gathering the Old Magic to her. She hugged her shawl back around her shoulders and walked to the border of the sacred place. A great void whispered to her from the blackness beyond.

She tossed her hair back and lifted her face, listening with more than her ears. Spirits rustled though the twisted trees guarding the pass, and they brought with them a taste of the *tacho Romano drom*—the true Romani path.

"*Shuv'hani*? Please. Guide me." Holding her hands out over the dark void, palms up in asking, she requested for the Old Magic to mend her broken heart and heal her soul. She promised to stay true to her path.

A sound of whispering wove with the wind and sang out, its harmony laced with the strength of wisdom. The song rushed up the mountain and blew over her. She resonated like the string of a mandolin with the music of the ancients.

The voices sang past her and up, up. Up to Jasper. On this night of answered prayer, her path was clear, her courage, once again whole.

She stood upon the edge of rock and lifted her shawl above her head. The wind whipped it about, and she let it go. The shawl sailed in the moonlight, across the black void, twisting and flying like a ghost on the wind.

Then it was gone.

"How far down are we planning to go?" Digger asked.

"This is the last tunnel. I want to be sure," Jack answered. Despite reason telling him Tom would never be down in the abandoned section, Jack was determined to search every inch. He owed that much to Tom, and more.

The mine was divided into two sections, working tunnels and the abandoned ones below. Teams searched the upper region of the mine while Jory had ordered Jack and Digger to search the lower passages. They were scheduled to be filled in next month, just like the first ones were years ago. The process of filling in abandoned tunnels was imperative to stabilize the mine, otherwise, a collapse might happen; a scenario no one wanted.

Jack crawled through the bent passageway until he reached the stope, a jagged cave at the spot where miners extracted the ore. He slid over the edge, his legs dangling. Holding his lantern high, he jumped, landed on his heels, and fell on his butt. Candle wax splashed over his hand.

"Ouch! Goddamn it!"

At least the light didn't go out. He lifted his lantern and stared into a gaping hole. A tunnel that shouldn't be there. Damned if he didn't feel like he looked down the huge maw of a creature patiently waiting for its next feeding. Light illuminated only a few feet in. Shadows wavered and whispers fluttered out and past him, as if ghosts spoke secrets in the dark. Empty tunnels played all kinds of tricks on a man's mind.

Digger dropped beside him. "Ain't no way he'd be down here. Even if he did get hurt and was mixed up and crazy in his head. 'Sides, how could he get down this far? I'm in my prime of health, and I barely made it." He eyed the passage warily. "Hey, Jack? Weren't this tunnel supposed to be filled by now?"

"Yeah, that's what I was thinking. Dig, listen. You go back up. I'll search this one, just to be sure."

Digger shook his head. "Lead on. We come this far together."

"You wouldn't be so far down here if you chose your friends with bit more discretion," Jack said, half teasing, half meaning it. Jory always gave Jack the dirty work.

"Well, you got one thing right. I'm the one to pick who I share my whiskey with. No one else. Besides," Digger continued, "whoever said I was your friend?" In the murky glimmer of candlelight, his grin flashed white in his dirt-darkened face.

Jack snickered and crawled up and into the slanted space, thankful for Digger's humor and praying he'd get to share a laugh with Tom again. Once the passage opened up, Jack reverted to his hunched-over miner's walk. He kept the lantern raised high.

"Tom!" Digger called. "Tom!"

A litany of airy echoes reverberated down the tunnel. "Tom! Tom! Tom!"

No wonder miners believed the tunnels were haunted. Not only did they twist through the dark and stretch on, seemingly endless, but men had died down here. Since Jack began working at the mine eight months ago, seven men had lost their lives deep within the mountain. Most not in easy ways. Panic for Tom rose. Jack pushed it down. Keeping his head would serve Tom best.

He got an uneasy feeling on the back of his neck again.

"Hey, Jack, stop."

He hunched over to the side, his back against the rock wall rather than exposed to the endless black and whatever else might be down here.

"Ain't this the tunnel where Eli got crushed?" Digger asked in hushed tones.

One of the worst things Jack had ever seen, and it happened when he'd been mining for only a week. An ore car broke loose, lost control, and smashed into the unlucky miner in its path, partially severing his leg. Jack did his best to stop the bleeding. They tried to get Eli up top, but he died on the floor of Tunnel Number Six.

Jack still smelled the coppery richness of lifeblood mixing with dust. Or was it just the stench of the mine? God, he hated this place. "Yeah, Dig, I think you're right."

Digger bowed his head and shut his eyes. "Lord, have mercy on your soul, Eli. Help us find Tom. Amen," he whispered.

"Amen," Jack said, resuming his troll-walk.

"Tom! Tom!" Jack called, feeling the emptiness as Tom's name repeated back at him in an eerie rendition of his own voice. He hoped he'd find the man alive and well or, at least, not hurt too badly. He sure didn't want to send word back to Nebraska of anything else.

The air down here felt colder, darker. Dank. Dead. Shadows danced at the edge of vision. He willed himself to relax. They were only shadows, images cast by flickering lamplight. Nothing more. This tunnel wasn't going to get the best of Jack Buchanan. He hoped.

The main shaft couldn't be too much farther ahead. A cold breeze blew past. Their lanterns and hat candles all blinked out. Jack's throat closed.

"Jack?"

"Hang on, I got a Lucifer." Using the term sent a fresh set of chills through him. "I mean match." Setting his lantern down, Jack fumbled in his pockets with trembling hands and peered into dark that was more than dark; a complete absence of light. A void.

When he struck the match, relief sprang into existence along with glowing light. He relit his lantern, took off his hat, lit the candle, and passed it to Digger. Jack's hands clutched the rim of his hardboil.

Digger lit his lantern. "You think that mighta been Eli? Or Tom?"

"That's foolishness, Dig."

"Is it? Foolish as a cold gust of wind this deep in the earth?" He handed the candle back to Jack, who fastened it back to his hat.

"Hang on, Dig. I think we're just about to the main shaft."

When they arrived there, sadness replaced Jack's moment of relief. These lower tunnels were probably their only hope, and they'd searched every one.

Tom Gallagher was still missing without a trace.

"Where is everybody?" Jack asked the small handful of men gathered at the entrance to the mine. At the time Jack and Digger descended, men were busily scouring every inch of mining property, searching for Tom. Mining operations were on hold and the night shift had joined in the search. Now only a few miners remained, huddled in a pool of lantern light by the gate.

"Creely called off the search. Work's starting up again with the day shift. Men're off catching a few hours of sleep," one of the miners answered.

"What?" Jack asked, incredulous. Frustration tied a knot deep in his guts.

"He said if you and Dig didn't find him, he weren't nowhere in the v'cinity. He figures Tom prob'ly just up and left," the man answered. "We looked ever'where, Jack, a coupla times."

"Then we look again," Jack said. "There's got to be places we missed."

"Creely says no. I'm surprised he let us go this far."

The knot of frustration catapulted into anger and launched Jack in the direction of the mine office. He knew Victor was there; the man arrived at his office no later than four in the morning on a regular workday, and this day was far from regular. Jack's boots thunked against timber as he strode across the porch. He hesitated briefly when he thought of everything he owed the man on the other side of the door. Despite his debt to Victor, a man was missing. A good and decent man. Jack would do everything in his power to find Tom. He opened the door without knocking. Victor looked up, along with Sheriff Cain. The two men had been deeply engrossed in conversation.

Cain appeared startled, but not Victor Creely. Nothing ever ruffled the mine president's smooth exterior. Victor was impeccable in his suit, as always, not a wrinkle or a speck of dirt anywhere, a neat trick in a town made of dust.

Jack tried to sound calm, but his anger broke through. "What the hell is going on? You called off the search?"

"Somethin' reeks like a dead skunk," the sheriff said, his craggy features twisting into a smirk. "You need a bath, Junior."

"Jack, there is no need for a show of emotion," Victor said, his voice smooth and cold, like polished steel. "Nothing was called off. The search has been conducted and completed. Twice, to be sure. I don't want any accidents or injuries at the mine any more than you do. Gallagher is simply not here."

"We figure he up and left," Sheriff Cain said.

Jack pushed his anger back down into a ball. "I'm not surprised you'd come to that conclusion, Sheriff. You always take the easy road."

Cain growled and reached for his gun.

Victor stopped the sheriff with a hand to his shoulder. "The men hunted for hours. There is no sign of Gallagher."

"He wouldn't just go, especially without his pay," Jack insisted.

Victor shrugged. "These men are not intellectual giants. Such forward thinking might not cross his mind. The miners are anything but reliable. Who's to say? He has no family here, no ties to Jasper."

"He might have got stuck in a whore," Cain said and laughed.

"I know Tom Gallagher," Jack said, ignoring Cain's crude remark. "He wouldn't just up and leave. His family back in Nebraska depends on him to send money every month. Something happened. Someone must have found something, seen something. Even the littlest clue." He looked at Cain. "You bother to ask anyone any questions, Sheriff, or check to see if his belongings are gone? Or is that too much effort?"

"You want to take over, Junior? You go right ahead, but I'll warn you, you need a set of knackers to do this job. From what I see, you don't got none of those."

"Gentlemen, please," Victor said, his voice silken yet leaving no room for argument. "I can't hold operations any longer. We lose money every minute. Everyone will keep an eye out for him. My guess is he's sleeping off a drunk somewhere. He is Irish, isn't he?"

"He's no drunk, Victor. He's one of the finest, most responsible men I've ever met."

"Regardless, we've wasted more than enough time. Try scouring the saloon. Everyone knows he's missing; word is spreading through town." Victor smiled a smile that didn't reach his eyes. "Believe me, Jack. I have everyone's best interests at heart."

"Speaking of best interests, did you realize Tunnel Six hasn't been filled in yet?" Jack asked. Cain's eyes shifted to Victor, and

Jack experienced a small surge of courage. "Any other tunnels open that shouldn't be, Mr. Creely?"

Victor's eyes hardened. "Six is scheduled for fill in with the other three above it."

"It's been removed from the tunnel map."

"You are obviously mistaken." Victor's smooth voice held the cutting edge of a razor blade. "Go home and get some rest. You're off for the day. There's no more to be done."

"I don't need to take time off—"

"You do. You're exhausted and overwrought."

"Mr. Creely, I—"

"*Two* days, Jack." Victor's hand still held to Cain's shoulder. The sheriff's eyes glinted with victory. Jack wanted to punch the expression right off his face. He locked eyes with Victor, and the mine president's gaze bored through Jack like a drill bit. Again, the deadly smile flashed. "Don't force me to insist on three days."

Jack relaxed his stance, but didn't look down. "Are you sure the entire mine's been searched?"

Victor sighed. "Jory assures me it has."

"And that's exactly what I'm trying to tell you," Jack countered. "He didn't even know about Tunnel Six. Dig and I stumbled on it. If this search was haphazard as—" Jack clamped his mouth shut.

"Haphazard as what?" Victor's words were even, but skin stretched taut on his face as he held something back. Like anger. "Please, Jack, finish your thought."

"I can't believe the way I've seen men die down there. This isn't a search; it's a travesty. Doing things the right way wouldn't take a whole lot more time and effort."

"Jack. Go home."

"Mr. Creely—"

"The search is concluded. Tom Gallagher is derelict, nothing more. I've half a mind to dock his pay for the money we've lost."

"Sir—"

"Jack. Go. And that makes three days off for you. Don't push me. The next step is I send you home. For good."

The three men stood frozen in the room; even the clock's ticking seemed to slow.

Three days' suspension. Like an errant schoolboy. As much as he hated working the mine, he needed most of his pay just to survive. Never mind his family's debt to Victor Creely. At this rate, by his calculation, he'd be working in Jasper Mountain the rest of his life. He had no doubt Victor planned it that way. Jack was stuck like the rest of the men. Walking away or getting himself fired meant losing the ranch. Again.

He was wasting his time. He swung around and left.

Call it what it is, Buchanan. Retreat.

He stepped out onto the porch. Behind him, the door *whomped* shut. With a final glance at the headframe of the mine shaft, he headed for home.

"I'll find you, Tom. Figure out what happened. I promise." He headed down the mountain. Time to search the town, ask questions. If Tom wasn't in the mine, where was he? He'd headed up top with the rest of the group. How did he disappear? What had happened to him? Men didn't simply vanish into thin air.

Jack remembered watching Tom and his light diminish to nothing in the tunnel. He sure hoped that wasn't the last he'd see of his friend.

He broke into a run down the mountainside. Finally, his house came into view. His big hound, Duke, ran off the porch, barking. Jack flung his hardboil and it sailed away, Duke chasing after it. The dog retrieved the hat and bounded to Jack. He couldn't lose this part of his life, no matter how much he wanted to. He ruffled Duke's head.

"Good dog. Slobbered all over this thing. Good enough for it, I guess."

Jack belonged to the privileged set; he lived in a house allotted for an officer of the company. He'd wanted to live at the Nugget Hotel, a dorm for miners. Victor wouldn't hear of it. No son of Buck Buchanan was going to live like a peasant. Never mind the house's rent came out of his wages and back into Victor's pockets like just about everything else in town. He stepped across the porch and saw a folded sheet of paper stuck in the slats of the porch swing.

"Somebody come by to visit?" he asked Duke, who stopped to dig behind his ear with his hind leg. At the sound of his master's voice, Duke trotted up beside Jack. "You're a terrible watchdog, you know that?" Jack asked, grabbing the note. Duke hopped up on the porch and rolled over on his back. Jack stooped to rub the dog's belly, and the letter flopped open in his hand. In a rough, black scrawl, words screamed across the paper:

"LEVE JASPER MINE NOW"

Below the demand, a crude sketch of a coffin scratched across the paper. Jack stood, a shiver curling up his spine.

Duke leapt to his feet and stared at Jack, his brown eyes questioning.

"Yep, I got a few questions of my own, fella. Like who left this? And where the hell is Tom?" He wondered if the note was a warning or a threat. "I sure wish you could talk, buddy." Jack shrugged. "Ah, well. Not the first time I've danced with the thought of death today." Hopefully, like Digger believed, Death was a lady.

Jack had every intention of standing her up.

Chapter 5

Mouse followed the men. The miners bubbled up from the mine after their work and flowed to the same place every day, taking the same path, stepping the same steps. This was as sure as a sermon on Sunday.

Mouse was the littlest miner, and they didn't invite him to tag along; still, he knew where they were going. He followed the group heading for the bar. The men didn't notice Mouse. He was quiet and small and this was his special gift. Da used to worry about his size, worried that days without food might be stunting his growth. He said Mouse should be bigger. Stronger. Able. But then Mouse got hired alongside Da to work in the mine just because of his smallness. That was his next-to-best day. His very best day was the first time they went down in the tunnels, and the shift boss, Jory, dubbed him "Mouse." Among the miners he had his own special name.

He has worked in the mine for two years, never once complaining. Da used to make fun of the constant bellyaching from the other men. Mouse imagined the miners were grumbling even now, on the way to the saloon, grumbling because they couldn't find the missing miner. But not Mouse. He never bellyached. He wanted Da to look down from heaven and be proud.

The miners approached, and Sam's was bright. Light spilled out of the saloon door along with three drunken men. They were fighting. Well, not so much fighting as flailing and falling. One landed face down in the mud right in front of the miners.

He saw the men from his shift laugh, so Mouse laughed too. The laughter came to him like tones of water, soft and round with no edges to tell one drop from the other. A deep and quiet rain. That's all the blast left him. The same explosion that had taken away the sound of wind and the peals of the church bell, took his da, too.

The preacher had buried Da's pieces while the miners said their prayers. Standing next to the new grave, Mouse watched the bowed heads and thought his own silent prayer. But not for Da. For the end of the thick silence. For music. Since he was a good boy who went to church every Sunday, God answered in his own way and gave Mouse the constant whispering sound of rain.

Mouse missed Ma too. She died on the way to Jasper, and they had buried her under a pile of rocks in the middle of nowhere. He will never find her grave again. He also wouldn't find the graves of Rachel, Annie, and little Bill. They were also piles of rocks, scattered on the way like the bread crumbs in the bedtime story Ma used to tell him, only Mouse couldn't ever follow the stones to find his way home. He had no home but here.

Rachel. Annie. Bill. Ma had said their names, over and over, before she died. Da told Mouse that losing them killed her. Ma missed her other three so much, she'd left. Mouse wasn't enough to keep her here. Then Da left. Right after the explosion, Mouse refused to leave his side in the mine; even so, he wasn't enough to keep Da to this earth, either.

All he had now were the miners, so he followed. The men

stepped over the flailing drunks and entered the saloon, Mouse so close behind them, all he saw was the back of Pete's sweat-stained shirt. As close and constant as the men were, both in the mine and coming down from the mountain, they spread and separated through the room. Then they were gone, devoured by the crowd. Mouse headed through smoke and the sharp smell of whiskey to the place he could find music. Just a little. Just enough.

He took his seat next to the piano and leaned his head to touch the side. The wood felt warm, like the night. A few globs of tone seeped through the rain, but more, the wood vibrated, a rhythm. Mouse knew the song. *Buffalo Gals*, his favorite. He was careful to keep his face serious. He didn't ever want to be taken for a simpleton. The piano-player man would let him sit however long he wanted. Mouse was content to stay forever.

Sally, the saloon whore, shoved through the crowd. Her salty sourness pushed a path before her, through the packed bodies. Her eyes found Mouse and lit up when she saw him. She headed his way.

Mouse bolted, and his smallness served him well. He crawled through legs, not stopping until he found a card game at a table big enough. He hunched beneath, hoping no one noticed him. He prayed Sally wouldn't ever catch him. He was afraid of her and what was upstairs. She led men up, and they all came back, not hurt, but still Mouse didn't want to go up there. He wanted Sally to leave him alone.

She would give up after a time, find a cowboy or miner, and then Mouse could return to the piano and again feel his music.

All he had to do was wait long enough.

Chapter 6

"Jesus, I'm glad you decided on a drink after all," Digger said.

The two men headed to town, and Jack took in clear mountain air, wiping the tunnels and the note from his thoughts. One thing he couldn't wipe away. Tom Gallagher. He'd spent hours searching the Nugget Hotel and questioning the miners who would speak with him, which weren't many. He'd used the first day of his suspension productively. Still, no results. Tom had simply vanished.

"How was work?" Jack asked.

"Oh, heavenly!" Digger clapped him on the back. "How many days' suspension again? Three?" He whistled low. "I guess I'm buyin'!"

They walked a few steps without talking, Jack listening to the barely controlled mayhem of the town. Shouts, horses, wagons creaking, laughing, and beneath all that noise, the steady thrum of the stamping mill. Sounded like the heartbeat of the mountain. He wondered if Tom's heart still beat or was silenced for good.

"What do you think happened to Tom?" Jack asked.

"Lordy, I sure hope we find him under a tree somewheres, drunk."

"Yeah, me, too."

"Think we will?"

"Nope."

Through the rough noise of the town, piano music drifted up the dirt street with a promise, drawing the two miners to the saloon. A crowd gathered outside as men strained to see inside. Jack heard shouts coming from within.

"Aw, not tonight," Jack said, elbowing his way through a mass of men. Another saloon fight. The miners enjoyed fighting as much as drinking. Jack pushed through the swinging doors and stopped. Digger smacked into his back.

An enormous stranger stood in the center of the room, yelling and gesturing. He reminded Jack of a raging bull. He'd make one hell of a strong miner if there was a tunnel he'd fit through. Jack thought it unlikely.

"Calm down, Rolf." A balding man put his hand on the bull's arm and the scene exploded into mayhem. The bull picked up Baldy and threw him over a table like a sack of feed. Several other strangers jumped the huge man. He stood, a mammoth covered with gnats. He flung one man away who crashed into the bar.

Jack launched himself forward just as Sheriff Cain strode in. Jack stopped short. Things were about to get interesting. Jasper certainly had its share of armed idiots, and Cain headed the list. Sure enough, the sheriff drew his gun from his side holster. Jack clapped his hands over his ears as Cain pointed the pistol up to the corner of the ceiling and pulled the trigger. The shot roared through havoc. One of these days, the imbecile would accidentally kill someone, but the sheriff achieved the desired effect. Everyone froze.

"Much better," Cain said. "Everyone sit down and shut up."

Digger snickered and gestured to the unconscious bald man lying in a heap on the floor. "I don't think he's gonna find a seat, Sheriff."

Cain swung the gun and pointed at Digger. "I said, everyone shut up. 'Specially you, dirt-hound. You and your friends are gettin' filth all over the place. What the hell you doin' here, anyhow?"

Jack pushed between Digger and Cain's gun. "How strange, Sheriff. We were under the impression this was a saloon." Jack smiled. Cain threw him a dirty look. The men who had caused the commotion busily picked themselves up, righting tables and watching Cain nervously.

"I'm gonna say this one time, Junior," Cain said, smirking at Jack. "Get your spoiled, good-for-nothing ass outa here. I'm sendin' you home, just like your boss did. And Creely ain't around to protect you now."

"Or you, Sheriff," Jack replied.

"I can take care of myself. I got what it takes, *Junior*." Cain squinted and returned his attention to the strangers. "I heard tell someone's wife is missin'. Whose?"

The bull clenched his huge, meaty fists. "That's me. Rolf Olsson." He glared at the Sheriff's gun pointing at him. "No need for that." The huge man pushed shaggy, dirty-blond hair away from his eyes.

"I decide what's needed, and I say I need it. Who's headin' up this settler party?"

Which explained all the strangers in the saloon, Jack thought. Another group of settlers filled with fools searching for a better life or, even more futile, chasing after the promise of gold. A promise breaking itself repeatedly over the backs of the desperate.

A skinny man with a hooked nose pointed to a heap on the

floor. "That there's the leader."

"We don't got time for this," the bull said, uncrossing his arms. "Laney's a tiny woman. She might be hurt."

"We seen her shawl on some rocks below Sunset Pass," the skinny settler whined. "She's prob'ly dead."

The bull moved closer to the skinny man. "You'd like that, wouldn't you?"

The sound of a gun cocking stopped everyone. All eyes in the room trained on Sheriff Cain. The bald man moaned from the floor.

"Everybody out 'cept him and him," Cain said, gesturing to Baldy and the bull.

"Hey, Sheriff, I'm open for business," Sam said from behind the bar. Cain aimed his gun at Sam, who gulped. "I mean, no need to empty out. Why don't you gentlemen retire to the back room for some privacy? No games goin' on."

Cain squinted.

"Free whiskey, Sheriff?" the barkeep added hopefully.

Cain nodded. "Thank you, Sam."

Two men pulled the bald man to his feet and dragged him to the back. Jack watched the bull follow. Activity returned and conversations began again.

"You ever see the likes of such a giant?"

Jack turned at the sound of Digger's voice. "He's a big 'un," he agreed.

"His wife, she prob'ly fell," Sam interjected from behind the bar. "They tracked her up the mountain, said she left the trail and wandered all over in the middle of the night. Musta fell right off. Damn shame to lose a woman in such a way."

"If I was married to that animal, I think I might jump off a cliff, too," Jack said, causing laughter to skitter across the room.

Piano music plinked again.

"Jack," Digger said, "you get some peculiar ways of seein' things. Buy you a whiskey?"

"Thanks, Dig, but I think I'll mosey on back and see what's what." Jack headed for the room in the rear of the saloon. A voice in his head warned him not to interfere. Cain would be furious. All the more reason to stick his nose in. He just couldn't help himself.

Jack slipped into the small room before the door shut. Cain stood with his back to the door, the stupidest thing Jack had seen yet from the inept sheriff. Cain may have been a gunslinger before he took on the responsibilities of Jasper law, but Jack suspected the only reason the man still lived was dumb luck.

"I tried to find a way down to where I saw her shawl," Rolf Olsson said. "Weren't no way to get to it."

"There is if you go down the north face," Jack said. The sheriff jumped, whirled around, and Jack again found himself on the business end of a Colt Peacemaker.

The sheriff glowered. "I thought I told you to git. You're lucky I didn't fire a bullet up your ass, Junior."

"Didn't anyone in Sheriff School teach you not to stand with your back to the door? And why don't you put that idiotic thing away before you hurt somebody?"

"You know a way down?" The bull pushed Cain out of the way.

The gun went off. Every man in the room dropped to the floor, including Jack. He lay there, numb and staring up at the ceiling. He patted his abdomen, his chest. No blood. No pain. Thank the good Lord in heaven, Cain missed.

No big surprise there.

Jack started to get up when a boot thunked in the middle of his chest and pushed him back down. He looked up into the

Colt's barrel. Cain cocked the gun. Jack focused past the weapon to the sheriff's cold gaze and saw murder in Cain's eyes. Realization washed over him like a frigid mountain spring.

"You really going to kill an unarmed man in front of all these witnesses?" Jack managed to say without his voice cracking.

A grin spread across Cain's face. He holstered his weapon and leaned his weight on the foot holding Jack. "Won't always be witnesses, Junior." The sheriff winked and lifted his foot from Jack's chest. "Well, not much we can do, Mr. Rolf Olsson. Treacherous terrain 'round Sunset Pass."

Jack jumped to his feet. "I've been down there dozens of times." He rubbed his chest, smiling sweetly at Cain. "It's a nice hike. That is, if you aren't scared of falling."

The sheriff glared at Jack.

"I'll pay anything you want," Rolf said.

"No, no. It's my"—Jack paused and smiled even wider at Cain—"civic duty. Someone has to help folks around here. As it happens, I have a few free days. Besides, a wife is a precious thing. We can't leave her out there. She may be hurt."

"I'll go with you," Rolf said.

"Mr. Olsson, the north face is pretty tough terrain, if you aren't used to it. I've been down that way a few times. If she's anywhere around there, I'll find her."

"I'm goin' with you. She's my wife."

Jack opened his mouth to protest again. The determination in Rolf's eyes shut him up. The big man wasn't about to take no for an answer. Jack was nimble, flexible. Rolf was merely solid brute strength. Hopefully, the bull would give up before he got hurt.

"Just let me get my gear," Jack said. Satisfaction lit Rolf's expression.

"Are you sure you're up to this, Junior? Hate to see you fall off the mountain." Cain grinned like he'd enjoy that very thing.

"I've climbed around the face a couple of times just for the hell of it. And somebody's got to step up and protect the good folks in Jasper. Don't you worry yourself, Sheriff. I'll find her." Dead or alive, he thought. Most likely, dead.

Jack possessed enough smarts to not say that out loud.

She walks in an Otherworld, not the one of spirits but of dreams. Milena approaches the blue castle with no fear. Not even the looming turreted towers cause her to hesitate, for the Shuv'hani *stands guard at the entrance.*

Milena remembers well the bright eyes of wisdom peering from the wrinkled face of her grandmother; yet the Wise One has shed the skin of old age. The Shuv'hani *wields all the strength and beauty of a priestess, drenched in youth and power so bright, Milena must shield her eyes.*

The Shuv'hani *stands aside and gestures for Milena to enter. She wishes to stop and hold her grandmother to her, but the Otherworld brightness burns with the heat of a thousand suns.*

Entering the castle, she walks into a dim and twisted hallway while unseen crickets chirp away in the dark as she passes. At the end of the tunnel, a room with a blazing chandelier calls her forward. Suddenly, a small, twisted figure lurches past her and into the room, moving so fast Milena barely catches a glimpse of the gnome.

He darts behind a queen with hair of crackling fire, who paints at an easel. She smiles at Milena, beckoning her to come closer. Before Milena reaches the queen, the gnome rushes forward and slams the door shut in her face. Milena reaches for the knob. It is gone, then so, too, the door. Milena turns. She isn't in a castle at all. She is on the top of a great mountain. The glittering chandelier explodes into a myriad of suns blazing across the sky.

Milena woke with a start in the full heat of the afternoon, still tucked away beneath the rocks where she'd hidden. It was difficult to sleep during the day, but she needed the cover of night for her travel.

Milena's stomach rumbled. She closed her eyes and returned to contemplating her vision. Dreaming of a castle meant a journey to an unknown place, certainly no great insight. The crickets in the tunnel foretold of happy times found in solitude, and the gnome warned of hidden danger lying in wait.

Despite the burning day, she fell back to sleep, waking when night finally arrived. She followed the sound of water and found a creek. Cool liquid refreshed her as much as the night air. Although dizzy from no food and stumbling from weakness, Milena's step lightened with the encouragement her dream brought her. She knew she neared Jasper. She moved fast, comforted by her cloak of darkness.

Jasper. Her freedom. Her destiny.

"Hey, Rooolf, your wife purty?" Digger used the big man's name every chance he got, holding out the vowel so he sounded like a moaning dog.

"None of your damned business," Rolf replied.

"Well, I need to know what she looks like, 'case I see her." Digger shrugged and stretched his hands out over the campfire.

"Dig," Jack said, "if you see a woman wandering around alone, I'm pretty sure it will be her."

"Oh, true, thanks for smartin' me up, Jack," Digger said. "So, Rolf, how long you been married?"

"None of your damned business."

"What kinda name is Olsson anyhow? Swedish? Norweedish?"

"None of your damned business."

Digger sighed. "Rolf? Don't you never say nothin' else?"

The big man glared.

"All-righty. Guess not." Digger squinted sideways at Jack, who busily stirred a pot of simmering stew over the flames.

The Swede had hardly spoken a word since they left, except for an occasional grunt or nasty remark. In complete contrast to the sullen bull, Digger wouldn't shut up. Amazingly, he possessed enough air to climb and talk nonstop.

They'd reached the lower plateau when Jack decided to stop for the night. Digger started whistling. Jack stirred the pot of stew, and sausages with fritters sizzled on a griddle to accompany Digger's out-of-tune rendition of, well, Jack didn't actually recognize a melody. Even though Digger couldn't afford to miss work, he'd insisted on accompanying Jack and Rolf. Considering the huge man's disposition, Jack was beyond grateful for Digger's company.

Digger stopped whistling. "So, Rooowlf, how long did it take you to get cross country?" That time, his pronunciation of the Swede's name sounded more like a moaning dog than ever before.

"You ever shut up?" Rolf asked.

"Not for very long," Digger admitted.

"Try," the Swede said, standing. He fisted his huge hands.

Digger stared up at the giant towering over him. His mouth dropped open. Jack stopped stirring. Time to remind the Swede who was in charge. Of course, one punch from Rolf would probably kill him. He hoped his thought hadn't registered on his face.

Jack jumped to his feet. "Digger and I don't have to be searching with you. We'd much rather be at the saloon or in a decent bed after a decent meal. You were in trouble, and we volunteered to help. I'm not asking for gratitude," he said with a bravado he didn't quite feel, "however, a bit of civility might be in order."

The Swede's anger melted into a perplexed expression, like he didn't quite understand.

"We're out here trying to find your wife," Jack said. "You could be a little nicer."

Neither man broke eye contact. The only sounds were sizzling sausages and boiling stew.

"Five months," Rolf finally said, unfisting his hands.

"What?" Jack asked.

"Took us five months to get to Jasper." He finished by sitting back down and glancing over at Digger.

Digger whistled low. "Golly! I ain't never done nothin' for five months." Digger grabbed a plate and dug in. "Bless you, Jack, you can even cook out in the wilderness. You'd make some man a fine wife! Even though you might look kinda ugly in a dress."

Jack laughed and sat back down. Rolf continued to scowl. Dull anger darkened the big man's face as he took the plate Jack passed to him and shoveled food into his mouth with his fingers. Jack wondered, not for the first time, what went on between this man and his wife. He must be difficult for a lady to abide. Jack's earlier statement nagged at the back of his mind. Did Laney Olsson throw herself off a cliff?

After dinner, the three men bedded down. Jack relaxed and his thoughts returned to Tom.

"Dig, at the hotel, where do you keep your stuff?"

"I got a cubby. We all do. Why?"

"Yeah, I saw them when I was looking around and wondered. I doubt Cain's bothered to search Tom's things."

"He'd have to shoot through the lock, and I don't recall such an incident."

Jack laughed. "With his aim he'd probably take out a few

men in the process."

"You think Tom left something that might point to what happened to him?"

Jack shrugged. "Probably not. But it might not hurt to check." He smiled. "'Night, Dig." He rolled on his side and let the breeze and chirps of the night music calm his thoughts.

"Hey, Jack?"

He rolled back over on his side and propped his head up on his hand. "Yeah?"

"Thanks for standin' up for me in the saloon. With the sheriff."

Jack smiled. "My pure pleasure, Dig. Cain's an idiot."

"Yeah, well, I don't much like the idear of a bullet in my gut, or spendin' the night in jail. I don't know what makes my mouth run off. I ain't so good at quiet," Digger admitted.

"Speakin' of that, you two gonna shut up anytime soon?" Rolf asked.

"Oh, don't mind us, Rolf. Go ahead and keep to yourself. We don't 'spect you to have nothin' worth puttin' your voice to," Digger said, tossing the comment over his shoulder. "Hey, I got me a grand idea, Rooowlf. How 'bout you do us all a favor and doze off?"

"Dig, please. Hush up. I'm not in the mood for a brawl," Jack said under his breath.

"Oh, all right. Anyhow," Digger said returning his attention to Jack, "thanks. You're a good friend."

"Why don't you just get up and kiss him?" Rolf asked.

Digger's eyes grew huge. "Hey, Rolf, you made a joke." Digger flopped onto his back. "Don't that beat all? A Swede with a sense of funny." He plopped his hat over his face. "'Night, Rolf. 'Night, Jack," Digger said, his voice muffled through his hat.

"Good night, Dig," Jack muttered, relieved his friend finally decided to settle down. Jack hoped for this search to end happier than his first one this week. He dropped off into the comforting hold of sleep.

Jack woke with a start, every sense snapping to sharpness. How long had he been asleep? Digger slept flat on his back, his hat still covering his face. Across dying embers, Rolf snored. Did Rolf's rumbling jolt him awake? Overhead, bats fluttered across the pale disk of the moon.

Something watched them. He felt it.

A branch snapped beyond his range of vision. Slowly, carefully, Jack reached into the pack beneath his head. His hand gripped the reassuring butt of his pistol. He just needed to pull it out without blowing his head off.

Another snap. Animal? Human? Comanche?

In one fluid motion, he rose to his feet. He'd learned long ago to sleep wearing his boots. No chance of a snake or scorpion crawling in them for the night. Jack took a few careful steps toward the sounds he'd heard. Someone watched, all right. He sensed a presence. Eyes, huge and dark, looked right into his soul. Whatever stalked him wove through his mind, prying it open, twisting, turning.

He stumbled back and his free hand grabbed his forehead. What the hell? His heart thudded in his chest.

Another bunch of bats fluttered through the night sky. What were so many of those critters flying around for, anyway? Jack saw them ever so often, but never so many. Some might label such an occurrence a bad omen. A shudder shook through him before he shut it off.

He crept forward, trying to discern shapes in the cold moonlight. All he saw were brambles and trees, twisting and entwining through the dark like misshapen skeletal arms. He took a few steps closer to the night maze.

Then Jack saw her, standing among the trees as if one of them. A mass of curls darker than the night surrounded her face, her skin glowing silver. An apparition made of moonlight?

In that moment, Shakespeare came to life. Jack understood how Nick Bottom felt when he first glimpsed Tatiana. Surely such a magical creature was not of this earth.

He shook his head and blinked. She was gone.

Confused, Jack scanned the landscape. Silence. No sound. No movement. He heard nothing beyond the cadence in his ears. Had she ever been there?

"Get a hold, Jack," he said aloud. "I'm losing my sanity," he whispered. Behind him, he heard someone stir. He whipped around.

"Jack?" Digger asked, breaking the unnaturally silent dark. He got to his feet and lit a lantern. Rolf lumbered up, slow as rising bread.

Jack returned his attention to the trees. A woman in the woods? A spirit? Some mystical forest creature, or nothing more than another Jack Buchanan flight of fancy?

Or perhaps the ghost of Laney Olsson.

Digger came with a lantern held high. Twisted shadows swung in the lamplight.

"You hear something?" Digger asked.

He lowered his gun and tucked it in his waistband. "I think I was dreaming. Maybe even sleepwalking."

"Laney!"

Jack and Digger jumped at Rolf's bellow.

"Jesus, Rolf. I bet they heard you in Jasper," Digger said. Nothing moved. At all. Unnatural stillness surrounded them. Once again, bats fluttered overhead. Rolf pulled his gun.

Jack grabbed at the big man's arm. "We don't need to start

shootin' at bats."

"Laney?" Rolf asked the dark. Still, no movement. "I'm gonna look myself," he said, raising his lantern higher and moving forward.

Jack gripped the Swede's arm. "No, Rolf, you'll kill yourself wandering around. Dig and I will be busy getting your sorry carcass back to Jasper instead of searching for your wife. Besides, daylight is in another hour or so."

Rolf's face scrunched in intense concentration.

"Do you hear anything? See anything?" Jack asked. "We'll continue right at daybreak. Trust me, if Laney's out here, we'll find her."

Rolf nodded, returning to his bedroll. He sat and continued to scan the landscape around them. Jack lay back down. This time, his hand stayed around the butt of his gun. His solid, real gun. He laid it across his chest, holding tightly to his only reassurance.

One thing was sure. He wouldn't get any more sleep.

Chapter 7

Isabella St. Claire strode down the main street of Jasper, as she did every Sunday morning. She was a beautiful woman, cultivated from a line of exquisitely bred women. But Isabella was determined to be nothing like her mother, a woman who allowed passivity to disintegrate her from the inside out like a perfect peach, rotting away.

Once her mother collected admirers without issuing so much as a sidelong glance or the crook of a brow. She married a fine, upstanding businessman who grew tired of his wife as their child, Isabella, blossomed into adolescence. He felt entitled to indulge his desires upon his young daughter. By the time Isabella fled her home, her mother was folded with bitterness and shame.

Eager to leave herself behind, Isabella headed west and changed her name. Molly Elizabeth Montfrow never suited her; it was way too plain and heavy. Isabella St. Claire she was now and, truth to tell, always had been deep inside, in her heart. A husband to pamper and finally betray her? Oh, no, not for Isabella St. Claire. She wanted life on her own terms and as much of it as she could get.

She was Jasper's leading businesswoman, and she wanted to

be sure everyone knew it.

Men she passed tipped their hats as their eyes lit with appreciation of one of God's finest pieces of handiwork. Almost six feet tall in her boot heels and dressed in imported silk the golden color of the setting desert sun, lace at her throat, feathers in a hat perched upon hair of campfire flames, Isabella knew she was the dream of every man in the West. An imposing and breathtaking figure, Isabella used her blessings to her fullest advantage.

After all, they were hers to use.

She did cause some trepidation, especially among the female population of Jasper, but there were not many women in the town. A situation that suited Isabella St. Claire just fine.

Church bells chimed down the mountain. She was late. She quickened her pace, difficult considering the steep incline of the walk. The Rock of God Community Church sat at the top of the town, looking down over Jasper. Probably some sort of sanctimonious statement by the builders, Isabella imagined.

The doors burst open. Reverend McShane headed the flood of the devoted. He frowned when he saw Isabella and turned to wish his parishioners well as they departed, one by one.

Isabella made her way up through the stream of churchgoers. She enjoyed traveling the opposite way of the majority. Women passed her, wearing their calico-ugly dresses and sour faces under bonnets; men wore their Sunday-best suits. Some crossed the street to avoid her. She clearly saw jealousy in the eyes of the women, as well as anger and disdain. In the eyes of the men? Desire. Appreciation. But honestly, mostly, above all? Lust.

Praise the Lord.

Isabella kept her head held high and her gaze locked on Pastor McShane. She took special care not to make eye contact with any of the Boarding House clients. That certainly wouldn't do, especially since a few of them escorted their wives. She waited until the reverend shook hands with the last of his flock before she lifted her skirts and climbed the steps.

Pastor McShane was a man of God. The man part, Isabella thought wryly, came first. His sculptured face and soulful brown eyes never failed to cause a jolt to run through her. She held an envelope out to him. He threw her a stern look.

"A donation, Reverend."

He took her offering. "I believe I've mentioned you don't need to come by so early. Or on a Sunday."

"I don't slink along the shadows, Reverend." She emphasized her words with her most dazzling smile.

He frowned, opened the envelope, and his eyebrows raised in surprise. "Miss St. Claire, this is quite generous."

"It's been a good week."

A blush ran up his neck and flooded his cheeks. So easy to embarrass, which made their Sunday morning exchange all the more fun.

"We appreciate your turning the wages of sin over for the Lord's work."

Isabella waved her gloved hand. "Please, Reverend. Save your pontification for someone who cares to listen."

Anger flashed into his eyes. Then compassion softened his expression and something she hated to see: pity. "I simply speak the truth," he said softly.

"Really. Well, allow me to speak some truth of my own, Reverend. These 'wages of sin' helped build this church and run the orphanage. You accept my money every week, yet I dare not cross the threshold of your establishment." She stopped and forced her anger into a smile. "But please understand, Reverend, you are welcome at my place any old time at all."

His blush deepened. He dropped his eyes to her feet, apparently struck speechless. She wondered if she lit upon a deep, dark desire in the good Reverend McShane. How very interesting.

Isabella spun, retreating down the steps, knowing he watched her. Poor man couldn't help himself. None of them could. And God didn't care to interfere with the will of any of them.

Quite a profitable situation for Isabella St. Claire.

Milena came upon a grand house with a blue tile roof on the edge of town. The blue castle. Her vision come true.

She scurried beneath the castle's porch. Her stomach rumbled. Ribbons of soft morning light slipped through floorboards, slicing through the dusky space. She was not the first to hide in this place. Remnants of food, some bones, and animal scat littered the dirt. She crawled into the corner farthest away from the road and brushed everything away, smoothing the dirt to lie down. Despite the hints of animals, the stench was not bad. All in all, she preferred this to lying beside the Dim Swede.

She curled up and drew her velvet bag to her heart. The bag held all the possessions she cared about. Her grandmother's gazing ball, her seeing cards, and a *choori*—a carved knife with a crystal handle Baba had forged with his own hands. The heaviness and shape of her grandmother's crystal gazing ball reminded her of her dream and its promise and warning. She did not know how her escape from the Dim Swede would be possible; she only knew she must believe such freedom was hers.

She tried not to think of Rolf and the strange men searching for her. Especially the one. When she'd reached out to get a sense of who helped the Dim Swede, a man startled her by waking.

Somehow, he felt her presence. He almost came after her, but she wove protection around herself, closed her mind to him, and he lost his awareness. He troubled her. Such a man saw more than with his eyes and was a danger, especially since he aided Rolf.

Rolf. Rolf, storming through town, coming for her. Furious. His hands ripping, tearing. His eyes, red with bloodlust.

She jolted awake, her heart pounding and her skin slick with fear. Darkness enfolded her; she must have dozed for most of the day. Even though she did not want to admit any weakness, her exhaustion must be great. Thankful that no one discovered a woman hiding under the porch, she concentrated on stopping the shivering from her dream.

Dream? Or vision? So hard to tell.

The *tacho Romano drom* opened before her to travel. The *Shuv'hani* brought her to the castle with the roof, blue like the sky. Blue, like freedom. And the gnome? The portent of hidden danger? The vision of Rolf? Words whispered through her like a relief, sweeping aside the gnarled foreboding in her dream. Trust.

"I will, *Shuv'hani*. I will."

She needed food and planned to appropriate it the way her people had for hundreds of years. Not stealing, really. Surviving. She did not come this far to starve to death hiding under a porch.

She would take care not to get caught, that was all.

Damn. The light was out again.

Isabella bolted up, clutching the covers around her in the dark, not sure if her nightmare had ended or if she continued on, trapped in her sleeping mind. A draft brushed through the room even though the windows were shut. The stench of a rotted soul rode the air. He must be here, the man who chased her night after night, through a landscape of dreams. She froze. A steady cadence pulsed deep inside her ear, echoing her pounding heart. Faster. Faster.

She reached for the derringer under her pillow. Cold metal and smooth pearl nestled in her palm. Well, that certainly felt real enough. So, she was awake. She pointed the gun out into the dark. Let him come. She'd blow off his useless Saint Peter and laugh while he bled to death at her feet.

From the next room thumping grew to a frenzied speed. Then, a muffled groan. Another satisfied customer.

Not about to sit awake all night in bed, she lowered the gun into her lap and lit the candle. The room filled with gentle light, and the glow expanded, searching out every dark, menacing corner. She was alone.

Relief sliding through her, she tucked her gun back under the pillow. Her earlier vision flashed across her mind. Him, lying, bleeding from his mangled manhood. Her, laughing.

"Good Lord," she said. What depths of her demented soul ushered such a vision? Honestly, she knew the twisted part of herself intimately. She could roll in chicanery with the best of them.

Rising, she covered her nightdress with a velvet burgundy robe, buttoned it, and pulled her hair from the lacy collar. The fall of red cascaded down her back, untethered. Much better. Dressed. Civilized. Beautiful and in control, her most natural state.

As Isabella glided down the hall, all manner of sounds emanated from behind different doors. The reverend could expect another healthy donation next week. She passed some rooms that were quiet; her girls done for the night, their benefactors rushing back to cold marriage beds.

Thank God she possessed enough sense to keep from that

path. Away from the vows women cherished and believed, finally learning the words were nothing more than a cobweb for husbands to clear away and do whatever they damned well pleased.

Once downstairs, she followed the back hall to her door. The key she wore around her neck slid into the lock, and she entered her room. Her parlor. Forbidden territory unless she issued an invitation, which she never did. This room, deep within the Boarding House, was her own. She lit the lamp.

In one corner, an easel and palette of paints waited for her to lift her brush and lose herself in the pleasure of color and creativity. In the opposite corner sat a piano, grand and ornate. Carved naked nymphs and satyrs danced within swirls of leaves and trees. For her eyes alone. The piano had been custom-made and cost her a fortune.

When she was a young girl, her father insisted she learn to play. She spent hours practicing, when she really wanted to stay in her room and paint. Her father refused to accept a less than perfectly accomplished daughter to parade in front of friends and business associates, so she sat, hour after horrid hour, tears falling on ivory keys. She tried her best. There was no music in her.

Every lesson unfolded in the same manner. First, disappointment. Next, Father's anger. Finally his cane whacked across her hands. Her mother never objected. Even when he broke Isabella's hand, her mother voiced no complaint. Her hand didn't heal correctly. Impossible to straighten it all the way, and it hurt, especially when she used it. And ugly, so very ugly. Thank heaven for gloves.

Isabella ran her once-broken hand over her piano. She never opened the lid; never saw the keys, trapped in darkness forever. The piano sat, beautiful. Useless.

She took a seat and lifted her palette. No sense in returning to bed; she knew who waited for her there, lurking within a nightmare. No, not sleep, but paint. Enter the world where she decided every detail, where she was the Great Creator. Completely in control.

God, one might say.

She touched her brush to the canvas with her silent piano for an audience. She stroked color on, so gently, sweetly. Benevolent as any creator.

Thumping. Shuffling. Sounds from the back of the house ripped her from her world of creation. A rear window opened, the sound unmistakable.

A prowler was invading the Boarding House.

A golden guard slept at the gate.

The man, huge, with yellow curls falling around his shoulders, snored in a tipped-back chair by a majestic front door. Milena wondered why she didn't hear him come out and sit above her while she slept. Then again, she was beyond weary. She was close to running into town and screaming for Rolf to come do whatever he wanted with her, as long as he fed her and let her sleep for a few days first.

A snore ripped through her moment of defeat. She worried such a thought crossed her mind. She needed food. Immediately.

She crept around the perimeter of the Blue Castle once again, hiding in the scrub, watching. She could not see in. Heavy damask curtains blocked any view. The fabric draped most of the windows so heavily, only the thinnest blade of light from the world slipped in or out. She'd wither and die in there, cut off from life, from the sky, the earth, the stars.

Milena made her decision. The entire back of the Blue Castle stood dark, with no guard to stop her. If her time in New York City taught her anything, she learned *gaujos* in grand houses kept to the top floors at night. She planned to tread lightly, to be in and gone before a moment passed.

Silently, she crept up the back steps. In the West, people were hung for stealing, their bodies placed in coffins and propped up for all to see. In the old country, the punishment was the hand, chopped off. Usually a death sentence, with blood flowing so freely, most did not survive unless loved ones were nearby and hadn't been beaten or killed for their association. More often than not, the "criminal" had taken a loaf of bread or milk to feed themselves and their starving children.

Milena shook the vision of nooses and severed hands from her mind. Fear must not guide her. She knew from her heavy limbs and the ringing in her ears, this was her only chance to keep moving. She was near to collapse but the call of the mountain sang continually, pulling her forward. She could not answer if she crumpled and became the food for crows.

The padlock on the door was at most an inconvenience. The window next to it slid open easily, and she lifted herself up and shoved her feet in. Sitting for a moment on the sill, she allowed a wave of dizziness to pass. She almost felt like she floated, her soul straining to leave her cumbersome and weak body. She needed food. Grasping the window frame, she lowered herself into the room. Her feet landed silently, without even a creak from the floor.

Now inside, she froze, listening. Nothing.

Scents surrounded her: spices, cooked meat, rising bread dough, sugar, all blending together and she almost passed out. The pantry was to the left and enticed her to see what treasures lay within.

Outside the room, wood creaked.

Milena froze. Felt a noose drop around her neck. She put her hand up, but nothing was there.

Another creak. The invisible noose tightened.

Isabella St. Claire learned early on to never be caught without a gun. Holding the trail of her velvet gown with one hand, she picked up the pistol she kept with her palette and headed for the kitchen, holding the weapon out before her. She'd heard the intruder come in through the back so she was reasonably sure it wasn't a client skulking about. Still, she planned to proceed with care.

She thought briefly about calling for help, but several screaming ladies wouldn't benefit the situation. Most, if not all clients had slunk back to their wives and homes by now. Luke, her strongarm man, obviously allowed the intruder past. She dismissed him as useless, like her ladies and clients. Luke most likely slept away on the porch. She wondered sometimes why she even bothered with him, but she'd think about that later. For the moment, she had a more immediate problem.

A scream might alert the prowler in the kitchen and cause him to run. Besides, Isabella St. Claire did not scream. She would teach anyone who dared encroach on her world quite the lesson. In fact, stories of this night might become legendary, with the right telling. Always good for Boarding House business.

She crept closer, through the hallway's dark, stealthily approaching the door to the kitchen. The sounds stopped. Silence.

Isabella kicked the door open. "Don't move," she ordered. Moonlight spread throughout the kitchen with colorless radiance, outlining a still, shadowy figure. A woman. Only a table stood between Isabella and the intruder.

"Open your hands and hold them up," she ordered. The figure complied. "There's a lamp and matches on the table," she continued. "Light the lamp. And move slowly."

The shadow did as she was told. Isabella held her gun, wishing it were bigger.

The figure struck a match. A flash of light revealed an oval face surrounded by cascades of curls the color of midnight. And those eyes. Deep, filled with sorrow and something else. Wisdom? Isabella felt she looked into the knowledge of the ages.

The lamp glowed. Light from the flame intensified, and she saw not just a woman stood before her, but a breathtaking creature. Something in her expression caught Isabella's attention. Desperation.

A beautiful, desperate woman in her kitchen. How incredibly fortuitous.

Isabella smiled. Then, realization faded her delight.

"Ah. You're the Gypsy," Isabella said. "From the settler party."

In reply the woman's eyes grew even larger, something Isabella didn't think possible.

"Everyone is searching for you, my dear."

"Please. No." And the voice. Bells on the wind. If Isabella were a man, she'd be hard as a stake. Such a shame this woman was married. What a waste.

"Your husband is turning Jasper upside down trying to find you." Isabella raised her eyebrows. "I understand why."

The woman's attention shifted to the gun, and suddenly Isabella felt silly holding it. She lowered it.

"I am wife to no man."

"Really?" Isabella asked with interest. "That doesn't make much sense, my dear."

"The man is not my husband. My father died on our journey.

Rolf took me in."

"I see. Not out of the goodness of his heart, I'll wager," Isabella said. "Imagine that. A man taking advantage of a helpless female. Such an awful situation. How horrible for you."

"He insists to make me his wife, here in Jasper."

Isabella found the woman's slightly awkward use of English added to the exotic mystery wrapping her like a delicate mist.

"And you, my dear?" Isabella asked. "What is it you want?" Isabella guessed by the Gypsy's air of desperation, she wasn't a willing bride. "What's your name?"

"Milena."

"Well, Milena, I am Isabella St. Claire, and you have come to the best place possible, considering your situation. No one understands fleeing from a man better than I." For a second he flittered through her mind, the pursuer in her nightmares. She pushed the thought of him aside. No matter.

"Please, some food? Only a little."

Isabella gestured to the table. "Have a seat, my dear."

The Gypsy sat, clutching her bag to her. She watched the room like a skittish cat about to bolt while Isabella opened the pantry door.

"I have no money," Milena said, settling the velvet sack into her lap. "I see the future. I can tell your fortune, for food."

Isabella placed cheese and bread before the woman. Milena lunged and ripped the bread apart with her filthy hands. She devoured the chunks like a starving animal, then lowered the bread, seemingly embarrassed.

"Please, continue. You must be starving."

Warily, Milena tore off another hunk, her dark eyes scrutinizing Isabella and the large kitchen. She ate, obviously assessing her situation. Isabella surmised the Gypsy owned a keen intelligence.

"However did you manage to avoid your—what did you say his name was?"

"Rolf."

"Ah, yes. Rolf. However did you manage to avoid him and Jack Buchanan? They set off to search for you, and there is only one way up."

Milena nodded. "I slip past them in the dark."

"I see." There was much more to this woman than the obvious, but wasn't that always true? And something the male of the species had yet to figure out, regarding all women. For their place of domination, men were unbelievably thickheaded. Luckily, Isabella didn't share such an unfortunate trait. She immediately recognized Milena's value. An exotic Gypsy. A fortune-teller. What wonderment she might add to the Boarding House's entertainment. The Gypsy would command the highest compensation from some lucky client. What man didn't want a taste of pleasure from another land? The problem would be deciding to which man to grant such a rare treasure. Isabella smiled. Then again, not a difficult decision at all. The one with the most money.

"Do you have anywhere to go? Any plan? Whatever will you do?"

Milena lowered her eyes.

"Marriage to Rolf is not a preferred solution?"

The Gypsy's gaze snapped up with anger. "I will not be wife to Rolf Olsson."

"Yes, well, I certainly can't blame you there," Isabella said. "Why don't you stay with us? This is a boardinghouse for ladies, and I am the proprietress. As fortune has it, I have an empty room. You'll need to stay hidden until the party leaves town. They should be gone in a day or so."

Milena closed her eyes and leaned back in the chair, cocking her head as if she listened to something. She nodded. Her eyes snapped open. Startled, Isabella jerked back.

Milena's expression melted into resolve. "I will stay with you."

"I'll explain to the other ladies my cousin has come to stay and fell ill along the way of her journey. She needs solitude. She must be left alone to recuperate. Besides, no one in town really pays much attention to our little boardinghouse." Isabella thought of her donations and the special attention her ladies provided to the sheriff any time he cared to visit. Money and services well spent.

"Why do you help me?" Suspicion curled through the question.

"Why, indeed? Milena, we are women trying to survive amidst the savagery of the West, without the protection of a husband. We women need to stand together." Isabella leaned forward. "I feel it is our solemn duty to help each other on the frontier."

Milena would help Boarding House business. Of that, Isabella had no doubt.

"I'm sure we'll discover some suitable manner for you to return my generosity." Isabella settled back into her chair. "But later. For now, relax and enjoy your meal."

Milena resumed eating but studied Isabella. The Gypsy's attention did not intimidate her. No one yet possessed the ability to truly see into her. Everyone saw exactly what she wanted them to see.

For all her obvious intelligence, her exotic and mysterious ways, the woman was no match for Isabella St. Claire. Besides, the Boarding House was much better suited to Milena than the dim-witted, lumbering Swede accompanying Jack Buchanan and Digger on their search. Isabella was providing a safe haven for Milena. Doing her a service. Saving her.

"You're safe, Milena. Trust me. You're safe now."

Chapter 8

"Jack, you are a cross to bear." Puffs of dust rose around Digger's boots as he trudged up Gooseneck Road.

"Yup," Jack agreed. The morning's walk up the mountain did not improve his mood, either. He was just plain irked at his own apparent uselessness. "Let's see, searched for Tom, nothing. Searched for Laney Olsson, nothing."

What he didn't bother to mention was his return to work after his "suspension." Not the best way to start the day. Jack turned at the sound of scuffling behind them. Mouse scurried up beside, then fell into their rhythm, two steps for each one they took. His pants tucked in his boots, canteen belted around a coat any man would wear, and a hardboil on his head, the boy looked more than ever like an adult diminished in stature by the rough life in the mines. The boy with the seriousness of a grown-up provided a hurtful reminder of the futility of this life. Or, at least, the futility of Jasper.

"Hey, kid," Jack said before remembering the boy couldn't hear him. Mouse wasn't interested in the two men, but mesmerized by the eastern sky. Jack followed his gaze. Color extended over the flatlands, and the mountain shone with the brilliance of white-gold morning light. Jack wondered if Tom or Laney Olsson were able to enjoy such a beautiful morning. One person he knew didn't see it was Victor Creely. The man started work before dawn. Jack didn't understand these "captains of industry"—men who sacrificed everything for the good of figures on a piece of paper.

"Well, leastways, Rolf didn't kill me," Digger said. "That worked out good enough."

"True. And if he'd tried, I might have been obliged to stop him—"

"Ain't no way you'd stand a chance."

Jack finally laughed. "Again, true. Hey, I don't suppose you checked Tom's cubby when you got back?"

Alarm flashed in Digger's eyes, then as fast as it appeared, the look was gone. "Hey," Digger answered, "I don't suppose I did. That thing is locked up tighter than a virgin's drawers anyhow." He grinned and began his hat throw trick. Jack wondered if he'd imagined or misread Digger's expression.

The boy followed Digger, the two of them tossing hats into the air and racing in zigzags around the road trying to get under them. For a moment they appeared so young and without a care in the world. Jack hated seeing them go down in the mine. No one should spend his days hunched down in the black of the mine. Not a young, carefree man like Digger. And certainly not a little boy.

Finally arriving, the three took their place in lines already forming; Digger, next Mouse, and finally, Jack. Other men fell in behind him.

Victor Creely came out from the mine office and stood on the spacious porch, the stone building being the only vantage point above the headframe. Jack was sure Victor built it on the highest point of the mountain on purpose.

"Jesus, Mary, and Joseph, Master Creely himself keeps watch upon us all. Look alive, all of you," Jory slurred from behind. Dull pain thudded into Jack's back. Jory's elbow. "Stand up straight, Buchanan. Show Creely what his pup's made of."

Jack clenched his hands at his sides. Balled them into fists.

Two officers emerged from the office and flanked Victor: to his left, George Barger, or Turtle, as the miners called him. Short, balding, the man tried to hide his hair loss and never went without his derby hat. His plaid suit might have fit in better days; now it stretched beyond decency. He was responsible for the day-to-day operations of the mine. He'd never been belowground.

Edmund Blum stood to Victor's right. His thin frame hunched over, but not from mining. Hours pouring over numbers and the weight of tracking the mine's profit slumped his shoulders. A young man, his demeanor echoed a much older gentleman. A sad one. The miners didn't see much of Edmund, but despised him nonetheless, just as they did every officer of the Jasper Mining Company.

How did a business thrive with so much hate?

"Ain't that a fetchin' group of ladies?" Digger asked, and sniggers erupted. Mouse stared up at the officers, his face like a soldier who lived too many years and saw too many battles.

The platform appeared and screeched to a halt, empty. Men stumbled onto the waiting wood. The platform filled, Digger stepping on it and turning to grin and wink at Jack. Jack grabbed Mouse's shoulders, keeping him from squirming his way through the men and jumping aboard. They ran these damned platforms much too full. Injuries mounted every week, torn arms, broken shoulders. Skin peeled from hands and faces. The deck filled enough for the plunge. Jack hadn't been able to help Tom, but he'd be damned if something happened to this kid while he was around.

Pain exploded in his back. "You and the boy get on the platform, pup! Now!" Jory yelled above the hum of idling machinery.

Jack dug in his heels and held tight to Mouse. The roar of a steam engine filled their ears and the ground swallowed the miners.

"Buchanan, let go of that lad," Jory said loudly. "Afraid he'll get lost? You can always go lookin' for him like you do ever'one else. Found anyone yet, pup?"

Laughter followed the comment, ramping up the heat under Jack's temper. "Mind your own business Jory," he said loudly and over his shoulder.

"You are my business, pup! We don't have all fookin' day to get down there."

Pain burst in Jack's back again. Same spot. Jack let go of Mouse and whirled around to face the shift boss.

"Do not touch me again," he said evenly.

Jory's eyes rounded with mock fear. And amusement. Jack turned back around.

Another burst.

Jack whipped around, launching himself into Jory, his anger torn free. The shift boss fell back, into the dust. The lines of men converged and circled, shouting insults, obscenities, and cheers. Jack jumped on Jory. The older man raised his knee, found leverage, and flipped Jack over. His face hit the ground. He tasted dirt. A heavy bulk landed on his back.

A roar filled Jack's ears, but not from a steam engine. Blood surged through his body. A year of watching men die and not being able to stop any of it. Investors growing richer while good men's spirits were ripped from them forever. Boys working to exhaustion when they should be playing outside and dreaming of futures filled with possibilities.

In one swift move fueled with fury, Jack rolled the bulk over, straddled, and punched, his fist meeting loose, whiskey-sopped skin. Jory's defiant face crumpled. Jack hit again. Tears spurted out of Jory's mean, piggish eyes, and blood from his nose. And again. More blood, from his mouth.

Jack stopped, his fist raised in the air. What was he doing?

Someone lifted him, dragged him through the crowd, and suddenly Turtle's face loomed in front of him. "Go home, Buchanan," spit from his pinched lips. "You're done here."

Jesus, he'd finally done it.

Fresh from suspension, he got himself good and fired. What the hell was wrong with him? Did he forget why he stayed; what he worked every day to keep?

Jack choked back his retort. Whatever came out would spew like lava. He kicked his hardboil and it skidded through dust. Leaving it behind, he shoved his way through the crowd and headed down.

He'd just lost the ranch.

Anger shot through him. He wanted to pound, to scream, to roar with it, but he'd be damned if he was going to put on a show. He stopped and bent over, hands on knees. Trying to calm panic. Pushing back anger. Frustration. All of it. He needed to get control.

A noise, a familiar one of feet scuffing in the dirt, made him glance over his shoulder. Mouse, eyes squinted and adult-serious. His hardboil candle listed at an angle. Melted wax adorned the rim of the boy's hat in drips of frozen tears.

Jack straightened and smiled. "Guess I'm a mess, huh, kid?"

Mouse's expression scrunched even more and he looked up at Jack.

"Oh, the hell with it. Let's go home." An idea broke through the whole, big, fiery ball in his chest. "Hey, you ever ridden a horse?"

The boy studied Jack with intense concentration.

"Horse. Ride. Horse." Jack galloped a few steps, holding imaginary reins. A smile broke on Mouse's face, just a hint of one, actually. More than enough for Jack. Between Mouse and the beautiful morning, he decided to leave his worries for later. Or at least until he was safe from exploding with frustration and anger. A fit would do him no good. He knew of one thing that might change his mood.

"Come on, kid. You're gonna love Willow."

Milena did not understand. Why did the *Shuv'hani* lead her to such a place? After a week, she understood this so-called boardinghouse for ladies. What about her dream, she wondered, the castle and the queen? This was no castle. And the proprietress was no queen.

She ran her hand along the print on the wall, a lattice of vines and blossoms. Exotic painted birds punctuated the pattern. They perched proudly, held for eternity in the lovely print. Trapped.

"Why, *Shuv'hani*? Why?"

A knock at the door jolted Milena from her thoughts. She'd learned a knock meant food waited for her in the hallway, and not just any food, but trays heaped with sumptuous feasts beyond compare. Already she saw fewer angles in the mirror, less of a sharpness to her face. The hollows of starvation had not quite faded away, but almost.

Another knock. To her surprise, the door opened. A young woman with hair the color of early morning sunlight entered carrying a silver tray bearing the extravagant food Milena came to expect.

"Oh, don't be afraid," the young woman said, her voice surprisingly deep for one so small. It reminded Milena of a smoky evening campfire. "My name is Beth, and I'm very pleased to meet you. Miss Isabella told me all about you and asked me to bring this and see if you need anything."

Milena shook her head.

Beth sat the tray on a small table in the corner. "Cook's outdone herself for luncheon. Roasted turkey stuffed with currants and sausages. Please." Beth gestured for her to sit. Milena's mouth watered at the rich, buttered scent of turkey and the spicy sausages. She kept her place, her back against the wall. She gulped, hoping her eagerness for food did not show.

Beth sighed. "I won't harm you, really. And I won't say a word about you to the others, although they are quite curious. The mysterious cousin in Deborah's old room. Miss Isabella trusts me; you can, too." Beth stopped as if she expected Milena to speak. When she didn't, the young woman continued. "Well, please enjoy dinner. I'll come back later and draw your bath."

Alarm rose through Milena. Bath? Was this the beginning then, of her offering to the men of Jasper?

"No," she said, stepping forward. "No, I thank you for the food. I . . ." her voice trailed off. She what? Could not stand another moment trapped in this fine room with its floral walls and ruffled quilts? Refused to give herself over to a man she did not love? What else was there for her? Where could she go? *Shuv'hani, are you certain I am to be here?* she asked silently. Tingles cascaded from her crown and skittered down her body in an affirming waterfall.

Yes, here.

"Miss Isabella has chosen a lovely dress for you," Beth said, confirming Milena's suspicion. She was to be primped and paraded like this delicate and useless flower standing before her.

"Actually," Beth continued, "the dress is one of mine. You'll be beautiful in it."

"I do not need your dress," Milena said despite how silly she sounded. After her journey across the country, her own clothes were tattered rags.

"Oh, I'm happy to give it to you. It's deep blue, like the sky just before night." Beth shrugged. "The dress is too dark for me. I've barely worn it at all. Besides, I have many more. I'll never miss one." Beth's dimples deepened. "Miss Isabella was right. Milena, you are very beautiful. Can you really see the future?" she asked.

The boldness of the girl's asking surprised Milena. Then she saw more than curiosity in the young woman's wide, blue eyes. A fragile hope glimmered, the kind that is afraid to come out for fear it might wither and die in the light of day.

Milena nodded. "I tell fortunes."

"Really? How?"

Milena shrugged. "Many ways. My gazing ball. Tea leaves. Seeing cards. Your palm."

"My palm?" Beth studied her hand, and then held it out reluctantly. Her eyes grew soft with unshed tears. Suddenly, she yanked it back. "I'm sorry. Your food will get cold." She spun around. "I'll come back later. Enjoy your meal."

Perhaps it was the girl's gentle compassion for a stranger, or the fragile yet vibrant hope running through her, but something caused Milena to reach out. Beth turned, a tear sliding silently down her cheek. The final persuasion. Milena rarely opened herself to anyone; the connection took so much from her. But she let herself open to the soul of this girl and took the stranger in her arms, holding her close. She felt Beth's heartbeat, her life energy, the strength of a young spirit. The joy, the hope. The fear. All so strong, intense. Alive.

Instantly, Milena knew her quick judgment of this girl was wrong. Not a useless, delicate flower, but one fighting for existence among weeds. Just like the birds on the wall, held in a lovely, yet choking lattice of life.

Beth pushed away from Milena, her blush deepening. "Oh, heavens, I'm sorry." She wiped tears from her cheeks. "I'm not usually such a goose."

"You are a young woman in love. Your love is for another, not the one who pays for your affection," Milena said. Beth's face filled with shock. Her tears stopped. Milena ventured forward. "And you are trapped. For all the comfort and the beauty, night after night the feel of a man's arms around you, you are alone, longing for the one who truly holds your heart."

Beth gasped. "How can you possibly know?"

Milena smiled. "You can trust me, too, Sunshine."

A bewildered smile bloomed on Beth's face. "Why ever did you call me that? My mama used to call me Sunshine."

Milena hesitated to say what came to her next, not wanting to broach such a sacred subject uninvited. The specter following Beth glimmered so clearly. Through her connection, Milena knew the girl needed to hear.

"Your mother, she keeps watch over you. She is very near."

Beth's face drained of all its color. "Really?" The word came out a sigh, a whispered prayer.

"You feel her, too, do you not?"

Beth nodded. "Yes. Sometimes, especially when I'm lonely. Or when I'm frightened. She used to sing to me, this lullaby." Beth hummed a snatch of a lovely melody. "She's been gone so long. I miss her very much."

Milena nodded. She, too, knew the feeling of being lost and alone.

"She is not gone. She is close. Strong. She stands beside you."

Beth shook her head. The tears in her eyes changed from pools of sadness to wonderment. "I . . . I . . . Oh, my. I don't know what to say." Her breath hitched in, almost a sob.

"Just hear her, Beth. Listen. You remain her sunshine. Always. She will help you, guide you. Of this, I am sure."

Jack often wondered if Mouse ever acted like a child. Played. Laughed. Well, the kid did know how to giggle, and Jack had proof. At first, Mouse hesitated, afraid of Willow. Jack climbed up and hoisted the boy up to sit in front. He held to her reins along with Mouse, and they trotted, slowly to begin. Mouse bumped up and down, his head bobbing like a rag doll's, but he finally got the hang of it and rode like he was born in the saddle. And that's when the sweetness of the boy's giggles rewarded Jack. They spent two hours riding away the frustration of the morning. The only thing better than riding Willow was hearing the joy of a boy who didn't often get the chance to be a child.

The two now walked to the Nugget Hotel, Mouse back to swaggering. Jack decided it was high time the boy take a nap. An honest-to-goodness, lie-down-and-go-to-sleep-in-the-middle-of-the-day nap. Just like every kid should have, every day. He wondered if Mouse ever experienced one before. If not, he was about to discover one of life's true pleasures.

They approached the Nugget Hotel, a wide, brick building hugging tightly to a lower tier of the mountain as if it were afraid it might slide off into oblivion. Jack and Mouse were coming from above the hotel and slightly west where officers' cabins dotted the mountainside. Farther beneath and off to the side sprawled spatters of crooked shacks where the Mexican miners and their families lived. Everyone called the area Tortilla Flats. Below the Flats, a field of tents lumped together in groups and was dubbed Celestial Alley. The Chinamen lived there, speaking their strange language and keeping secrets to themselves. No one breached the invisible borders between any of the levels. Jack thought of Leno Santiago and his family. One thing life at Tumbling Creek taught him was how much a man learned from different cultures and each other. But not in Jasper. People were filled with fear and therefore disdain of anything unlike themselves.

Mouse lagged behind as they approached the dorm for miners. The Nugget Hotel. Jack snorted. The only thing hotel-like about the place was the frequency people came and went.

"Come on, kid." For about the tenth time today, Jack felt like a pure idiot. Why didn't he remember Mouse's world was silent? He circled his hand in a "hurry" gesture. The boy looked down, dragging his feet through dirt. Obviously, he didn't want to return to the hotel. Guilt stabbed through Jack, but the last thing he needed was a kid in his life.

A group of men sat on the steps leading into the building, and they watched Jack and Mouse approach. One of them, an old grizzled night-shift miner named Stoop, rose to his feet and stared. Jack figured Stoop got his nickname from his hunched shoulders, his thin frame bent like a C. The man wasn't able to stand up or walk straight, thanks to years of working at the mine. Long wisps of hair floated around his balding head like a tangled web. A long, gray beard hid his facial features, making his huge, buggy eyes pop even more. Stoop always looked like he'd been caught by surprise. Clothing hung on his thin frame, making him not only seem ancient, but frail. Stoop was forty-two years old.

The miner broke his trance, spit in the dirt, and disappeared inside. Then three men, including Stoop, appeared in the doorway and planted themselves across it, shoulder to shoulder.

"What do you want, Buchanan?" Stoop's tangled beard flapped when he spoke.

"I'm bringing Mouse back to take a nap."

That elicited a laugh from the group of men. Stoop's eyes nearly bulged right out of his head. "Nap? For that critter?"

Jack turned. Mouse pulled out and lit his pipe, puffing away. Jack reminded himself he looked at a seven-year-old boy.

He faced the men. "Yes, for him. A nap. A thing little boys do."

"Heard you got yourself in a speck of trouble this morning."

"Mind your own business, Stoop. Now excuse me." Jack climbed the few steps and shouldered his way past the men. To his surprise, they let him pass.

He stopped, always taken aback at what he saw. From the outside, the Nugget Hotel looked hospitable, almost graceful, with brick walls and large, half-moon windows up high. Inside, the walls closed in a rough-hewn wood floor, and the windows let in plenty of light. And heat. The place was hotter than a blacksmith's oven and smelled like rotten human waste. Row after row of wood platforms tilted on stacks of leftover bricks. Fully clothed and wearing their boots, a miner sat or reclined on every wood platform. Some slept on the floor. There were no mattresses. A few men slept on bedrolls or a thin blanket. Junk heaped everywhere. Tin plates, cups, piles of clothes. The building stretched out long, but only about thirty feet deep and resembled a never-ending hallway filled with junk, filth, and men. And not an interior wall in the place. Forget privacy. Or quiet.

The sunlight pouring in might have made any other place hospitable, but the night-shift miners were trying to sleep. Apparently, no one thought of them during construction. Jack remembered why he'd agreed with Victor and, despite the cost, took a cabin. This place was as bad as living in a barn. Worse.

How did they manage? How did anyone live like this? Mouse. Digger. And Tom.

Tom. Damn it, Tom.

"Where is Tom Gallagher's cubby?" Jack asked. Silence fell around him in the immediate area. The rest of the place still hummed with rough voices.

Stoop came up behind him. "Sorry. I'd help, but I'm mindin' my own business." He glared at Jack.

"Come on, Stoop. I'm looking for Tom."

"He ain't here."

Jack sighed. "You know what I mean. Looking for clues. Anything. I'm trying to find him. I'd appreciate any help you might give me."

"Not sure I got any help. I'll give you some advice, Mr. Dandy Britches. You're the one should mind his own business. This ain't affairs for a spoilt rich kid."

And there it was, laid bare. The reason Jack stayed on the outside, why the miners would never accept him. Then he cracked a smile. "Mr. Dandy Britches?"

Stoop shrugged. "Best I could think up quick-like."

"Okay, I'll give you some leeway. Next time, if you want me to be offended, you'll have to do better."

Under the beard, Jack thought he might have seen a small grin. Stoop nodded to the far end of the building. "Cubby's down that-a-ways. Tom's is the fourth from the east wall, three rows up. Thar's a lock on it."

"I don't suppose you have a key?"

Stoop pulled a gun from somewhere in his baggy clothes and cocked it. "I reckon I do."

He followed Stoop to the row of cubbies. "Plug your ears, boys," the old man said. He shot off the lock and the explosion reverberated. Jack opened the cubby and looked in. Some coins, a Bible, a gun. A cross on a chain. Tom never missed services on Sunday.

He took the Bible, flipped through it, and a photograph of an older woman with three girls slipped out. Three gorgeous girls, despite the grim expressions. Tom didn't exaggerate; his girls were downright beautiful. But pretty as they were, and getting a peek into Tom's life through his possessions, Jack found nothing to help him.

Holding the Bible and cross and chain, he turned to leave and stopped short. A wall of men surrounded him. Stoop cocked his gun with a click. He leaned over and spit on the floor.

"I'll return all of this when I find Tom. To him, hopefully. You have my word."

Stoop squinted. "Jest what do you think your word's worth 'round here, Buchanan?"

Mouse chose that moment to break through the knot of gathered miners. Pipe hanging from his mouth, he stomped over and stood in front of Jack, spinning to face the other men. His face scrunched in defiance as he blew out a puff of smoke.

A voice sliced through the haze. "Coward. A man standin' behind a kid."

The anger Jack had fought to keep down all day reared up, red and hot. "I don't hide behind anyone," Jack said, scooting Mouse to the side. "Who said that? Come on up and say it to my face!"

He waited for someone to own up to the insult, and he clutched the Bible and cross.

A voice shot through from the back of the crowd. "I'd be

careful, fellas. Mr. Dandy Britches beat the bejesus out of Jory this mornin', the way I heard it told."

"Any one of you'd do the same. He pushed me. And stop calling me Mr. Dandy Britches."

"Mr. Dandy Britches!" A chorus of voices reverberated through the huge hall.

Jack grimaced and nodded to Stoop. "Thanks."

"Any time, Buchanan."

Jack took a step forward. "I mean to leave this place."

Stoop held his ground. "Well, that's a simple enough thing. Put them items back and you kin go."

Jack considered. He didn't think anything here would help him in his search. Certainly nothing worth dying over. He held the Bible out, tossed it on an empty wood platform next to him. It landed with a thud. The chain slid from his hands and dropped on top of the holy book.

Stoop nodded and moved aside. Jack took a few steps forward, and true to Stoop's word, men opened up a way to the door. He walked, each step deliberate, expecting someone to jump him, or for the crowd to close up and crush him. Neither happened. He reached the door. Mouse followed close behind him, a reminder of why he'd come in the first place. He wasn't about to stop and tuck the kid into bed. The way he figured, he was lucky to get out of the Nugget Hotel in one piece.

Outside, the two walked along in silence, heading for town. Jack wasn't sure why he didn't just turn and go home. His feet were leading him somewhere else.

Some coins, photos, a Bible, a cross.

He stopped. Mouse did, too.

A Bible. A cross. Tom never missed services.

"Come on, kid," Jack said. "Let's go to church."

Chapter 9

The church building stood like a white beacon in the sunlight. Perched at the very top of Jasper proper, it sat between the Nugget Hotel and the town. Jack suppressed a grin at whoever thought of placing the house of worship right where the miners passed to get into town and to the saloon.

The church huddled in a grouping of three whitewashed wood buildings. Mouse and Jack passed the orphanage first, next the chapel with its steeple stabbing up at the sky, and finally came to the parsonage tucked away on the far side. The door sat open, and Reverend Taryn McShane rose from his desk and came to meet them.

Jack and Taryn had become friends immediately when they met, both arriving in Jasper at the same time and both feeling completely out of place. The town found the good reverend to be as patient as he was pious, and he easily won over the Jasper congregation. The town adored their Reverend McShane, and Taryn was perfectly at home. And Jack? Still an outsider.

"I do hope the ground doesn't open up and swallow you," Taryn said, grinning.

"Yeah, I've missed a few services." Jack held out his hand and they shook. "How the hell are you, Reverend?"

Taryn's grin grew. "I am, as always, blessed. What are you doing here? Shouldn't you be about a mile underground by now?"

Jack shrugged, pushing thoughts of the morning aside. Time for that later. "I need your help."

"With the shadow you've picked up?" Taryn asked, nodding to Mouse. Jack glanced back. The boy sat on a rock and puffed away on his pipe. "Really, Jack, you shouldn't allow him to smoke."

"The kid is not my responsibility," Jack grumbled.

"Are you sure?"

"Oh, for God's sake, I just took him out riding. And anyway, if he belongs anywhere, your orphanage makes a far more suitable place than my cabin."

Taryn's eyes filled with guilt, and Jack regretted his words. Since Mouse worked and paid his way, he'd been swept into the world of adults. Taryn tried, when he arrived, to get Mouse to stay at the orphanage. The boy struggled, fought, and ran back to work at the mine. None of the officers were about to stop him. They needed the boy, because of his small size. Child or no. Taryn's hands were full with the children who didn't have the wherewithal to make their way in the world.

"Tare, I'm sorry. I'm just getting cranky. But I have no intention of becoming a nursemaid."

"Doesn't look like he needs one."

"That's where everyone's wrong," Jack said softly, and then focused on the reason he came. "I need to ask you a few questions. About Tom."

At the miner's name, the guilt in Taryn's eyes intensified. "So he is missing. For certain?"

Jack nodded. "Without a trace."

"It's only been a few days. It's not unusual for people to come and go, and—"

"Trust me, Taryn. Something's happened to him. He isn't the kind of man who comes and goes."

Taryn nodded. "True."

"Do you know anything that might help me figure out what happened to him or where he is? Unlike some of your parishioners, he came to church religiously." Jack stopped and cracked a smile. The reverend didn't return it. Taryn's look of guilt collapsed into serious thinking. Jack waited a few seconds. When the minister looked back at him, the plea for help etched on his face shouted louder than words. "Taryn, what is it?"

The reverend shook his head. "I don't know. I . . . I keep hoping Tom will reappear. I'm not sure what to do." He looked over Jack's shoulder at Mouse, and then gestured for Jack to follow. The rectory office drew him in, promising mysteries, dark and cool. Small, shuttered windows held secrets inside. Taryn shut the door and faced Jack. "Tom gave me something for safekeeping. He told me not to turn it over to anyone, no matter what. I've been praying and praying for an answer."

"I'll make it easy. Give it to me."

"Jack, he trusted it to me."

"What is it?" When no answer came, Jack pushed. "At least you can tell me what it is."

"Actually, I can't. I don't know. It's sealed up in newspaper."

It might have been the cool air, but Jack's skin tightened and tiny bumps raised on his arms. "Taryn, you have to show it to me. It might have something to do with Tom's disappearance."

"That would be a horrible breach of confidence."

"Don't you think the situation warrants it?" Taryn still appeared undecided, so Jack tried a different approach. "Reverend, you say you prayed for an answer. Well, I came to you and asked. Don't you think that's something, a sign or whatever?"

"You think you are sent from God to help me with this?"

"I do think things happen for a reason." Again, getting fired and his fight with Jory crept into his mind. "My day brought me to your doorstep. Any other day I'd be down in the mine, but I'm aboveground, asking you to help me with Tom. A lightning bolt hit me at the Nugget Hotel when I held his cross and Bible. I think that's as close to Divine Intervention as I'm ever gonna get."

Taryn's face held his perplexed expression.

Jack put his hand on his friend's arm. "Tare, you can trust me."

He watched the decision emerge in the reverend's expression. Taryn walked over to one end of his heavy oak desk. "Help me." Jack went to the other end and they scooted the desk forward a few feet, revealing a break in the floorboards.

"Why, Reverend McShane!"

Taryn knelt with a letter opener in his hands. "Yes, apparently the last minister kept his poker winnings and libations hidden in this spot." He slid the opener between floorboards and lifted. "I stumbled across the hiding place quite by accident."

"No wonder they rode the poor guy out on a rail," Jack said in a teasing voice.

"The town tarred and feathered him first, from what I hear," Taryn said. "And he died from it."

Jack stopped smiling. "Mobs can be a dangerous animal."

Taryn extracted a package from the dark hidey-hole and stood, clutching the bundle, looking anything but sure.

"Why don't you open it and we'll look at it together? I'll leave it up to you to decide whether or not to give it to me or hide it back away."

Taryn leveled his gaze at Jack. "But then you'll know what

it is."

"You've known me since we came to this miserable town. You come to my house every week for dinner. Tare, you can trust me. I'll do what's right. You have my word."

"I'm putting a lot of faith in you."

"I won't let you down."

Nodding, Taryn handed the package to Jack.

Jack glanced from the boy sleeping in his bed to the sheaf of paper on his table, the pages still trying to curl in and hold secrets. He walked to his window to look up at the Creely Mansion. And to think. A speck scuttled down the mountain. Turtle. Jack wondered if the operations manager headed his way, to do some managing of him.

Turning back to the table, Jack unrolled the papers once again. And wondered for the hundredth time what to do. He knew, yet deliberation seemed prudent. What he held in his hands would begin something. And it meant the end of Tumbling Creek Ranch, if he hadn't ended it already this morning. No turning back if he acted on this.

A petition. Shorter shift hours. More safety parameters. Better pay for the more dangerous jobs. A list of things that should be a man's God-given right, things the miners should never have to ask for, all words printed out in neat, careful letters. Tom, in addition to being a decent, honest man, was one of the few miners who knew how to read and write. The penmanship definitely belonged to him.

Most of the miners signed an *X* following their formal names. Obediah Bailey's *X* slashed across his printed name. Digger.

Now his panicked look this morning made sense. Hurtful sense. His best friends didn't trust him enough to tell him about the existence of this piece of paper.

Demands screamed across the page from workers. Instead of calming miners and making things easier for Victor and his officers, Jack would bring a petition to the mine president on the men's behalf. If he had the nerve to do it.

He glanced back out of the window. Barger scuttled ever closer. The operations manager who'd never been below and had no idea about conditions beneath the surface.

The entire mining operation trudged on, day after day, completely unfair. There was no real decision for him to make. Just the right thing to do. Everything he owed Creely settled around his conscience, and it wasn't just the money weighing on Jack. After Victor saved his family, their home, didn't he at least owe the man some loyalty?

Oh, what the hell? He held the fate of the petition in his hands. The way Jack figured, he was out of a job anyway. The ranch was as good as gone. Yep, what the hell, indeed?

Turtle was definitely coming his way. And Jack was in the dubious position of representing a bunch of miners who didn't trust him. What a mess. He rolled up the petition and put it in his bureau drawer, then reached down inside to find the strength to face what was coming, one disaster at a time. Duke began a frenzy of barking. He must not like turtles, either.

"Down, Duke!"

Duke trotted over to Jack. The knock came. Duke growled.

"Mr. Buchanan?" Turtle's nasal voice came muffled through the door. "Shall I return another time?"

"No, hold on." Jack patted Duke on the head and lowered his voice. "We can't kill anyone today. Get over to your quilt and be a good boy." Jack swung the door open and steeled himself. Turtle squinted through his spectacles into Jack's cabin, paying close attention to the huge hound in the corner.

"Is it safe to come in?"

"Absolutely." Jack gestured for the man to enter. "Duke's eaten lunch already. Can I offer you a libation, Mr. Barger?" Jack crossed the cabin to pull out a bottle and two glasses from his small cupboard. A shot made the perfect accompaniment to a man losing everything. "Genuine Kentucky bourbon," Jack continued. "Care to join me?" He sat at the table and poured. "An officer of the mine is always welcome." He lifted a glass and threw the drink down his throat. It burned the whole way.

"There is no need for sarcasm, Mr. Buchanan. And thank you, but no, to the offer of a drink. I never imbibe prior to evening hours."

"Damned noble of you." Jack picked up the glass he'd poured for Turtle and threw it back, too. It burned a little less. A man could get used to this stuff.

Turtle's eyes slid over to the bed where Mouse slept. "What is the boy doing here? He should be on shift."

Jack echoed his earlier confrontation with Stoop. "Mr. Barger, I suggest you mind your own damned business."

Turtle gasped. When he spoke, his words were edged with ice. "Mr. Creely requests your presence. Not at his office. He awaits you at his manor."

Jack sat back in his chair, wood scraping against his spine. So, the big man would do it himself. And how damned civilized, in his home. To take away Jack's. Ironic, too. Jack leaned forward and poured another shot. Mr. Barger huffed and walked backward, keeping his eye on Duke. He tossed a disgusted glance at Mouse before he slammed the door. The dog laid his head on his paws and looked over to Jack with misery in his eyes.

"Don't look at me that way, Dog. You can't kill every ass in the world." He retrieved the petition and sat back down. Stared at it. These miners, despite the threat of losing everything, were standing up for themselves. Asking for shorter workdays, more pay. Their list, their demands, their words were courage, plain and simple.

Jack downed the whiskey and looked over at Mouse, now asleep. He thought of the little boy riding a horse, giggling. Like little boys should.

Tom had found courage enough to make the document. The miners had possessed courage enough to sign it. Well, he'd find the courage to take it to Creely. No, more. He signed his name, his full name, Jack Horatio Buchanan Jr. to the petition and rose from his chair.

He didn't want to keep Victor Creely waiting.

Creely Manor.

Although Jack had been in Jasper for months, he'd never received a summons until now. Set away from the road and perched on a rock ledge, the Gothic structure of impenetrable stone sat, imposing and ominous. A figure in the window moved away from slightly swaying lace curtains. Someone had watched Jack's ascent up the road. Mrs. Creely? No one ever saw the woman. Victor claimed her frailty and illness kept her housebound. With the stronghold in front of him, Jack wondered if she really chose nonexistence over moving freely about.

The rock used to erect the fortress had been ripped from the core of the mountain. But the inside, Jack discovered when he crossed the threshold and nodded at the boy who opened the door for him, reveled in opulence. Marble floors, majestic spiral staircase, wood walls polished to a sheen, no expense was spared to build the palace. Yet, the place felt like a mausoleum. Cold. Hard.

The boy, dressed formally in a morning suit, led him into Victor Creely's library. Around Jack towered shelf after shelf of books, leather-clad volumes punctuated by gold letters calling to him with a tempting chorus of titles. More books than a man could read in a lifetime covered the wall. Jack would give anything for a chance to try.

The miniature butler bowed slightly. "I'll inform Mr. Creely you are waiting," he said, his voice cracking. The kid looked odd, like a child playing dress up in his daddy's clothes. The fancy version of Mouse.

As the boy-butler backed out of the room to the rhythmic ticking of an ornate grandfather clock, Jack took stock of his surroundings, trying to quell his nerves. His presentation of the petition would sure add a touch of interest to the scenario Victor had planned. Mr. Creely hated surprises.

A stuffed peacock in the corner spread its colors, suspended for eternity in a mocking moment of life. Busts of philosophers and generals watched him with blank, sightless eyeballs, causing his neck to itch. The carpet beneath Jack's boots told of exotic lands in a woven tapestry story. In the center of the room, like a guardian of rare treasures, sat an imposing mahogany desk.

He stepped closer to one of the walls of literature to see who populated the shelves. Shakespeare, Thoreau, and one of his personal favorites, Poe. Nathaniel Hawthorne, Herman Melville, Horatio Alger, Charles Dickens, Thomas Moore. Authors Jack loved, some he'd yet to read, all with whom he desired a close acquaintance.

"Impressive, isn't it?" Victor said, and Jack jumped. The exotic Persian carpet muffled the fall of his footsteps, and it seemed he'd just appeared in the room. "Imagine the intellect lining these walls. The ideas, philosophies, wisdom." Victor's eyes lingered over the books, then he turned back to Jack, his attention piercing like a drill bit.

"Very impressive, sir," he agreed.

"Please, Jack, sit." Victor gestured to chairs on the visitor's side of the desk. "I trust you are well after this morning's altercation?"

If Victor played a game, the concern in his eyes made no sense. He walked to the corner of the room to pull a silk cord, and for a second Jack thought he and his chair might drop through the floor into a dungeon. Instead, the child-butler appeared at the door.

"We'll have tea, Jamie. And please, close the door behind you."

"Sir," the boy said, nodding.

To Jack's surprise, Victor didn't walk around the desk. Instead, he settled in the chair next to Jack, concern still in his expression. Victor's demeanor didn't make any sense. Jesus, this was a game. One where Jack wasn't privy to the list of rules.

"Sir, I know you're gonna sack me, so go ahead and get it over."

Surprise. Something Jack had never seen on Victor's controlled countenance. Then, a bigger shock. Victor burst into laughter. Even his eyes crinkled, his mirth genuine. "Why on this earth would I fire you?" Victor asked.

"You saw the fight."

"You stood up for yourself. Didn't let a drunken sot pick on you. I've been waiting to see the Buchanan spirit, and at long last, it finally emerged. I wondered how long I'd have to leave you down in the mine."

"I don't understand."

"Do you really think I'd bother to bring you all the way to

Jasper, consider your services payment of debt, if all I wanted was for you to serve as a dirt-hound? Really, Jack. You are hardly a half-wit." His voice softened. "That fire really took its toll on you. I was there when you came into this world. Knew the curious boy. So bright, full of life, eager to take on any challenge, intellectual or physical. Quite a youngster." He paused. "Quite frankly, I've been surprised at the man who came with me to Jasper. I never thought I'd see the son of Buck Buchanan so"—his lips pressed into a thin line—"damaged," he finished.

The word clutched Jack's windpipe.

"Joellyn's death. The demise of your ranch. These tragedies aren't on your head, Jack. Somewhere inside, you know it, too."

Surprised at the emotional ambush, a lump grew in the back of Jack's throat. He tried to swallow it down and pull up a shield, but he wasn't successful. Victor's words just plain hurt.

"Jack, I love Buck dearly. He's like a brother to me. But he is a stubborn bastard; you know that. And between us, hardly the embodiment of intellectual prowess. You knew, didn't you? Knew you all should evacuate." Victor paused and shook his head. "Buck didn't listen to you, did he? If anyone's to blame—"

"Here." Jack pulled Tom's petition from his pocket and thrust the papers out, the only way he could think to stop Victor's words.

Victor took the sheaf and leaned back in his chair, his puzzlement giving way to a look of interest. "Ah," Victor said. "I've heard about this petition." He flipped through the pages. "Pathetic, isn't it? Most marks are an 'X.' Men who can't even sign their own names." He flipped to the last page, eyes stopping on the last signature. Victor aimed a sharp look back to Jack.

Jack struggled to find his voice. "Do you think this has anything to do with Tom being missing?" he asked, nodding at the papers. Silence stretched, the only sound in the room the ticking grandfather clock.

Finally, a chuckle. "Whatever are you suggesting?"

"I honestly don't know, Mr. Creely. I'm just looking for some answers."

"I doubt you'll find any from this insignificant list of *X*es. And your name? Did you add it because you thought I would fire you? Is this an attempt at retribution?"

Jack persisted. "Did you know anything about the petition before Tom disappeared?"

"Don't you realize I sent you home today to protect you? I wanted to give you some room; let the tempers of those animals die down. Spare you any more humiliation. Although you aren't grasping this, I'm on your side." Victor rose, tossed the papers on the desk, and walked over to pull a book from the shelf. "Have you read Shakespeare?"

"Yes, sir."

"*Julius Caesar*. One of my favorites." Victor looked pointedly at Jack. "A story of great betrayal."

A sharp rap on the door caused Jack to jump. Victor didn't flinch. "Enter."

Jamie came in, barely able to carry the tray laden with china, silver, and food. It tipped precariously as he placed the tray on the desk. Silence stretched through the room. When Jamie left and closed the door behind him, Victor snapped the book shut and slammed it on the desk, causing Jack to jump again. He scrubbed his hand down his face. Lord, his nerves were rubbed raw.

Victor held up the petition, the stuffed peacock staring lifelessly over his shoulder. "For some reason, you believe this has some sort of meaning." He tore the papers down the middle, and then tore them again. And again. He didn't stop until he'd ripped the petition into bits that he tossed into the air. Jack watched the pieces flutter and land on the Persian carpet. Victor smiled. "There. Gone. Problem solved. And less complicated than killing a man, don't you think?"

Heat flooded up Jack's neck. "I didn't mean—"

"Yes, you did." Victor picked up *Julius Caesar* and replaced the volume in the wall of books. He spun around to face Jack. "Do you really think I'd kill a man over a piece of paper? One with no meaning? No point?"

"There is a point, sir, an important one. The miners are unhappy and growing more so by the day. Their lives are hell."

Victor shrugged. "So? What do they expect? They are tunneling through rock with explosives, not peddling candy for a living." Victor grabbed the back of the chair and leaned forward. "It's hard work in the mines? Difficult? You don't say? Who would ever imagine such a thing?"

"You haven't worked down there, sir. The mine is worse than you can imagine."

"They can always quit."

"No they can't!" The words exploded from Jack.

"Ah, yes. This is the only job they can do; I'm the only one who will hire them. They aren't fit for anything else."

Jack glared, his frustration straining against a wall of guilt. He worked to keep calm.

Victor continued. "A few rabble-rousers won't change the fact that the miners are well paid and have decent jobs despite their momentous shortcomings." He gestured to the bits of paper beneath his feet, eyes snapping with disgust. "They don't even possess the ability to sign their own names. The cart mules I own are more intelligent than most of these men. Jasper Mine gives them the opportunity to make something of themselves."

"Mr. Creely, if they're so well paid, how is it they live like they do? Sharing beds at the Nugget Hotel? Some of them are so deep in debt at the company store they'll never get ahead."

"You're a compassionate man, but you empathize with those who don't deserve your concern. Where are the miners after every shift? What do they do with their precious earnings? Drink and gamble and whore. If they live poorly, it is their own fault."

"Mr. Creely—"

"I can see you're frustrated with the simplicities of your job. Men like us bore easily when left unchallenged. You have much too much potential to spend another moment blasting rock." Victor smiled, just barely. "You are hereby promoted to shift boss."

Jack tried not to stare, but his jaw dropped. He closed his mouth and gulped.

"This afternoon I did fire someone," Victor continued. "That worthless piece of drunken rubbish. The man actually cried. Begged for his job. Disgusting." His smile widened. "Congratulations, Jack." He clasped Jack's hand and pulled him to his feet. "This will give you the opportunity to shape these men. Mold them. You are a fine example for them. I'm sure you will lead as brilliantly as you blasted tunnels. And tonight we'll celebrate." He put his arm around Jack's shoulder and led him into the entryway. "We'll announce your promotion at the Boarding House. All the officers are meeting there. Be there at seven. Supper is served at eight."

"Sir—"

"I know you're not actually an officer yet. You are on your way. You belong with us. Time for you to begin your rightful path within the company."

Damn it, where the hell was his voice? Jack wondered. His words?

"Oh, and Jack? Wear your Sunday best. Miss St. Claire is quite particular in the matters of appearance and dress. We'll discuss all the details of your new duties tonight and the additional benefits of your position, some of which you will welcome this evening." Victor's smile seemed genuine. Just like the stranger rolling through town last month selling Miracle Cure-All Elixir. "Congratulations, Jack Buchanan. You've more than earned this."

Jack stepped out onto the porch. Behind him, the door shut, a heavy sound. He turned. And found himself standing on the outside, his nose inches from a solid, closed door.

Chapter 10

"Well, well," Isabella remarked when she entered the bedroom. "I see we're prepared for the evening. Milena, you'll be pleased to learn your party left town this morning. You may officially come out of hiding. You're free."

Beth smoothed Milena's skirt and stepped back. The Gypsy was stunning in Beth's midnight blue dress. Distrust snapped in her black eyes. And perhaps, Isabella thought, even a little well-harnessed anger. And after such a happy announcement.

Midnight curls swept away and back from the woman's magnificent eyes. A few strands escaped her elaborate upsweep, promising a touch of unbridled wildness. The black lace trim on the dress echoed her crown of hair and hinted of elegant darkness within. Isabella had been mistaken when she labeled the Gypsy breathtaking. There were no words to describe this. Well, no, perhaps there were.

Gold mine.

Milena held her chin a bit higher. "I took your bath. I wear your dress. I will only do this. Not your service."

"Ah, my dear." Isabella smiled and shook her head. "You agreed to tell some fortunes, a little mysterious hocus-pocus. A lovely addition to the evening. However, I certainly don't expect any more of you. Not every woman is Boarding House quality."

Milena's eyes flickered, but her neck remained stiff.

"Beth dear," Isabella said, "will you excuse us?"

On the way out of the room, Beth touched Milena's arm. The two shared a moment of support, as if they were old friends. Interesting, and after such a short time together. Isabella tucked the observation away for later thought. Behind her, the door shut. Time to bend this one's stiff neck, just a bit. But not break her. Isabella knew the regality with which the Gypsy held herself was a selling point. High-spirited women were always worth so much more.

"You've become acquainted with Beth. Tonight you will meet the other Boarding House ladies. They are refined. Educated. Able to discuss matters social, literary, political, all with great insight and candor. They work to be perfect companions in every way. Milena, you are quite lovely, but a bit, please pardon me, rough-hewn."

She got the desired effect. Milena's expression melted into an unsure look, perhaps even hurt. Still, she held her jaw stiff, clenched. Good. Metal ran through her, something she'd need to survive. But Milena also needed a benefactor. Isabella knew she was the best deal in town, especially for a woman as intriguing as this.

"Not to worry. You'll do fine telling your fortunes." Isabella walked to the dresser, where Milena's velvet bag sat, crumpled. She picked it up and held it close. "In fact, I predict you'll be quite successful in adding a certain, shall we say, excitement to the evening." She clutched the bag tighter. "I'm sure you passed the cribs on your way up. The whore shacks? That's not what this is. What we are. We entertain gentlemen callers. Occasionally romance ensues. Intimacy for each lady to decide for herself.

No one is forced into anything she does not wish." Not quite a lie, Isabella thought. Not really.

The Gypsy held steady, but her eyes flickered to the bag. Everything Milena owned, and Isabella held it in her hand. How incredibly pathetic.

Time for the final persuasion. "You recall, my dear, the man searching for you? What was his name, Rolf?"

Milena's expression turned a touch anxious.

"You remember, I'm sure, what you were about to be forced into?"

Milena dropped her gaze. No, this little Gypsy and her misbegotten pride were no match for Isabella St. Claire. No one was.

"I would never, ever ask that of you, my dear, nor anything you weren't comfortable with. Just fortunes. Just what you wish to offer."

"I am sorry. I thought—"

"Of course, my dear. The conclusion the ignorant come to when regarding us."

Again, hurt in her eyes. Time to build confidence and dangle the prize.

"But you aren't really ignorant, are you? In fact, I find you to be quite intelligent. Capable. You've made it this far. Many women don't. Can't. You've seen them, I'm sure. Women working in factories, households. Selling their lives for a few coins and a meager existence in an attic or cellar. Or the crib whores." Isabella allowed herself a shudder. "And let us not forget the wives whose husbands abuse them in so many ways. Force themselves upon them, convince them they are worthless, no better than laboring animals. Women who bear child after child, growing weaker with each. You've passed their graves, unmarked places with rocks piled up, a wooden cross stuck in the ground." Her words struck a chord as Milena's expression grew troubled.

"You, my dear," Isabella continued, "managed to escape from all that. You stand before me, wearing a stunning silk and lace dress, about to spend the evening enjoying good food and fine wine. You will entertain and tell the fortunes of handsome, intelligent, and well-mannered gentlemen who will, I promise, treat you with dignity and respect. Like a queen. And you deserve to be treated like royalty, Milena. We all do. The difference is most women don't realize this. They sell their souls for nothing more than a broken vow." Isabella harnessed her growing anger. This was not the time, nor the place. Not here. The world within these walls, what she offered to Milena, she'd built with her strength, her intelligence. Her soul. This deserved world of dignity, of respect, came at a price. A very steep price, yet worth everything, this place Isabella St. Claire made for her ladies and herself.

"I gave you my promise you'd be safe, Milena, and I am a woman of my word. You can absolutely trust me." Still holding Milena's hand, she held the Gypsy's bag out. Milena grabbed it with her free hand and clutched it close.

"Come along, dear. This will be marvelous fun. I promise."

"Whoa, girl."

Jack pulled up his horse at the top of the ridge and looked down. He'd faced mountains, stampedes, fires, explosions, and endless hours underground in the mines, yet all that was nothing compared to this. The thought of approaching and entering the house below terrified him. He wasn't sure if it was Victor and his pack of officers, or all the beautiful Boarding House ladies who scared the bejeezus out of him.

Or something else entirely.

He felt like he did the night on the mountain, when he searched for Laney Olsson and he woke up in the middle of the night, aware of—what? The Faerie of the Forest. Why did he feel the same way now, like he stood on the verge of pushing aside a curtain and beholding a world he'd never seen? Well, that description certainly fit the Boarding House and its beautiful occupants. But this felt like more. Different. Something here was important. If only he could figure out what.

Few men held the honor of a Boarding House evening. Honored wasn't exactly how he felt. Duped was more like it. He spurred his horse on, feeling he was riding straight into an ambush, of what intrigue and manipulations he could only guess.

Luke, Miss Isabella's strong-arm man, looked up from his post when Jack approached. A wry grin spread across the hustler's face as he took Willow's reins. Jack dismounted.

"Well, looky, Buchanan, you're all gussied up. How long did it take you to dig rock dust out of your ears?"

Jack smiled at the formerly rough and grizzled Luke. A tall and muscled man with a thick beard and hair that had never been cut, Luke worked on Jack's shift until a few months back. When one of the Boarding House customers got rough and beat a girl halfway to death, Miss St. Claire stopped the man by shooting off his knee. She hired Luke the next day with a few requirements: a bath, a shave, and a haircut.

The barber shaved the three years of beard, but Luke refused to cut his hair. The result, a thick golden mane and the handsome face beneath it, caused ladies to swoon. Now Luke guarded the Boarding House, his powerful frame straining against his cashmere suit.

"You got no room to talk, Goldilocks," Jack answered. "You're pretty as a girl at her first dance."

Luke laughed, then sobered. "You know, Jack, I never figured you for one of them." He tied Jack's horse to the post.

Jack's smile faded. One of them.

Luke continued. "Guess I never figured on me openin' doors and smellin' like a flower, either. Even bought my own damned bathtub. Barber cost me a fortune. I don't own nothin' in this world but a bathtub. Not enough space for it in my room, so Mrs. Peabody moved my bed out. I even sleep in my goddamned tub. Christ, Jack. Amazing what a man will do for a woman, even one he works for." He grasped the ornate gold-plated knob and swung the door open.

The stained-glass doorway framed an impossibly elegant world set against the filth of Jasper. Evening sun flooded through glass designs, reflecting patterns of color onto a white marble floor. The melody of female voices spun around the heavy murmur of men's discussion, and every so often, a trill of soft feminine laughter danced in the air. The rich scent of cooking meat and the sweetness of baking chocolate broke through, and Jack's empty stomach rumbled. He thought of Digger, eating mush at the Nugget Hotel, and Reverend McShane and his orphans, eating whatever the good citizens of Jasper saw fit to donate for the week.

In the entryway to the parlor beyond, dressed in green silk and lace with her red hair piled high, resembling a very rare and expensive rose, stood Isabella St. Claire. She smiled dazzlingly and came to him, holding out her gloved hand.

"Jack, welcome." Her voice was lyrical music. What did they call such a creature in Greek mythology? A siren. Only this one didn't exist on a faraway ocean, this one lived on an enchanted island, in a sea of dust and dirt.

"Miss St. Claire." Jack stepped over the threshold and took

her proffered hand. Panic lurched his gut. Should he kiss the glove? Lord, he'd never done such a thing before. Thankfully, in one graceful motion she squeezed his hand and drew him close to take his arm.

"I understand congratulations are in order."

They walked together to the parlor. Through the archway the room teemed with people: Turtle, Edmund, other officers of the mine, the mayor, and beautiful silk-clad ladies with upswept hairstyles and soft, bared shoulders. A mist of cigar smoke and sweet perfume hung like a veil protecting this other world.

"To tell you the truth, Miss St. Claire, I feel fairly out of place."

She stopped and faced him, her smile turning genuine. "That's what I've always liked about you, Jack. You're honest." She took his hand again. "You're to feel perfectly at home. Everything will be fine. It's what I'm here for, what we're all here for. All you need to do is relax and enjoy yourself." She led him into the parlor. "And please, I think it's high time you call me Isabella."

Soft candlelight, leather chairs, and wood-paneled walls made the room one any man might be comfortable inhabiting. Jack had no doubt Isabella planned it that way.

"I see you've found our new shift foreman." Victor's voice cut through the haze of gentility like a knife. Isabella dropped away from Jack's side, and Victor shook his hand. Jack couldn't get over the feeling he performed an intricately choreographed ballet, one where he didn't know any of the steps.

"Jack, congratulations." A lovely blond woman with wide-set blue eyes came to Victor's side. She took the mine owner's arm, leaning into him. Jack almost didn't recognize the polished and perfected woman on Victor's arm, and suddenly he realized it was little Beth Freemont. Beth used to be a scullery maid at the Creely estate. She became one of Isabella's ladies soon after Jack arrived in Jasper. Apparently, she still served Victor, but not in the matters of housecleaning.

"It's good to see you, Beth," Jack replied. At least he knew one of the ladies. Isabella and her flock were well known in town, but they always stayed discreetly on the edge of Jasper life, not coming close enough to cause any complaints. Jack not only recognized Beth from her scullery days, but he remembered Digger and Beth grew up together in the Jasper orphanage. He wondered if Digger even recognized her now.

"Delighted you join us this evening, Jack," Turtle said, his face pinched as though he smelled something foul.

Jack grinned and nodded. "Mr. Barger. The pleasure is entirely mine."

"And Jack is precisely who we're celebrating tonight," Isabella interrupted, handing Victor, then Jack a glass of champagne. The other ladies drifted about the room, dispensing glasses to the rest of the assembled men.

"To Jack," Victor toasted, "and his very hard-earned and, I must admit, a bit delayed promotion."

"To Jack," the room chorused. Not only did everyone dress for effect, they spoke for effect, as well. Jack wondered if he might count on anything in this world as genuine. Only one thing to do. Time to toss a rock of reality.

"Quite amazing," Jack said as glasses were raised to lips across the room. "Just a few days ago we searched for a missing man, and now we join in a toast, as if in celebration of finding him, safe and sound. Shame the man is still missing."

Silence fell.

"That reminds me," Victor said, his voice immediately cutting through tension. He handed Jack a book. *Julius Caesar*. "From my private collection. To commemorate your promotion and continuing success. A special gift, from me. Enjoy. To you, Jack, my godson, and the offspring of my most trusted friend."

As if on cue, talking and laughter began, attentions focused back to small, scattered groups of conversation. Victor's recovery impressed Jack. He managed to regain control and at the same time made Jack feel like an ungrateful jackass. The man was a master.

"To Junior!" Sheriff Cain held up a glass of champagne.

Isabella slipped between them. "I have a surprise before we serve dinner. And this is especially appropriate in honor of Jack's promotion and his bright future."

Jack clutched his glass, wondering what was coming next.

"We're all going to have our fortunes told," she said, then lowered her voice to a stage whisper. "That is, if we dare!"

Several feminine giggles of delight rose along with one of Victor's eyebrows.

"Ladies and gentlemen, I present for your amusement and pleasure, the mysterious and gifted Madame Shabanov!"

Jack felt her before he saw her. A presence so strong it filled the room, announcing her with more flourish than Isabella's dramatic proclamation. Despite her enormous presence, a tiny, delicate woman walked into the room. Jack fell into her black eyes and was instantly lost. She was real. The Faerie from the Forest stood before him, not a mythical creature, but a flesh-and-blood woman.

He felt like he did when the platform pulled him up from the mine, and the sun blinded but reminded him there was light, life, and the taste of sweet air above the existence of smothering darkness.

Everything has changed, Jack thought, as the reality of her existence sparkled through his soul. Everything.

Chapter 11

Milena entered the parlor, acutely aware all eyes appraised and judged her. Silence drew across the room like a curtain, followed by glances of curiosity, surprise, appreciation.

Suspicion. Envy.

She admired the dramatic abilities of the proprietress. The madame had orchestrated quite an entrance. One by one, Milena boldly met each person's gaze, determined not to show fear to these wealthy *gaujos* who, in any other circumstance, would not allow someone like her to walk among them.

A man watched her along with all the others, his eyes lit with the fire of a predator. On the outside, he appeared calm, but a dark and persistent power exuded from him. Everyone else in the room fell away into the shadows.

Suddenly, she felt another commanding life spirit among these people, someone other than the predator. Alarm filled her. In a flash, she knew. The man who had hunted at Rolf's side, who sensed her presence despite her cover of night, was here.

Frantic, she ripped her awareness away from the predator and settled on blue eyes, wide with wonderment. She froze. The Hunter.

Her panic changed to confusion. No man had ever looked at her with such bewildered joy. Not lust, not desire, but awe, as if she were a rare and never before seen treasure. And his boyish face, handsome, open, and shining with honesty. Kindness. Although the room glowed only with lamps and outside dusk swept the sky, sunlight sparkled in his hair.

Had he hunted her that night on the mountain? Tracked her like some animal, some prize to be dragged to Rolf's bed? The man standing in the group before her and what she knew of the Hunter did not match. At all.

His kindness. His light. One explanation. A trick.

Isabella grasped Milena's hand. "Ladies and gentlemen, who will be first? Who possesses courage enough to allow Madame Shabanov a peek into their soul?" The proprietress's voice rippled with dramatic excitement.

Immediately, the predator came forward. All else in the room dropped away. As he approached, his desire, forceful as a deadly avalanche down a mountainside, rumbled over and almost knocked her from her feet.

Isabella squeezed her hand. Milena tried to take a deep breath, made impossible by the ridiculous undergarments the proprietress had forced her to wear. The corset—an implement of torture, Milena thought—made an impenetrable shield against the taking in of air. The petticoats, more than any amount of skirts worn by a Romani woman, weighted her down. No wonder these American women chose to sit most of the day. Who possessed the unending strength to move against such restrictions of dress? The clothes held Milena in a frightening grip. She fought the urge to flee.

"Madame Shabanov, it is my pleasure to present Mister Victor Creely, the president of Jasper Mining Company and, if I may be allowed a small digression of affection, my very dear friend."

Smoothly, Victor took Milena's hand from Isabella's gloved one and brushed his lips across her fingers. He searched her face for her reaction; perhaps he expected a giggle, a blush, a smile. She wanted to shudder with revulsion at his touch. She showed nothing.

"I'm charmed, Madame Shabanov." His voice was smooth, alluring. The soft rattling of a deadly snake.

Isabella ushered them to a small, velvet-draped table, and Milena caught a glimpse of Beth, her eyes downcast and hurt on her pretty face. Beth had been at Victor's side when Milena entered the room. How quickly he came forward for a taste of something new, leaving the lovely young flower to wilt by the wall.

"I tell your future with seeing cards, my crystal ball, or I read your palm," Milena said just like she'd rehearsed earlier with Isabella. She pulled each one out of her bag and set them on the round table, grateful to concentrate on something other than the man before her. When she looked back at Victor's face, she saw him measure her. In turn, she decided to measure him.

Rich, his expensive clothing told her. Particular, from his neatly barbered hair and smoothly shaved face. Powerful. She wasn't sure if that came from his broad-shouldered body, his decisive movements, or his overwhelming presence, but in this pack of jackals, he reigned king.

"Oh, please," Victor answered, "read my palm. I've always been sure my future's in my hands." He turned over his hand and presented it to her.

"Both," Milena corrected him. He raised his eyebrows and held his hands over the table, palms up. She hesitated. His eyes glinted with interest, and he dared her with his look. Showing a confidence she didn't really feel, she took them in her own and lightly caressed his palms with her thumbs, sparking the slight and guarded connection she used to tell fortunes. His expression flashed alarm, but he smoothed it over, strong and in charge once more. He hid the tremor well, but not from her. She would see much about this man others did not. His palms were smooth, yet hardened. Not exactly those of a working man, but once they had been thick with the calluses of labor.

"Hard work has brought you far," she said.

"Don't need no fortune-teller to know that," a voice scraped with skepticism.

"Sheriff," Isabella admonished. "Hush."

"No," Milena said, "I mean very difficult work."

His hands bleed, and he swipes them down dirty pants and reaches to pick up another crate. He is starving, afraid, alone. Tears stain his filthy cheeks. He is exhausted. This job is his only way to survive. Without it, he will die. He works furiously. Determined. He is not a man. Only a boy. A little boy.

Her voice softened. "You were very young. Just a child."

Victor's eyes lost their harsh glare. He nodded. "That's true."

"You spoke correctly, Mr. Creely," Milena said. "Your hands tell your future, but much more. Your emotions, health, talents, strength." She stopped for effect, then continued. "Your fears."

Concern flashed in his eyes. Then they drained of everything except his wall of confidence. "I have no fears, Madame Shabanov."

She dropped her attention back down to his hands. Oh, yes, he had fears. Isabella warned her of being too personal, especially with the men. Compliment, admire, praise, and flatter them, the proprietress advised. That's what they sought from the Boarding House and its occupants.

"You possess a great prowess with details, your mind is powerful, your memory strong. And," she said, her voice light so not to offend, " I see a great love of argument."

The men in the room, Victor included, burst into appreciative laughter that died down in the next moment.

"You are a man of strong will. You have a love of perfection. You possess much confidence." But the line on his palm stretched across, broken in several places, hinting of doubts he held deep within. She did not mention the distrust of himself that must haunt him. Interesting. Not even Victor Creely trusted Victor Creely. Milena continued. "You love your work."

"So inform us of something we don't know." Again, the rough voice.

"Cain, quiet," Victor said in a low tone. Milena did not speak of the extremes she saw in his hands. Strength leading to ruthlessness, confidence growing to a pride that devoured character. Not only a man who loved his work, but a king who must rule, at all costs.

She raised her eyes. His gaze bored into her, searching. This man was not merely strength. This man was danger.

"What else do you see, Madame Shabanov?" he asked. She returned to studying his palm.

A tuft of hair springs out. Fingernails grow and curl into claws. The beast springs and rips into her flesh.

She blinked her eyes against the vision. His hands were again normal. He smiled. "What else?" he persisted.

"You have great command of words. You are able to use them to your advantage," she said. *Deceit*, his palm told her.

"You insist to get what you want. Within you is endless desire," she said, as again his hands spoke. *Bloodthirsty. Merciless.*

"Calm. Patience." *Cold-blooded. Relentless.*

"Passionate." *Vicious.*

Victor's eyes held her, pinned. The room dropped away and

the King of the Jackals overwhelmed her. She must end this.

"Great vigor and success," she said. "Riches. Prosperity." Safe, empty words with no meaning. Words the *gaujos* always preferred to hear. She tried to pull away from him. He tightened his grip.

"I couldn't ask for more," he said and raised both her hands to his lips. This time, his mouth lingered. He tasted her. She saw from his expression that if he could devour her, he would.

"Jack," he said, looking up from the table. "Jack must be next."

The crowd shoved Rolf's hunting companion to the front. Victor relinquished his chair and, to Milena's complete dismay, Jack Buchanan took his place. Determined not to let him sense her fear, she met his gaze.

His face broke with a slight smile of shyness. She wanted to believe what she saw; yet she knew better than to believe such deceit. She did not want to touch him, this man who hunted her like an animal, yet came to her, his true spirit hidden in a cloak of kindness and a mask of honesty. She recognized this one as a master of trickery. He must be, to wear such a disguise.

"Give her your hands, Jack," Victor prompted.

"If it's all the same," he said, shaking his head. A blush ran up his neck. An accent of America, once she'd heard before from the southern regions, colored his voice. Still shaking from her connection with the Jackal King, she imagined a wall erected between herself and this Hunter of Women and concentrated on strengthening the barrier. She must not open to him. She must not.

"Give her your hands, Jack," a female voice echoed.

"He's skairt!" the sheriff called out. "Junior's skairt of a little girl."

Milena lifted her head and glared at the haughty face that matched such a rough voice. "I am not a little girl."

Her statement elicited laughter, particularly from the men. Jack shoved his hands onto the table. Summoning all her defenses and protection, she reached out and gently touched him. He jumped like a bolt of lightning hit him.

His hands were rough, calloused, cracked. They'd bled, and recently. New scars covered old. Compassion grew for the kind of life that caused this, but she pushed her feelings aside. She must not allow empathy to open the door between them, and she must not let him see she knew him, or that they had already met on the side of the mountain beneath a full moon.

From under his cuff peeked the tip of a scar puckering his wrist, a burn. She shifted her attention to the other wrist and saw the same. More scars. An echo and memory of flames so intense they burned cold, like ice. A terrible fire destroying everything. Everything.

A wall of flames. The scream of a woman rips through his soul. Horror, frustration, he can't reach her in time. He doesn't reach her at all. An expansive desert of emptiness. A heart, barren and lost. Guilt crumbles his soul, pain burrows deep. Her children want their mother. They look to him for answers. He has none. He should have insisted they all leave. They would be safe. Alive. He can't live with this. He simply cannot.

Coward.

Connection with him transported her back to the *MoortYak*, her own experience of death and fire, sorrow without an end. She curled in against the memory and fought against reliving it.

"Madame Shabanov? Milena?" Isabella's voice called her back. Milena shook her head trying to shake away his vision and her empathy. Their two tragedies melted into one and she lived his every pain.

Despite her resistance, she'd never experienced a connection so strong. This man knew the *MoortYak*. He'd lived through

DeathFire himself. He was a survivor, like her.

Their eyes met and he trapped her in shared sorrow.

She pushed her back to the chair, and he grasped her hands. How did he pull out her most horrible memory, the most intimate of pain from her, and present it as his own? Could his be real? Did he share the devastation of such a loss, hold it inside, in a small, black space threatening to open up and become endless? Or was this a trick?

How did he manage such a thing? Who was this man?

"Are you all right, ma'am?" he asked her as if she'd stumbled during a stroll. She pulled her hands away from his and shook her head, trying to clear it.

"What'd you do to her?" the voice of the lawman called from the edge of her consciousness. "Jesus, look at that, touching Junior almost kilt her."

"No, no, I'm fine. I only . . . " She searched for something to say, something to cover this most personal and unwelcome moment.

"What about your cards?" Jack asked, gently. "She can't see anything through all these calluses." He held up his hands. "Cain, some of us actually work for a living." He laughed along with everyone else, and the moment of awkwardness passed.

Milena gathered her wits enough to pick up her seeing cards and hand them to him. She watched him shuffle the cards, and he glanced up at her.

This time, she jumped when his look bolted through her.

The dinner bell sounded lightly, like a prayer. Sounds of disappointment skittered across the crowd.

"Dinner, everyone," Isabella said. "Jack, you'll have to wait. I'm sure after some sustenance, Madame Shabanov will be ready for you."

Isabella threw Milena a look of warning that sliced through

her panic. Milena would never be ready for this man. Never.

Victor slid between Jack and Milena as they stood and he offered her his arm. She reluctantly accepted his touch and entered the dining room with the King of the Jackals. They sat, and she watched Jack escort Beth into the room, chatting away like old friends.

"Milena, I find you incredibly fascinating," Victor said with his deceptively soft voice. "You must tell me everything about yourself."

She wished, with all her heart, for this awful evening to end. Isabella sat to Victor's other side, and he angled to speak with the proprietress.

Her face itched. Did the Hunter watch her? She glanced over and met his blue eyes. Again, the open honesty on his face struck her. This false cloak of kindness was beyond the powers of a trickster. Was he a *beng*—a demon in human skin? A warlock?

"Milena . . . may I call you Milena?" Victor's question brought her back to him.

"You may."

"Where are you from?" His question demanded. An interrogation and not any true interest in her. He leaned close to hear her answer.

"From everywhere. From nowhere."

Victor raised his eyebrows.

"I warned you; she is mysterious," Isabella said, leaning forward to smile at Milena and lifting a glass of red wine to her lips. Isabella had warned Milena to speak evasively when discussing her past.

"Well, perhaps you might enlighten me as to how you came to arrive in Jasper?" Victor asked.

"I am Romani. A traveler," she answered. "It is what I do. Travel."

Milena spent the rest of dinner dodging Victor's questions and Jack's wistful glances. When the piles of rich food came, she barely ate.

Milena silently prayed, again, for the night to end. Inside the Boarding House, smelling rich, decadent food, listening to cultured, educated voices, and wearing the finest silk, she'd never been more pampered.

Or more trapped.

"Have you completely lost all reason?" Victor's voice, unusually harsh, cut through the room. Fine, she'd match his mood. Isabella thought there may be trouble of some sort when he pulled her into her office immediately following dinner. Trouble, or he was in the mood for a jounce. Or, perhaps, both.

Isabella knew better than anyone that without Victor, the Boarding House would be nowhere near as exclusive. His meetings, influence, invitations, and parties supported this world Isabella built and protected. Only one man in Jasper owned enough power and money to touch her. And he knew it. He stood before her, his anger and desire almost tangible.

"Whatever do you mean?" Isabella asked, all innocence.

"The Gypsy. Madame Shabanov, or whatever the ridiculous name. She's the Swede's missing wife."

"She's no such thing. She was traveling with her father. He was inconsiderate enough to perish somewhere back in Nebraska and leave her on her own."

"So you maintain she is not Laney Olsson."

Isabella sighed with impatience. "Really, Victor, do you think the woman in my parlor, entertaining and telling fortunes, is really mundane enough to be 'Laney Olsson'? And do you think me foolish enough to recruit a married woman?"

"Do you take me for an idiot? Two Gypsies arriving in Jasper is mere coincidence? Isabella, you and I both know, there is no such thing as coincidence."

"Perhaps not. But there is such a thing as a big, stupid Swede with the arrogance to believe he can force a desperate woman into marrying him against her will." The words tumbled out before she could stop them.

"Aha!"

"Aha, yourself. She is a free woman and you may find this difficult to accept, but Milena Shabanov may do exactly what she pleases!" Silence stretched. Isabella worked to rein in her emotions.

"As long as you turn a profit from 'what she pleases.'"

Isabella allowed herself the pleasure of glaring at him, this man who assumed he owned the world. "Quite the rude statement, and not at all the gentlemanly behavior I expect from you, Victor Creely. Really, most unbecoming."

He laughed and crowded closer. "You sound more like my mother every day."

"Fitting. You act like a spoiled boy." She held his gaze. "I will force Milena into nothing, unlike the hordes of men with whom I am familiar."

"The important word being *familiar*."

"Did I say spoiled boy? I meant arrogant bastard."

His eyes flashed desire and he moved close, leaving almost no space between them. She knew his need for her. And her power over him. Despite what was to come, Victor Creely was right where she wanted him.

He spoke, his voice a husky whisper. "Now, now, my sweet, your fangs are showing. It is fortunate for you they are so very lovely."

She knew what he desired just as she knew this would come the moment she watched his frustration during dinner. Well, Isabella St. Claire would give as good as she'd get. She smiled and removed the glove, one finger at a time, from her good hand. His eyes lit with desire. Her smile sharpened into a snarl and she slapped him, just as he wanted. He grabbed her wrists and pushed her down, across the desk. She allowed anger to explode into her struggle against him. Her efforts in his iron grip were useless, she knew, but she fought anyway. That, he desired, too.

This was best, she told herself. Beth would crumple in the wake of his unbridled passion. Isabella knew from experience she was best at withstanding Victor Creely. Usually this scene played out after a discouraging meeting with his officers or a threatening telegram from the board of investors in New York City.

He clawed at her bodice, tearing it away. She'd add the cost of her dress to his monthly bill, something she'd done many times. His rough hands couldn't breach her corset, and in his frenzy, he wouldn't bother to take the time to undo the stays. He never did.

He grabbed her skirts and yanked them up, ripping the delicate fabric of her drawers. Then he was on her, ravaging her mouth, biting. He bit her jaw, her neck, her shoulder. *No matter*, she repeated in her head as she struggled against him, *no matter, no matter*. She imagined her next painting. She'd paint the portrait of a gelded stallion, harnessed and pulling a plow like a common mule. Oh, and driving it? A lovely, innocent girl with red hair.

He rammed into her, and she cried out. He flailed upon her, this upstanding businessman, this mogul of mining, this *gentleman*, and thrashed against her like a convulsing animal.

She gasped out his name, begged him to stop, then to continue faster, harder. Just the way he expected. Heavens, she really was the most amazing actress. Perhaps she'd look into it for her next career. His thrusts grew brutal, and she clawed his neck in return. He growled, releasing the beast he usually kept hidden. The real Victor Creely.

Her painting, she thought, her painting. Not the stallion pulling a cart. She'd capture it at the moment of gelding. The girl with the red hair holding a blood-soaked knife above her head. The horrid image helped her hold to sanity while she acted out her part against the onslaught of him. And hold on she would, for her life, for her ladies, for her world. For herself.

Pleasure and pain mingled and exploded through her in one thought, one feeling.

Power.

He collapsed on her with a groan, the sweat of his face stinging her bitten neck and shoulder. Thank heavens when he was in the mood for a rough tumble, he was also quick. He raised himself to look down into her eyes.

"I want the Gypsy," he said, still inside her.

"Milena is rare," she answered, her voice even. "Expensive."

"I expected as much." He withdrew and stood straight, fastening his pants. "How expensive?" he asked, smoothing the vertical tucks in his shirt. "I want her exclusively. No one else is to touch her."

"That will be twice what an exclusive contract with a young scullery maid is going for these days," Isabella said, and raised herself to sit up on the edge of the desk, wincing. She realized the error of her expression when his eyes lit with satisfaction. He returned his attention to straightening his shirt. There was no point in even attempting to fix herself. Her dress hung in ruins. Tendrils of hair fell to her shoulder. "And Milena is not ready yet."

His head snapped up. He glared at her, his expression dangerous. "What do you mean?"

"I'm sure you'll agree, it won't do to frighten her away. She will run and is quite a capable woman." *Unlike Beth*, she thought. *Unlike your wife.* "Accepting you must be Milena's decision. At least, she must think it so. But," she said, delicately touching her swollen and bleeding lip, "I'm sure with your overwhelming charm, it shouldn't take long."

"Ah, well, there is still Beth to ease my tensions." He wiped away the remnants of blood from her claw mark and wound his cravat around his neck.

"May I help you with that?" she asked.

"I don't believe that's wise. An accidental strangling might have an unfortunate impact on your business, my dear." He smiled and picked up his waistcoat, inspecting it before putting it on. "So, Madame Shabanov is mine." A statement, not a question. As usual.

"Of course." Isabella felt a bit sad for Beth, tossed aside in one, brief moment. But wasn't that the way of this business?

He came at her, and she thought he might push her back down and have at her again. She jerked back, her eyes widening. He smiled, self-satisfaction oozing from his grin, and he offered her his hand. She took it. He kissed her gloved fingers, gently.

"We understand each other," he said.

"Always."

He lifted the palm of her ungloved hand and kissed it, then pulled her close and brushed her lips with his. Then he kissed her. So tender. And again, like the gentlest of lovers. He smoothed back her hair, ran his thumb along her jawline, and stepped back. "Now, if you'll excuse me, I have a young scullery maid to find." He turned, took a few steps, and faced her again, his eyebrows raised. "Oh, and Isabella?"

"Yes?"

"A warning. Rolf Olsson. He hasn't left town. We hired him to work in the mine. Seems he likes Jasper. He wishes to remain." Victor grinned, then turned his back on her and left. She listened to his boots click down the hall, echoes mingling with the light laughter of the parlor.

"Well, Mr. Creely," she said to the empty room, "if that's true, I wouldn't want to be the man enamored of the Swede's object of desire." Or more to the point, she thought, she wouldn't want to be the big, stupid Swede in the way of Victor Creely.

Chapter 12

One look from Suzanne and Jack knew how a steak felt when a starving rancher, fork in hand, came at it. The moment Beth left Jack's side, he supposed he became fair game for all the ladies. He'd been reluctant to enter this seemingly genteel lair, and his instincts were right on the mark.

Suzanne tilted her head to one side, smiled fetchingly, and headed his way. Jack didn't feel at all like being fetched. He managed to dodge her and duck through the kitchen. An older woman cooking at the stove glared at him.

"Pardon me, ma'am," he said, and darted through.

Jack escaped out to the back porch, the door clacking shut behind him. Night air coursed around him. Out here wafted no suffocating smells, temptations of the palette mixed with the perfume of ladies. The dirty, work-sodden, metallic, and animal stench of Jasper didn't sink this far down. Pure, sweet mountain air hit him in the face. One thought clung stubbornly. *Milena.*

He wanted to sit before her again, take in her face, and lose himself in her eyes. She seemed a mystical creature, not of this earth but somewhere unseen. From somewhere magical, the type of made-up places he'd read about, but had grown too jaded to believe in. When she'd taken his hands, eternity tumbled through his soul.

God, he wanted so badly to touch her again it hurt.

One difficulty. For all her otherworldly beauty and mysteriously gentle demeanor, she was in reality a fancy lady. One for hire. Victor Creely had the money, not to mention, first choice.

Jack came down the steps, intending to follow the stone path around the house to the front, find his horse, and gallop away. Light spilled out through lace curtains, illuminating the side yard in soft, webbed pools. A perfectly tended side garden glowed in the splashing light. He almost didn't see her.

Like a wild elfin queen communing with her subjects, Milena sat, circled by plants and flowers. Diffused light barely painted her and the surrounding foliage in muted, silvery tones. Ghostly color emerged from shades of black. She held her eyes closed and her head tilted at an angle as if she listened to whispered secrets. Zebra grass swayed around her, communing with her magic. Purple rain sage flickered at her feet, leaves rustling and shimmering in the moonlight. Her calm beauty ached through him. He did not want to move for fear of disturbing her. If she woke, she'd disappear forever.

Before he knew it was coming, he sighed. Her eyes opened and she jumped to her feet. He hated what he saw constricting her face. Fear. Of him.

"I won't hurt you," he said immediately. "I was just coming around to leave."

She was very real, and very afraid. The pulse in her throat pounded. He'd startled her, sure, but why did he frighten her so thoroughly? What had this woman been through to make her this terrified of him? He watched her steel herself, composure replacing her alarmed expression.

"I won't hurt you," he repeated, spreading his hands apart, palms up. He needed to start some conversation. Something meaningless to calm her down. "So what are you doing out here?" What a stupid question. She was doing the same as him. Escaping.

"I come for solitude," she answered back, her words soft, round, with a tinge of wariness around the edges.

"My apologies for disturbing you, Madame Shabanov." But, Lord, he wasn't sorry at all. He didn't want to leave, or for her to go. He took a step forward and paused. She didn't run. "You never did finish my reading."

Her eyes widened and she shook her head. He remembered her butterfly-light touch across his palm, and knew he'd sell his soul to feel the spark of her sizzle through him again. He would never forget the moment when her eyes met his in understanding. For the first time since the fire and all his loss, he didn't feel alone. Someone else knew.

She must be magic. The only explanation that made sense, yet made no damned sense.

"You do owe it to me, Miss . . . er . . . Isabella promised." A bit of shame twinged at how he pushed, but his need to be near her overpowered any regret.

Another thought crossed his mind. He did need her. For a very real reason. If her jabber was nothing more than imagination, at least he'd get to talk to her some more. He took another step forward, deciding to take the honest approach.

"I've lost a friend. A good one. He disappeared about a week past. I've been looking all over for him and I can't find him. I'm afraid he's . . ."

She nodded and sank to the bench. "In the spirit realm?"

"What?" Then he realized what she meant. "Oh, yeah. Dead. It sounds much nicer when you say it." He nodded to the stone bench. "Do you mind if I join you?"

Her eyes skimmed down to the space by her side and back to him. Her look begged him not to come any closer.

"Or, I can stand here, too." He shrugged slightly, only making small motions, like a man discovering the presence of an exotic bird. He didn't want her to flutter away. "Can you help me, do you think? Can you do that with your fortune-telling?"

"A woman stands beside you. Not a man."

He took stock of the area around them. They were alone. He looked back to her. "What?"

"A spirit. A woman." A smile softened her face. "She looks very much like you. Perhaps a twin?"

He froze, chills sliding through him. "Jo." His voice broke when he spoke his sister's name. In this garden of moonlight, saying her name sounded like a sacred prayer, a song of memory.

"Jo," she repeated. "You keep her tied to this world with your sorrow."

Everything around him seemed to brighten, then faded back into night. "I don't believe in ghosts. I believe in what I can see."

Milena held her gaze steady. "I see her. Your sister. Your twin."

Brushing Milena aside as insane, touched, would be much easier. Yet she looked back at him so calm, so sure. He'd never said anything to her or any of the ladies about Jo. A lucky guess? Did the information come from Victor to aid her parlor trick? Jack wondered if he was being played, not an unusual occurrence in this place. And honestly, Milena's appearance worked in her favor. Not just pretty. Beautiful. Damned beautiful. She used all her talents to keep him unbalanced.

He decided to call her bluff, even though he hoped she somehow really saw his sister. He approached Milena and sat beside her, carefully and as far from her as possible. Perhaps a foot separated them, but he felt her soft, radiating warmth. He wanted to wrap his arms around her. Instead, he lifted his hands, palms up. She studied them, finally taking them in her own.

"What happened to you?" she asked.

He followed her glance to the scars on his wrists, twisting and creeping up under his shirt cuffs, then raised his eyes to look squarely into hers. "You tell me."

"Fire." The fear on her face softened into compassion, and then pain. "I, too, have seen flame devour loved ones. Is this what happened to your Jo?"

Another flip response froze on his tongue. He didn't answer. Didn't trust his voice to speak steadily.

"It was," Milena answered for him. "The fire. It brought you here, follows you, consumes you even now."

Everything in him closed. Again, frustration bloomed. Anger. Suddenly it didn't matter how damned beautiful she might be or how badly he wanted to touch her; he didn't want to play this game anymore. He snatched his hands away and stood. "This wasn't such a great idea, Madame Shabanov."

"No," she agreed, "it was not." Her eyes traveled past him and she rose to her feet.

"I thought I heard something, wanted to make sure everything was all right," Luke's voice intruded. Jack spun around to face the former miner. He'd forgotten all about the sentry at the gate. When he did look back around, Milena was gone.

The back door clacked through the dark.

Milena slipped through the kitchen. The cook, used to flouncing ladies flitting about everywhere, did not even glance her way.

Milena took the back servant steps, praying not to stumble across any randy men, beautiful seductive women, or definitely not the proprietress.

She slowed her climb when she came to the hall. Sounds intruded, ones she did not want to hear, the unwelcome noise she heard every night. She clamped her hands to her ears and hurried to her room. Closing the door quietly, she leaned against it.

Jack Buchanan. Who was this man who wore the mark of fire on his skin? Evil or friend? She wanted him to leave her alone, be gone from her, yet he followed her, first in the hunt, and now in a different landscape. But a hunt all the same.

Yet his sorrow. His pain. These were true. She'd felt the depth of him in her own despair. She slid down and lowered her head onto her arms, trying to shut out the *MoortYak*. Like the holocaust itself, the memory advanced, unstoppable and on a surge of hate and fear.

At first the Romani are welcome, their blacksmithing skills, sewing, and wares much needed by the residents. Rumors begin and the town turns inhospitable. A few grumble about the filthy Gypsies. Question their ways. Their beliefs. Distrust grows and hate spreads like a sickness. Soon the entire town is angry. They want the wares and services for free. Greed glistens in their eyes as they watch the coins Milena and the others have sewn to their skirts glitter in the sunlight. Who are these Gypsies to wear gold that clinks with every movement? The people insist the Romani are rich, have stolen from them, do not give fair trade.

They refuse to realize Milena's people carry everything they own in wagons and on their person. This is the Romani way and has been for generation after generation.

The Romani circle their vardos—wagon homes—as the kampania *holds a council. Milena is invited and watches beside her grandmother, the* Shuv'hani. *When members of the council turn to the* Shuv'hani, *she nods approval. They must move on. Immediately.*

Milena and the Shuv'hani *return. Baba begins to load their vardo and Milena tends to her sister. Sasha is about to give birth. Sasha's husband helps Baba with the packing while his wife cries with the pain of bringing new life into the world.*

It begins with the sound of thunder. Hooves pounding. The ground rumbles.

Baba screams, "Run!" but Milena cannot. Sasha writhes and the child is almost here. A tiny head peaks out into the horror of the night. The Shuv'hani *turns to Milena.*

"Leave, child. Run. Someone must live to tell of this night. The MoortYak *is upon us."*

The legend of the MoortYak—*the night of death and fire—has been passed down through their history, its story told around the campfire on the darkest of nights. A creature born of lust and greed with a need to possess everything, the* MoortYak *comes when least expected at the hands of people who destroy all they see. They plunder and murder and burn what is left to ashes, concealing what they have done.*

Her people did not expect this nightmare to happen to them. Now or ever.

The MoortYak *falls upon them through the swords and torches of handsome men with blond hair and bloodlust in their eyes. They rip into the* vardo *and before Milena can move, Sasha screams and she is butchered like an animal. The man who kills her sister turns to finish his job, and Milena recognizes him. He danced and flirted with Milena only a night ago and now grins at her with the fever of death burning in his eyes. She breaks through her shock and dives out of the* vardo *as he plunges his sword into the floor where she knelt only seconds before. He murders the* Shuv'hani. *With her dying breath, her grandmother looks at her and mouths, "Run" before she falls. Milena leaps to her feet. The man dives out of the* vardo *after her, but he is too late to catch her. He mounts his horse and chases her, his sword held high. He yearns to kill her; she can feel lust and hate run off him in rivulets. The woods are ahead; if she can only run fast enough, she will have a chance.*

Shrieks of pain and dying follow her as she darts into the trees, no words for the horror of this night but one.

MoortYak.

Milena raised her head, tears falling freely. She lost everything that night. Finding Baba, although broken and his eyes echoing horror and loss, had been a miracle. Her father had cried and taken her in his arms, thanking God for saving his daughter and bringing her to him.

Milena did not remember much other than chaos, screaming, and the massacre of her people by tall, strong, sure men with pale, white skin and sunlight in their hair. The same men who smiled and bought jewelry from her people, whose clothes the Romani women patched and sewed. Men who had flirted and clapped at their dancing, laughed at Romani stories, broken bread with Milena and her family.

These men brought the *MoortYak* and after, returned to their loving families and comfortable homes, their souls soaked with the blood of her people.

"Awful interesting," Jack answered Luke. The side garden continued to sway around him in cool mountain air. "This kind of thing goes on every night?"

Luke shrugged as they walked around the house to the front. "More or less." He jerked his thumb over his shoulder to the back of the house, where Milena had disappeared. "The Gypsy, she's new. First night I seen her. She's a beaut. Miss Isabella's got strict rules. I can look, but no touchin', much as I'd like to taste all she's got to offer."

Jealousy rose in Jack, shoving away any leftover wonder from the last few moments. He'd like to smack the grin from the sentry's face. Instead, he headed for the front steps of the huge wraparound porch before he did something he'd regret. He reminded himself Luke was on guard for the ladies' protection. For all the lovely trappings, this was a rough life for a woman.

"Guess I saved you a heap of trouble," Luke called, catching up. "Word from dinner is Creely's marked that one. Don't worry, there's plenty more to choose from." Luke climbed the steps up the front porch, but Jack stayed at the bottom. He'd best get home and immerse himself in one of his favorite books before his manhood did take over. Fighting or whoring, either way, he'd get into trouble.

"Think I'll head home."

A leering grin spreading across Luke's face. "Nothin' to your liking inside? I find that near impossible to believe. Miss Isabella's got everything imaginable in there, even if wholesome ain't your appetite."

A blush started up Jack's neck. To his relief, Beth emerged from the front door.

"Jack!" She extended her hand, and he climbed the steps. She took his hand. "Come over this way. There are some chairs on the side of the porch. Such a beautiful night to be out." They walked around to the other side of the house and some wicker chairs surrounding a table, forgotten poker cards scattered over its top.

"Seems I keep running into you." He leaned against the porch rail. Beth sat down, spreading her silk skirts around her. She smiled brightly but didn't fool him. He sensed the sadness running beneath her guileless exterior like a muddy current. "I can't get over how pretty you are."

She blushed. "A little different from the scullery maid," she said, smoothing the light blue satin skirt of her dress. She laughed and the sound took the edge off his frustration. Beth looked past him, into the night. His thoughts wandered back to Milena. Inside which room of the house? And with whom?

He shook his head, trying to knock the thoughts right out of it.

"Are you happy?" he asked Beth. She seemed so young. Despite her place in the Boarding House, naïve. Innocent. Honestly, Beth reminded him of his sister. He wanted to keep her safe.

"It's a good life."

"That doesn't exactly answer my question."

She shrugged. "Is this my dream come true? No. But whose life is?"

Damned good question, Jack thought. *Sure as hell not mine.*

Beth continued, "It's the best I can do. For now."

"Well, I know exactly how that feels." Jack thought of his endless hours underground. What was the difference, really? Beth was Creely's mistress. Jack dug through Creely's dirt. Who was he to judge these women, anyway? They were all doing their best.

"Heavens, Jack, we must switch to a happier topic," Beth said. "Why don't we discuss your wonderful promotion?"

"Why don't we not?" Jack answered. Between Victor Creely, his promotion, and the woman inside, his head spun. The thought of Milena. Was she now with Victor? The thought made Jack want to storm in, beat the smug smile off Victor's face, and carry her away from this miserable town.

"Jack?"

He snapped back to the present. "I wonder why life has to be so hard."

"You aren't helping me to lighten our conversation."

Jack smiled. "Let me finish by saying if you ever need anything, and I mean anything at all, you come to me. We're friends,

Beth."

Her eyes softened with unshed tears. Perfect. She was going to cry, thanks to him. To his great relief, instead of weeping, she stood and threw her arms around his neck, hugging him.

"Thank you, Jack. No one's ever offered such a thing to me."

He put his arms around her tiny figure and drew her to him, tightly. "I mean it, Beth. Anything." He closed his eyes. It felt good to hold her, protect her. Like hugging his sister again. God, he missed Jo. Squeezing Beth to him, he tried to close the wound in his heart. Just a little.

Jack opened his eyes and looked into the grim expression of Victor Creely.

Chapter 13

Watching Victor, Jack untangled Beth's arms from his neck and gently set her back from him. Beth turned, and a small gasp escaped her lips.

"Beth and I were saying good night," Jack explained.

Victor's expression was a stone in winter, cold and unforgiving. The mine president reached into his jacket, and for a moment, Jack thought he might draw a gun. He certainly saw the chill of death in Victor's expression. Instead, Victor withdrew a small black box and held it out to Beth, all the while observing Jack closely.

"A gift, my angel."

Beth accepted the box and opened it. "Oh, Victor." A sapphire necklace sparkled in the porch lamplight. "It's beautiful."

"Allow me."

She turned and faced Jack, an uneasy smile on her face. Victor, on the other hand, glared at Jack while he clasped the gems around her neck, as if he hooked the collar on a favorite pet.

Victor turned Beth around to face him. "Wait for me upstairs." A command.

She nodded and stood on her toes to kiss Victor's cheek.

"Hurry," she whispered in Victor's ear.

Jack dropped his gaze to his shoes. Heat flooded into his cheeks. Perfect, blushing like a schoolgirl. He listened to Beth's footsteps reverberate away from them, and he heard the door shut somewhere around the corner.

"I'm losing patience with you," Victor said.

"Beth and I are old friends. We were only saying good night."

"I don't give a damn. Listen to me very carefully, Jack. You do not touch her again."

"Sir, I didn't—"

"I repeat, I'm losing patience. Quickly."

Jack clamped his mouth shut. He didn't know what else to do. One wrong comment might turn this smoldering tinder into a raging fire. Beth was a part of this, and Jack didn't want to risk spilling any of Victor's anger onto her.

"Jack, explain something to me. Why are you hell-bent on mistreating me?"

The question doused Jack like cold water. "Sir?" Mistreat Victor Creely? Jack doubted anyone possessed any such ability, least of all him.

"You are familiar with an accounting register, are you not? Columns of numbers, deficits and gains?"

Jack nodded.

"Allow me to clarify. On one side, gains. Positives. For instance, I save your father's ranch from ruin. He is my best friend, my oldest and dearest. Positive, from me." Victor paused. "Against my generosity, a deficit. He's such a poor businessman he can't possibly pay back what he has promised to me."

Jack fought the urge to come to his father's defense. Victor was right. Buck was a poor businessman. He'd trusted Victor Creely and signed his son's life away to the mining mogul. Jack admitted to himself he was a poor businessman, too. He'd agreed to everything.

Victor continued. "Next a positive, again from me. I agree to accept the work of his son in lieu of interest. After all, you are the son of my oldest and dearest friend. And not to mention, my own godson. I take you in, teach you, and guide you to make a success of your situation. Learn a business from the ground up. Find out there is more to the world than cactus and steers. Again, a positive. Again, from me."

Jack clenched his hands at his sides. His stomach soured.

"I promote you quicker than any other man in my employ; you are the son of my oldest and dearest friend. Once more, a positive. Oh, and not coincidentally, from me." His voice iced. "You accuse me of murder, when really, the disappearance of a drunken miner is the actual mystery. I'd call that a deficit, and quite a large one. And straight from you."

"Sir—"

"And lastly," Victor interrupted, "I share with you this elite social arena. A place few are privileged enough to experience. How do you repay me, abuse my kind and generous disposition? I find my paramour in your arms."

Silence fell. Jack heard the clicking of distant night insects, and from even farther, strains of piano music echoed down the mountainside from the saloon. Jack wished he were up there, drinking whiskey and betting his week's wages on a card game instead of on this porch, feeling like a vile thing Victor scraped from the bottom of his boot.

"Victor, I'm only trying to find some answers. And Beth, I haven't seen her in a while. I almost didn't recognize her tonight," Jack said, everything he owed Victor settling on his shoulders with twice the weight as before. "Sir, I will take care not to offend you over Beth, but Tom is still missing. I'm worried about the men. So many have died, and more will follow. It's a matter of time. The petition made some valid statements. Points you need to consider."

Victor sighed. "Jack, we've discussed this. Mining is dangerous."

"It's more than that. Men's tempers are heating up. This isn't a good situation, not for anyone. You said you wanted me to understand this business thoroughly, eventually work as liaison. Well, I'm ready for what you hired me to do."

"And I will decide when you are ready for increases in responsibility. You have too much empathy for these animals. You still don't see the reality. I will leave you down in that mine until you understand the situation. The miners aren't paying you, Jack. I am." Victor stopped and pierced Jack with a cold stare. "Allow me to grant you some excellent advice. Workers always complain; they have the need to blame someone for their miserable existence. They refuse to take responsibility for themselves. Subject closed." Victor relaxed, looking at Jack like he was an errant child. "You're like a son to me, Jack. At the moment, I'll admit, a rather unruly one. Make no mistake, I've placed quite a bit of faith in you. Do not disappoint me." Victor held out his hand. Jack took it. The mine president grasped, hard. "I don't take disappointment well at all." Victor dropped Jack's hand and disappeared around the corner of the porch.

He heard a rustle from the darkness in the trees beyond the Boarding House light. Another rustle. Then, a snicker. Cain came into view.

"Whore ridin' always gives me a powerful need to piss, and good thing it does. I wouldn't have missed that ass-whompin' for the world. Nice show, Junior."

What more perfect end to the evening?

"Why don't you go to hell, Cain," Jack said, and shot off the porch, no need to control himself anymore. He craved a brawl, especially in this stupid Sunday suit. With any luck, he'd rip his jacket to shreds pounding the smirk off Cain's face. He turned, opening his arms in welcome. "You keep telling me how tough you are. Come and prove it."

The sheriff stood, crossed his arms, and laughed. "No thanks, Junior. I think I'll go prove myself with the much prettier things inside. Not that you got that figured out." He walked past Jack and turned. "You really ain't no man, are you, Junior?" He retreated into the house, shaking his head and laughing.

Jack closed his eyes, wishing the entire night away. When he opened them, the Boarding House beckoned, lights blazing, inviting, promising all manner of pleasures within. This night at the famed Boarding House of Jasper might well be the most miserable night he'd yet experienced in the deplorable town.

Except for her. Milena. God, what was she doing in there, in the midst of that spiderweb? He glanced down at his palms, difficult to see in the dim light. Didn't matter. Not much to see past the calluses of manual labor, of work that, as Victor so clearly pointed out, any animal like him had the capability to perform.

"Stop it, Buchanan, you're pathetic enough already," he said. The glow of the Boarding House dropped away when he turned to get his horse. He and Willow followed the tinny piano music up and back into Jasper, leaving the Boarding House and Milena Shabanov behind.

The saloon was perfect. Bright, garish, noisy, smelly. The cadence of rough voices peppered with an occasional shout, and offensive obscenities tumbled through the open doorway. In short, a rowdy, raucous mess. Exactly what Jack needed.

He took in the comforting odor of smoke, sweat, and whiskey. This place smelled real. He made his way around tables clustered with filthy miners and saloon girls in skirts and embellished corsets. They held trays heavy with drinks. Jack searched for Digger in the barely controlled mêlée.

A few men eyed him up and down, and he realized how ridiculous he looked in his Sunday suit, but not silly enough to inspire him to turn around and leave. He yearned for a shot of whiskey to burn all the way down to his gut. He needed to talk to Digger about the petition. Torn up or in one piece, it stood between him and his friend.

"Sam," Jack said when he slid up to the bar, "where's Dig?"

Sam's eyes flickered to the closed door of the back room. If Jack had blinked, he would have missed it.

"He ain't here," Sam lied. Jack headed to the back of the saloon. "Dig ain't back there, Jack, he left," Sam called after him, still lying, and Jack thought he knew why. If Digger was dealt into a card game, then the miner was in big trouble. He was the worst poker player either side of the Rockies and famous for losing every penny he owned in a night. Sam received a generous cut of the spoils.

"Jack!" Sam called. "Here's a shot. On the house!"

Jack knew something was wrong. Sam never offered up booze unless a gun was pointed in his face. Jack catapulted himself the rest of the way across the room and slammed the rear door open.

Six miners sat around a table in the small back room. There were no cards, no coins stacked. Nothing but grim faces, and the big Swede leaning against the wall.

Rolf pushed off and came at him.

"Hold up, Rolf!" Digger called from the table. The Swede froze, his flat eyes squinting. Noise and music clamored in from the saloon, a backdrop to the silence. Jack closed the door behind him and the din lost its edge.

"Rolf, I thought your party left," Jack said, distracted by the presence of the huge man.

"Rolf decided to stay on; he signed up," Digger announced. "We need another on our team to take Tom's place."

"Kinda late to still be in church duds," Rolf said.

"They ain't for church. He's all purtied up for Creely," Pete spat out.

"Go back to your fancy whores, Buchanan," another miner grumbled.

Jack didn't answer. He stared pointedly at Digger who returned his look, edged with guilt and defiance all at once.

"What's this about, Dig?"

"Nothin' you need to know about," Rolf said, stepping so close, Jack smelled the sourness of whiskey on the Swede's breath. Jack had itched for a fight all evening, but not with Rolf. The Swede could probably kill him with one punch.

"Back off, Olsson," Jack said with false bravery.

"Jack," Digger finally said, "this is a meetin'. We're talkin' on some minin' business, that's all."

"You ain't invited, Buchanan."

Jack turned to the man who tossed the comment. "You got something to say to me, Pete? Then say it, plain and simple."

Pete stood. "I got plenty to say. Jory lost his job thanks to you."

Jack was a patient man. This was where it ran out. "Jory lost his job because he's an incompetent drunk."

"You aimin' to tell me you got nothin' to do with him getting fired? 'Cause I think I smell a liar."

"Funny, Pete, all I smell is a hypocrite. You constantly complained about his drinking. Well, the problem is fixed. Solved."

"And you think you're the answer?" Pete asked.

"I can tell you one thing. I'll do my best, and I'll do everything in my power to make the mine safer. More fair to us all."

Rolf snorted behind him.

"Why should I believe Creely's pup?" Pete crossed his arms.

Jack stepped forward, close as one man could get to another. "I think it's about time we drop the nickname. It didn't make any sense, anyway. I'm no one's pup."

"Prove it."

"I will."

"Pete," Digger said, trying to wedge between the men, "Jack don't deserve our anmimosisity."

"Animosity, Dig," Jack said softly.

Neither man moved. Digger stepped back.

"Yeah, that. It ain't his fault Creely likes him. Why shouldn't he? Jack's a good man," Digger said. "You've seen him work. Why, his first week he tried like hell to save Eli."

"Eli died."

"Yeah, and no one else carried him up to the top. Jack did. He's right about Jory. We all know that. By the way, congratulations, Jack. When I heard you was promoted, I figured ain't nobody deserves it better. Come on, let me buy you a drink." Digger thumped Jack on the back, turning him around and opening the door.

Jack turned back and faced the table of miners. "If you all think I'm some kind of snitch, running back to Creely with anything I hear, it just isn't the case. I'm not sure what you're talking about. I wonder if it has something to do with a petition."

Uneasy silence blanketed the room. Pete broke it.

"Forget that, Buchanan, tell us about the goin's on down at the Boarding House. I bet it weren't discussion on a raise in wages for the rest of us."

Jack opened his mouth to tell him nothing more than fortune-telling happened when Rolf filled his vision. Rolf. His missing wife. Missing Gypsy wife, Laney. Jesus, Milena. Jack froze. The pieces connected.

Avoiding facing the big Swede, Jack looked Pete in the eye. "Nothing at the Boarding House, only fancy ladies and their offerings."

The faces in the room reflected varying shades of disbelief. This was pointless. He was exhausted, mixed up, embarrassed. Most of all, he was tired. Tired of everything.

"No thanks to the drink offer," he said to Digger, leaving and slamming the door behind him. He worked his way through the saloon and decided he did need a drink. Maybe a few.

Sam poured the whiskey, and Jack threw it back, enjoying the burn. Maybe several more would burn the whole night out of him. Jesus, Milena was Rolf's wife. Why didn't he figure that out? Only one answer. He didn't want to.

He watched the teeming ruckus of drunken men for a few moments when Sally, the saloon whore, rose above the crowd and led Mouse up the stairs. The boy pulled back and Sally jerked, practically dragging him the rest of the way.

Anger mixed with shame from the past. When Jack was eleven, Buck took him to Boonville to "make a man of his son." The whore—Nasty Nan, as the saloonkeeper introduced her—was at least three times Jack's age and had no teeth. She laughed when she saw his "baby diddler," and afterward announced to the entire saloon she would only charge him half on account of not being able to feel anything.

Sam poured Jack's shot glass full again, dribbling some across the bar. "You look far the hell away from here. Good for you," Sam said without humor.

"Yeah, good for me." Jack threw back his whiskey and plowed through the crowd, following the path taken by Sally and Mouse.

When he reached the top of the stairs, he didn't bother to knock. He kicked open the whore's door. The dark, stinking room hid many secrets, the least of which was a man lying naked on a bed. He grabbed the sheet to him and scrambled up against the headboard. Mouse stood in the corner and backed into the wall, like he'd disappear if he pushed hard enough.

Sally sauntered forward, hands on hips, fully clothed, thank God. Well, as clothed as a corset and bloomers made her. "What the hell you think you're doin'? You ain't invited."

"That boy's seven years old." Mouse scurried behind Jack, head hung low.

"You don't bother much about using a kid," Sally answered. "Least this is easy money. Ain't no black death 'round here."

"You leave the boy out of any of your sick, twisted games," Jack said, surprised at how deadly and calm his voice sounded. "He's off limits."

"Who'll stop me?"

Jack reached for his gun, but too late, he remembered. The gun hid where it usually did. In the top drawer of his bureau.

Sally laughed. "Missing something? Other than your prick?"

"Let me make sure you don't miss something. If you so much as look at him, I'll be the one you have to deal with. And trust me, Sally, you don't want that." Jack glared at the man trembling behind a sheet. "And before I deal with her, I'll come for you."

"Why don't you show me what you're made of now, cowboy?" Sally asked, her voice soft and low. "The boy can go; I didn't touch him. Some customers like a watcher, and I figure some education'll do the bugger good."

"You're a sick woman," Jack said.

She smiled. "You wanna free poke?" She gestured to the man on the bed. "'Sides of bein' watched, he likes to watch, too." Her words were welcoming, but her eyes were like her skin: dull, slack, and tired. They stood opposite each other, in the same room, in the same town, yet a chasm separated them. Jack hoped he escaped Jasper before he saw a bridge.

"No thanks, Sal. I'm not buying. Ever."

"You better remember to bring your shooter next time if you plan to play like a big boy." Sally unbuttoned her corset, and Jack's eyes drew down to the small derringer nestled inside. He raised his eyes back up and held hers for a moment. Then he turned his back on her and gently pushed Mouse out of the room ahead him, putting himself between Mouse and her gun.

He tried to shut the door behind him. It swayed on a torn, rusty hinge.

Mouse had never felt so much shame.

Jack saw him in Sally's room. She'd finally caught him and Jack saw it. Mouse didn't think he could ever look him in the eyes again. He knew going to her room was shameful, but he didn't have a choice.

Did he?

Head hanging low, he followed Jack and was surprised when they passed the Nugget Hotel and headed up the mountain. Maybe Jack was taking him to his house? But why? Da used to give him a whipping when he'd been bad. He'd tell Mouse it hurt him worse, but Da had to whip him to raise him right. Was Jack going to do this? Even though it would hurt, he hoped Jack would give him a whipping, because right now Mouse had no one to raise him right.

Jack turned and waited until he caught up. Then, Jack walked so fast, Mouse had to run to keep up, hot tears threatening. He couldn't cry. He didn't want Jack to see that he was no more than a big old crybaby.

Jack's house came into view, a black mass in the night. Mouse wondered what Jack would use for the whipping. A switch? A brush? A wooden spoon? There was nothing that hurt like a whack with a wooden spoon.

They entered the house and the big doggie, Ook, bounded up and licked his face. Mouse didn't laugh. It would not be right, to laugh before his whipping.

He watched Jack build a fire and Ook trotted over to sit at his master's side. Mouse kept back in the corner, out of Jack's way. He didn't want to be any trouble at all. He watched Jack make a bedroll on the floor, but then Jack gestured for Mouse to take the bed.

He didn't want to, because Jack would have to sleep on the floor and why should he? Besides, more often than not at the Nugget Hotel, someone took Mouse's cot, and he ended up sleeping on the floor. He was good at sleeping on the floor. Then he had a thought. Was Jack's bed where he would get his whipping?

Mouse didn't know what to do. Jack hiked his shoulders and finally gestured to the bedroll. Relieved, Mouse obeyed. He flopped facedown, hoping Jack would see he really was a good boy. Jack was strong and brave and nice and Mouse didn't want to be trouble for him. In fact, he planned to stay perfectly still for his whipping. And surely, he wouldn't cry. Only babies cried.

The punishment didn't come.

Instead, Jack slung the biggest, softest quilt over him. It felt like a warm cloud. The doggie came and stretched out next to him, making him even warmer. He prayed Jack would forgive him. He hated Sally. He hated that she caught him and Jack saw. He hated that Da left him all alone. The big doggie yawned. Mouse buried his face in Ook's fur.

The doggie's heart beat and Mouse thought that was about as good as the piano music. Jack got into his own bed and extinguished the light.

Mouse's tears came after all. Mad at himself, he cried, just like a big baby.

Chapter 14

A new morning. Not a time for questioning, demanding answers, or judging. A time to listen. To clear the mind and heart. Milena held her velvet bag and closed her eyes, determined to summon all at her disposal to find what she sought. Clarity.

She opened her bag and removed her special set of cards. Created more than a century before by her many times great-grandmother who was also *Shuv'hani*, each card a work of art in its own right. Together they possessed the power to reveal a multitude of secrets from the Otherworld. Anyone could look upon the cards, yes, and admire their rich colors, meticulous detail, but for the cards to speak, for Old Magic to reveal itself, the reader must listen.

These were not the cards she used for fortune-telling. Too precious for the touch of *gaujos*, these were for her and her alone. Her mother presented them to Milena on her arrival into womanhood, as her mother's mother did years before, and so on, and so on. Created and painted in the old times, the cards were proclaimed illegal in ancient days. Legend told of a crusader, a Christian ruler coming into power in their country, determined to destroy all that was labeled "pagan," which in reality meant anything unlike his own beliefs. The penalty for possession of such cards, crystal balls, or beliefs other than the ones he held, was death. The *Shuv'hani* of her time held to the precious cards while her people fled, but not before many were massacred, those escaping sought out and burned alive in front of screaming crowds of devout and pious followers.

So the legend of the first *MoortYak* was born, to be passed down and retold.

Milena knew of the legend's horror firsthand, and when she held the cards, the fragile spirits of those who died to protect them swirled around her. Shuffling them with care and reverence, she knew she held the most delicate of treasures.

She spread them before her in the pattern her mother taught, the Path of the Moon, with all the cards facedown. Each one she chose to turn would speak a truth including insight into herself, the forces circling her, a warning of evil to beware, and finally, the outcome to expect.

She fought the urge to go straight to the end and turn over the final card. As important as choosing it might be, she must travel the Path, step by step. The card's meanings were easy to memorize, but to interpret correctly, one must be open to receive the messages without the clouded veil of hope, the power of desires, or the finality of judgment.

First, she flipped over the one signifying her. She gasped.

"This cannot be," she said and looked down at the priestess of the Old Religion. She shook her head, incredulous. This card, meant to signify her, encompassed all the faith and power of a *shuv'hani*: healing powers and wisdom without end. A woman able to walk on this earth as well as through the Otherworld. One with strength enough to bring significant and meaningful change to the world around her. All the things she admired in her ancestresses. All the things she searched to find. All the things she was not.

She jumped at a rap on her door. She knocked the table and her cards fluttered, landing facedown. Only one landed faceup.

The card of death mocked her from the floor.

Miners lined up at the platform like they did every morning, but this was hardly every morning. With Mouse practically glued to his side, Jack searched for Digger, his stomach in a ball of nerves. Shift boss plus damned petition, and Digger hadn't shown up for work. Perhaps he merely ran late. Jack watched anxiously while the miners gathered. Rolf lumbered up toward the headframe. But no Digger.

So much for friendship.

Rolf glared at Jack and took a spot in the center of the platform. Men fell in around him. Jack forced his feet onto the hanging wood floor, Mouse following. Others crowded close, but the platform seemed empty. No Digger. As usual, no one said a word. No matter who left, who came, who was fired, or who died, this moment never changed.

Jack gulped back the slightly nauseous feeling that rose when the lift lurched, then dropped. He reminded himself he was responsible for a team, their leader now. Time to start acting like one. They plunged past a lighted working tunnel. He closed his eyes, determined to settle his stomach. There were better ways to start his illustrious career as shift boss than puking all over his men.

They jerked to a stop. The men dismounted, the platform shaking with every step. They congregated in the cavern, hanging lunch pails and taking turns lighting the candles in their hats. One glow spread into many. Together they made enough light to see, barely, in the murk. Uncanny silence folded around them. Faces looked to Jack. Some interested, a few angry. Most uncaring. Mouse watched Jack with rapt attention. Pete and Rolf glared.

Jack swallowed. Hell, what to say?

"Gentlemen," he began, because the men were never called that. Dirt-hound, moles, tugger heads. There were scores of names for the miners, none carrying respect or dignity. Well, the lack of respect for miners ended today. He continued, "You all know what needs to be done. You all have your posts for the day."

"If you're takin' Jory's place, we'll find you at Sam's?" a voice asked. A few men laughed, a few sniggered. Pete grimaced.

"I'll still be blasting, and if anyone is interested in being trained for the position, let me know."

"Trained?" Rolf asked. "Ain't that for dogs?" Other murmurs rumbled beneath the question. Jack wondered if Victor hired the big Swede with the intention of complicating Jack's life. Who knew what other moves the Chess Master had in store for him. Well, he was up to any challenge. He hoped.

He answered Rolf's defiant question as honestly as he could. "No, Rolf, training is for men. Skilled men. From this moment on, no one will start work until he understands the job, inside and out. At least, not on our shift. Especially in a position as dangerous as a blaster. Someone will take my place, but not until I'm convinced he knows what he's doing."

"Who'll take Tom's place?" Pete asked.

Silence filled the cavern. Jack banished it. "No one can, Pete. I haven't forgotten. We'll find him." Grumbles rose and Pete crossed his arms, looking skeptical in the back of the group. He hoped his shift boss speech wouldn't end with a hanging. His.

"Well, gentlemen, we have a quota to reach. Let's get to work."

No need for more words. The men needed every penny of their pay. If they failed to reach quota, well, Jack didn't want to face this pack under those circumstances. He hoisted his sledgehammer onto his shoulder and gestured for Mouse to follow. They headed down the tunnel, Jack acutely aware of who was missing. Digger.

Jack stopped, panic a twisting knot in his chest. They'd lost Tom. Surely, Digger was playing hooky. He'd done it before, almost to the point of being fired. Damn it all anyway, Jack was shift boss. He couldn't very well leave his team the first day, running after a truant worker.

Mouse looked up at Jack, eyes huge in the murk.

Jack decided on the side of responsibility. These men needed him. Digger was probably playing poker or drinking.

"Come on, kid. We've got a job to do."

Still, panic squeezed a bit tighter.

The card of death grinned at Milena from the floor.

The rap repeated. "Milena?" Beth's voice asked, muffled through the door.

Death screeches, the sound splitting sanity. Ruination of fire engulfs the landscape. Flames flicker and dance and devour. The skeletal figure in its tattered cloak raises its face to her. It reaches out. Beckoning. Mesmerizing. Holds open its arms of bone to embrace her in a lover's grasp.

Milena backed away from the vision. Her chair fell over.

"Milena!" Again, banging on the door.

She dropped to her knees and gathered up the cards, saying a quick prayer before she touched the card of death. The knob rattled against the bolt holding the door in place. Milena rose, slid the cards into her bag, and flung the door open.

"Are you all right?" Beth's eyes were wild with worry.

"Yes."

Beth looked like she didn't quite believe the answer. Milena concentrated on bringing her breathing back to normal, but her heart pounded in her ears.

"Miss Isabella requests for you to join us for breakfast." The young woman, wearing a beige cotton dress, looked more like a schoolgirl than a fancy lady primed for men's pleasure. "Milena, are you positive you're all right?" Beth asked again.

Milena nodded her head, closed the door behind her, and followed Beth down the long staircase. She contemplated the card of death. Sometimes it simply meant change, but her vision, the face turning to her, the flames devouring everything . . .

Isabella rose when they entered the dining room. "Ah, Milena, welcome."

The faces around the table did not echo Isabella's greeting. A few watched her suspiciously, a few, guarded. Milena took the seat Isabella gestured for her to claim. Beth took a seat at the far end.

"Time for formal introductions, now that the gentlemen are gone and we may indulge ourselves with some honest discussion." A few ladies giggled. "Milena, may I present Suzanne, Pearl, Gay, Claire, Estelle, Cassandra, Mimi, Frances, and you already know Beth."

As Isabella spoke each name, a head bowed and eyelashes fluttered. In the light of day the women were tired, worn. Hardly the sparkling specters of the night. Milena noted Isabella used extra face paint under a slightly swollen lip. The table of lovely women was really a gathering of the battle-worn and weary.

"Ah you really a Gypsy?" the one named Suzanne asked with

an accent the same as Jack Buchanan, "because you look ever so much like you might have some Negrah blood. You show up at my daddy's estate, he'd put y'all to work scrubbin' pots."

"I am Romani," Milena answered. Suzanne's eyes narrowed in an immediate challenge.

"Leave her alone, Suzanne," another woman said, one with intelligent brown eyes and hair pulled back in a simple braid. Milena searched her memory to recall the name of this woman. Claire? She smiled at Milena. "Suzanne hasn't been anything other than rude since the South lost the war."

"We didn't lose. We succumbed to Yankee treachery," Suzanne said, her face pulled taught by a too-tight bun as she glared at Claire.

A thin scrap of a man with limp white hair entered the dining room. He carried a tray piled high with eggs and sausages. The portly cook followed, with bowls of steaming gravy, and a mound of biscuits. Milena realized she was starving. The man and woman served each lady, and Milena caught the proprietress observing her.

"Suzanne," Claire said, "didn't they allow you fluttering belles any education at all? I read all about Gypsies in school. They are wandering bands of Egyptians. You see, gypsy, Egyptian. That's why her hair and eyes are black." Claire delicately scooped a forkful of eggs into her mouth.

"Is it true, Milena?" Beth leaned forward. "Are you Egyptian?"

"I am Romani," Milena repeated. "A traveler." She shrugged, not willing to share her history with this group of *gaujos*. Information became a weapon turned easily upon the giver. Milena had no intention of trusting these strangers.

"Can you really tell fortunes?" another asked, a raven-haired young woman whose round pale face supported a mass of dark hair.

"Of course she can't; it's all for show, Cassandra," Suzanne answered. Milena took note that Cassandra's mystic name fit her lunar beauty perfectly.

"I can tell anyone's future," Milena answered for herself and silence fell, all faces at the table turning to her. She observed Isabella, who leaned back in her seat. The proprietress did not interfere, but watched.

"That's the most ridiculous statement I do believe I've ever heard," Suzanne said. "Then again, I did gasp in delight last night when Mister Barger lowered his britches. I told him he was in possession of the mightiest man-piece I'd ever laid eyes upon. I do suppose that was a bit more absurd." She stabbed her fork into a small sausage and held it up. "Yes, I do believe this is about right." She bit the end off.

"How did you keep from laughing, Suzanne?" Claire asked. "I never can."

"Perhaps that's why he never asks for you, Claire. I almost lost my voice moaning with delight. Can you even imagine?"

The ladies giggled and a few laughed outright. Shock silenced Milena as she listened. Did the men know of such discussion? Surely not, for what man would give himself over to this humiliation? She thought of the strict rules governing her people, and the most important rule of all, not allowing Romani to mix with *gaujos* and their corruption. She reminded herself she sat at a table full of women like her. Women with no choice.

"She really can," Beth said. "Tell fortunes. She did for me."

"And whatever did she see in your future? A sapphire necklace?" Claire asked. "It is such a lovely piece of jewelry. You're so lucky."

Milena thought Beth was not at all lucky. The price of the bauble was to couple with the King of the Jackals.

"Don't be envious, Claire," Suzanne said. "Perhaps you'll get a necklace of your own soon. Once y'all learn how to please a man."

"Will you tell my fortune, Milena?" Cassandra asked.

Milena nodded her head and smiled. "I will be happy to do this."

Cassandra returned the smile and blushed.

"Well, I suppose you can tell mine, too, Gypsy," Suzanne proclaimed. "Although I do doubt I'll believe a word of it. Oh!" she said, bolting upright in her chair. "I don't have to actually touch you, do I?"

Milena wondered when this woman grew picky over what she touched.

During the remainder of breakfast conversation, the ladies discussed all manner of topics, including their clients. Milena noticed not once did Beth mention Victor Creely. Nor did the proprietress bring up his name. Milena clearly sensed his influence although no one mentioned him. The King of the Jackals ruled even when absent.

"Milena, fortunes are a marvelous idea. And don't forget, ladies, Dr. Kline will pay us a visit this afternoon," Isabella announced after the breakfast dishes were cleared. "Milena, every month the doctor comes to make certain we are all in the best of health. So please, ladies, be sure you are available by late morning. He hates to be kept waiting."

Anxiety bolted through Milena. What new horror was this? A *gaujo* doctor? A man to practice his sorcery and potions upon her?

"Ambrose is no one to be frightened of, Milena." Isabella smiled in understanding. "He is quite kind. Gentle."

"Who will pay him this time around?" Cassandra asked, hopefulness laced through her question. "I will be glad to." The pale moon waned no longer, but flushed with emotion.

"Y'all'll do no such thang. It's my turn," Suzanne said with an edge of jealousy in her voice. She turned to Milena. "Ambrose is a scientist and quite inquisitive about the functionality of the human body. I am more than pleased to allow him all manner of experimentation with mine. He certainly adds to my repertoire, not to mention . . ." She sighed and shivered. "Sometimes I think I should be paying him."

"You are, idiot," Claire interjected. "And please don't include me with those pining away for Dr. Kline. I find him as revolting as every other man in this town."

"Why, Claire, you're sour as a rotten grape," Suzanne said, sneering. "I imagine a good dose of Ambrose might cure what is ailin' y'all. He can cure just about anything wrong with me."

"Ladies," Isabella interrupted. "Have we forgotten payment is at the discretion of the good doctor? He is the one to choose. Haven't I taught you anything, Suzanne? Never, ever become enamored of a customer. Such emotions will only cause trouble."

"I'm not enamored of anyone," Suzanne said. "I simply enjoy Ambrose's bedside manner."

Cassandra kept her eyes downcast, and Milena noticed the girl's shoulders drooped.

"Cassandra," Milena said softly. The pale face looked up, sadness heavy in her eyes. "May I tell your fortune now?" Milena asked. The girl nodded.

"What a glorious idea," Isabella said, rising. "And, Milena, perhaps the doctor would enjoy a reading."

From what Milena had heard, the good doctor would enjoy just about anything. Milena hardened with resolve. She refused, under any circumstances, to become part of the Boarding House offering.

Dr. Kline would not have the opportunity to enjoy her.

Chapter 15

Beth stood in the back of Angelina's tiny shack, listening. What was she doing down in the cribs? This was a place for fifty-cent whores, not a Boarding House lady. She took a terrible risk being anywhere near here, let alone inside one of these hideous shanties.

But what else could she do? She was in love.

She was also one of Miss Isabella's ladies, at least as long as no one caught her here. She'd almost been found out when Luke, the Boarding House guard, came to visit Angelina. When Luke pushed open the door, he stopped, his head turned to talk to someone outside, and Beth dove for the back room.

Now she stood on the other side of the wall with no choice but to listen to Luke and Angelina. Miss Isabella would never understand. As if to punctuate the threat, Luke howled like a coyote from the other side of the wall, then his voice broke into giggles.

Beth rubbed her sweaty palms against the plain brown dress she wore. She'd left all her beautiful clothes behind and covered her blond hair with a brown bonnet. She wished she'd worn one of her fancy outfits so Digger would see how pretty she could be.

Beth met Digger after her father died in the mine explosion of

'65. Two weeks after her father's death, her mother jumped from the north face of Jasper Mountain. When Beth entered the orphanage, Digger was thirteen and about to leave for his grown-up job. For both, it was love at first sight. They became best friends, joined by loss and childhood laughter.

Beth's heart broke when Digger went to work in the mines, but they found secret ways to meet. When she was finally released from the orphanage, she went to work for the Creelys. Eighteen hours a day of the worst kind of work, scrubbing all kinds of filth from someone else's clothes and home, with only Sunday mornings off for church. She lived in the Creelys' attic and worked every day until exhaustion, her hands raw and her eyes bleeding tears. She lost track of time. She found it near to impossible to see Digger. Her life as a scullery maid trapped her, a sentence for eternity.

After church, Beth used to take a stroll through town, free from the Creely Mansion for one precious morning. She met Isabella face-to-face when the madame waited for her in Husband's Alley, a small wood walk leading behind the town and straight down to the Boarding House.

"My dear Beth," Miss Isabella said. "You are much too lovely to be emptying chamber pots and scrubbing floors."

Beth wholeheartedly agreed. Miss Isabella was not only beautiful, but rich and smart. She longed to live a luxurious life like this stunning woman.

Ironically, Beth left the employ of Victor Creely's household to become Victor Creely's mistress. Not such a horrible trade-off. She made more money, which meant she and Digger could be together all the sooner. Once they saved up enough, he'd take her to San Francisco. They would get jobs, respectable jobs, and live happy and have babies.

Beth heard the front door creak open.

"Digger! Come on in!" Luke's voice welcomed.

"Oh, beg pardon. I thought you was ready for me, Angelina."

"She is, Dig. I got her warmed up for you," Luke quipped.

Beth's stomach dropped right down into her boots at the life these women of the cribs were forced to lead.

"Why Luke." Digger's voice was tinged with sarcasm. "That is very kind of you."

"I'll leave you to your pleasure," Luke said.

Beth heard the front door shut, and she leaned against the sink, thinking she might faint. The door swung open, and Beth's heart climbed up from worry when she saw Digger's grin. She threw herself into his arms.

"Oh, thank God. This was a crazy scheme!" She buried her face in his neck. He'd taken a bath and been to the barber for her; he smelled like soap and cologne. When Beth looked up, she saw Angelina leaning against the door frame, watching them, a cold, mean flash in her eyes. Beth let go of Digger and he dug two dollar bills out of his pocket.

"Thanks, Angel," he said, handing the bills over. Angelina tucked them in the waistband of her skirt. Digger turned back to Beth, excitement animating his boyish features. His handsome face made her heart flip. His misshapen nose—broken twice in brawls—and the scar running along his cheekbone from a knife fight only added to his charm. Beth knew exactly why she came. When she gazed into his face, she knew she'd always take such a risk. He was worth everything.

"Ready?"

She shook her head. "We can't go anywhere. I'll be seen."

"We're goin' on a walk, down away from town. No one'll see us."

"What if someone does?"

"We're safe outside of town. Let's go down to Sunset Pass. When Jack and me looked for Rolfie's wife, I saw a place where fluoride is runnin' up the rock face. I need to take a close-up look. This might be it, Beth. Our strike!"

Digger constantly searched for a vein of gold to make him as rich as Victor Creely. Beth believed in Digger and his dreams. So much so, she built her own dreams on his.

"I have to be back before three or I'll be missed," Beth said.

A shadow passed over Digger's face, and Beth regretted reminding him of her Boarding House life.

"I'll go if she don't want to," Angelina piped in.

For a moment, anger twisted through Beth, then a pang of guilt and sadness replaced the hot feeling. Angelina wasn't to blame. Life in the cribs made a girl mean.

"Beth," Digger said, taking her hands in his, "I didn't show up to work. I might get sacked."

She'd only risked sneaking away from the Boarding House for a few hours. He was right. No one would see them. Digger grinned and led her out the back way. She held tightly to his hand. She was so lucky to have him. She would follow him anywhere.

The doors of the church stood open, most likely in hopes of catching the cool breeze coming down off the mountains. Instead, the open doors of sanctimonious welcome caught none other than Isabella St. Claire. She stopped at the threshold of the rectory office, where she knew he'd be. Indeed, there he sat, the good Reverend McShane. He appeared lost in a world of his own, a world contained in a sheaf of papers he held in his hands. Most likely, he prepared some devout dribble for Sunday services. Beyond the rectory the side door to the church stood open in sacred acceptance, but not, she knew, for someone like her.

"Reverend McShane?" Isabella's voice echoed through the austere office, no carpets or draping to soften noise. The preacher's head snapped up from the manuscript he held, and he leapt to his feet, his papers scattering across his desk.

"I don't dare come in any farther." She arched an eyebrow. "I'd hate for your church to be struck by lightning or the walls to come tumbling down."

The reverend's face turned a shade of crimson. She knew she appeared particularly stunning, covered in ivory silk and lace that matched her skin, making her green eyes and red hair the only color in a field of milk and honey. She'd adequately covered Victor's rough play of the night before. Isabella was smart enough and had the wherewithal to hide this side of her business, the ugly side that constantly lurked just below the surface of the lovely evenings, polite conversation, and delicate laughter. Like a hideous, twisted creature, it watched, waited for a moment to attack. Although it didn't emerge often, the threat constantly lurked, and Isabella strived to be always ready.

It wouldn't do to show the ugly side to the world. Not at all.

"Miss St. Claire," Reverend McShane said, his voice sweet and hushed. God indeed possessed quite a sense of humor, creating such a beautiful man and then giving him a misguided sense of faith, keeping him out of her reach.

She smiled and held her envelope out like bait. "I don't want you to think for a moment I forgot you."

He came to her and took the envelope. "Thank you." He paused and glanced uneasily around. Propriety barred her entry. God forbid anyone should see him consorting with the likes of Isabella St. Claire.

"Hypocritical motivations always feel rather uncomfortable, don't you think? Like rough clothing that doesn't quite fit. Not to worry, I wouldn't dream of keeping you from your duties of the divine. Good day, Reverend." She pivoted and walked down the stone path the way she came. Suddenly, he stood next to her. She stopped. "Why, Reverend. Did I forget something?"

"No, I did. Miss St. Claire, I wanted to . . . I mean . . . I need to . . . oh," he stumbled. Dear Lord, how did this man, with his misguided virtue and pious judgments, endear himself to her? He cleared his throat. "I want to apologize to you for the last time we spoke. I was unforgivably rude."

Startled, she searched her memory. Rude? She ran through the last time she delivered her donation. "Ah, yes, I recall the Wages of Sin speech. Don't concern yourself, Reverend. I find slogging through meaningless pontification tiresome. I don't really listen. No harm done." She granted him her most radiant smile.

He held up the envelope, ignoring her verbal slap. "You are so generous. I have no right to treat you with anything other than gratitude for your kindness to us."

Isabella St. Claire found herself in a state she rarely experienced. Speechless. The reverend? Apologizing? To her? And a genuine apology at that. She realized she stared, the smile wiped from her face by his honesty and humility. Neither were attributes she expected to come from a man.

He continued. "You always give me so much." Color rose in his cheeks. She imagined a few other things to make that gorgeous blush of his grow even deeper. He dropped his gaze to the toes of her boots, then startled her by looking her straight in the eye. "I'll be honest with you, Isabella. I need every cent you donate. I'd be lost without you."

His confession cut right to her heart. How interesting. She

hadn't realized, until this moment, she even possessed one. She'd grown used to the lovely numbness she usually operated within and found she actually didn't care for this mixture of pleasure and pain he evoked.

A group of children tumbled out from the orphanage building attached to the other side of the church. They ran in circles, calling each other names and screaming. From the same building lumbered a portly woman who waved her arms in an attempt to get them under control. Isabella thought of a rather fat goose with a gaggle of unruly goslings. The woman barked out an order, but the children continued running in circles, a blond boy dropping to roll in the grass.

Isabella returned her attention to the reverend. He watched the children, and the compassion in his eyes melted the edges of her guard. She struggled to pull herself back into tight control. Truly, these feelings he evoked, no matter how glorious, were becoming quite complicated and more than a bit bothersome.

Reverend McShane turned to her, and she experienced a swoon. She thought it must be some residual weakness from Victor's ungentlemanly behavior. That, or she'd pulled her corset too tight.

"I should clarify," he continued, bowing his head to the group of children. "We need every penny you give us. And we thank you."

"It is my pleasure," she said softly, shocking herself. She spoke without sarcasm. She actually meant what she said.

Before she realized what he was doing, he took her gloved hand. Her right hand. Her weak hand. She snatched it back so violently she lost her balance, and he grabbed to steady her. She straightened herself and stepped away, recovering her wits. She was Isabella St. Claire. She didn't need him, or any man, to help her stand. Best not to forget that, not even for a moment.

"I suppose it wouldn't do at all for me to collapse in the churchyard," she said. "People would believe that God struck me down and that I got what I deserved."

"Not me." Again, that bare honesty. Indeed, his best weapon, and she found there was nothing in her arsenal to withstand him. Her only answer: retreat.

"Good day, Reverend McShane."

"Good day, Miss St. Claire. Thank you again." He held up the envelope, smiling at her as though they shared something more than a few words and a few dollars.

She thought of several snappy retorts, perhaps another invitation to the Boarding House to turn him back to the color of embarrassment. Give her the last word.

She nodded and left, saying nothing, feeling that somehow God had won that round.

Beth watched Digger swing the huge pickaxe that was almost as tall as him. He repeated the same motion, a human metronome ticking away their precious moments together. Sweat glistened on his naked torso; he'd taken off his shirt and undone the top half of his union suit. It hung upside down from his waist, like a deflated body dangling in surrender.

He swung and a huge chunk of rock lost its grip and came away, tumbling onto the broken pile at Digger's feet. When they had first arrived at Sunset Pass, he pointed out the vein of fluoride running through the rock, glistening in the sun. Taking her hand, together they ran their fingers along the rough edge, tracing the purple and white crystal shooting through the sparkling granite rock face. She had shivered with a luxurious longing for him. He didn't notice. Instead, he explained to her, veins like this sometimes indicated gold deeper within. A hot flush of shame had coursed through her at her overwhelming yearning for him. Thank heaven he was so strong and knew better than she did. He possessed imagination enough to dream and desire enough to make it real. He was so smart. So very clever.

"This is it, Bethie. Our answer."

Now she watched him pick away at rock. She sighed. Not exactly what she planned for the day, but perhaps best. Victor had been more forceful than usual the night before. Angry. She knew she'd have a rough night when he caught her with Jack, innocent as their embrace was. If Digger saw the bruises on her, it might set off his pouting. He was so sweet, but the life she led was almost more than either of them could bear.

He swung again. Another chunk gave up and tumbled away to join the ruined pile at his feet. She rose from the shade of an aspen. He swung the pick in an arc above his head, his torso stretched. Beth's heart twinged to see the ridges of his ribs. He swung the pick down, and his body shook with the impact when it hit rock.

"Digger."

He lowered the pick and grimaced, wiping sweat from his face with his arm. "I still got a ways to go. I can't tell yet."

"I have to get back."

"I can't leave now. Someone will see where I've been workin'. They'll get my strike."

How many times had she heard this same longing, the same sureness that this time they'd find the big bonanza? This time they'd win.

"We don't need much more money to get to San Francisco, do we?" she asked. They must be close. Except for the dresses she'd bought right away—and yes, they had cost a small fortune—her few expenses were relatively minor. She turned all her money over to Digger to keep locked away, safe in his cubby.

"We ain't close." He refused to look her in the eyes and again raised the pick. The afternoon sun beat down, warm. Still, she shivered. He couldn't hide anything. He was keeping something from her. Something about their money? Digger often played poker, losing his mining wages. Surely he wouldn't risk what she gave him, their future?

"We must be close. I imagine we can afford to leave soon." She tried to add it in her head, wishing she'd kept better track of what she gave him. "Why don't you count it when you get back?"

He lowered the pick, but didn't face her. "I can't do that, Beth." Frustration grew under his voice. "I don't want no one to see what I got in my cubby."

Turn to me, she prayed silently. *Please, Digger. Just look at me. Then I'll know you are telling me the truth. Please.*

"All I know is we ain't got it yet." Deception stiffened his voice. He still stared at the rock before him. He was the worst liar in the world. Surely he hadn't lost it playing poker. He'd learned his lesson after that first time, hadn't he?

Beth's heart fell right into her stomach. All her money? All their dreams? "Digger?" she asked, willing him to turn around and smile in the way that made her heart flip. Grab her, kiss her, and tell her he only teased her, then ask her to marry him.

He stared at the rock.

Tears built, deep, fast, and unexpected. She swallowed and blinked them back. If she read Victor's mood last night, she might not enjoy her exclusive contract much longer. Milena clearly infatuated him, and why not? The Gypsy was beautiful and exciting, not at all the faded little rag doll Beth knew she'd become.

That frightened her most of all. When Digger looked at her now, did he see the same thing she saw in the mirror?

How would Digger feel when Victor lost interest and she was forced into the life of the other girls? How would he react when she bedded the mayor, the sheriff, and one by one, the officers of the mine? What about Jack, his best friend? Would he still insist they didn't have enough money? Would it still be worth it for him to stay, to keep searching for gold?

He swung and chipped away another piece of rock. The once beautiful rock face was scarred for good, its destruction easy, really, one small piece at a time. It would never again be whole.

"Digger, I have to get back," she said.

He turned and threw the pick. The tool fell, useless, in the grass a few feet away. His eyes pierced through her, miserable, wounded. He huddled in on himself and sat in gravel, his head buried in his hands. All the thoughts of Victor and Jack and lost money swirled away at the sight of his skinny, curled-up frame. She dropped down beside him and gathered him in her arms.

How could she be worried about herself when she lived such an easy life, and he worked so hard? Even if he came safely to the top at the end of every shift, life in the mines was slowly killing him. All the while, she enjoyed all the finest things life offered. The worst she faced was a rough bounce on her feather-down mattress.

She didn't deserve him. Not at all. She pulled him closer and rocked him. "I'm sorry, Digger." Tears built a hurting pressure deep inside.

"Bethie, I just—"

"I know, sweetheart. I'm sorry."

He looked up at her, his blue eyes honest and sad. "I want everything to be right for us."

"I miss you. I only want to start our life together." She let him go and stood. "I'll get myself back." She spun away from him and her tears pushed over. She hated that she always cried. She didn't want to add her tears to his burden. He had too much to carry already.

"Bethie!" he called after her.

She waved, picked up her skirts, and broke into a quick trot. She didn't want him to see her cry. Not again.

"Bethie!"

She brushed her tears away and turned to see him coming after her. She waved to him, walking backward. If he came closer, he'd see through her false bravado. She tried to smile to reassure him.

His face wrinkled to horror. "Bethie!"

Her heel hit rock, and she tumbled backward. She grabbed, but there was nothing to hold to, nothing at all to catch her from falling.

Chapter 16

The afternoon air in the Boarding House grew dense, thickening like clouds in a darkening sky. From downstairs firm footsteps drummed, underlined by the rumble of a masculine voice. Around deep male tones, feminine laughter fluttered.

The doctor had arrived.

Milena dragged her chair to the opposite corner of the door and sat with her arms folded, watching. Waiting. She stared at the door, willing him to stay away while she listened to him move through the house. His footsteps and voice drew closer, his laugh billowing through the hall, and finally right outside her door. She jolted at the sound of a knock. Did not answer. Another rap invaded the solitude of her room.

"Milena?" Cassandra's muffled voice asked.

The time had come for Milena to face this new threat. "Enter."

The door swung open, and behind the muted joy on Cassandra's face stood the dreaded Dr. Kline.

Except he appeared nothing to dread. Wavy brown hair framed intelligent eyes and a curious face. This man was a seeker, Milena knew immediately, always one with a question. Her spirit reached out, examined, but she felt no danger from him. A confirming tingle flooded the surface of her skin.

"Milena Shabanov, it is my pleasure to present Dr. Ambrose Kline."

Dr. Kline stepped forward, but Milena did not rise. She kept her arms crossed and gave him her fiercest look. The doctor cleared his throat. "Thank you, Cassy. We'll speak later."

Cassandra blushed and shut the door, the doctor watching.

"You will not touch me."

His attention snapped back to her, his black bag swinging when he turned to face her. He smiled. "Have you ever had a physical examination before, Milena?" He spoke easily, friendly yet strong, as if to an unruly child.

She shook her head. "I do not intend to have one."

He chuckled and sat on the edge of her bed like a trusted member of her family. "I've been told you are wary of me. Rest assured, my only interest is to keep you in the best of health."

"I care nothing of your interest," she said, her words angrier than her tone. In fact, his cordial manner made her want to relax, but she didn't dare give him an invitation to come closer. "You will not touch me," she repeated.

He sighed and sat his bag next to him. "Well, that's a difficulty. Miss St. Claire insists I monitor the condition of all you ladies and honestly, my dear, this is in your best interest."

"I have seen how the West honors the interest of women making their way alone."

He blinked, looked down at the floor, and back to her. "I understand you tell fortunes."

"I do."

"Read palms?" Curiosity lightened his voice.

"I do."

"Will you read mine?" He extended his hand.

To do this, she would have to cross the small space and sit beside him, on the bed. She narrowed her eyes. "This is a trick."

"No trick, I assure you. In fact, I do hope you possess the ability to answer questions about my future. I need all the free advice I can get." He gave her a shy smile. "And I need a friend. Someone to trust."

She recognized his method to tear down the barrier she'd placed between them, yet an earnestness ran beneath his words. She moved to the bed, his black bag between them.

"You are a shrewd man."

He laughed. "Just curious."

"So I am told. Give me your hands."

She took them, examined his palms. Not the hands of a workingman, no, these hands were pampered, the nails clean and trimmed. Gentle hands. Hands of care.

"What is your question?" Looking into his face, she saw he didn't know how to ask. His brows knit together as he contemplated his words. This man moved about the world in a deliberate and thoughtful way.

Suddenly something rustled outside her window. The doctor jumped to his feet, and in a quick, protective movement, pulled her behind him.

A mop of blond hair popped over the sill, followed by a face, scarred and young. Blue eyes widened in surprise.

"Oh, damnation! Hey, Doc." A young man hoisted himself up and climbed the rest of the way through the window. Dr. Kline grabbed his arm and helped him through.

"Digger? What on earth are you doing?"

"Shhhh!" The slight young man hissed with his finger to his lips. He glanced sheepishly at Milena. She noticed, in addition to a scar running the length of his cheek, his crooked nose betrayed many fights and a rough past.

"Ma'am?" he asked. "Are you Miz Milena? Beth sent me."

"Beth? Where is she?" Milena asked, sensing not only discomfort in this young man but a bit of panic.

"My apologies, ma'am, Doc. Beth's hurt. Not bad," he added, "but she made me leave her. She's afeared Miz St. Claire'll find out." Anxiety colored his features, and his words tumbled out, faster and faster. "We went on a walk, talkin'. Nothin' else, I swear, but Doc, I never thought you'd be here. Beth told me to come for Milena, and—"

"Simmer down, boy," Dr. Kline said, grabbing the young man's shoulders. "Take a deep breath. There, that's it. Nice and slow. Now, where is Beth?"

"We was on a walk. She fell down Sunset Pass, slid down the mountain a bit, not bad. She caught a branch. But she can't stand."

"Where is she?" the doctor repeated, his voice sharpened.

"Wait, Doc! Miz St. Claire can't see you leave; she'll figure out somethin's up. Bethie says there ain't nothin' the woman misses."

Milena thought the proprietress did an admirable job of missing a man climbing through a second-story window of the Boarding House.

"Digger, we don't have time if Beth's truly hurt," Dr. Kline said.

"She ain't hurt bad. Twisted her leg's all. I left her back aways from the main road."

Milena was concerned for Beth, but also troubled that a man had just climbed into her window. "How did you get past the guard?"

"Luke? Last I saw he was . . . I mean . . ." The young man's voice tapered off and his eyes shifted into deception. Milena wondered what secrets he hid, and not very well. Digger sighed. "Oh, hell, Luke ain't nowheres around anyhow. That's the part that matters. Bethie told me which window's yours. Milena, she said we could trust you. She said you'd help." The young man's eyes pleaded when he looked to the doctor. "Doc? Please, this has got to keep quiet. Miz St. Claire'll throw Beth out for sure if she finds out about us."

Dr. Kline regarded the young man sternly, shaking his head. "Digger, have you lost all reason? Beth is Victor Creely's mistress."

Pained anger racked the young, scarred face. "She was mine way afore he took her. She loves me, not him. She's got no choice with him."

So. Before her stood the reason for the constant sadness Milena sensed in Beth.

"Please, Doc."

Milena watched Ambrose Kline calculating, creases deepening between his eyebrows. Every thought reflected across his face. The doctor's expression finally softened with sympathy. Milena knew his decision before he put it into words.

"Milena, if you will distract Isabella, be sure she stays away from the windows, I can help Beth."

Milena nodded.

The doctor leaned and looked out of the window, then straightened. "Is there any other way out? Surely you don't expect me to climb out of the window and down that wall?"

"We got to," the young man said, relief threading through his voice. "I'll take your bag," he added hopefully. "The side porch roof is right below. Even if you fall, it won't be bad."

The doctor sighed. "It appears I am about to engage in the sport of wall-climbing. Hopefully, my injuries won't end up too terribly serious either."

Digger grabbed the doctor's bag and patted him on the shoulder. "Don't' worry, Doc. You won't fall."

"Yes, well, thank you for the vote of confidence." He bent

over to look out the window one more time. "Good luck, Milena. We'll wait five minutes for you to distract Isabella. Then we are off to rescue our ailing damsel!" Despite his reluctance, Milena saw the light of adventure in the doctor's eyes.

"How will you bring Beth back inside?" she asked.

"You let me worry about that. You keep Isabella occupied. I'll take care of everything else." The doctor's face burned with the excitement of his quest.

She opened her door and scanned the hallway. Empty.

"Milena?" the doctor asked. She turned to the sound of his voice. He sat on the windowsill, half in and half out. "We're not finished."

"Yes, Doctor," she said, stepping out into the hall. "We are. I will tell your fortune later, as long as you do not fall out of the window." She shut the door as his eyebrows rose.

Jack always felt like he'd keep rising and catapult into the air when the platform broke the surface to pop him into the real world. The contraption stopped, jolting the miners. A few stumbled forward, and the men in the front rushed off the wood disk. Autumn crept closer, and the light had already started to soften, but it still blinded Jack. His eyes barely slit open and tears stung, falling freely. God, he hated this part, the crying and not being able to see after coming up from the mine. He wondered if tunnel blindness would ever hit him for good, especially since it took him longer and longer to adjust to daylight each time he came up.

Jack's turn finally came and he hopped off the platform, with Mouse close by. He took a few steps and stopped short, as did everyone. He shielded his eyes from the light with his hand, hoping he might see better, or at least stop the stabbing pain and burn. Through bright haze, he saw a form moving. He recognized Turtle scuttling around on the office porch. A tall, skinny blur followed Turtle out on the porch, Edmund Blum. Others came out to stand in a fuzzy, watery line.

The blur around them cleared slightly and he saw four men holding rifles. He recognized another of the rifle-toting men, a huge bulk called Bear, so named because he was big, fat and hairy. And mean. Jack's vision cleared enough to see Bear sneer. Hoping for a fight, Jack thought. The man loved nothing more than to pound miners into dust.

"What's going on?" Jack asked.

"Like you don't know," Pete grumbled back.

"Oh, Christ, Pete, I don't."

"Gentlemen, today we are instituting a new process," Turtle began, projecting his nasally voice, "one to ensure your safety and sanitation in addition to the well-being of The Company."

"He says 'The Company' like it's God Almighty," Pete said. The miners around him mumbled in agreement.

"Please form a line to the left of our newest building." Turtle gestured to the structure they'd watched go up over the last several weeks, an assayer's office or some other such nonsense, they'd been told. The raw wood building, not yet grayed with age, suddenly took on an ominous look. The men all stood, not moving, and a hush fell over the knot of miners.

"Once you step through the door, please strip. We'll show you where to hang your clothes for inspection."

"What?" Jack asked, and the other miners' voices raised with questions. Turtle gestured for them all to be silent. "It has come to our attention some unscrupulous workers have been stealing ore. From this day forward, no one will be allowed to leave mining property until properly searched."

A chorus of dissent rose on the air, the shouts speckled with a few choice words. Turtle winced, yet held steady. The men with the guns didn't flinch. Bear grinned.

"All this for a few missing chunks of copper?" Pete leaned over and spit in the dirt.

"They discover a lode again? Gold?" a voice asked from the back of the group of men.

"Prob'ly. Creely gits richer and we git to strip nekked."

Turtle waved his hands for the men to quiet. "Anyone who objects to this process is free to quit today. However, we will require a search before you leave."

"This ain't fair," one miner shouted.

Bill Sutcliffe—Gentleman Bill as the miners called him, due to his proper dress and polite manner—stepped forward. He kept his hands in his pockets and bowed his head slightly. "Beggin' yer pardon, Mister Barger. I ain't pulling my pants down for no man. Not even one fetchin' as you."

A few men laughed uneasily.

"Really. Sutcliffe, isn't it?" Victor Creely stepped out on the porch. Voices immediately dropped. Confidence oozed from Victor. He looked from one miner to the other, locking eyes with several, demanding respect. Jack watched while some men who met the mining president's gaze looked down. Others, the outspoken, kept their heads up, and Victor's look lingered, as if remembering them for future reference.

Victor planned this, surprising them with the announcement before their eyesight fully returned. When they felt the most vulnerable. Jack had no doubt the purpose of this search was to extend even more control over the miners and make them feel helpless by stripping them of everything. Even dignity.

Victor's attention settled on Jack. His look asked a question. Jack could choose where to stand: with the miners and their strip search, or step back and take advantage of his special status at the mine, and declare his loyalties to its president. Victor's mouth tweaked slightly, an invitation.

Jack held steady.

Victor's eyes hardened. Power glinted in his expression and something else dark and mean. His gaze settled on Gentleman Bill. The only sound, a slight breeze rustling the aspen trees.

Victor broke the quiet. "Mr. Sutcliffe?"

Bill gulped and took off his hat and held it in his hands. "Yes, sir, Mr. Creely?"

"I suggest, if you want a job come tomorrow morning, you step up to the change building. Speaking of tomorrow, everyone is to bring a set of clothes to work in and then to leave for inspection."

"Beg pardon, sir," Gentleman Bill asked, "but what if we only own one set of clothing?"

Victor smiled. "The General Mercantile. Since this is a newly instated policy, I've instructed the store to extend credit to anyone who needs it, at a modest interest fee. That is, if you still wish employment at the mine."

A chance to sink these men further into debt. No one said a word.

Victor continued, "Some men are robbing me blind, and it hurts everyone. It simply must be stopped, and I can think of no other way to insure success for us all." Victor turned around to go back into the mine office, then stopped and faced the group of miners again. "And the company is offering a reward. Fifty dollars to anyone turning over names of thieves." He smiled and retreated into the office.

Another masterful move. Setting the miners against each

other. Not overtly; such was not Victor's way. He planted several blades of suspicion with a few words, and in moments, tested Jack's loyalties. The man was a master.

Gentleman Bill broke away first and walked up to the Change Building. Except Jack knew this change was not for the best. Not at all.

Milena searched the house and crept to the front door, careful to make no noise. She couldn't find the proprietress anywhere. She glanced behind, down the hall. A locked room near the back of the house was off-limits to everyone, and Milena did not know if the proprietress was locked away on the other side of the door or not. If so, as long as she stayed, Milena's job was simple. Cook worked diligently in the kitchen, the aromas wafting out thick and rich. The ladies napped and would continue to sleep well into early evening, like they did every day in preparation for the night ahead. They reminded Milena of bats in a cave, hiding, sleeping during the day, then free to flutter with unencumbered grace across the sky once nighttime fell.

The Golden Guard did not protect from his post, just as Digger had reported. Nor did he return while Milena waited. Fidgeted. Watched. She walked through the house several times, boots off to slip about without detection. Finally, after a hundred years it seemed, a figure skirted the road, hugging to the pines. The doctor held Beth in his arms. Thankfully no one was around; his covert actions were more obvious than if he had walked up the center of the road.

He stopped, apparently not sure what to do. It appeared the hero needed assistance. Milena waved him to come ahead, and on tiptoe she sprinted through the first floor of the house once again to be sure. All clear.

As he approached, she held the door open for him, gesturing for him to follow. They climbed the steps, Milena scouting ahead and watching all around. The hall remained empty.

Once inside Beth's room, Milena sighed with relief when she closed the door. The doctor set Beth on her bed. The poor girl's face puffed red with scrapes and many shed tears.

The doctor opened his bag and lifted from it a bottle of clear liquid. "Milena, will you hold her head for me, please? I'm going to clean her face. We don't want to risk infection."

"Milena?" Beth asked, her voice shaking.

"Hush, Sunshine. All is well." Milena sat and helped ease Beth down, resting the girl's head in her lap. She gently brushed Beth's hair back from her injured face.

"Miss Isabella—"

"She is not here," Milena answered. She thought of the young man with the scarred face. "Your secret is safe." She looked straight at the doctor when she spoke, and he nodded in agreement.

"This will sting, Beth. Close your eyes and please try to hold steady." He spoke softly. "Breathe deep. It helps sometimes."

Beth shut her eyes tight and groaned with pain before the doctor touched her. When he attended to her face, she only managed to whimper.

Milena helped Beth undress down to her shift. The doctor checked her bones for breaks but, thankfully, found only sprains. Beth nodded, staring far off while the doctor explained her injuries to her. Numb with misery, the girl looked somewhere into the air, not focusing on anything and not really responding to the doctor's words.

Milena assisted Dr. Kline as he attended to every scrape and bruise. She noticed how gentle and adept he was at his craft. Some of Beth's bruises were older, their color already blossoming into sickly shades of blue and brown. A bruise shaped like a hand wrapped around her upper arm, a grip of iron, took Milena's attention. The doctor noticed it, too. Their eyes met over Beth's head in shared acknowledgment. Milena held fresh disdain for the King of the Jackals.

Milena wondered what caused Beth to fall. Where was Digger when she sustained the injuries? What was wrong with these men of Jasper?

The doctor gently covered Beth with a quilt, as if he tucked a child away in safety. He gave her a teaspoon of tonic to help her sleep. A kind and decent man. Apparently, in Jasper, an exception.

When he finally left, a tear slipped silently down Beth's cheek. She brushed it away, but not before Milena noticed.

"What happened?"

"I fell walking backward. Can you believe how silly?"

"Your tears," Milena said gently, wondering what might cause a young woman to back away from her lover.

"Oh," Beth said and looked away. "Nothing." She turned her face to the wall and closed her eyes in dismissal. Milena opened her mouth, but decided against further questions. Best to let the girl sleep.

She worried about Beth as she returned to her room and opened the door. She froze when she saw who sat upon her bed. The doctor.

"You owe me, my dear."

Owe? Milena recalled the breakfast discussion concerning the doctor's payment. She shook her head. "No." She backed against the wall.

He sprung to his feet, towering over her. "This will go much easier if you cooperate, Milena."

So. The doctor did possess a black heart. Why didn't she realize? What happened to her sight? Frantically, she looked around the room for a weapon. She grabbed a chair and held it up between them.

"You will come no closer."

The doctor took a step back, a perplexed look wrinkling his brow. "Honestly, my dear, a physical examination is nothing to be this frightened over."

"What?" She suddenly felt quite foolish. "Oh. Doctor, my apologies. I thought we were discussing terms of your payment."

"Oh!" His eyebrows shot up his forehead. "Oh, no, my dear. No." He sat back on the bed and laughed uneasily, his face the color of embarrassment. "Only an examination, Milena. You can put down the chair."

She held her shield. "No, Doctor. I refuse."

He shook his head and sighed, his shoulders drooping slightly. "Milena, not only does Miss St. Claire insist upon this, I wholeheartedly concur. This is a matter of public health."

"My health is of my own concern."

"My dear? Have you forgotten the gentlemen you entertain?"

"I tell fortunes. I touch hands only. Nothing more." She put down the chair, sat on it, and held her hands out to him. "Here. You may examine these."

"Your work, er, consists in matters of fortune-telling only?" He looked at her skeptically. The shade of crimson in his cheeks turned deeper.

"Yes," she finally said, dropping her hands. "It is the truth. I do nothing else."

Again she saw the deliberation of his thought as skepticism changed into an uncertain belief. "Are you positive?" he asked.

"I believe I would know this."

The doctor looked thoughtful. "I suppose. I must have misunderstood Miss St. Claire."

She allowed her defensive shield to soften. "I do owe you a reading."

The doctor pulled out his pocket watch. "Yes, and it is nearing the Boarding House hour of festivities." He smiled. "Milena, thank you." He took her hand and squeezed it. "I appreciate all you did to help me today. You make a fine nurse."

"Does a nurse require a health examination from you?" she asked. "Because if one does, no thank you to that, as well."

Jack's clothes might be on his back again, but he wouldn't feel right until he took a bath—a hot one with lots and lots of soap. He wasn't sure if he was angry, upset, sad, humiliated. Furious. Or all of them rolled into one. Mouse, bless his heart, scooted alongside. He'd taken the search completely in stride.

Jack's anger built with each step down Gooseneck Road until his house finally came into view. Relief swept over him, a very welcome feeling. His mood lifted along with one of the sweetest sights he'd seen that day, not that he'd ever admit it. Here came Digger up the road, fine and no longer missing.

Anger returned. The son of a bitch had scared him to death.

Digger walked slower when he saw Jack and Mouse. Jack stopped. Mouse looked up to Jack, drew in from his pipe, and puffed a tiny cloud out of the side of his mouth.

"You really have to stop that habit, kid. It's for grown-ups." Jack wondered if he'd ever remember Mouse's deafness, but decided his talk was mostly for himself anyway.

Digger approached, guilt written all over his face.

"Dig, I need to ask you something."

"Yeah, sorry I missed my shift. I know it was your first day and all, but I went prospectin' last night after Sam's and sat down to rest. I fell asleep. Din't budge 'til roundabout noon."

"About the saloon last night," Jack said, ignoring Digger's flimsy excuse and lie. "The meeting. The petition. We've got much more to talk about than a missed day at work."

"A petition?" Digger attempted a poor show of wide-eyed innocence. He dropped his eyes and stared at the ground between Jack's feet, shifting his weight from one foot to the other.

"The petition," Jack answered. "Tom's. The one everyone signed. The one you signed. Why didn't you tell me, Dig?"

The miner shrugged, his eyes still lowered.

"Digger," Jack said.

"'Cause," Digger answered, his head snapping up. His eyes leveled with Jack's. "I couldn't say nothin'."

"I'm your friend," Jack threw back.

"Yeah, well, you may be my friend, but you're—"

"Creely's pup?" Jack asked, realizing Digger really, truly didn't trust him. Not completely.

Digger flinched and turned away, surveying the landscape. When he looked back at Jack, his eyes held a steady honesty. "Jack, I'm sayin' sometimes it's hard is all. Tom asked me not to say nothin' to you, so I didn't."

"Digger, the man disappeared! Didn't you think that might be an important piece in the puzzle?"

"Whose puzzle, Jack? Yours? You gonna figure this out and find him? You know well as I do he's a dead body. Like anyone who stands again' Creely. Look around, Jack," Digger answered, his tone of guilt replaced by annoyance. "You ain't like the rest of us. Look where you live." He gestured back to where Jack's modest cabin sat. From inside the house came Duke's muffled barking as he sensed his master coming near.

"Where I live? It's a house, Dig. What's that got to do with anything?"

"This is a goddamned palace, Jack. I share my bed. Another man sleeps there when I'm workin' my shift. All I own I fit in a cubbyhole. I been workin' in the mine seven years and I got nothin' to call my own. Nothin'."

Duke's distant barking built into a frenzy and grew louder. Mouse watched, his eyes round. The boy might not be able to hear, but he obviously felt the tension.

"Hell, even your goddamned dog lives better than I do," Digger said. "Look at the kid, followin' you around. Even he wants to join in on a dog's life. It's better than anything we can ever hope for. Mouse and me and Tom, it's different for us."

Digger's words stunned Jack, but his sense of betrayal and anger softened under a light of realization. Jack didn't really know what it felt like to live the way the miners did. Theoretically, perhaps, but not really. Yes, he worked alongside them, breathed the same dust, did his best to ignore cramps in his legs and back that grabbed so bad some days he thought he'd never make the walk home. He dealt with the constant sting of scraped and infected hands, of bruises in places where a man ought not to be bruised, but when he got through, when he came up to the surface, he lived in a decent home. Slept in a decent bed.

Jack swiped his hardboil off his head, knowing his leather-brimmed hat waited to take its place once he returned home. The hat he wore when he forgot the mine and his life under the earth and reminded him of a future waiting. Something the other men didn't have. And his future came courtesy of Victor Creely.

That's what he owed the mining mogul, really, something going way beyond money. Thanks to Victor, Jack had a future.

No wonder Digger didn't trust him, why no miner trusted him. How could they, as torn as he felt?

"I didn't realize you felt that way, Dig," Jack said, sensing his friendship with Digger slipping away, powerless to stop the slide.

"It ain't no way." Digger shrugged. "Sometimes it's hard. What happened to the petition anyways? When Creely takes a look at it, every man on that piece of paper will suffer like we always do."

Jack's frustration resurfaced. He was the only one trying to make the situation at the mine better for all concerned. "I agree with that petition, and I signed it like I would have if anyone bothered to show it to me. Hell, I took it to Creely and told him I stand behind it. Which I would have done if anyone gave me the chance."

"Signing a piece of paper don't prove nothin' to no one. There's a whole bunch more needin' fixin' at Jasper Mine. Things is boilin' up. When it comes down to it, you're not gonna be sure which side to stand on."

"I stand where I always do. Always, always with my friends." Jack forced the anger in his voice to ease off. "I'm sorry you weren't comfortable coming to me."

Digger's guilty look came back with more intensity than before. He shoved his hands in his pockets. "How did your first day as shift boss go? I'm sorry I missed it."

Jack buried the rest of his frustration and smiled, even though it didn't feel quite right on his face. "We have lots to catch up on. Dinner?" Jack asked.

"Oh, Jesus, Jack." Digger pulled his hands out of his pockets. "I jest about forgot why I was comin' to find you. It's Stoop."

A cold wind flipped the hardboil out of Jack's hand. He didn't bother to retrieve it.

"What is it, Dig?"

"He's missing. At the last part of his shift last night. Jest like Tom. Ain't no one seen him for close on to twelve hours."

Chapter 17

Healing energy radiated from the doctor's palms. Holding his hands were like suspending hers over a campfire, Milena thought, or soaking up the warmth of a vibrant source.

They sat on the side porch, no table between them. Dusk deepened around them, one of Milena's favorite moments of the day. The perfect time to do a reading.

"You have followed your path, Doctor. All is true and right. Except for love."

He smiled sadly.

She enjoyed her easy connection with the doctor. Earlier today, she'd done everything possible to prevent him from entering into her life. She was grateful for the decision, whatever inspired it, to allow him through her door.

"So, about this love? Where, exactly, do you see that?" His attention dropped back down to his palm.

She traced the uppermost horizontal line across his hand, the heart line. His ran solid. "Here, you see? This line. It reveals your love is strong. True. Your feelings of the heart run deep, and you love with great passion."

He grinned.

"But," she said, and his eyes widened, "see where the line branches? This part of your palm is ruled by Jupiter, this part by Mars. Your love cannot decide in which place to dwell."

"What does that mean?"

"There is an ideal for which you search. A woman who is all things." Milena shook her head. "There is no such ideal woman, Doctor. Life forever leaves its marks upon those who live it. Perfection is possible only in the spirit world. In this world, you search for the woman with no failings and miss the one who is mate to your soul."

"Oh," a small voice gasped behind her. The doctor's head snapped up to look beyond Milena. His face crinkled with surprise, then grew tender. The very thing he searched for shone in his eyes, brighter than the clearest answer. Milena did not need to look to know Cassandra uttered the small cry. The doctor jumped to his feet and Milena looked over her shoulder, but there was only thin air to behold.

"Cassy," the doctor whispered.

Milena turned back to him. "It seems you find your own answers, Doctor."

He shook his head and sat back down, his eyes downcast. "It's complicated, Milena."

"No. It is not."

He jerked his head up to look at her. Helplessness flickered on his face. "I shouldn't keep you. I'm sure there are many waiting for your attention."

Ah, a retreat. Often men chose this when faced with a conflict of emotion. She stood, and the doctor with her.

"Consider what I told you." She took his arm.

"Um-hmm. And when did you say you were free for that

physical?"

She smiled to herself and they headed around the porch. Luke leaned against the front banister. He leered at her. Milena dropped her glance. Deception glistened from his skin and wove through his ridiculous yellow mane. Although his professed purpose, he did nothing to protect the women of this house. Despite his constant grin, meanness poured from him.

She quickened her pace and, with the doctor, entered the house. The parlor lay beyond, music, voices, and laughter leaking from it, sounds of joy swirling the air softly, like a breeze.

Yet a chilling cold curled around Milena. Something wrong. Here? No. Approaching. An affirming tingle fell over her, but this time it offered no comfort.

This time, the feeling prickled with warning.

Milena enjoyed the dark and quiet. There were no lamps lit in her room. She retreated once she finished telling the future of the doctor and four others. After the doctor, she gave the kind of fortune Isabella wanted the men to hear. Victor watched her constantly, and she sensed the King of the Jackals tightening his circle around her.

Her knees gave way and she sat on the edge of her bed, her head spinning with questions. If ever she needed guidance, the time was now. She needed to leave. Soon. But where to go?

Closing her eyes, she reached out to the Otherworld. *Shuv'hani, what am I to do?*

Silence. No answer.

She stood and retrieved her bag from the dresser, intending to ask the Old Magic to help her through her cards. She slipped the bag's cord around her wrist and turned.

A man of darkness stood against her door. He took a step forward and kicked the door shut with finality. He took yet another step forward and moonlight fell across his face.

Victor Creely.

Desire and purpose poured from him. And something else. There was a darkness to this man, a thousand darknesses, and they skittered from him and scurried around the room, circling her. She knew why she couldn't hear the *Shuv'hani*. Victor wove black magic stronger than her own.

"I'm sorry, Milena. I didn't mean to startle you." His voice, silk. The lure of a rattlesnake. He took another step. And another.

She pressed against the dresser and shook her head. "No." Her voice came out in only a whisper.

He closed the space between them. "My dear, why are you frightened of me? I would never, ever harm you." He drew his finger down her cheek, her chin. She raised her hands and pushed against his chest, her velvet bag dangling helplessly, its magic lost. His hand circled her neck, barely touching her. The contact was just enough. Evil poured from him, dripped down her neck, over her shoulders, under her clothes, coating her, reaching into forbidden places. She shuddered. He smiled.

He pressed against her. No heat came from his body. Only ice. "I have so much to give you, Milena. You cannot comprehend what your life will be, with me." His face stretched with a grin; his smile no smile at all.

"Please," she managed on an exhalation. "No."

His thumbs caressed the pulse in her neck. He looked down at her, the cold of his barren soul leeching her warmth. Her life.

He slipped his hands up her back, entangling her hair. His lips brushed hers, and he spoke. "Harm is the last thing I have on my mind." His mouth closed on hers, his thumbs pressing into the tender flesh of her neck.

He tasted like ashes. Dust. Death.

She cried out, but he swallowed the sound. She pushed against him, but he locked her tighter in his arms and raised his mouth from hers, looking deeply into her eyes.

"No," she said again, this time with her voice strong. To her relief, he loosened his hold and took a step back. Still smiling, he hit her. Her head snapped back and a bolt of hot pain stabbed down her neck.

"*No* is hardly acceptable, Milena. Especially when issued from the lips of a common whore." He grabbed her throat and squeezed.

She clawed at his hand, trying to pry it from her throat, her effort a brush of butterfly wings in a tempest. He chuckled. Her struggle peaked, crazed. Black closed in. Sparks danced at the edge of her vision.

His eyes lit with exhilaration. Passion.

He kissed her again, even as he choked the life from her. He bit her mouth. Blood. He licked it from her lips. She was going to die in the arms of the King of the Jackals.

Shuv'hani! Help me!

He lifted her and threw her to the bed. She gasped in a grateful gulp of air but he fell upon her, crushing her beneath his weight. He bit her again, his teeth piercing the flesh of her neck, his knee forcing her legs apart.

No! her mind screamed. The cry did not reach her voice. He clapped his hand over her mouth. With his other hand, he ripped her drawers and then unfastened his pants.

Her bag. Her crystal ball. She closed her hand around velvet and swung with all her strength. The bag cracked into his head.

Instantly, he dropped on her, dead weight. Summoning all

her strength, she heaved him over. He thudded onto the floor like a sack of filthy laundry.

She rolled to her side and drew a gulp of air. It seared down her throat. She took in another. *Run!* her mind screamed. No sound came from the floor. None at all. Leaning over the side of the bed, she looked down. He wasn't moving. She backed away and sat up against the headboard. Trembling, her body jerked with each heartbeat.

He did not move. He looked strangely like a pile of clothing. Except his hand turned up, almost reaching for the ceiling.

She'd killed him.

She laughed, a crazed, hysterical sound, and then crammed her fist in her mouth to keep the wail within her. She'd killed him. The hangman's noose would finish what he began if she didn't gather her wits and do something. But what? Someone might be in the hall, and even if she did get out of the Blue Castle, the Golden Guard waited below.

She looked over to the window where the doctor had exited that very afternoon. She slid along the wall, keeping as far as possible from the body on the floor. His hand still gleamed, oddly twisted up.

She climbed out the window and dropped to the roof. The ground stretched below, more than ten feet away. She tucked her bag into the waist of her dress and hesitated, but the bulk on the floor of her room provided enough inspiration to jump. She landed on packed dirt, the impact pounding through her. Stones stung into her hands and knees in sharp, hot points. In an effort not to cry out, she bit her lip and scrambled away from the light of the Boarding House.

Keeping beyond the light, she crawled until she saw around the corner, to the front of the house. Luke sat on the porch, looking straight ahead. If he saw her, there would be no escaping. She hesitated, not sure of what to do. She stayed that way for what felt like eternity.

A voice whispered through the night, waking her. "Hey, handsome."

Milena almost shrieked.

"Hey, Angelina." Luke glanced back, into the Boarding House. "Right on time. We been busy tonight."

A thin waif of a girl appeared at the edge of the light. Blond hair tangled to her waist and she sucked on a cigarette glowing red. She threw it down and crushed it out.

Luke jumped to his feet. "Get back, you stupid bitch! Someone might see you," he hissed.

The girl backed away silently, disappearing into the dark. Luke visibly relaxed. "Give me a second," he whispered out into the night and, turning, clomped through the front door.

Milena hugged the ground, praying the young woman would not come near her. The chill of night seeped deeply into her, and surely the girl heard her thundering heart or chattering teeth. She desperately tried to calm herself, to stop shaking.

After a few moments she was able to listen. Nothing other than her heart slamming inside and silence outside. All night creatures were silent. She clenched the ground, her fingernails digging into dirt. Finally, Luke clomped back out and headed for the dark. The waif ran to meet him, jumped up, and wrapped her legs around him. Giggles and hushes came, and they disappeared.

Milena heard low murmurs. Silenced laughter. Then a noise she'd become used to hearing from behind the doors of the Boarding House. The sound of mating.

This man was responsible for the safety of the women in the Boarding House? Although grateful for Luke's female diversion,

Milena was angered at such a showing. The Golden Guard was as inept as he was treacherous. A dangerous combination. Others were at ease around him, but Milena felt brutality ooze from him constantly.

At least tonight he provided her the perfect opportunity to escape from the nest of horror and the body upstairs.

"Jesus, Luke, you're gonna buck me clean across the yard!"

"Shut up, you dumb bitch! You want someone to hear us?"

"Ain't no one gonna—"

"I said, shut up! I think I hear someone."

Milena froze.

"Ain't no one around. Lessen you want me to bring some help next time." A giggle and Luke's grunting began again. Milena crept quietly. She must get closer to them before she'd reach the main road.

"Hang on, girl!" Luke whispered huskily and loud enough for Milena to hear. She fought the urge to cover her ears and block out the nightmare, but she needed to be completely aware of everything around her.

Luke groaned. "Not so fast. I ain't done all the way."

"You are lest you got another fifty cents," Angelina answered.

Milena heard a dull thud and the woman gasped out. A fist against her flesh, no doubt.

"You ain't nothin' but a cheap poke," Luke's voice slobbered through the dark.

"Ain't cheap. Fifty cents more," she said, "and another fifty for hittin' me."

"What makes you think you're worth another dollar?"

"Oh, I am, and you're about to agree. How much you think Miss St. Claire would pay to find out one of her girls is cheatin' on her?"

Silence. Milena wanted to quiet the girl before she betrayed one of the ladies. But she dared not move.

"What're you sayin'?" Luke asked.

"Just what you heard, cowboy. One of her ladies came down to my place today. I'll tell you which one, but you gotta make it worth my while."

Chills cascaded down Milena's spine, and not good, affirming tingles. These were cold and shot through with the feel of death. Surely Beth had not come from the cribs. She'd been with Digger.

Luke's voice broke the night. "I smell a whore trick."

"No trick. I got much better tricks for my favorite man."

"I got five bucks with me," he whispered hoarsely.

"Sounds about right. You already owe me a dollar fifty. Give me the whole five dollars, and you git her name. Trust me, she's worth every cent."

"You throw in one of them 'better' tricks and you got yourself a deal, Angel."

Angelina laughed. Not a sound of joy, but a sound of conquest and anger. "Here we go, cowboy."

Luke's grunting punched through the night. Milena wanted to stay and hear the name of the Boarding House lady soon to be in trouble, but this might be her only opportunity to get away. And what could she do? Once Victor Creely's body was discovered, she would be hunted. Beth would have to take care of herself. She crept through brush until she met up with the road, and once she passed far enough out of the pool of Boarding House light, she stood up to travel. She looked behind her. The Boarding House seemed like another world, remote and unreachable. A faded painting, its details nothing more than some suggestive smears. Clutching her bag to her heart, she faced ahead and walked, not feeling, not thinking. She welcomed the numbness and did not want to push it aside. It wrapped around her, the most comfort she could hope to have.

She'd lost everything. All her long and arduous travels, away from all she loved, across the ocean, across this country. The loss of her family and friends, Baba, even the loss of the proprietress and the ladies, and nothing ahead for her. Nothing. Night insects sang, and from far away she heard piano music. There was nowhere but Jasper.

She looked behind. The cribs hunkered beyond the Boarding House. After that, wilderness stretched across the country. Death for one such as her.

Would death be so unwelcome?

She knocked the thought aside when another hit her. Was death unavoidable? She'd killed the King of the Jackals. All of Jasper would cry for justice.

Justice. Milena knew no such thing existed for a woman alone. Especially a foreign-born woman. Death in the wilderness felt like a better choice than hanging from a rope for all to see.

The sounds of a horse and carriage rumbled from behind her. She dove to the side of the road and scooted down. Hoping she wasn't heading for a sheer drop, she settled into the crook of a strongly rooted tree and waited. The clacking grew louder until she thought they might be on top of her. Victor's carriage passed, a blur. Behind it swept the chill of death.

She lowered her head onto her arms. For the first time during this journey of insanity, Milena truly could not hold her tears.

She did not try.

Chapter 18

A severed hand floated in a jar. Suspended in liquid, its fingers spread in a gesture of surrender. Milena almost cried out. Almost. She stumbled backward, into the dark beside the building, and looked around. No one saw her. Heard her.

She hugged her arms around herself. She must not make a mistake. Discovery meant death.

The town's activity finally settled in the hours before morning. She'd kept back into the pines and emerged only when she could skirt the town without risking discovery. She slipped from alley to alley, building to building, holding herself out of sight. Keeping away from the main street, she made her way by slinking along the outskirts of town.

She did not travel the back alleys of the town alone. Spirits, a myriad of them, wandered, eyes blank, hollowed by whatever despair haunted them from this world. The further into town she'd come, the more specters roamed, hanging on the edges of life. Even in the crowded New York City, she'd not seen so many restless souls.

What did Jasper do to these people? What might it do to her?

She longed for the rambling rivers and gentle hills of Bukovyna and the time in her life when people were few, at the most a small village. Contacts with spirits was rare, considered a sacred moment to be revered. Time and energy to help the spirit on its journey to the place of peace. These specters of Jasper, rife with anger and hatred, drained her.

She vowed not to become one herself. If she died in this place she would move through the Otherworld with great eagerness. Fear, anger, hate, revenge, all these kept a spirit from traveling to the final destination.

Also, caring for someone in this world, like Beth's mother or the twin of Jack Buchanan, meant entrapment between the two realms. Love could be as strong of an imprisonment as hate. Sometimes stronger.

She pressed closer to the simple wood jail and again observed the hand. She shivered. These *gaujos*, they called her people barbarians. Yet in the window of the jail sat the sheriff's most grisly trophy. She wondered what the owner of the appendage did to earn such a fate. As if to answer her, a spirit came around the corner of the jail and looked longingly at the jar. His left wrist dripped blood that didn't pool on the ground but faded away into nothing.

She turned away from the sorrow on his face. These spirits—*devi*—spoke everything through their eyes. They no longer possessed the words of this world to convey the price Jasper exacted from them.

Flexing her fingers, she imagined her own hand in a jar. She shook the vision away. A severed hand would not be her price to pay. She'd killed a man. A *gaujo* man.

Do not fool yourself, a voice wisped through her mind. *Not just a man, but a king.*

Thank heaven she didn't run into Victor's apparition, although she expected him at every turn. Yet knowing the man, she suspected he stood in Hell at this very moment, challenging Satan himself. If Milena were to bet on which king operated with more ruthlessness and evil, she would advise Satan to find another home.

Hopelessness rose, and instead of allowing fear to join, she focused on her purpose.

Jasper Mountain.

The giant rose up behind the town, darker than the night. No matter what the hour, the mountain's presence overshadowed all else, the town of Jasper cradled in its arms like a wailing, troubled babe. At any moment the mountain might tire of its charge, let go, and cause the town to slide down into oblivion.

Take the next step, she reminded herself. Night offered its cloak, and she must be gone before daybreak. She must continue. Hard as she tried to concentrate on the task at hand, the handless man followed her. His stump dripped, a nagging reminder of the barbarian souls hiding beneath cloaks of civilization these men of the West wore around their shoulders.

Piano music and voices leaked around the buildings from the saloon on Main Street, but not so loud as before. The town had quieted finally. The men still speaking slurred their words loudly, sentences stumbling and making no sense. A few lamps on Main Street glowed, casting sickly light.

Looking both ways, she darted across the alley to the back of the General Mercantile. Hoping to stay hidden, she stayed back in the shadows of the night.

Milena was not alone. A woman spirit stood tucked between the two buildings. She lit a cigarette, her eyes not blank at all, but filled with barely contained and deadly hate. Familiarity tingled, and Milena looked closer at the specter. The spirit sucked on her cigarette, her cheeks sinking in. Her angular face revealed, among other hardships in life, this woman had faced starvation. Her blue eyes were the only color piercing through silvery hair hung in ropey tangles to her waist.

Her beauty had not faded, though. She drew in another drag from her cigarette and smoke billowed out from her chest. Milena's eyes drew down to the hole. Bullet? Most likely. The wound gaped, torn and uneven. Someone had shot this woman at very close range.

Recognition gripped Milena and she gasped. The waif she'd just seen with Luke a few hours before. Angelina nodded as another web of smoke leaked from her chest.

Milena staggered back, wanting nothing more than to flee this town. Evil pervaded. Brutality always won in Jasper. She swallowed back nausea and tried not to look Angelina's way. If Milena had the time and wasn't afraid of discovery, she'd help the woman move on. For the second time this night, circumstances forced Milena to put her own needs before any others.

The specter continued to watch her.

Milena spoke in a whisper, "You face an eternity here. Of this existence. Let go and travel forward. Move on."

The spirit continued to suck the cigarette, her blue eyes burning with hate.

Noise and shouts interrupted from Main Street. A fight broke out. The shouting rose to a crescendo, and taking advantage of the ruckus, Milena smacked her velvet bag into the mercantile back window. She reached in and opened the door with a click. She paused, listening. Angelina and the handless man watched her. Did anyone else?

No sound came from inside or above.

In the tradition of her people, she planned to gather only what she needed to live. She entered the back of store. Angelina followed. The handless man stayed back, and Milena did her best to ignore the specter following her.

Through the large window at the front, the saloon spewed men out the door like a great creature with indigestion. Watching the saloon while she moved about the dark store, Milena took only things she might need. A canvas bag first. Candles, a blanket, some food—bread, dried meat, cheese. A knife. The sack grew heavy with the tools of survival. The fight across the street died down, and men entered and left the saloon, some standing in groups on the wood sidewalk. Angelina drifted to the window and watched the men pour out, a webbed cloak of smoke hovering around her. Milena smelled a faint whiff of tobacco. This woman's sorrow permeated, potent indeed.

Milena recognized Digger when he came out. Angelina watched the young miner and a tear streaked down her face, but her expression of anger and defiance did not change. Her eyes blazed although tears fell. Milena felt very exposed with Digger close.

Hide. Now.

Someone else was here.

Danger. Close.

The sheriff appeared, moving into view right outside the store window, his attention on the group across the street. Milena gasped and backed behind a counter. Slowly, he turned and cupped his hands around his face, pressing against the glass to peer inside.

She dropped to the floor, motionless. Her heart thundered so loudly, she was afraid he might hear it. She wondered if, before he hung her, the sheriff would cut off her hand.

After a few moments, his footsteps reverberated away on the

wood walk outside. Angelina continued to watch the street and smoke.

Milena recalled a Boarding House dinner conversation regarding the recent hanging of a man. The sheriff described the occasion and laughed, telling how the dying man's heels kicked in the air. Many times since, Milena watched the dance of death play over and over in her mind. The sheriff bragged of placing the dead man in a coffin and propping him up for several days of display as a warning to others. A warning, indeed, Milena thought, of the cruel nature of the West. She swallowed. Her throat burned.

She remained hunkered down for a bit to be sure he was gone. Finally, she rose to her knees, looking at the window. Nothing. She and Angelina were alone.

She must move. When daylight came she would lose her cover. She must get to Jasper Mountain before morning. Retreating to the back door, she tiptoed over glass and looked outside. The street stood empty. She hoped. The hand continued to float in the window, across the street. For a moment, she thought it waved to her to join it.

Had the sheriff gone back to the jail? Did he watch out his window?

"Are you planning to stay until daylight?" she whispered to herself. Searching for enough strength, she tried not to let the consequences of getting caught stop her, and she slipped out the door and around the building. After another minute or two, she then sprinted across the street, running away from the main road and veering to the north through scrub and rocks. Once on the outskirts of town, she slowed, surveying the landscape around her. No one followed. Not even Angelina. She clutched the canvas bag of survival in one hand and her velvet bag of magic in the other.

She wanted to give up. Turn herself over to the *gaujos*. Justice would never hear the words of a woman alone, but what of that? The serene cradle of the Otherworld waited to catch her, and she grew tired of this world, exhausted from struggling. Tears pressed behind her eyes and spilled over for the second time that night.

No time for such self-indulging. This was a time to—

Survive.

She wiped her tears away. "*Shuv'hani?*" She did not know where the voice came from, the Otherworld or inside herself. It did not matter. Only one thing did.

"I will survive, *Shuv'hani*. I will," she promised out loud, more to herself than to her grandmother. She had nothing left within, yet she would not give up. She was Romani, she reminded herself. Romani could endure anything. She must not forget the strength of her ancestresses running through her, the Old Magic guiding her, the *Shuv'hani* walking beside her. As long as she took another step, there was no such thing as hopelessness, or surrender. Not for her. No matter what horrors came after her from the town. She turned, and Jasper wavered before her in spots of lantern light. Distant, dark voices spattered through air.

She left them behind, where they belonged.

"Are you sure she was there? Beth?" Isabella St. Claire was nothing if not brilliant at detecting deception. Luke stood before her, his bright blue eyes glinting with fortitude and probably a bit of whiskey.

"Yep. I followed her, ma'am. I seen her myself, ridin' them miners like the whore in heat she is." Luke laughed.

Isabella kept her expression stone. She did not find herself amused by him. At all.

Luke's face betrayed the realization of his error. "I mean, beg pardon, ma'am. I ain't got nothin' 'gainst no whores. My favorite type of woman. Whores, that is." Luke grinned.

He'd come before dawn, pounding on her door despite the indecent hour, and insisted on meeting her before she properly dressed. Isabella decided it was high time she sacked him. She was tired of coming upon him, sleeping at his post. All he was good for was sleeping, and like all men, rutting. Luke smelled sour and dusty, like the cribs and those cheap whores he constantly visited. Isabella's stomach turned. Just what she deserved, really, for trying to help a miner out of his lowly position. Those filthy dirt-hounds were all the same. Fit only to wallow through the underground.

But not to get distracted. First, Beth. At the cribs. The girl's condition and actions of the previous day supported Luke's story, the main reason she'd listened to him at all. Isabella recognized truth, especially when it slapped her in the face.

"When she rises, at the usual time, will you request for her to come down to my office?" No need to wake the girl at such an hour. She'd let her sleep a bit more, secure and safe for the last time in her life. Besides, Isabella needed some time to ponder over this most distasteful news and to properly dress and groom herself. She needed to be a picture of cold perfection. She knew her little Beth would crumple, and she needed all the strength she possessed to stay the course.

"When you return with her, please leave immediately. Go back to your post by the front door."

"Ma'am." Still grinning like the town idiot, he nodded and winked at her, backing out of her office. He shut the door.

She sat at her desk and dropped her head into her hands.

Really, this day was becoming most disagreeable. And so early. She wondered how Victor fared at the clinic. She thought she'd have heard if he'd died.

She raised her head from her hands and smiled despite the stormy waters she found herself navigating. It was actually lovely to see Victor underestimate someone for a change. Especially a woman. All the times Isabella fantasized about killing him, and the Gypsy struck the blow.

Of course, Milena's life was forfeit. One did not merely wound a lion. No, the only way to insure survival was to kill the beast completely, guarantee its destruction. Especially one with wounded pride, a beast with a taste for twisted torture, and sick revenge. No, she didn't envy Milena's future at all.

Victor Creely must be alive. And if Isabella knew him at all, very much in a mood.

Milena watched the sky. Night began to fall away. She barely made out shapes and rocks in the landscape. A few black wisps swelled continuously, churning into a thick blanket of cloud, heavy and oppressive in the dark. Strange. A storm must be about to pass through. Despite the spinning cloud, the air felt cold and still. Once the wind whipped up, the way would be treacherous. She needed to find shelter, and quickly.

Milena shivered, pulling her blanket closer around her shoulders, grateful for the canvas bag and treasures from the store. She breathed heavily, not used to the altitude. She'd journeyed through the remainder of the night and made it to the back side of Jasper Mountain. On this side, the mountain didn't seem quite so imposing. The ground she traveled rose well above Jasper, and more mountains surrounded her. No spirits wandered here. She imagined no one else on the earth existed, and after the last few days, she found such a daydream comforting.

Suddenly, the black of the sky solidified, gathered into a roiling whirlwind, a storm of clouds circling into a funnel. She frantically searched for cover. Then paused. She felt no threat from the cloud. No tempest announcing the onset of a storm. Puzzled, she kept watching. The cloud pulled in on itself, the edges coming closer and the cloud growing thicker, taller, swirling faster and faster until it towered. A high funnel, the kind that if it touched the earth, it destroyed everything in its path.

No warning came to her, no air surged, yet she clearly saw the spinning mass and heard its whispering howl. As instantaneously as the funnel came into existence, the mountain inhaled and sucked it deep within. The cloud shrank until it no longer existed.

No, not a cloud, she realized. Bats. Thousands of bats.

They were leading her to sanctuary, inviting her within the mountain. The bats were her welcome. They revealed the threshold, and Milena stepped forward, she hoped, to a place of wonder, where mountain spirits danced and magic sang.

A tentative rap sounded at the door. Isabella stood.

"Come in."

Isabella noticed Beth's eyes, huge, on the verge of tears. She approached the desk, limping slightly. Isabella struggled to reinforce her wavering determination.

The girl tried not to cry, her lips tense in her bruised and scraped face. Best to move quickly, Isabella thought, to strike at this situation, immediately. No preamble, no questions, no explanations. And certainly no compassion. She'd never get through this otherwise. She wasn't about to allow anyone, not even her dear Beth, to chip away at the foundation of the Boarding House.

"You were at the cribs yesterday."

Beth flinched like she'd been struck. The wariness in her eyes sharpened into panic. She shook her head. "I . . . Isabella, I—"

"Miss St. Claire."

"Yes, ma'am," she said, her voice small, hanging her head like a child waiting punishment.

"There is no explanation I will accept. Don't waste your breath. Or my time."

Beth's head snapped up, her eyes growing ever wider in a face draining of color.

Isabella continued. "Pack your things. I want you gone inside the hour." She did not miss the irony of the situation. If Victor was the least bit interested in Beth, this scene would play out much differently. The way things stood, the girl had no value to Isabella, to the Boarding House. Especially with the taint of the cribs clinging to her. Isabella must, at all cost, keep out anything cheap and tawdry. She had a sanctuary to protect. For herself and her ladies.

The girl had turned herself into a liability, one Isabella could not afford.

"Please, Miss St. Claire, I can explain. It's not what you think," Beth said, her voice barely above a whisper.

"Tell me, have you honored your contract with Mr. Creely? Have you remained faithful to him?"

Beth's face finally crumpled in the wake of tears. They fell, an answer. The only one Isabella needed.

She inhaled deeply and hardened her resolve. "Get out."

"I love him."

"Victor?" Isabella asked, surprise rushing through her.

"Digger. That's who I went to meet." Angrily, Beth swiped her tears away. "It's Digger I betray. Every time. Not Victor." Another tear spilled down her cheek. "And you. I betrayed you. For that, I am sorry."

Closing her eyes, Isabella willed her chest to quit hurting. There it was again, that bothersome heart of hers. It kept rearing up, insisting she feel. But damn it, didn't she tell the girls a thousand times not to become attached? Not to care? And above all, not to love. Men didn't love; they weren't capable of such a thing. Men used, and the sheer joy of this business was using them right back.

Isabella opened her eyes when she heard the rustle of skirts. Beth opened the door to leave. A small sob clung in the air. Isabella opened her mouth to call out to Beth, bring her back. Give her another chance. But the cribs. The cribs! And Digger. A miner. A filthy, stinking dirt-hound.

She simply had no choice in the matter. None at all.

Paint, she decided. Yes, begin another painting. This time, a beautiful sunrise, bursting with color and light. A lovely herd of deer in a distant meadow. And in the front? A hunter. Yes, that was it. A woman hunter. What was the name of the goddess? The one who both hunted and protected? Diana?

Isabella smiled to herself, her calm once again in place. No tempest. No feeling. No hurt, the pain in her chest gone. Yes, she would paint Diana, the huntress with a bow and arrow. At the feet of the goddess, a fawn with an arrow through its heart. A baby deer, ignorant of any danger, separated from the rest of the group, inviting predators and giving away the location of the herd. A fatal mistake, leaving Diana no other choice.

And the sweet herd of deer, continuing to graze in the gentle light of dawn, blissfully unaware of any danger. But, no matter. The huntress would protect them.

Isabella sighed. Another masterpiece in the making. Really, she was amassing quite a collection. She rose and fingered her key as she walked to her parlor. Her easel called to her from the corner of the room, and the promise of her new painting lured her to begin its creation. She returned to bolt the lock at the door.

Nothing could get in.

Amazing what a man could accomplish in a night. Jack walked to the mine, proposal in hand. Only a bit late. He'd sent Dig on with explanations to his team. He didn't think anyone would fault him for trying to figure out what happened to Stoop. In fact, his actions might actually garner some trust from his men.

Then again, maybe not.

The whole mess wore him down. When he went to the Nugget Hotel to question the miners about Stoop, they weren't especially forthcoming. Jack pieced together enough to understand Stoop's disappearance was similar to Tom's.

Jack walked across the yard to the front office. Time to talk to Victor, make him understand and stop operations for a thorough search. Organize teams to map the tunnels. Jack worked out the entire process. His proposal would make the mine much more productive in the future. The only cost to production: two days. Two lousy days. He'd documented the time, the expense of a shutdown, and extended the savings over the next year. Surely, Victor and the investors would agree to a few days of stopped operation for an increase in efficiency.

Then again, maybe not.

Jack knew the missing miners in the equation didn't matter to Victor or the officers. But Stoop and Tom mattered, damn it.

He was ready for Victor to punch holes through his proposal, but he was more sure about this than anything he'd ever done. As he approached the main office building, he slowed, trying not to let his newfound confidence erode. Tom and Stoop couldn't afford it.

Jack opened the door. The front office, a wide and shallow room, shouted functionality. Desks lined the walls, and housed the officers, the self-proclaimed planners and thinkers. The inhabitants all looked up. Almost in unison, they returned to their work when they saw who it was, dismissing his existence. Another thing Jack was sick and tired of seeing, the arrogance of these men. The way they looked down at the workers who were the backbone of the business.

Turtle did acknowledge Jack's presence, wrinkling his nose like he smelled something foul. Edmund Blum, the mine's accountant, at least nodded to Jack before returning to busily scratching away at his ledger.

Behind the columns of officers, an ornately carved door stood in the center of the far wide wall, like a portal of wonders. The entrance to Victor Creely's office. A door few ever entered.

Edmund looked up again, sighed, and rose from his desk, a thin pipe of a man with black hair and eyes. He looked like a human version of Poe's raven. The young man appeared much older than his years, just like the miners. Perhaps the burden of numbers and profit for Victor was a difficult job, too.

"Jack, can I help you?" The man's voice drew out, tired. For a moment, Jack felt a kinship. He relaxed his shoulders, and the painful throb in his neck faded.

"I need to see Victor," Jack answered, hoping his familiar use of the mine president's name would bypass any need for further explanation. It did not.

"And what may I tell him this is regarding?"

"This is regarding the mine."

Edmund smiled thinly, like he wore his britches too tight. "I need a bit more detail than that."

"I'll save the details for Victor. Thank you."

The accountant pursed his lips. "Well, discussion with Mr. Creely will be a bit difficult."

Despite Jack's earlier empathy for the man, frustration took hold. Enough was enough. He took a step forward. "Listen, Blum—"

Edmund retreated and his eyes widened. "Jack, Mr. Creely is indisposed."

The statement took Jack completely by surprise. "What do you mean?"

"What it usually means. Indisposed."

Tired of excuses, lies, and being put off, Jack pushed past the accountant. Summoning whatever fortitude was left in him, he swung open the president's door.

Victor's office was empty, the mahogany desk sitting alone in the center of the room, surrounded by deeply stained wood paneling. Paintings, pastoral scenes dotted the walls with tranquility.

Jack spun around. "Where is he?"

Edmund smirked. "Are you having difficulty hearing this morning, Jack? I told you. Indisposed."

Jack headed for the accountant, who scuffled back, beyond the threshold. Before Jack had the chance to say another word, shouts punched through the air, coming from the headframe. The shrill of the lifting engine cut off. Yelling rose in pitch and fever. Turtle rose to his feet. Jack changed direction and just about catapulted across the office when the door slammed open.

"Somebody fetch the doc, and right quick. Jack, you'd better get out here. The platform collapsed. Your entire group was on board."

Chapter 19

Plenty of times, Jack imagined the mountain was a creature consuming him. At this moment, he almost believed it, and this time the mountain not only devoured his body but his soul. He dropped another few feet, rope burning his palms. Below him, a thousand-foot fall. Pete controlled his lifeline. If that wasn't a test in trust, Jack didn't know what was.

Pete explained the incident to Jack. The platform had started to split just when it reached the collar. Miners scrambled off. Only one didn't make it off in time, a boy not big enough to push his way to safety.

If Mouse fell to the bottom, he'd been killed, no question.

The only hope was that the kid caught the mouth of a tunnel. Jack swallowed back fear, and clung to the thin hope like he clung to his rope. He tried not to see visions of a little boy, hurt. Broken. Tingling pushed behind his eyes. No time for tears, not even the kind that didn't fall. Mouse needed him like he'd never needed him before.

Miracles happened. He'd seen plenty after the ranch fire: Leno and his family, Willow. But miracles were in short supply in Jasper. He willed Mouse to be alive. More, he believed the boy was alive, believed it with everything in him.

Jack dropped another several feet, gripping the cable tighter. If he wasn't all tangled up in rope, he'd kick himself in the ass. He'd been tied up with his stupid proposal and then ran off to the Nugget Hotel without a second thought for anything, especially not the child sleeping in his bed. Mouse could take care of himself. No surprise the kid rose, made his own breakfast and went to work to do his job. Seven years old, and this was his life. While Jack postured with Edmund Blum and battered down the door to an empty room, his team had been on the way up in preparation for a blast. Mouse, usually glued to Jack's side, had been at work due to a sense of responsibility way beyond his years. His reward? He'd fallen, the latest victim to the mine.

Jack's feet hit rock. He pushed off and slipped down farther. Chanted in his head. *Mouse is alive.* Swept aside everything else for those words.

Mouse is alive.

He let them fill him, become him.

Mouse is alive.

Suddenly, he swung into the dark, no wall beneath his feet. A tunnel.

"Ho!" Jack yelled. The rope stretched taut. He bounced and started swinging like a pendulum. It took him a moment before he faced the right way, the candle from his hardboil illuminating the mouth of the tunnel. Empty. And mouth it was. An infinite, dark gullet, yawning wide, hungry for a sacrifice.

"Not Mouse. Mouse is alive," Jack muttered. "Ho! Ho!" he hollered. A damned inefficient way of communication; a problem preplanning might solve. Yep, he'd add that to his stupid proposal. How to communicate, dangling above certain death, while searching for a deaf child. Jesus, what a place.

His feet found rock, and he pushed off, slipping down to the next tunnel. He gauged the drop to the next opening fairly accurately and didn't swing so helplessly, his spin controlled.

"Ho!"

He hung, peering into the black. Nothing. His heart sank. This was about as far a fall as Mouse could have survived. A slight breeze came from the tunnel, thankfully, not enough to blow his candle out.

"Ho! Ho!" he boomed, like some insane incarnation of Saint Nick. Along with the gentle caress of wind from the tunnel rode a scent. Lilac, meshed with a chill.

He began dropping and pushed out. The lip of this tunnel jutted a few inches. He realized the last time he'd smelled a lilac scent. Her perfume. Jo's.

"Ho!" he screamed. He stopped, his eyes level with the tunnel floor. Grabbing the rock, he pulled himself up and hooked a leg over the lip. He crawled in a few feet and sat back on his knees, feeling a tinge of relief he wasn't dangling over the seemingly bottomless drop.

A figure loomed in the dark. He squinted. Someone was just at the point past where he could see. No, nothing. Wait. Yes. A figure.

"Jo?" he asked, and was about to kick himself again for being an idiot. Or was he so desperate, he imagined such a thing? No, he definitely saw something. He dropped his gaze and almost saw her on the edge of his vision.

Every muscle in his body tightened.

Dear God in heaven, it looked like her outline, but when he looked straight at whatever it was, nothing was there. He glanced back to the side and the figure again formed on the edge of his vision. He thought he saw a flash of eyes, looking at him. Green. Piercing.

He held perfectly still, afraid whatever was there might dissipate into nothing. He kept his vision locked on the rock on the ground right in front of her, if it was her and not a figment of his insane imagination.

"Jo?" Jack asked again. She faded. His eyes bored into the space where she'd stood. Nothing. "No! Jo!" he called. The rope behind him began to drop into the tunnel. He leaned back and called up the shaft "Ho!" then gave a yank, the signal that he was going to get out of the rope harness. He coiled the line at the mouth of the tunnel and rose to take a few steps forward. Of course, nothing. She'd probably never been there.

Another Jack Buchanan flight of fancy? Yes, a logical explanation, but it didn't feel right in his heart. He was sure he'd seen her.

"Nothing here."

It must be Milena and all her talk of Jo standing beside him. The Gypsy tricked him, entertained him with her stories of twin spirits. She merely did what Isabella paid her to do: entertain gentlemen callers.

He took a few more steps in. Mouse's life depended on him, and here he was, seeing ghosts. Jack kicked at dust, angry at the substance coating the tunnels, him, the rope, his clothes, gritting in his eyes, his lungs. He kicked again. A haze puffed up. Fury bit through him, and he kicked again. Another puff rose. And again, again, until a fog of rock dust floated in the air.

The dark stone, marking the place where Jo had been, moved.

Jack stopped, focused on the dusky form, and rushed forward. He dropped to his knees. The rock unrolled, loosened and transformed, not a rock at all. A boy. The candle on Jack's hardboil illuminated enough for him to see Mouse's pale face, a tiny moon in the dusty dark. The child panted, his body shuddering.

Gently, Jack laid a hand on the boy's chest. "Hold steady, kid.

I'm going to get you out."

Mouse's eyes were open and glazed, as if he didn't see Jack, or anything at all.

"Hold on, little man," Jack said, gathering Mouse in his arms. "Just hold on. That's all you have to do. I'll take care of everything else."

Milena slept for hours, waking to complete dark. Although wrapped in the intimate black of a cavern, she knew sunlight reigned outside. Beyond, the world of men pushed on in daylight, fast and mean and hard. Unforgiving.

Within the safety of the mountain, constant rustling overhead reminded her she was not alone. The comings and goings of her companions indicated the cycles of the sun and moon. She decided she wanted to stay here forever.

She'd found a cove where she could stretch out at the other end from where the bats nested. Although the nook was cold and hard, she'd slept soundly. For the first time in a long while, she felt completely safe.

Yawning, she lit her lantern. Light skimmed along the floor, and mountain gems glittered. The lantern illuminated enough of her surroundings to reveal not just a cavern, but a sacred cathedral. No structure built by man would ever rival the beauty of this place. Towers speared up, and others dripped down, fluid caught by time and hardened into rock. Centuries of painstaking artistry. Every so often the light caught a reflection of imbedded crystals and flung a sparkle through the dark. The cave's ceiling vaulted up into endless black.

Curiosity to explore farther and deeper pulled at her, but

something else as well. Since the night of the *MoortYak,* she'd never felt safe, or that she belonged anywhere. Until this moment. She was meant to be here. The pull from the mountain folded around her, calling, beckoning. She was almost to her destination.

Holding the lantern before her, she ventured farther inside. The tunnel's ceiling lowered until she dropped to her hands and knees, pushing the lantern ahead. Although she wandered through the tunnels for hours, she was perfectly content. Some stretches allowed her to walk, many forced her to crawl. Rivulets of water dripped, adding to the sounds of life filling the mountain. The sound of bats rustling fell off, diminishing to a whisper.

She came upon a pool, black as obsidian and still as night. Her reflection regarded her from the underground lake, and she smiled to think how the proprietress would disapprove of her wild hair, disheveled velvet dress, and smudge of glittery dust on her face. She wished for her own comfortable clothing, but wishes were useless and she needed to push on. She left the pool behind as the mountain called to her with more intensity than ever before. Her own excitement built, sparkling through her. She was almost there.

She crawled through a low channel and the mountain opened, its walls soaring up. Milena sat back on her heels at the threshold, and although she had anticipated wonder, she paused in shock with what she saw before her.

Light flashed off crystals crusting the walls of the cave. Translucent rock seemed to drip down from the ceiling. Light and color danced through and off facets. The entire chamber swirled with brilliance.

"The Chamber of Jewels," Milena whispered. Such places were spoken of among her people with hushed voices; these caves were rare and their magic, strong.

This was the heart of Jasper Mountain.

Centuries-old spirits whirled in the dance of lights, and their song whispered in the air. Their presence permeated the cavern, and rising above them, holding them close inside its heart, the magnificent and ancient spirit of the mountain. It hummed with wisdom in the deepest and eldest of voices.

Magic of the Ancients and the secrets of mystics whirled. She closed her eyes, stretching herself out to touch them, to connect. The spirits danced around her, fizzled through her like bubbles in champagne, and they tickled over her skin. Every part of her awakened to them. The curtain to the Otherworld swept aside.

When the anthem began, it did not startle her. It rose, a mixture of the rush and whistle of air. Strands of a deep and ageless voice wound through, with spirit song sparkling in harmony. The anthem skimmed along an undercurrent of sacred and ancient chant.

The Song of the Mountain, sung for countless centuries.

She closed her eyes, humbled to hear such sacred music.

For the first time in her life, Beth truly felt like a whore. She wasn't used to the stares of men, certainly not these unabashed leers, accompanied with hoots and whistles. She almost wished she'd stayed hidden in the small grove of pines, but she'd waited for hours and watched the miners come from their shift.

The second she recognized the slim figure of Digger, her heart lifted for the first time in hours. She loved him so much. And what she had to tell him would destroy his hopes and dreams. Maybe even him.

He stopped short when he saw her, just stared, like he didn't quite understand that she stood in front of him.

"Bethie?"

The sweet familiarity started her tears again. She didn't know how to tell him. He approached her, the catcalls of his friends growing louder.

He did nothing to stop them.

"What's going on? What are you doing here?"

She'd never seen him so filthy. Or tired. She swiped away tears. She wanted to lighten the news and tried to smile but only managed a pathetic grimace.

"Miss Isabella. She found out about us, Digger."

His face went slack with shock. Disbelief, and finally distress. "Oh, God."

"I'm ruined," she managed to get out before a sob broke through, and she gasped it back. She put her head in her hands. Waited to feel his arms around her. Nothing. She cried for a bit, and looked back up.

He stood there, shoulders caved inward, eyes miserable, staring at the ground as though an answer might spring up through it.

She shook her head. "I can't think. You have to tell me what to do."

He grabbed her arm and pulled her back into the trees. "How? How did she find out? What did you do?" He gritted his teeth and spit the words. "What . . . did . . . you . . . do?"

She tried to pull her arm from his grip, but his fingers bit into her flesh. "I didn't do anything! Luke must have seen us down by the cribs. Nothing else makes any sense."

Digger flung her arm away from him. "Unless the Gypsy whore told her."

Beth gasped. "Milena did no such thing. We can trust her, Digger."

"She didn't like me no how, no way. I saw it in her eyes. I knew it was a mistake to ask her for help the minute I saw her."

He looked at Beth, his eyes burning with anger. "It was a stupid thing to do, trust her."

"Why are we fighting over this? What difference does it make how Miss Isabella found out? She did. That's all."

Digger scuffed his boot toe in the dirt.

"What will we do?" Beth asked, afraid to hear his answer.

He shook his head. "Bethie, I got nothing to give you. Nothing. I don't even got a place where you can stay."

"Do we have any money left at all?" She didn't have the strength or energy to spare his feelings. She needed to know what their situation was; they both needed to face it. "You've lost all my money at the tables, haven't you?"

He didn't answer. The look on his face, even through dirt, was enough.

"I have nowhere to go," she added.

"You can't stay with me."

As if to back up Digger's proclamation, a passing miner hollered, "Drop yer pants and do it, boy. She din't come to talk!" Laughter, mean and harsh, followed.

For the first time in her life, anger surged up at him. "All our money! How could you?"

"How could you let Miz Isabella find out about us? This is a disaster, right sure."

"You don't need to tell me. I'm the one who got thrown out, remember?"

He shook his head. "Can you go to the church? Reverend McShane might help."

"Last I knew, he was running an orphanage, not a home for wayward whores."

"Don't you start blamin' me for this mess," he said, sharpness creeping into his voice. "You're the one who got yourself fired.

You're the one who opened your legs for Creely in the first place. I loved you, Beth, and lookit you. You ended up a whore."

Something started to crumble, deep inside. She gasped, not able to speak.

"I loved you so much, and there you were, one of Miss Isabella's fancied-up whores, and layin' under Victor Creely, no less."

A dull noise roared in her ears. She finally found her voice. "I had no choice. Victor was determined to take me, no matter what. The Boarding House was my only way to ever see you again, give us some time together. You never managed to figure out anything better."

"You didn't give me a chance!"

The roar grew to a frenzy and she felt something she hardly ever did. She was hurt, yes, but something else foreign to her. All these past years of pleasing Victor, pleasing Digger bubbled up and sharpened to fury. "I worked for the Creelys for years! Scrubbing their filth until my fingers bled, trying to stay hidden from Victor's looks. What choice did I have? What choice did you give me? Other than taking my money and losing it at poker? How dare you blame me for any of this? Miss Isabella was right, I was insane to have anything to do with a dirt-hound."

Shock registered on his face. The look of a man hurt in his pride. He slapped her. Turned his back to her. Walked away.

A miner grinned at her, leered, and waved as he passed. "Hey, girlie, don't cry. If he ain't buyin', I sure will!"

"Jack, let go."

Jack held tightly to Mouse's hand, as he'd done for, Jesus, how long? The evening and night, anyway. He watched and counted each breath the kid took, in, out. Seventy-six. In, out. Seventy-seven. He needed to be sure.

Ambrose shook his shoulder, gently. Jack ignored him; he had to count. In, out. Seventy-eight. In, out. Seventy-nine.

"Jack? There's nothing more you can do."

"How the hell can you say that?" Jack barked, talking for the first time in several hours. The doctor had finally broken through the fog he'd pulled into place when he took the post by Mouse's bedside. He willed himself to not feel anything, to just be there, with the boy. Save all his thoughts and emotions for another time, when Mouse didn't need him. He'd begun counting, to keep from screaming, ranting, punching the wall. As long as he counted, Mouse was fine.

"Jack?"

"What time is it anyway?" His voice sounded raspy to his own ears.

"Four," Ambrose answered. "In the afternoon."

"Missed my whole damned shift."

"Jack, he's doing fine. I think rest is probably the best thing for him. You could use some yourself."

Sounds interrupted from the room next door. Victor's room, where throughout the night and into today, an endless parade of people passed. Jack finally realized what Edmund meant when he said Victor was "indisposed." Someone had attacked the mine president.

Ambrose nodded to the wall separating Victor's room from the main clinic space. The doctor had given up his quarters for Victor to have privacy. "I don't think anyone will care you took the day off. Especially not your boss."

Jack was ashamed at the feeble smile playing around his lips. It disappeared when he looked down at the tiny miner in the bed before him. Mouse's hand. It was cold. So cold.

He felt the familiar knot of frustration, the one he got every time he thought about Jasper Mine. "Ambrose, please tell me he'll be all right."

"Jack, I just don't know. He might be fine. He may never wake up. The next twenty-four hours are important."

"Not the answer I asked for."

The doctor sat on the edge of the bed and looked straight into Jack's face. "I'll always tell you God's honest truth."

"And I do appreciate that, Doc. You're one of the few who do."

Jack resumed his watch over Mouse, silently asking God to keep the boy with them. If there was a God. Jack wasn't sure he believed anymore. He watched the boy who dodged death in the mines. Twice. Death was a jealous mistress who insisted on taking Mouse's hearing with her the first time they danced. He hoped this time she'd leave him intact.

Gently, Jack tucked Mouse's arm back under his blanket.

"Thank God the lip of the tunnel jutted out." Jack shook his head. "Even so, it was only a few inches. I can't believe Mouse ever hit that and hung on."

"Miracles, Jack. They happen all the time," Taryn McShane's voice said from behind.

Jack shifted around at the sound. The preacher stood in the doorway, his brown eyes rife with understanding.

"Miracles?" Jack said, turning back to the boy. "None in the mine, Reverend."

"There's one, sleeping right in front of you." Taryn came forward and placed a hand on Jack's shoulder. He found it amazing, how Taryn's presence made him feel better. Calmer. Like things might work their way back to right. No wonder the man was a preacher.

"You think you can put a word in for him?"

"God is always watching us, Jack. Always with us. Whether

we realize it or not." Taryn pulled up a chair beside Jack and sat down. "Shall we pray together?"

Jack figured praying for help at this point would make him the biggest hypocrite in the world. He shook his head. "Nope, but you feel free."

Disappointment weighted down Taryn's sympathetic expression.

"Actually," Jack said, "I'd really appreciate it if you do it. I'm not good at anything like that. My faith's shaken loose. I guess I need proof God gives a damn at all." Jack thought of the image—Jo? Standing above Mouse. Making sure Jack reached him. "Tare, I'm sorry. Been a long day. I was up all night before last working out a proposal for the mine and planned to talk to Victor yesterday. But the platform collapsed."

"And you've mostly been up the entire night with Mouse," Ambrose said. "I'm trying to convince our hero to get home and get some food and sleep."

Jack shook his head. "I couldn't sleep even if I wanted to. Damn it, I'm so mad, I can't think straight."

"Could be you're so tired you can't think straight," Ambrose countered.

"Proposal?" Taryn asked.

Jack put his head in his hands and rubbed his eyes. "Oh, just one of my idiotic ideas." He lifted his head to look at Taryn. "I made a list of everything the mine needs and ideas to implement different things. Mapping, safety procedures, working procedures. Rescue and search procedures. I even managed to show cost benefit to the mining operation in case Victor tries to summarily dismiss the whole idea."

Taryn smiled. "I think it hardly sounds idiotic."

"Well, I thought it was a good idea at the time, but Victor will never listen."

"Which is why you wrote it down. He can read it at his leisure."

"That's pretty much next to impossible to hope for."

"How do you know that?"

Jack laughed. "Well, minister, what do you think the odds are?"

"The odds? Victor, I'm not sure about, but if you don't ask, you will never receive. You say these miners don't trust you, but I'd wager if they don't already, they will soon. Especially when they realize what you are doing for them."

"Now, I didn't think preachers were the wagerin' type." Jack found himself relaxing. And after the last few days, it felt good. "You're right. I can do so much for the men, or at least try." Talking made him feel so much better. Gave him the illusion he was doing something. Gave him hope. "You're one hell of a preacher, Taryn McShane."

Taryn laughed. "The perfect immortalization. Be sure to remember it for my tombstone. Why don't you go have a meal and then you might feel like sleep. You'll do much better for Mouse if you aren't worn down. I'm happy to stay, and Ambrose and I can take good care of him."

"What about your orphans?"

"Mrs. Beauchamp has them well under control. I asked her to take them for the evening and tonight. I figured this little fella is in need. This is where I belong. If you don't mind my telling you, Jack, you look terrible. I believe the doctor is correct, you need sleep. Go home for a while. It will do us all some good."

Jack smiled weakly. "I do feel like I've been put through the stamping mill."

"I'll stay with him. We'll do some of the praying that makes you so uneasy."

Jack shook his head. "I'm not going anywhere. You go ahead and pray, Reverend. I'll just count."

Chapter 20

Mouse twisted and wormed through the blackest tunnel, so dark he couldn't see. There was no light ahead, or anywhere. He wasn't sure what had happened to his hat candle, which was an awful shame considering he was lost. And not only lost, but bad lost. He couldn't hear or see either.

He felt like those children in his favorite fairy story who wanted to follow bread crumbs but the birds ate them all up. Well, some big old bird had eaten all Mouse's light, candles and everything. He didn't know what he was going to do, or how he would ever get back.

He had never been this lost or alone. Ever.

He felt sort of like he was floating, but that couldn't be true. No one floated through the mine. He was being silly again. Jack seemed to like it when he acted silly, laughing or playing. He tried not to do that kind of stuff, though, because he thought he might seem a simpleton. He was already deaf and if they thought him a simpleton, too, they wouldn't let him work at the mine, and if he couldn't work at the mine, then where would he go?

How did he get in this darkest place? He tried to recall— hadn't he been with somebody? When he became the boss, Jack paired everyone up, and Jack was his team-buddy so where was he? Mouse couldn't figure out why he was down here alone.

He remembered. Jack hadn't come into work today.

He remembered more. The platform. It broke. He fell.

He must be dead.

But if he was dead, where was Da? Where was Ma and Rachel and Annie and little Bill? They should all be here. Not this dark. One thing Mouse knew for sure, he didn't much like the dark. Especially not this dead-dark. And he was floating but he couldn't move his arms or legs; someone had tied him up. Or maybe he was petrified because he was dead.

This sure wasn't fair.

He didn't like this dead. He squirmed. Nothing. He started to panic and squirmed more. Nothing. He tried to break free. He couldn't. At least someone was holding tight to his hand.

Hand?

Did the dead have hands, because someone was holding his, awful hard. He wriggled again. One thing he knew for sure, he wouldn't be dead quietly. No, sir.

"Did you see that?" Ambrose jumped to his feet.

"He's squeezing my hand," Jack said. "Talk to him, Ambrose. I think he's coming around."

"Jack. He's deaf."

"Oh, yeah. Seems I can't get it through my head. It's just this kid is . . ." *Special. Incredible. He doesn't seem at a disadvantage at all.*

He clutched Mouse's hand, and the boy squeezed back. "He's coming around, Ambrose, I'm sure of it."

Suddenly, Mouse sat up. He blinked, looked at the doctor, at

Taryn, and finally, at Jack. He let go of Jack's hand. Jack wondered if he'd held to the boy for Mouse's sake, or for his own.

It didn't matter. What did matter was the existence of miracles in Jasper after all.

Beth swiped tears from her cheek. Even through walls and stacked supplies, she heard everything. She stayed quiet, what she was best at, she supposed. But she wanted to clap when Mouse woke to face the world again. Wanted to hug Jack for having the tender, kind heart he did, even though he did his best to hide it. The doctor, who diligently stayed with Jack and Mouse, and who took her in when she had nowhere else to go. The preacher. Such a kind, kind man.

Why hadn't she fallen in love with one of them instead of Digger? Selfish, irresponsible, thickheaded, funny, sweet, wonderful Digger.

Of course she needed to stay hidden. Victor Creely was somewhere in the clinic. She didn't want to be trouble for the doctor after he'd been so good to her. Honestly, she didn't want to get out of this bed, either. Every time the doctor peeked in on her, she'd stop crying enough to feign slumber. It became easier to pretend; she went inside herself for hours on end. Not move, not hear, speak, feel.

She wanted to sleep forever.

Mouse mimicked the action of lighting and smoking.

"He wants his pipe," Jack said.

"I simply will not have a child smoke in my clinic." Ambrose shook his head firmly at Mouse, who crossed his arms and scowled.

"Look at that. He's already starting to act like you, Jack." Ambrose rose, rushed to the other end of the room, and started clinking bottles.

"Well, I'd say the last hour proves there is nothing wrong with him," Taryn said.

"Can I take him home?" Jack asked, taken aback at his own question. He thought of his house as Mouse's home. On second thought, he wasn't surprised. Not really.

Ambrose returned, armed with a bottle of greenish liquid and a spoon. "I'd like to keep him tonight and watch over him. Think he'll take this?"

Mouse's expression scrunched down even further until his face seemed to be made of dried fruit.

"I'm sure going to have fun watching you try," Jack said.

"I'd like to see you go home and get some rest," Ambrose answered. "Maybe I'll have better luck with my patient once you're gone. I think half of this is a show for your benefit."

Most likely true, and there was nothing for him to do here, not really. But there was something he could do up at the mine. Something he'd contemplated between counting Mouse's breaths. Why wait? Why ask for permission? Why not start mapping, at least begin it so he'd know exactly what he was talking about. His argument would be much stronger when he presented it to Victor. He needed all the facts he could get for that discussion.

If he found a few tunnels that shouldn't exist, well, it might stop Victor's insistence the maps were up to date. And Mouse was the answer to any proclamation of a safe mine. Hell, Mouse, along with an ample list of dead, injured, and just plain missing. Tom and Stoop.

He got a strange queasy feeling when he thought of the two men. Searching through the mine might settle him down a bit. He'd return in the morning and take Mouse home. Besides, he'd sat at the boy's bedside for hours.

"I'll be back to get you in the morning," he said to Mouse. The boy kept his face scrunched and shifted back to watching Ambrose. Jack moved to the door. "Doc? Don't skimp on anything. I'll pay for everything."

Ambrose's serious countenance broke into a grin. "You? On a miner's salary?"

"Don't forget my promotion. I'm living ace-high nowadays."

"Go home and get some rest," Taryn said. "I'll stay, too."

"Mouse will most likely sleep through the night," Ambrose said, "if I can get this concoction down his throat. The reverend and I will keep watch. He's in good hands."

"Yeah, he is." Jack gestured to the direction of Victor's room. "Do you think he's up to a talk on my way out?"

"Planning your attack when the enemy is weak?" Taryn asked.

The doctor chuckled. "Sound thinking, but he's fading in and out quite a bit, and when he's lucid, he's in quite a nasty mood. I think between the two of you, he might be able to out-jackass you. Although you have become fairly astute in the area yourself."

"Ah, Doctor, the perfect parting comment," Jack said. "And I'm too damned tired to return an insult."

"I knew I'd wear you down one of these days."

"What happened to Mr. Creely anyway?" Taryn asked.

Ambrose shrugged. "Story is, a group of miners attacked him on his way home from the Boarding House. Luke saw a few of the men. He hasn't named names, but he swears they were miners."

"Why didn't Luke stop them?" Jack asked.

Ambrose cocked an eyebrow. "A good question."

Taryn shook his head. "Tempers are flaring in the town. You can feel it everywhere."

"Yep, and that's about the last thing I want to talk about. You're right, some sleep will do me good." Jack gave a quick wave. Mouse waved back.

He glanced inside when he passed by Creely's room. Edmund leaned over Victor's bed, speaking low. Whoever smacked the mine president upside the head did one a hell of a job. Pillows propped Victor upright. His eye was swollen shut with a bruise spreading over the right side of his head like merging blots of sickly colored ink. His pallor, tinged with the gray of middle age, usually reminded Jack of the steel running through the man. Now his coloring made Victor look old. Tired. Sick.

Jack looked at the savior of Tumbling Creek Ranch. His father's oldest and dearest friend. The man who took Jack under his wing, promoted him, reassured Jack he was like a son. He wondered if Victor would recover. An empty space sat inside him, where he should feel something. Anything.

Jack realized he plain old didn't care if Victor ever got out of his bed again.

The inside of Jasper Mountain was as stable as a structure made of lace doilies. The so-called maps had maybe one-third of the tunnels notated. Man-made passages tore through delicate catacombs and caverns created by Mother Nature. In true form, man simply blasted through whatever looked like it might make some profit.

Lifting his lantern high, Jack put his other hand up against rock. He stood at the end of a mining tunnel that should have been filled in years ago, but was left dead, cold, its mouth a gaping hole in the cavern soaring before him.

No wonder why wind sang here. The sounds racing through were damned eerie, like voices humming. He almost imagined he heard chanting. Weird.

A shame, actually, all these tunnels punching through caverns. He wondered how much beauty the quest of gold destroyed. The haphazard way the tunnels were blasted through and not filled back in appalled him.

He had more than enough proof for Victor, should he care to listen. Jack's own sense of responsibility fueled to a feverish pitch. This place was a disaster waiting to happen, and he wasn't about to let go of this issue.

He glanced down. The fall was only about six feet. Curiosity got the best of him, and he wanted to explore, take the time to see what else was around. It had been a while since he'd wandered simply for the thrill and pleasure of it. He blew out the flame in his lantern and hopped down. Dark didn't usually bother him, but this dark pulsed, alive with something. Was the creature he kept imagining waiting for him in the tunnels? Spirits darting through the air? Ghosts wandering?

Any or all of these diabolical happenings?

He relit his lantern, trying his best to ignore a shaking hand. God, he really could be an idiot. The small bit of light didn't do much to slow down his beating heart, but the beauty of the place drew him forward. Plus, he reminded himself, he wasn't a scared little girl, but a big, strong, brave man.

He laughed at himself and felt a whole lot better.

Ahead an underground lake glistened, still as death and black as Satan's heart. He kept a few steps back, wondering what, if anything, lived beneath. Probably nothing. A blurp broke the surface and he stumbled back, imagining an aquatic dragon rising out of the black mirror from hell.

"I'm in the wrong business. I should write spook books." His voice bounced off the walls and came back at him.

He shouldn't get himself lost. He possessed a pretty good sense of direction, even in these tunnels, and he wanted to wander a bit farther. He skirted around the small lake and ahead to another mouth to probably yet another cavern.

He wondered how Mouse was doing. It was time to go back. He'd found all the fortitude he needed and was about to become Victor's nonstop, nagging nightmare.

He hoped he didn't simply disappear, like Tom, Stoop, and anyone else who crossed Victor. Did he really believe that?

No.

Well, maybe.

All right. Yes.

There were no more questions about which side he stood on. The biggest question was how it might affect the life of the ranch. Buck and the boys. He'd do his best for them, but he knew Victor could be vindictive.

He laughed to himself, this time at such understated thought.

He turned to retrace his steps, but something caught his eye. A flicker at the other end of the cavern. In the dark, a flash, small, subtle, fast. But there. He saw another. Colors.

He froze. Listened.

Yep, chanting. But how?

And above the chanting, a voice, sweet and pure as sunlight, began to sing in a language he didn't understand. The words sounded ancient and mystic and from somewhere exotic.

He crept closer to a small entrance. Beyond the opening, more tiny colors sparkled against the floor, a swirling prism. He imagined tiny fairy critters, darting around.

What the hell was going on?

Carefully, he moved forward, the real world falling away with each step.

What was this place?

He checked behind, the black pool troubling him, but nothing rose from it to breathe fire or bite his head from his body.

The singing grew louder. Every step closer revealed more flashes of lights, the place within ablaze with jewels and colors. The chamber mouth was small, and he dropped to his knees to look inside.

Looking in was like being in the darkest night and gazing through a spyglass at another world miles away, full of light and wonder. In the center of it all, eyes closed, kneeling as if in prayer, Milena.

If he needed any proof she was not of this world, it unfolded before him. No question. This woman was magic. Spellbinding. Like a statue carved from the crystal rock, she glowed, translucent. Hair dark and shining like the mirrored pool. She seemed of this place, perfectly at home.

He couldn't move. Couldn't breathe.

She sang in a strange language. Romani. At least, he remembered her insisting that's what she was. Romani. She wove exotic intonations, not the simple melodies he was used to hearing, but sharps and flats twisting, combining to sound like a language all its own. A language of marvel and enchantment.

He crawled in until he cleared the mouth of the chamber. Colors danced around him. Everything was crusted with fluorite, pyrite, crystal quartz, and did he see chunks of gold? Stalactites, stalagmites, boulders, all glistened and glittered. Milena's lantern lit a dance of color. He'd never seen anything like it.

He didn't question what she was doing here. She belonged,

surrounded by a world she fit. She seemed sprung from the minerals around her, made from the same luminous material. He didn't know how long he sat, watching her. Time didn't exist in this place. He would have gladly stayed forever, but she stopped singing and opened her eyes.

Instantly, she jumped to her feet, her black eyes snapping with fear. She pulled a huge knife from her side, no longer the gentle, magical creature, but something that might have risen from the black hell-pool.

She raised the knife, murder in her eyes.

Chapter 21

Mouse swaggered into the bar, just like any miner. He'd show them. He wasn't a little kid. Even though he was puny and fell off the lift, he wasn't some baby to lie in a bed.

He walked into Sam's, unnoticed, and glanced around for Sally. Thankfully, she was nowhere in sight. He wanted to sit by his piano, feel the tones, and, most important, keep away from the preacher.

He had escaped, and he figured they wouldn't look for him here.

He wove through the forest of men and finally reached the piano, all the while watching for Jack. He thought Jack might be in the saloon, but he wasn't and maybe he went home to Ook. Disappointment raced through Mouse, but Jack's place was not his home and he was probably sick and tired of Mouse hanging around. That was okay. He could take care of himself anyway.

Mouse sat and leaned against the warm wood, just happy to be there. He wondered how long it would be before the doctor noticed he was missing. The preacher had fallen asleep in the chair and hadn't stirred when Mouse got dressed. He was easy to fool but the doctor wouldn't be, and he hoped the doctor wouldn't figure out where he'd gone.

Rolf, the giant miner, stood at the bar. He was so big; Mouse could see his shoulders and head above everyone else's. Luke, the curly-haired man who used to be a miner, was with Rolf, talking and buying him drinks. Mouse didn't like Luke. Although Luke grinned and laughed all the time, he was mean. He didn't fool Mouse. He had been the object of Luke's tormenting, and he, for one, was glad Luke didn't work at the mine anymore.

Luke shoved money to Sam and a shot to Rolf, who threw it back. Rolf looked mad. Mouse planned to stay out of the giant's way. Mostly Rolf left him alone and that was fine.

Mouse had tried to stay out of Luke's way at the mine. Luke always played tricks, like crashing something loud behind him for the other men to laugh at Mouse's deafness. Once he tripped Mouse and then one time set his lunch pail out of reach. That wasn't the worst ever. The worst ever was longer ago when he had asked Mouse and Da to shovel out after a blast although it was his job. Luke had told Da he'd pay him the money he owed from poker if Da did this for him, and they needed the money bad, so they agreed. That day, the explosion had happened and Da died and Mouse lost his hearing.

Nope, Mouse didn't like Luke at all.

Luke bought another drink for Rolf and talked a whole bunch. Rolf turned redder and his fist clenched around the glass. He threw back his whiskey. He seemed to get madder and sadder the more Luke talked. Mouse wondered why such a giant would be sad. Sure, plenty of things could make a giant mad and mean. But sad? Mouse thought he saw tears in Rolf's eyes. They didn't fall.

Rolf slammed down the glass and headed out the door, Luke right behind him.

Sally came down the stairs, a miner tagging behind. She

scanned the room, probably looking for new quarry. Mouse didn't want it to be him. He darted through the crowd, headed for the door and ran out, glad to be safe, out of Sally's reach. He saw Rolf and Luke walk down the main road, heading out of town. Mouse knew he should just go home, but he couldn't help it, he was curious. Where were they going?

The giant staggered a bit. Luke laughed and kept talking. They were up to something. It might be best if he kept these two men in his sights. Mouse was the smallest of the miners, and he could follow and they wouldn't see him. He might find something out and then wouldn't Jack be proud of him and think he should keep Mouse around?

He sure hoped so.

Music fell away and the tickle of bubbles slowed. The deep tones of the mountain died as silence consumed the cavern. Milena fell into place as a mere mortal. She opened her eyes.

The Hunter of Women kneeled at the mouth of the Heart, the candle in his hat an intrusive and accusing eye. How did he find her? She unsheathed her father's *choori*. She had survived the *MoortYak*, and she intended to survive the Hunter. Most important of all, she must protect this sacred place. She sprang to her feet.

"You will die."

Amazingly, Jack Buchanan sat back on his heels and tried not to laugh, the mirth in his eyes unmistakable. Shock caused her to hesitate, only for a moment.

She narrowed her eyes. "You find this situation worthy of laughter?"

"No, no, not at all." He put his hands up, palms to her. "I'm unarmed. I won't hurt you." He kept grinning, as though he found her most entertaining.

She did not flinch. "How did you track me here?"

"Actually, your music brought me. I was investigating the mine, trying to find some tunnels . . . oh, never mind. It doesn't matter. I heard you singing." His amusement wore off, and the look of wonderment he wore the night at the Boarding House softened his face. "Milena, it was beautiful. What kind of song were you singing? Your people are Romani, right? Was the song from them?"

She sensed no threat from him, yet he was the Hunter of Women and friend to Rolf and the King of the Jackals. She'd seen handsome faces masking evil and cruelty before.

Beth, too, was friend to this man, which did give her pause.

"I swear I heard other voices." He shrugged. "Probably the echoes." He looked around the Heart Chamber and lowered his hands. "This place is incredible, isn't it? I've never seen anything like it. How did you ever find this place?"

She refused to be lulled by his babble or distracted by his questions. "You hunt me. So here I am. I will not allow you to take me to the sheriff to hang."

"What?" Confusion replaced the look of awe. "Hunt you?" he asked. "I'm not hunting you. Why would I do such a thing?"

"You did before. With Rolf."

He hiked his shoulders. "Milena, he told me you were his wife. I thought you were lost and might be hurt. I only wanted to help."

"And you hunt me down to aid the sheriff," she challenged, raising the *choori* higher, to point right at his face.

"In case you haven't noticed, there's no love lost between me and Cain. The man is an idiot and a bully. Even if I could, I wouldn't help him with anything."

She wanted to believe him, and sensed no deception from him. However, her life was at risk, and he might have the powers of a sorcerer. Perhaps that was why she felt no threat from him. She refused to lower her guard, no matter how honest and friendly he might appear.

"What are you doing here anyway?" he asked. "I thought Isabella kept you ladies close at hand."

Not close enough. She'd killed a man. Although she did it while defending herself, guilt washed through her. Her anger faltered and she dropped her gaze to look at the floor. "I am no longer welcome at the Boarding House."

"Why not?"

She knew the shame of her crime showed on her face, but if she would be forced to kill this man, she owed him the truth. "I killed the King of the Jackals. Victor Creely."

Jack Buchanan looked at her in shock, his mouth dropping open. He closed it, seemingly bewildered. Then he started laughing. This time, he laughed so hard he fell back to a sitting position.

This was insanity. She was now forced to defend her life and perhaps to murder yet another man, and he was acting like a fool.

She watched. Without humor.

He wiped his eyes. "You? Milena, you're the one who brained Victor?"

"I do not expect you to understand." She met his eyes. "He attacked me."

He rose back up to his knees, all merriment gone. "Did he hurt you?"

"Why do you care? It is only a matter of time. I will be hung."

"For braining Victor?" Jack shrugged. "The official story is some miners attacked him. I'm serious, Milena, I'll kill him myself if he hurt you."

The *choori* shook. Was this a trick to lower her defenses?

"Besides," Jack continued, "there are about a hundred people who'd like to take credit for thrashing Victor right into the clinic. My guess is it serves him best to say it was miners." Jack smiled at her, a faint one, but a smile just the same. "Especially since it was really a woman who put him there. He'd never admit to any such thing."

Blood rushed from her head and she felt dizzy. "Serves him best? Admit? He still speaks?"

"It'll take a whole lot more than a thunk in the head to keep Victor Creely quiet."

She sank back down, her legs no longer having the strength to hold her. "The King, he is not dead?"

"Dead? Hell, no, whoops, pardon me," he said taking off his hat. "Where are my manners? I forgot all about this." He set the hat beside him, the flame of its candle flickering. "Milena, you didn't kill anyone. Victor was alive and raising a ruckus when I last saw him at the clinic."

She lowered the *choori*, not sure why she held it up She pondered Jack's honesty and sincerity. Were they real? Was he genuine? Was this a man to trust? She did not forget she'd seen men smile and speak pretty words one day and murder her family the next.

She opened to him and sensed no false flattery, no lies of charm covering horror of the soul. This man's heart stood behind the words he spoke. She froze with uncertainty, not knowing what to do, to think. Should she trust what she felt or her life's experiences?

"Milena, are you all right?"

"I thought . . . I thought I killed a man. You tell me I have not. I thought you hunted me to aid Rolf." She looked at Jack's face, gentle with understanding. "You did not. How could I be this wrong? I am supposed to understand. To see." She shook her head. "I see nothing."

"Fear can get in the way of anything. I don't profess to understand any of your mystic stuff. I imagine fear can block that, too. Milena, considering everything you've been through since you arrived in Jasper, it's amazing you even realize what day it is."

"It is day?"

Jack smiled. "Well, probably night."

"I will not hang for the murder of the King of the Jackals," she said, just to put her relief into words.

"He'll never admit a little woman like you put a dent in that hard head of his. I think you're safe on that count."

She relaxed, soothed by the warmth of his easy humor. She wanted to move closer, but instead shifted back, not ready to forge an open connection. Not yet.

He watched her intently, his face flushing red from the neck up.

"Your face burns, Jack Buchanan."

"It does that when I get embarrassed." He spoke just above a whisper. "And I have to tell you, no one flusters me the way you do." He cleared his throat. "Milena, may I change the subject for a moment?"

She nodded, relieved to talk of anything other than sheriffs and jackals. She sensed something was coming he found difficult to discuss. He struggled with the words. She prepared for anything, and found herself hoping, for what, she wasn't sure. But still, hope filled her, wide and warm and wanting.

"With all your background in hocus-pocus, I need to ask you something."

She wasn't sure what she wanted, but this wasn't it. She hid her disappointment. "Hocus-pocus? What is this?"

"Uh, magic."

"Oh."

"Yesterday, in the mine, the platform slipped and one of my men fell down the main shaft."

"I am sorry."

"Well, the good news is Doc Kline thinks Mouse will make a full recovery. What I want to ask you about is what I saw." He shook his head. "Mouse was in a tunnel, and I was about to pass him up. I had a hard time seeing real good. I saw, I saw—"

"Jo," she finished for him.

He nodded. "I keep thinking that Victor told you about her, that's how you know I have a twin sister and how she died."

"You doubt yourself, your abilities to see into the Otherworld. This is what keeps you from her. She needs you, Jack Buchanan. She must settle with you before she moves on."

Red drained out of his face as he paled. "You really saw her?" he asked. "In the garden?"

"Yes."

"Is she here?"

Milena shook her head. "This place is sacred. A sanctuary. Not a place for restless spirits. In Jasper, she is almost always by your side."

"Oh, God."

"You spoke of fear as a barrier. This is true for you, too. There is no reason to be afraid, especially not of your Jo."

"I'm not really, but I don't think I believe any of this."

"Do not think. Feel." She smiled faintly. "Why is it men deny fear as well as the unknown? It is no shame to be afraid or see the unfamiliar. You have every reason to believe in the Otherworld. You have heard, you have seen, yet you look away. The choice is yours, Jack Buchanan. It always is. It always was."

Mouse followed Rolf and Luke to the grand mansion below the town. Mouse used to hear tell of it, when he was able to hear. The Boarding House, full of fancy ladies. Da had told him never, ever to go near the place, although he couldn't figure out why. It was such a nice house.

Luke clasped Rolf on the shoulder and handed him a bottle. Had he brought more whiskey from the saloon? Mouse hoped not, because Rolf had drunk enough. Luke turned around and headed back up to town. Mouse was relieved he was hiding in the bushes when Luke passed.

Rolf hunkered down behind some trees near the house. It was raining. Why didn't the big man go in? It must be too late, except the house was all lit up. There was a couple on the porch. Rolf stayed crouched and Mouse did, too.

The couple went inside. The rain let up. This was good, because he was getting cold.

Rolf rose to his feet and hunched over, creeping to a side window. He raised his bottle. Then Mouse saw the wick. Rolf struck a match and lit it.

This was not good.

Rolf threw the lit bottle through the window and jogged back to his place in the trees and hid.

Inside, light grew as the fire did, too.

Chapter 22

Jack didn't want to walk away and leave her inside the mountain by herself, but Milena insisted. She'd wanted him to leave. She felt safe in her chamber, and once she was convinced he wouldn't drag her back to town to hang, she seemed completely content to stay there.

Working his way back down the mountain was peaceful until the chaotic jumble of Jasper reached him. Wagons creaked, horses clopped, shouted obscenities sailed through the air, hollers of drunks echoed up the mountain. The stamping mill pounded a steady beat under the din. So much noise, and constant.

Compared to Jasper, inside the mountain was heaven. Bat guano and all.

What a switch, thinking of the inside of the mountain with fondness. The mines were hell; he'd thought so since the first time he dropped down the shaft. Now he realized man made them that way. He figured the mountain didn't like miners tunneling through it any more than the men who did Victor Creely's dirty work.

At the thought of the mine president, Jack increased his stride, wanting to get down to the clinic. With every step, anger built. Never mind about all the dead and missing miners thanks to Victor's love of money over everything else. He'd attacked Milena. Jack had a pretty good idea of what Victor wanted from her. He felt pure disgust for a man who thought he had the right to take anything from any woman he desired.

He wondered if he'd be able to control himself or if he'd burst into the clinic and finish the job Milena began. Victor would be an easy target. Probably the only time in his life the mine president would be in such a position.

Nope, Mouse would see it all. What kind of example would he be?

The drum of the stamping mill pounded reality right back into his head. He'd have to show up for work in the morning. If Victor had been on his feet, it would all be over for him, he'd missed so much work.

He saw his house ahead and decided, since it was late, he'd go home instead of the clinic. Mouse was most likely asleep, along with Taryn and Ambrose. The best plan was to catch a couple hours of sleep and go down to the clinic before his shift. He took in a deep breath of cold night air, wondering how he'd become a caretaker to so many. "A dog, a deaf kid, and a bunch of dirty miners. No wonder I'm feeling so damned needed."

From the other side of the door, Duke barked out his welcome. Jack *thunked* up onto his porch, relieved to be home, if only for a few hours.

Except he wished he held Milena's hand, wished he was bringing her home. Why the woman stirred so much in him, he didn't know.

Well, sure he did. With all her claims to knowledge of the future, her discussions with the dead, her heavy silences, those dark eyes looking right into a man's soul and turning it inside out. And she was so damned beautiful. All in all, a pretty terrifying combination.

He reached out to open his door when he heard someone running, behind him. He turned. As though he'd wished her into existence, she emerged from the dark. Milena stopped, out of breath. Her hair curled and tangled, wilder than her eyes, which were sharp with distress.

"Milena?"

She tried to speak, and Jack came to her side. She grabbed onto him.

"Milena?" he asked again. A chill brushed over him.

"Something," she managed. She doubled over and gasped. "Danger," she whispered. "Death."

"Milena, calm down. I'm not the only one who's had a rough couple of days. You've been through a lot. You must be imagining things."

She shook her head vehemently. "No. No. Something—" she cried out, pointing past his shoulder. "No!"

Jack followed her gaze, down the mountain, past the town. A small flicker. Flames.

"What the—" Jack asked.

Fire bells screamed up Jasper Mountain.

Smoke billowed up the road. The smell of burning wood and brush flung Jack back into the past. Fire. Hell.

He shook his head and concentrated on the Boarding House. "This ain't the ranch," he murmured and urged Willow to run faster. Red flickered through the night, and air thickened with smoke stung his nostrils.

He knew the smell. The smell of death.

Jack thundered past the fire department, two men on horses

pulling the water wagon, and two more men jogging next to the contraption. He passed several others on the road who were running down to help. Or to watch.

Jack dismounted and threw his reins to one of the bystanders.

Flames completely engulfed the Boarding House. The main windows on either side of the door blazed with fire and smoke. The door flapped on one hinge, the doorway a large, open howl of surprise, the house astounded it was burning.

"Is everybody out?" Jack yelled. People ran, and screams pierced through smoke. A window popped, showering hot glass out several feet.

Lead in the stained-glass transom melted, dropping beveled glass on the porch. The glass shattered with a cry of artistry dying, a delicate sound glimmering through the roar of destruction.

No more beautiful rainbows skimming over a marble floor.

Jack ran around the perimeter of the house, trying to see if there was any easy way to get inside, but it was too late for heroics. Fire engulfed the entire structure. Sweat ran down his neck and back. He circled to the front, desperately searching for a way to help while the firemen arrived and began pumping water, fighting the roaring inferno with a pathetic stream of spit.

Nearby Suzanne clutched a tree, holding it to keep upright, her face white with shock. A stunned and frightened girl replaced the usually perfect and poised woman.

"Suzanne! Suzanne!" Jack called out. She didn't hear him. He ran to her and grabbed her arms, gently shaking her. "Suzanne! Is everyone out?"

"What?" Her gaze circled.

"Suzanne! Look at me. Look at me."

"Jack?"

"Where is Isabella?"

She stood and gaped, mouth working. Nothing came out.

"Listen to me," he commanded. "I need you to gather up the ladies. Take a head count. Tell me if anyone is missing." He shook her again, trying not to handle her too roughly.

Her eyes finally focused on him. "Jack?"

"Can you do that? Gather up the ladies and take a head count?"

She nodded. He steadied her, and she nodded again.

A few men shoveled around the house, intent on digging a trench to contain the fire. Jack thought of the trenches dug around the ranch buildings. They hadn't done a thing to help. The fire had hopped over them.

As if to agree with Jack, a demon of flames leapt from the roof of the house and landed on a tree, igniting the branches.

"Andy!" Jack shouted to the nearest fireman, who immediately aimed his hose at the burning tree. The fire extinguished and Jack thanked the good Lord it had rained a few hours before. The damp brush might keep an inferno from racing up the mountain and destroying the town.

Ambrose arrived on the scene, sweating and out of breath.

"Ambrose," Jack said, running to him. "You better set up a ways back. This smoke is getting fierce."

"Injuries?"

"I'm not sure."

Ambrose turned, but Jack grabbed his arm. "Mouse?" Jack asked. Guilt shot through the doctor's expression and just when Jack thought he couldn't feel any more panic, he did. "Doc?"

"Jack!" Suzanne ran up to him. "Isabella! Isabella must be in there! No one has seen her. Jack, she's not here!"

Jack looked from the doctor to the house and realized he was a religious man, after all.

"Jesus, God, have mercy," he whispered.

"Hellfire came all the way up the mountain to take its own!" a woman shrieked and tied her bonnet tighter around her sharp face. The flames reflected in her unforgiving eyes. She looked at Milena smugly. "I hope all them whores are inside!"

Since the woman spoke, Milena knew she wasn't a restless spirit of Jasper. Many apparitions mixed about with the scores of people in shock, making it difficult to tell the dead from the living.

Milena backed away, aware she shouldn't be here. Where else could she be? The proprietress and her ladies were in trouble. Terrible trouble.

Ambrose Kline knelt by a grove of trees, his form orange and flickering in the fire's light. He'd spread blankets and treated one of the firemen whose arm blistered raw and shiny. Ladies sat or lay around him, some coughing. Some moaning. Someone was crying.

Milena went to Ambrose and dropped to her knees beside him. "I am here," she said.

"I see," he answered, his voice deep and controlled. "Here, can you do this?" the doctor asked, applying salve to the wound.

"Yes. And bandage?"

"Exactly. I knew you'd make a fine nurse."

"Yes, Doctor."

Ambrose moved on to the next person, and Milena began her treatment, appreciative of the trust the doctor had in her.

A man emerged from the curtain of smoke, carrying a limp figure. He gently laid her down on the blanket.

"Cassy," Ambrose said, and immediately went to her. The girl was pale and unconscious. "Cassy!" the doctor repeated.

Suddenly a scream ripped the air. No, not a scream. A wail.

Of sorrow unimagined. Milena recognized the voice. Isabella ran to the burning house like a mad woman, small bits of ash snowing around her. Everyone watched in stunned silence, the roar of fire and rush of water a backdrop to destruction.

"Crazy whore," the fireman beside Milena muttered. Then Jack Buchanan ran from the other side of the house.

Isabella almost reached the porch when Jack launched into the air and tackled her. They rolled in the dirt, and somehow she ended up on top of him, her fists thundering down on his chest. He held tight and rolled again so she was under him.

The house seemed to take in a deep breath. Wood creaked and crackled, and with a sigh, it gave up and collapsed to the ground. Smoke billowed out, covering everything and everyone. Milena and the firemen threw themselves to the ground. Ambrose covered the inert form of Cassandra. Fire rained everywhere. Screams ripped through the night as a dingy cloud ate up the ground and consumed them all.

Pieces of hot pelted down on him. The woman beneath him didn't move.

"Jo," he said. "Jo, please, hold on. I'll get us out of this." He couldn't let anything happen to her. He just couldn't. "Keep your face close to the ground," Jack shouted into her ear. "I'll keep you safe. I promise."

Wait.

The house had collapsed. Almost a year ago. With Jo inside. Yet there was a woman beneath him. He held her tighter. "Jo?"

He fought to cling to logic. That's right. He was in Jasper.

This was the Boarding House. The woman underneath him was Isabella. Not Jo. He'd lost his sister forever.

"Keep your head, Buchanan," he muttered to himself. He dragged in air, but heat seared his throat and it constricted in defense. Beneath him, Isabella's chest heaved. She'd stopped struggling to get away. He wrapped his forearms around her head, a last feeble effort to protect her.

Jack thought he was on fire, but smoke billowed thick, and he didn't dare roll off her. The house pelted them with shards. He gasped in stinging thickness, and his eyes felt like a thousand bees swarmed in them. Tears streamed down his cheeks.

It looked like hell had finally caught up with him. At least he'd die protecting someone.

He was lying on sand, the sun warm on his back.

Home. The ranch.

He was finally home.

"Jack!" Jo called from far away. A dinner bell clanged across the landscape. "Jack!" she called again, her voice sweet, beckoning him to come. Come home.

The sun grew bright, tears kept streaming down his face. He closed his eyes against beautiful gold light. Thank God, he was home. The ground beneath him moved, breathing. Alive. He stretched himself over it, sinking into it, becoming part of it.

Suddenly, a waterfall splashed over him. Cold, drenching, reviving.

Then someone tried to drag him.

He didn't want to leave. He was home, damn it, finally, home. Digging his arms into the earth, he held on. He refused to leave.

"Help me, I got two here!"

Jack held tightly to the ground. The ranch melted around him and washed away in a downpour. His soul screamed out with loss and heartbreak as he jolted back to Jasper.

He sobbed, his arms wrapped around Isabella. More hands, pulling both of them out of the smothering dark.

He thought he might go blind. Tears streaming down his face, Jack tried to look up through them to see his savior. At first, a figure clothed in light towered over him. His vision cleared enough to see Cain, sneering down at him. A piece of cloth dropped into his lap.

"Here's a hankie for your little-girl tears."

Jack tried to answer, but coughed up mud. Bands of steel wrapped around his chest, and they slowly shrank, squeezing the life right out of him. Coughing racked his body, and came from deep down, making him retch. He collapsed at Cain's feet.

This was hell. Had to be.

"Isabella—" he managed to get out before another cough cut him off. Tears streaming, he gagged and coughed, a downright mess. He gave in, letting his body collapse.

They weren't tears. They simply weren't.

Isabella hugged her knees to her chest. Her eyes burned. Because of all the smoke. Not tears. Never tears.

The crackling fire groaned, and the heap that used to be her beautiful house sighed and sank even farther into the earth. Another blanket of smoke spewed into the night. Her world. Her entire world, the one she'd built for herself and her ladies. Their only safe place. Gone.

She heard him. God. Having his last laugh.

Divine retribution, some might say. Well, God damn every one of the sanctimonious faces surrounding her, coming closer and closer like predators closing in on weakened prey. She'd show them. She was far from finished.

Isabella searched for the figure of the pastor. Surely he would come to help her. She looked and found nothing around her except those hateful, horrid faces drifting in the acrid fog. Fine. She closed her eyes. Her house. Her world. Her paintings. All gone.

No matter.

"Diana," she said, recalling the detail of her latest work in progress, her heart aching from the loss. "Forest in the Spring." While painting that one, she discovered how to add detail to the leaves of the trees, rendering them much more lush, full of life. A world of exquisite colors and sensual textures. Her world. "Ariadne," she whispered to herself. One of her favorites. A strong and beautiful woman on the cusp of destruction, a woman denying her fate with the fury of passion in her eyes.

"Proprietress?" The Gypsy kneeled down beside her. Isabella's eyes snapped open and she drew back. The movement caused her to cough without control. So unbecoming, the cough. Not to mention the dirt. The lace of her gown was torn. She was filthy.

"You're supposed to see the future." She managed enough words to accuse. "Why didn't you warn me of this? Or were you in too much a hurry to desert me?"

Milena shook her head. Her eyes must be stinging from smoke too. She looked to be on the verge of tears. And they were filled with—what? Pity?

How dare she? Isabella preferred a thousand smug faces to one look of pity. She drew her hand back and slapped the Gypsy across the face. Milena fell back, watching Isabella with those black eyes pretending to see all. She sat back up, and after such a slap, no anger on her face, not even pity. Compassion.

Something inside Isabella weakened, cracked. She felt it give way. Something she'd guarded and kept safe for so very long.

"Proprietress?"

Isabella focused on the Gypsy's face. Only kindness. Concern. The crack within her widened and broke. Isabella fell into Milena's waiting arms. She sobbed. No, that was wrong. She wasn't crying. Her eyes were simply stinging from the smoke. No tears. Never tears.

Broken or not, she was still Isabella St. Claire.

Chapter 23

Unbelievably, Jack forgot how badly burn wounds hurt. Until now. Pain crackled hot and cold over his skin. His arms and back screamed, not with memory, but fresh agony. Waves of hurt prickled over his arms and back, keeping him sharply awake.

"I don't need a bed," he insisted, although he certainly belonged in one. As one of the more severely injured, the doctor had immediately ordered Jack to one of the few beds in the clinic. For Jack, lying on the damned thing felt like surrender. He sat on the edge, fighting the temptation to lie down and sleep.

With his arms crossed, Mouse watched, leaning against the wall. Why the kid was dressed and tooting around, he didn't know. But really, seeing him up and about bolstered Jack's spirits. Nothing kept that kid down.

Moans and crying permeated the clinic, an undercurrent reminding him of the horrors of the night. At least the entire town didn't burn to the ground, only the Boarding House. Jack looked across the room, makeshift beds and floor filled with former fancy ladies—now dirty, disheveled girls with fear and misery etched on their faces. Also present and under the doctor's care were the officers of the mine and so-called gentlemen, at least the ones overcome with smoke and unable to run and hide. The main room of the clinic overflowed. People sat, stood, milled about anywhere and everywhere Ambrose managed to fit them.

Cassandra was the only silent patient, unconscious and on the bed next to Jack's. Her face waned paler than usual. No matter where Ambrose worked, he checked on her every few minutes, not letting her out of his sight or, obviously, his mind.

Jack wanted to rise to his feet, free up a bed. If he could only stop shaking.

Milena sat beside him, bottle and glass in hand. "The doctor insists you take this."

"I don't need it."

Mouse grimaced and shook his head.

"See," Jack said. "He agrees."

"He is only pleased to see a kindred spirit, a child who will not do what he is told."

"What I need is a shot of whiskey."

"What do you think this is?" Milena asked. He took the shot and gulped it down, sour curling his gullet.

"If that's whiskey, it's the worst I've ever tasted."

"Lie down. You need rest."

"No, what I need is to get home. Next I have a mine president to see."

Milena shook her head. "You must rest or your body will stop for you. Even I see your exhaustion," she said in her soft voice. Her fingertips brushed his leg, one of the few places that didn't hurt. Although featherlight, her touch shot through him. "At least stay until you stop shaking."

"I don't think that will be any time soon," he admitted. His shakes were growing progressively worse. He trembled like a hundred-year-old man.

Jasper took everything from him and everybody else. He surveyed the myriad of people and wondered who else might be here. He thought of people beyond his seeing, not sure if he believed Milena and her visions of the dead. But damn, she'd seen Jo.

"Milena, I have to ask . . ."

"She is with us, yes."

He turned from her sympathy and looked around. Ladies crying, men injured while helping, gentlemen caught off guard. The doctor and Taryn moved among them, giving whatever aid they could. No shadows lurked in any corners, no matter how hard Jack tried to see.

"Really? You see her?"

"She stands beside Mouse." Milena's voice sounded hesitant, like she wanted to hide something.

"What is it?"

She shook her head and would not look up at him.

"Someone else is here, aren't they?"

Her eyes returned to him, boring deeply. "There is another who is intent upon keeping track of you."

Although Jack thought such a thing impossible, he shook harder and gulped air to steady himself. His throat dried up. He swallowed and managed to croak out a question.

"Who?"

"I have never seen him before."

Jack trembled to his core. "Describe him."

"Kind eyes. Sad. They are very large. Brown, like his hair, which he wears long, to his collar. It curls."

Might be anybody, Jack thought.

Milena continued. "He wears the hat with the candle, like the one you wore when we met in the chamber."

Jack's blood ran cold. A miner. Tom?

"His face is long, sad." She stopped, smiled wistfully, and took Jack's hand. "With his long face and curling hair, he reminds me of a sheep." Her voice deepened into melancholy. "A gentle, kind sheep. One who follows and is happy to do so."

The temperature in the room dropped a few degrees. "Where is he? I mean, is he on the bed? Across the room?"

"Standing to the other side of Mouse."

Jack studied the space on the wall. Nothing. Not even a hint of any sort of image or movement. Logic denied her words, yet how could he not believe her? She described Tom as if he stood right in front of them.

His entire existence shifted. Changed. Life beyond death, the future, seen. Magic. The impossible. All real. All truth.

His voice came out a reverent whisper. "Tom, I'm sorry. I've let you down. I promise I'll figure all this out."

Mouse followed Jack's gaze and looked at the space next to him. He squinted.

Jack turned back to Milena and spoke softly. "Can they speak? These ghosts?"

"No. This is not the way those in the spirit realm communicate. And not all spirits see us. Some do. This man, Tom, he watches you as though he wants you to understand something."

"Yeah. I'm the one who let him down." Jack's teeth started clacking. "Oh, Christ, I'm chattering."

Milena wrapped her arms around him and he leaned into her, finally giving in. He closed his eyes and felt her brush his hair with her lips.

"Now I might be able to stop shaking."

He didn't know if he had spoken aloud, or if he held the thought of her deeply in his heart.

Or both.

Isabella abhorred this lack of privacy, but she really didn't have much choice. At least the doctor allowed her and the ladies into his clinic. Took them in without hesitation. Most people refused to have anything to do with them, not even the "gentlemen" she'd known for years. She'd seen such disdain in the people standing around, watching her home burn to the ground, the gleam in their eyes proclaiming Isabella St. Claire got what she deserved.

Not the doctor. He'd jumped in, working diligently, and brought them all to his clinic. When she rebuilt, she'd have to give him more attention. Perhaps even personally.

Ah, but she must be in a weakened state to entertain such a thought.

Isabella had a fairly good vantage point. She could see almost everyone in the large, depressing room. The good Reverend McShane also clucked about, tending to her wayward ladies. He would receive nothing but trouble from his pious and pathetic parishioners, yet it didn't stop him. He ministered to everyone, no matter his or her station. She'd love to repay him for his kindness. As if he sensed her longing, he glanced up at her, his gorgeously soulful eyes questioning.

Oh, and she had an answer. One he'd never believe.

Isabella decided to busy herself and encourage her continued welcome at the clinic for herself and for her ladies. Mindful not to step on anyone, she moved to stand behind the doctor.

"Ambrose?" she asked softly. "Is there anything I can help with? Anything I can do?"

The doctor straightened from his table of concoctions and

looked at her, seeming not to see her, then his eyes focused. "Oh, Isabella. Thank you, no. Just rest, my dear."

"I believe you need some of your own medicine, Doctor. She touched his arm, lowered her head, and lifted her eyes, sorrowfully, she hoped. "I am worried about Cassandra. Do you think . . .?"

His expression hardened and he shook his head. "Reverend McShane and I are doing all we can. If you will excuse me, I have injured to attend." He gestured to the room of sick and moaning. Suzanne cried out as if proving the doctor correct. Ambrose brushed past Isabella to rush to her aid. Silly girl. She didn't have a scratch on her.

Isabella thought about sitting for a bit with Cassandra. She changed her mind the moment the thought surfaced. Cassandra's already pale face blanched whiter than the sheets, not a good commentary on the girl's complexion or the doctor's laundering abilities.

Across the room, Milena helped Jack to the floor when he gave up his bed to Claire. The chivalrous Jack surrendered it the first chance he got. The man was so predictable.

Isabella closed her eyes, and let the thoughts in, the ones making her sick to her soul. Not that she had one. What she did have were suspicions. The fire. The timing troubled her. She knew from experience anything coincidental usually was not. The destruction of her Boarding House might have come from anyone, but somehow she didn't think so. If Victor was involved, and she suspected he was, Jasper was now a different world for her. Well, she'd rise to any task.

It was time she see if the Gypsy was worth her weight in crystal balls. Isabella headed for Milena. The Gypsy made her way across the room and leaned over the bed of Mr. Browsly, whose hair and eyebrows had been singed off. A homely man, his missing eyebrows actually improved his appearance. Milena administered salve to the man's face. A natural healer. What a shame she hadn't been born a man. She would have made a wonderful doctor.

Finally, Milena finished and stood.

"Milena, do you have a moment to join me on the porch for some air?"

"Yes, Proprietress."

"Really, you don't have to call me that anymore. I have nothing left to proprietor over."

Glad to be away from the fluttering moans of ladies, Isabella felt herself relax once she crossed the threshold of the clinic. A cough exploded from her. She pulled out her lace hankie, as bedraggled as everything else, and she wondered if she'd ever get all the smoke out of her lungs.

Isabella continued, "I apologize for striking you. Most uncalled for and uncivilized."

"You were upset."

"Certainly I know you aren't responsible for the future."

Interesting, the slight flash of guilt across Milena's features. "I did know something was coming," the Gypsy said, almost apologizing. "I just did not see what. Or from where."

"How terribly frustrating for you." Isabella watched her sarcasm hit the mark. Milena's guilt intensified. "At least you and Beth were not in residence, didn't have to go through this."

"Beth was not there?" Milena asked in complete surprise.

"Luke disclosed a most distressing subterfuge. Beth took a filthy, foulmouthed miner as a lover. I couldn't very well have such a liaison going on beneath my nose. I sent her packing. But Victor couldn't possibly know. You, my dear, smacked him right out of action, didn't you?"

"He attacked me."

"He didn't realize you were gone, either."

Milena's expression turned thoughtful, widened into shock, and finally, disgust tinged with some disbelief. "Proprietress, do you believe he set the fire for revenge? On me, on Beth?"

"I have my suspicions. Milena, can you really see things? Can you see if he had anything to do with this?"

Milena shook her head. "He is evil, Proprietress."

"Yes, well, you haven't told me anything I don't already know. I suppose I'm fortunate," Isabella continued. "Victor called me to his bedside just as this happened. I would have tried to save my paintings. Very well might have been my undoing."

Milena raised her eyebrows. "Victor Creely called you away before the fire?"

"Yes. Actually, my dear, it strikes me as very unusual. He rarely summons me out of the Boarding House. I suppose I have him to thank for my life, what's left of it." She looked at Milena intently. "Are you sure you can't see anything? Do you need to look in your crystal ball or something?"

Again, Isabella's acerbic wit was not lost. Milena had the grace to look embarrassed.

"Here is what I really wonder. Luke, my strong-arm man. He's been with me for some time. The only way Victor would find out about Beth and her miner is if Luke told him." She watched Milena closely. The Gypsy didn't know a thing. No matter. She would figure out who was responsible. Who destroyed her world. And make him sorry forever.

"Heavens, I do hate men. They are so overt in their dealings, don't you think? Their callous ways must come from their sex dangling in their pants. Must be awful for them."

Isabella left Milena immersed in propriety's shock. Really, these women crumpled too easily. She thought she'd taught them better.

Something was terribly wrong.

Jack sensed it, even in his sleep. He opened his eyes to morning light. He lay on his side, his back burning. Jesus, he was sick and tired of pain. He tried to move, but his joints had stiffened almost to beyond moving. Served him right for sleeping on the ground, but he wasn't about to sleep on a bed with a woman on the floor, so he'd traded last night with Claire. He creaked up to a sitting position and saw Claire, sleeping soundly on the bed to one side of him. He turned to the other bed, Cassandra's.

Empty.

Panic pushed him to his feet. Despite light pouring in the windows, most everyone in the room still slept. Taryn sat propped against the wall, dozing, and Milena curled around Mouse. His heartstrings pulled to see them together, but worry kept him focused.

No doctor. No Cassandra.

Carefully, Jack stepped over inert forms, making his way to the doctor's private room. Victor being long gone, the doctor must have moved Cassandra there for her comfort and privacy. As Jack rounded the corner he first saw the long table with bottles, concoctions of who-knew-what, sparkling with different colors and sending up an antiseptic and pungent scent.

Next, the bed came into his view.

A sheet completely covered a body on the bed. The doctor leaned his elbows on the mattress, his head buried in his hands.

"Oh, God, no," Jack whispered. Ambrose didn't move. Jack pulled a chair up next to him. The doctor didn't even look up.

Jack remembered the girl under the sheet, Cassandra. Quiet,

unassuming, so young for the life of the Boarding House. Weren't they mostly very young? Cassy was shy, too. She didn't flirt or demand attention. A gentle girl living a lonely life the best way she knew how.

"Doc?" Jack asked softly, mindful he was in the presence of the dearly departed. Dear, indeed. "Ambrose? Can I help?"

Ambrose raised his head. Sorrow haunted his eyes. "I loved her."

"I'm sure she knew," Jack answered.

Ambrose shook his head, staring at the far wall. "No. She didn't. I never told her." His voice sharpened with shame. "One mustn't admit to loving a whore."

"Ambrose—"

"I knew I loved her. I'd never admit it, not to her, not to me. Let me tell you what else I knew. Cassy loved me." His voice broke. "She was brave enough to tell me. Brave enough and honest enough." He laughed, a sound so bitter it curled through Jack's heart. "Me? I'm a coward. The worst kind."

Jack had no answer, no words of comfort. There were none for this.

"There's no excuse. Especially for me." The doctor put his head back in his hands, muffling his words. "Go away. Please. Just go away."

Jack knew how it felt, losing someone you love and the heaviness of regret. He thought of the mysterious, quirky woman sleeping in the other room, taking care of others, holding a little deaf boy through the night.

Did he need to admit something, to himself at least?

He sat beside Ambrose, trying to feel something and name it. The only thing in him was an empty place in his chest. He decided not to break into the doctor's mourning, not to tell him he'd survive, he'd go on, that time would help. Really, there was nothing to do. No way around such pain, except to hit it straight on and push through it.

Taryn appeared in the doorway. At the sound of rustling, Ambrose looked up. "Reverend," he said, and stood, walking to look out the window as if he searched for answers somewhere in the landscape of Jasper. Jack knew there were none.

"You did everything possible for her," Taryn said.

"Did I?" The doctor whirled to face them. His hip bumped the table, and bottles clinked in a chorus. "I'm not sure of any such thing, Reverend."

"She's in a good place, Ambrose," Jack managed to say.

Anger sparked, extinguishing the dull misery in the doctor's eyes. "Surely she's in hell. Ask the minister. Cassy was a whore."

"She was a gentle soul who did no harm," Taryn answered back without pause. "God is forgiving. She's in a good place, Ambrose. I have no doubt."

"And I have nothing but doubts!" Ambrose clenched his fist and pounded the table. Bottles knocked over and one fell to the floor and shattered. "I'm not even sure there is a God. Not after this."

"There is. Especially when you need him." Taryn moved close to the doctor and laid a hand on his shoulder. Jack stayed back. The minister should handle this, and Taryn, up to the task, continued. "I'm also sure of your skill and dedication and Cassy's kind heart. She didn't suffer, Ambrose. That's what matters."

"She never woke up." He put both hands on the table and leaned over it, his middle caving like someone punched him.

"Sometimes we don't know why things happen. God has a divine plan, and Cassy is part of it. She's with him and, finally, has peace."

"And the Boarding House fire? Someone started it. That's what they're saying. Someone threw a flaming bottle through a downstairs window. People heard it. Saw it. Was that part of God's plan?"

"Ambrose—"

"And what kind of God stands by and watches this happen? Watches a young girl die?"

"I won't deny the evil in this world, Ambrose. In our line of work, you and I both face mankind's dark side every day, but there is good, too, great good. Cassy was human; she had her failings, her frailties. We all do." He stopped for a second, gathering his thoughts. "Ambrose, do you remember your trip on the stagecoach?"

"What does that have to do with anything?"

"Humor me."

"Of course I remember."

"And the stations, each with its own laws? Different flavors, completely different ways of living?"

Ambrose nodded.

"This life is like one of those stops at a coach station. It has its own rules and laws and ways. We feel isolated and are afraid this is all there is, but this life isn't the end. There is so much more beyond. If one is brave enough to go."

Ambrose blinked.

"Cassy was brave enough to board the coach, move forward," Taryn said. "Her journey is just beginning, Doctor. Not ending. Not at all."

The doctor turned away. Taryn placed a hand on his back.

Damn the minister. Jack found himself comforted by his words. Almost back to believing in something again. Thanks to the woman in the other room, he knew something existed beyond this world, things he didn't see or sense. Just when he'd thought this miserable life was not worth living, Milena came. With her came complications he never asked for, but somehow, knew he couldn't live without. He needed her. Plain and simple.

Jack thought of Jo, Tom, Stoop. The dead walked through Jasper, searching, but Jack hoped God existed, too, and would gather the ghosts at some point, end their helpless wandering.

He prayed the master of the stagecoach stop believed in forgiving.

Chapter 24

Jack limped, but by God, he was on his feet. Walking hurt like hell, but it was a damned sight better than lying around feeling sorry for himself. And he'd come straight to the lion's den. Of course Victor made him wait. Jack cleared his throat and Edmund once again looked up from his desk, along with the entire room of pinched-nosed officers.

Jack was in a terribly uncharitable mood. Funny how a raging fire, death, and destruction did that to a man.

"Are you sure I can't get you anything, Jack? Do you need to sit?" Edmund asked.

"No, thanks. Victor knows I'm here?"

Turtle sniffed. "He has quite important matters to attend to since he's been absent for some days."

"You docking him?" Beyond giving a damn what any of the officers or Victor thought of him, Jack didn't care how bad the question sounded. He knew the mine president left him waiting on purpose.

"No, however I have notated it's afternoon and you haven't clocked in yet." He returned to his ledger.

Cretin. Yep, bad mood for sure.

A bell tinkled from behind the closed door of Victor's office.

"You've got to be kidding," Jack grumbled.

Edmund jumped to his feet. "One moment, Jack." He slipped into the office and closed the door behind him. A few seconds later, he came out. "Victor will see you."

Jack summoned up all his courage, his anger, and his frustration, and entered into the upper-crust world of Victor Creely.

The mine president sat behind his expansive mahogany desk, nothing about him friendly or welcoming. The bruising on his face had changed to a sickly yellow color, and his skin looked waxy. His eyes burned.

"Jack."

He came farther in, his footsteps muffled by plush carpet. "Victor. How are you?"

"Never better. You?"

"I kinda hurt some. Quite a fire down at the Boarding House."

"I've heard all the accounts and actually, I'm very busy." Victor returned his attention to the ledger before him.

"Everyone's trying to figure out who's responsible. They say someone tossed a torch through the window. Who would want to burn the place down?"

"Every woman in Jasper. As I said, I'm very busy."

Jack flopped his packet on the desk and Victor stared at it. "I'm a mite busy myself." He nodded to the papers, bound together by twine. "This includes everything."

The mine president raised his eyes to Jack's. They iced cold, no hint to betray what Victor might be thinking. "What is it? Other than a stack of ragtag papers?"

"Proposal. Process for mapping out the mines. I took the liberty and checked the old maps out myself. They are useless. There are scores of tunnels down there, and they are a huge safety hazard. Tom and Stoop are probably somewhere down there. At the rate we're going, which is backward, we'll never find a sign of them. Or of anyone else who might disappear."

Victor leaned forward. "You trespassed? Went down in the mine on your own, without prior permission?"

Jack ignored the question. "These proposed processes will save you money in the long run. The numbers, the time involved, all included. The savings will recoup your time investment in a year and a half, and then the program will start paying out for something you should be doing anyway."

Victor glared at Jack. The look used to stop him, but all it did at this point was kindle his determination.

"Processes detailed for search and rescue procedures, too. Again, time and cost estimate attached. Your men will be trained, your officers will know what to do and each have a function in an emergency situation. You'll recoup these costs during the first incident. Which will happen any day."

"You have no idea," Victor muttered.

"Is that a threat?"

Familiar silk tones coated the mining mogul's words. "Would I threaten the son of my oldest and dearest friend?"

"Let's stop the games. Just once," Jack said. "Oh, and security procedures, too. You have tons of explosives anyone can get their hands on. Other than dandies at desks and rifles in a cabinet, there is nothing in place, nothing thought through. This operation is a bunch of disasters waiting to happen.

"Very well." Victor leaned back and steepled his fingers. "I must admit, I am impressed, but disappointed with your priorities. If you used even part of your wit for the good of the mining operation, you'd make me, and therefore yourself, very rich."

"This will enhance the mining profit as well as the safety and the well-being of the men." Jack sighed, tired of dancing around the main issue. Nothing like hitting something head-on, and it was high time he did it. "Doesn't it mean anything to have employees who are treated fairly? Who work under safe conditions?"

Victor shrugged. "There are always more half-wits for hire." He leaned forward. "I never took you for such a soft, ridiculous man. I must have left you down in the mine too long, and you have lost all reason. Do you have any idea what line you are drawing? What exactly you are walking away from?"

"How much money is enough for you, Victor? How many numbers on a page do you need before you feel like a man?"

"If you were more of a man, Mr. Buchanan, *Junior*, you'd be much happier and richer. I guarantee it." Victor rose and picked up the papers, slamming them back to the desk. "Goddamn it, Jack, I brought you here to be my right-hand man, to help me with this business." No silk to his words, just clenched fury, barely kept under control. "I thought I held the answer to your problems as well as my own. I bailed your family out of ruin, taught you my business, and this is how you repay me?"

"I know what you have done for my family, Victor, you remind me every chance you get. And I'd be happy to cooperate and give you all the support you need. You have to realize, you'd have someone who would honestly work to implement what's right for both profits and the miners. Not another bug scuttling around to do your dirty work. You've got plenty of those, a whole, goddamned infestation right out there, in the front office."

Victor stared. "All I ask from those in my circle is loyalty. A concept you don't appear to understand, let alone practice."

"I am loyal. I'm probably the only man in this company who has been honest and truthful with you. Seems you don't like it so much."

"And it seems you don't like your ranch *so much*."

Jack stared, not speaking. Victor did the same, and suddenly there they were, locked once more in a child's game.

Victor broke the standoff. "Get out of here, Jack. Consider the possibilities I offer you. Ponder what you are throwing away. And ponder well. I will give you no other chances."

Victor sat and swung his chair around to look out the window. Jack's tattered, smudged packet of papers sat on the mahogany desk, out of place. Just as out of place as he was.

The papers' edges curled in defiance even as twine attempted to keep the packet tied down. Jack turned and left the office, paused, and closed the door quietly behind him.

Slamming it would be just plain rude.

"Hey, Jackie!" Digger straightened and grinned. "About damned time you show up."

Jack clapped him on the back as he passed and walked along the tunnel where his men worked. Pete stopped swinging his sledge and turned.

Gentleman Bill bowed politely, a chunk of rock still in his hands. "How's the back and arms?"

"Never better," Jack said. As much as he hated the mine, he felt good to be with these men. For the first time, Pete tempered the suspicion in his expression. However, it hadn't completely disappeared.

"Pete, Gentleman Bill, Dig, you guys come over here?"

Bill loaded the rock into the mule cart and stood. Mouse worked at the far end of the tunnel with Rolf. Neither looked over at him. Mouse couldn't hear and probably didn't realize Jack was even around, or he'd be swaggering over. Rolf, well, anyone's guess as to why the big man was surly. It was, after all, the man's constant state.

Once they were far enough down the tunnel for privacy, Jack stopped.

"I just came from a meeting with Victor Creely."

"We should be impressed?" Pete asked.

Jack shook his head. "No, Pete, not yet, but you might be if you just listen. I gave him a proposal. On everything the petition asked for and then some. Plans, numbers, everything he needs to change this whole operation around into a decent place to work."

Pete laughed, a sound without humor. "Oh, I bet he'll get to it the quickest he can."

"Actually, I'm guessing he needs some encouragement."

Jack watched his words sink in. Pete seemed bewildered, then looked at Jack with a reassessing expression.

A smile grew across Gentleman Bill's face. "What do you have in mind?"

Jack took in a deep breath. Once he formed these words, there was no going back. "I think we should start by meeting with some of the night-shift miners. Especially the shift boss, Harley Quade. Can he be trusted?"

Bill and Pete exchanged looks. Neither talked, but both looked full of things to say.

"Gentlemen, if we all stand together, we can get Victor to take my proposal seriously. The one thing he resists, time after time, is a shutdown. He rolled over the searches for Tom and Stoop to keep this place going, and that made me realize we held the power all along. We can stop production and hit him right where he'll hurt. On his precious ledger."

"You hear what you're sayin', Buchanan?" Pete asked.

"Yep."

"How do we know we can trust you?"

Jack sighed. "I'm not sure what else I can do, Pete."

"Jack's already been to Victor to start all this," Digger said.

"Yeah, well, how do we know he's tellin' us true?" Pete asked.

Jack shrugged. "What would I have to gain by lying?"

"Like I said before. Our trust."

"I won't deny, I need it. Like you need mine." Jack stopped to look each man in the face. "Do we accuse each other of everything we are scared of, or do we start taking the steps to change the way things are done?"

Sounds of mining echoed down the tunnel.

"Look, we been talkin' on this for a good while, and it's Jack Buchanan who is tellin' us to find our hearts and walk out," Digger said. "If we spread the word and the mine shuts down, we'll be able to get more money!"

"Well," Jack interjected, "we might end up there. Showing a united front will force Victor to realize we're not a bunch of useless animals. And that's a start."

Gentleman Bill shook his head. "We've been talking about this for a long time, Jack. You do know things will get ugly if we push?"

"The first step will be a request," Jack answered. "We won't start with walking out; we'll start with talking. Maybe Victor will listen."

"Do you really think that's possible?" Pete asked.

Jack shook his head. "No. I agree with Bill. The situation is bound to deteriorate. But the alternative is business as usual, a hell of a rotten option." He looked into each man's face. "If you or anyone else doesn't want to be part of this, I understand. We'll be threatening Victor's profit, and he won't take it well. Or quietly."

"From here on out, we'll have to watch our backs," Gentleman Bill said.

"I think, as of this moment, we stay in groups. Two, three, or more. Never walk alone. That's the whole point anyway. Banding together," Jack said.

Digger's eyes rounded, huge, but Jack didn't miss the glimmer of excitement in them. Taking back control was heady stuff. "What about you, Jack? You live on your own."

"Actually, I'm not worried about me. But I'm going to turn Mouse over to you guys and you'll have to watch him, keep him at the Nugget Hotel. We might as well start before anything heats up. The kid has a way of doing whatever he wants, and I won't see him get hurt. Ever."

"We can meet at Sam's tonight," Pete said. "I'll get Harley and a few others to come. They'll miss their shift, but it's worth every penny for them to be in on this."

"Just keep it quiet," Bill said. "No one but us."

Digger and Pete nodded.

They all shook hands. Jack felt the ranch take the final slip away from him. Maybe his life, too. Yet his job, money, not even the ranch was worth selling his soul. He simply could not turn away. No more than he could have run from the Boarding House fire, although getting in the middle of it returned him to the worst day of his life.

Hiding wasn't his way. Especially when it really mattered.

The ranch was as good as gone. He hoped Buck would understand.

Chapter 25

Beth drifted across the alley, her face pale, drawn, her eyes burning and haunted.

Milena's heart sank. A spirit. Wherever she'd wandered, Beth had died. Or more likely, someone killed her. The girl was too gentle a being to survive a place like Jasper.

Perhaps Milena could have done something, but she'd been intent on fleeing the Boarding House. At the time, she believed her life depended on escape.

A tear slid down her cheek, for her inability to help Beth. "Forgive me, Sunshine."

Beth approached the back of the clinic. Milena took a closer look. Although her eyes were haunted and her spirit waning, Beth did appear more solid than an apparition. The girl moved out of Milena's sight. A door, in the back of the clinic, creaked. Spirits did not open and close doors. Not to enter a building.

Relief tingled through Milena. Beth must be alive. Then worry followed. Milena had never mistaken someone alive for a spirit. The girl's will for life had withered to nothing.

Milena backed away from the window, wondering how long Beth had hidden in Ambrose's supply room. He kept a lock on the door, stating the need to keep his medicines safe.

Medicines and the leftover shell of a girl.

Milena picked up the tray she'd piled with clean instruments and made her way through the room of women. Most of the men were gone, none hurt terribly and most anxious to return home, especially those with wives. Their spouses were not happy with a clinic full of fancy ladies also housing their husbands. Ambrose refused to allow any visitors in, citing the crowded space as enough reason. The doctor didn't back down when one of the wives insisted he throw the ladies out. Instead, he'd shooed her from his doorstep.

"Here you are, Doctor." Milena lowered the tray and sat it on the table next to Ambrose. He didn't look up, but concentrated on changing Claire's bandages.

"Are you in great pain?" Milena asked her.

"What do you think?" Claire sniped. When the doctor pulled at the bandage, she shrieked.

"Oh, for heaven's very own sake, do stop dramatizing your injuries," Suzanne said, turning away on the other bed.

"Bitch," Claire threw out. Ambrose finished the unwrap. Milena watched and understood Claire's cranky mood. Her skin blistered and oozed, thin blades of white streaking across her burns.

"And why is it you are still in bed, Suzanne?" Claire asked. "As I recall, once the fun began, you ran, fast as you've ever moved. Thank heavens no one got in your way; you might have flattened them. And I don't recall as you have anything wrong with you other than a fat behind."

Suzanne rolled over to face Claire. "Your wound has brought out the very worst in you, Claire. Your injury is nothing. You should have been in Atlanta when it burned to the ground. That was an event to bemoan. The Boarding House was quite lovely, but we all should have realized it would never last. Not in a town like this." She flopped back over, away from them. "Not in any place where men are free to destroy."

The doctor finished treating Claire in serious silence, no sign of his buoyant temperament. He nodded to Milena and she took the instruments back to clean them. She picked her way around ladies and plopped the tray down, dumping the instruments into a bucket of soapy suds. The doctor insisted this was the most sanitary way, according to his fine medical school, to keep instruments clean. He told Milena many didn't believe in such cleansing details, but he did. He kept the entire clinic meticulously scrubbed and neat.

As she exchanged the cloth, balling up the old one and tossing it into a basket for future laundering, she wondered how to broach the subject of Beth in the supply room. The girl looked so pathetic, Milena knew she needed someone. Something.

Milena wondered where Beth's prince hid. Digger, the man with the scarred face and quick laugh. Where was he, now that his love needed him?

Danger. Smother. Death.

Milena stumbled back. Foreboding dropped and wrapped around her. She looked at the ladies, then searched outside the window for anything to account for the warning. She tried to keep panic at bay. Surely no one would set fire to the medical clinic?

No. Not here. Not now.

Chilled air circulated around her. Something was forming. Beginning. Something bad.

Leaving the utensils soaking, she hurried to the front of the clinic. "I must leave you for a time, Doctor," she said, stepping over an inert lady to reach the door. On the way past, she glimpsed into Cassandra's room to see the proprietress sitting next to the body. Milena didn't stop to offer comfort or aid. Panic pushed her forward. Where or to what, she did not know.

"Milena?" the doctor called after her. She did not pause to answer.

Outside, the sun hung low in the sky.

Danger. Smother. Death.

She turned, trying to feel where the threat came from, who it was aimed at, anything other than a disembodied thought.

"*Shuv'hani?*" she asked aloud.

Nothing.

A wagon rolled by and splashed her with mud. Milena took a few steps. The town teemed with people and animals. And spirits. Angelina leaned against a post by the saloon, a group of men around her, not aware of the spirit in their midst. She sucked her cigarette, her eyes burning through Milena, to communicate—what? Milena found her gift more frustrating than ever at this moment.

She needed to get to the mountain. To the heart.

Yes.

Putting her head down, she headed through town when one name hit her.

Jack Buchanan.

She stopped. Turned. Angelina continued to watch her.

Jack Buchanan.

Again, confusion. Surely, Jack wasn't involved in the death of Angelina? No, Milena suspected the last man to see her alive, the Golden Guard, held the answers to that specific mystery. Then why Jack's name? Was he the one in danger?

Yes.

A strange sensation bolted through Milena. Fear clenched a fist around her heart as she worried for the safety of Jack Buchanan. Another strange sensation tumbled through her at the thought of him. A strange and powerful feeling.

Jack Buchanan, the Hunter of Women, but he'd hunted to help her. Jack Buchanan, *gaujo* with sunlight in his hair and the blue of the skies in his eyes, like the men of the *MoortYak*. Yet not at all like them. Hadn't hurt anyone. Quite the opposite, time after time he jumped in to help, especially those who weren't as strong and able as him. He was a man, and could do anything he wished, like many of them did. He could simply take what he wanted, whether offered or not. Instead, he gave. Constantly.

She picked up her skirts and ran, heading through the town in the direction of his home. Mud sucked at her boots and slowed her. She hopped up onto a wood sidewalk, dodging people to make her way.

Finally to the edge of town, she kept her pace quick, praying she wasn't too late to deliver her warning. Once more a fist squeezed in her chest at the thought of him in any sort of danger. When did she come to care so much for him?

Stopping for a moment to catch her breath, she recalled the look on his face every time he beheld her, his kind, gentle manner, the deprecation of himself he delivered with humor. The way he rushed to cover the proprietress from burning debris, not caring about himself or any injuries he might suffer. Somewhere in all this, in him, she'd learned there was someone she might be able to trust in this town. In this world.

Picking up her skirts again, she ran with renewed vigor. And prayed she wasn't too late.

"I promise I'll provide the finest funeral this miserable town has ever witnessed," Isabella whispered to the serene girl. Like the moon,

Cassandra had always glowed with an unassuming and fragile beauty. Not at all like the sun, blazing and showy. Indestructible.

"Not at all like me," Isabella whispered.

How strange. Cassandra merely slept, or so it seemed. Why couldn't she reach over and wake the girl? Helpless in the face of death, Isabella certainly didn't appreciate the feeling. Thank heaven she seldom experienced it.

She pulled the sheet back over Cassandra's face, and then slipped outside to watch the setting sun. It blazed with intensity all summer, never wavering. At this time of year, its light glowed weakly. Tired. And strangely, most beautiful.

In a way, Cassandra was lucky, Isabella thought. Done with this wretched world, this disgusting town, Cassandra no longer struggled for a place, for survival. She slept. Forever peaceful.

Sleep called to Isabella, but she had no time for it. Not for a while yet. She longed for her silk sheets, rose-scented perfume, and her silver-gilded hairbrush. And something to wear that didn't smell like a smoldering ruin. Smoke and antiseptic. She was weary of them both. She sighed and pulled back her shoulders, reclaiming her familiar, confident stance. To the task at hand. So much to do.

A funeral to plan. A world to rebuild.

The serenity of a finished day surrounded her. Isabella always looked forward to evening. Everything appeared much more civilized in the night. One minor difficulty: the night cloaked threats. Like the man who destroyed her home.

A knot tightened deep within her and twisted tighter. And tighter. She'd find him. Discover who killed Cassandra and ripped from Isabella and her ladies the only sanctuary they'd ever known. No matter who he was, he had no idea of what he called to himself. No man was a match for Isabella St. Claire. She planned to make him pay. Dearly.

Even if it did turn out to be Victor Creely.

"I will find you," she whispered into the dark. "I will find you."

Jack tossed his untouched steak to the dog and pushed away from the table. He might as well clean up the dishes. In a few hours he'd meet the other men at Sam's. Something hooked into him and pulled him—he didn't know where, or to what, exactly. He'd find out soon enough.

He loved being home with his dog again. He admitted to himself, with a bit of guilt, he was relieved Mouse wasn't underfoot. Pete, Digger, and Gentleman Bill were apparently as good as their word and much more capable of keeping a hold on the kid than Taryn and the doc.

He lifted a bucket to the counter and his thoughts rambled to the clinic and how the ladies might be doing.

"Who are you kidding, Buchanan?" he asked out loud. "You wonder about her."

He strolled out to his front porch, looking down to the lights of Jasper. A backdrop of faraway sounds beckoned. His future, or lack thereof, waited for him down there.

A small rustle shushed through the dark.

Animal? Assassin?

There he was, his imagination running wild again. His eye caught a phantom figure. Then nothing. Ghost? It reappeared and he realized that, indeed, someone headed in his direction. He squinted. He'd recognize her anywhere, even if he couldn't quite see her.

"Milena."

He remembered the first time he'd seen her, in the woods, when she appeared magical. She came closer, lamplight transforming her from a creature of magic to a woman. Warm and real. And God Almighty, so desirable, it hurt him to see her.

She must have run the entire way to his cabin, frightened. The last time she'd run to him, the Boarding House burned to the ground. Something was wrong. All his instincts sharpened to protect.

"I come to warn you, Jack Buchanan." She stopped and took a few gasps, her eyes wild, worried. "I feel something. Danger."

"Oh, magnificent."

"Not quick, like the Boarding House fire. Something waiting. Stalking."

Jack nodded. "Yeah, I actually know what you're talking about, and I can't even see the future." He smiled, but she still seemed worried. "Milena, please don't be concerned. I am walking into some trouble, but I know where any threat might come from."

Her chest still heaved and her lips parted. Lust bolted through him, and although he should be ashamed, he wasn't. Lordy, he wanted to touch her, taste her. In the middle of all his problems, one thing pulsed through him stronger than any other.

He wanted her, plain and simple.

He moved closer, and she didn't back away. Her eyes widened. He pulled her in, holding her until her breathing came down to even. She trembled and he held her tight, afraid she might dissipate into thin air. He felt every part of her in his arms. A living, breathing woman. Real, warm. Her heart beat under his, and slowly the two met, coming together to strike the same rhythm. He buried his hands in her hair and the curls twined around his fingers, soft as a whisper. Gently, he tugged. She raised her face to his.

"Jack—"

He silenced her with a kiss. Light at first. She responded, and he delved in, deeply. She tasted like sweet, spiced wine. Passion grew along with a yearning so deep he thought it might explode through him, but instead it rose until he took in a breath against her mouth and moaned.

He remembered the doctor's regret. He would not make the same mistake.

"Milena, I'm in love with you," he said, his voice husky. She gasped a small sound of surprise, her eyes questioning, not quite believing. "But," he continued, "you probably already knew that, being able to see the future and all."

Her astonishment softened into a smile.

"God, you're beautiful when you smile. You need to do it more often." He lowered his head and kissed her again, feeling her smile under his lips. He was content to lose himself to her forever. He nipped at her jaw and brushed his mouth down her neck.

She shuddered. "Jack, please."

He pulled away to look at her.

Her eyes, warm and soft, contrasted with her words. "You are in danger. I feel this very close, this warning."

He stepped away from her, mostly to think straight and put a sentence together. He needed to get hold of himself. Big night ahead.

"I'll be careful."

"This is not enough."

"It will have to be. I know what you're trying to tell me. I'm about to put something in motion, something I should have begun the moment I arrived, if I'd had the nerve."

"You are not the same man who came to Jasper."

Jack chuckled. "No, no I'm not. I guess that's good."

"I am frightened," she whispered.

He took her hands. "Don't be. Not for me. Consider your warning delivered. Come on, I'll walk you back to the clinic. I'm heading into town anyways."

Despite her foreboding warning and his uncertainty of the future, Jack felt the most contented he'd been in a very long time.

"Oh, hold on," he said, and cracked the door open an inch. "Be a good dog."

Duke didn't even lift his head to look, the steak not much more than a bone.

"We'll spread the word among the night crew." Harley puffed as he spoke, wheezing. He coughed into a soiled rag Jack supposed was a handkerchief.

Pete caught Jack's eye. "Tuesday night, then. We'll draw it up and take a vote on who'll take it to Creely."

Another petition. To replace the one Victor had torn to shreds. Except this document would never hide under the floorboard in the church.

"There is always the chance Victor will read my proposal and decide to implement it."

"No offense, Buchanan, but he's probably wipin' his ass with it," Harley said. His comment drew sniggers and barks of laughter.

"I hope not." Jack grinned, a twisted expression, he knew. "But you're probably right."

"I pity the idiot who agrees to take the petition to him," Digger said.

"No need to wonder. I'm the idiot who'll take it," Jack said. "And I'll do a better job this time. Especially when he rips it to shreds."

"This time you'll have us all openly behind it," Pete said. "Nothing held in secret after tonight. He'll have all of us to answer to. By the time he sees the petition, we'll be done with closed doors."

"If he does tear it up agin, what'll we do?" Digger asked.

"We'll decide on Tuesday. My vote will be to walk out," Jack answered. "Shutting down the mine is the only thing Creely's gonna understand."

Everyone shook hands, Digger, Pete, Gentleman Bill, Harley, and Jack. Once they left the room, something big and unstoppable would spring into motion. Jack certainly wanted to be around to see it all. He thought of Tom and Stoop, and hoped he wouldn't be the next in a lineup of disappearing miners.

At least if he vanished, everyone would have some idea of what happened. Jack Buchanan would live on forever, a martyr. Perfect. How did he ever get to this place?

He regarded all the faces, character carved by the hardships of life, and he knew this was where he'd always choose to stand, and should have a long time ago.

The group decided to leave, slipping out at different times and spreading around the bar. Jack was the first to go, the plan to bellyup for a drink while the others ducked out after him, one by one with plenty of time in between. When Pete left, he'd be the last one and join Harley and Gentleman Bill outside to walk back to the Nugget Hotel. Digger would collect Mouse and wait for Jack at the clinic only a few doors down. Quite a bit of choreography, but everyone was intent on working together, and it was amazing what they accomplished when they weren't arguing and accusing each other.

The plan was perfect and included a chance to see Milena again. Even if it would be in a clinic with others around, he wanted to be near her as much as possible before . . .

Before what? This direction didn't feel good. Right, but not good.

It annoyed Jack that Mouse hung around in the saloon tonight, but Jack knew keeping him away was next to impossible, especially with Pete and Gentleman Bill here. Jack slipped out into the noise. His eyes skimmed over the crowd to the piano. Mouse leaned against the console. Good. Sally had kept her word, as had the piano man. He passed and dropped a dollar in the jar, a tip for keeping watch over Mouse.

"Hey, looky who's granting us his presence. Howdy, Jack." Luke slapped an empty space beside him at the bar. "A whiskey for my friend, and make it top shelf, Sam."

Sam turned over a glass and filled it.

Jack wandered over. "Not much to do with the Boarding House gone, huh?" Jack asked, needling Luke.

"Nope." He tossed back his shot. "Isabella St. Bitch fired me. Said I shoulda been at my post. She's cheap is all. Tired of payin' me."

"My guess is her money burned down with the whorehouse," Sam said.

"By the way, Luke, where were you that night?" Jack tossed back his own drink.

"I was there, helpin' out. Where the hell else would I be?"

Funny, Jack didn't recall seeing Luke anywhere near the chaos. Then again, Jack was in no position to remember much of anything.

Luke giggled and slapped the bar. "Keep 'em comin', Sammy boy."

Jack hoped he blended in and was acting normal. He felt as obvious and unnatural as a snowstorm in July. Sam poured Luke's glass first and then grabbed the Kentucky bourbon.

"Just give me the usual," Jack said.

"No, no, the best for Jack Buchanan," Luke insisted, and that's when Jack paused. He and Luke were drinking from different bottles. Luke and Sam might be in on it.

In on what? Victor Creely's henchmen were officers. Like Bear, whom he'd seen when he came out of the back room. Jack looked behind him. Sure enough, Bear leaned against the wall, scowling at him. When Jack caught his eye, the big man grinned, revealing several missing teeth. Jack turned back around and Luke slapped him on the back, grinning. Jack grimaced as his burns pained under Luke's palm. Sam smiled, too, and refilled Jack's glass. Christ, what was this, a smiling contest? Something sure didn't feel right.

With Bear keeping such close tabs on him, naturally he'd feel uneasy. He'd known Sam and Luke since he'd come to Jasper. Both had become friendly acquaintances when others shunned him. A bit of guilt bolted through him at his disloyal thoughts. Didn't matter. He'd had enough anyway. Only one drink and he felt fuzzy.

"Guess I'll get going," he said.

"Hey, what about this one?" Luke asked, gesturing to the filled glass.

"One's enough for me tonight, but thanks."

"Anytime, Jack." The sardonic grin again. Why did all of Jasper seem like he viewed it through a freak-show mirror? He was relieved to step out into the clear night, and in a few moments he'd see Milena. It might take some time to make Mouse understand he needed to stay at the Nugget Hotel, but really, communicating with the kid wasn't difficult. Jack guessed he dreaded the look of disappointment he'd see on the kid's face.

He stepped off the wood walk and crossed the muddy street.

Suddenly he slammed up against the side of the General Mercantile. Behind him, Luke laughed.

"Jack, I really wished you'da downed that second drink. I wouldn't have to do this."

The night exploded into a million shards.

Then black.

Chapter 26

"Hold!" A faraway echo.

Black. Then red. Next, pain. Jack thought he might be stuffed in a barrel. He was bent double, his knees tucked up under his chin. He leaned forward and fell, smacking his already throbbing head. Dirt. Nausea. He rose to his hands and knees in time to throw up.

Clinking on rock. "Hold!"

An echo-edged voice sliced through his pain. Closer. Still only black. Jack crumpled to his side, careful not to fall facefirst into his own vomit.

A flicker from a distance. A cart clattered on a track.

Lord, have mercy, he was in the mine. But where? Why was he separated from his team? His head burned like a pile of hot coal, dizziness and nausea twirled together. He rose to his hands and knees and threw up again, this time, loud and coughing.

"Hey, I hear something."

A dim glow down the tunnel. Jack wanted to shout out, but he couldn't. He crawled a few inches, leaned over on his side, and closed his eyes. He wanted to die.

"Careful," he warned himself. Pain shot through his head,

but at least his stomach didn't roll as violently.

"Anyone down there?" Pete hollered from somewhere down the tunnel.

"Pete," Jack murmured, too quietly, he knew, for anyone to hear. What happened to him? Was he working and a rock hit him in the noggin? Where was his hardboil?

"Anyone down there?" Pete yelled again.

"Here," Jack spoke with all his strength, which was almost none. He moaned.

"Bill, I think someone's down there."

The dim glow grew bigger, brighter, and then separated into floating lights coming closer.

"It ain't Jack, is it?" Digger's voice, hopeful.

"Here," Jack said a bit louder.

"Hallelujah!"

"Jack!"

Someone lifted him to his feet, arms held him. Mouse hugged Jack around the waist, tightly.

"Glory be, we thought you was dead!" Digger said. In the background, Rolf looked on, his face sour beneath his hat's candle. Gentleman Bill was just about to giggling.

"Where you been, Buchanan? How did you get down here?" Pete asked. "We thought you were a goner when you didn't show up at the clinic."

Clinic? Milena. The meeting. The drinks. Christ, Luke.

Panic shivered through him and he tried to yell for them all to get out. Instead, he retched again. Dry heaves. Pete and Digger lowered him to his hands and knees.

"Out. Out," was all he managed.

"Jesus, Jack. What's wrong with you?" Worry shot through Digger's voice.

"Let's get him up top," Pete ordered.

"Get. Out. Now!" Jack finally managed.

Pete hauled him to his feet. Suddenly from beneath them, a deep rumble grew. The mountain shook. Impossible, yet it shook. For a split second, no one moved. Jack locked eyes with Digger, whose face tightened with disbelief. Then the tunnel floor bucked. Digger tumbled backward into Rolf. Mouse lurched and fell to the ground.

A huge, invisible hand swept through and knocked down every man standing. The ground opened up, and the floor dropped into nothing. Dark exploded. The mountain finally claimed retribution and wrapped them all in its smothering grip.

"How long has she been back there?" Milena asked the doctor.

He sighed. "Since Isabella tossed her out. She has nowhere else to go." Ambrose's eyes, lately sorrowful, looked apologetic.

"You are a kind man, Doctor."

"And it gets me nowhere, Milena. This is not a kind world."

She touched his hand. "Yes, it is, as long as there are men like you in it." She nodded at the back room. "Why has she not come out? Because of the proprietress?"

"I can't even get her out of bed. She just stares at the wall. Other than wandering every so often, she is completely uncommunicative. I'm not sure what to do."

"Perhaps I can help."

"I'm ready to try anything, and I will admit, you do have a way about you, my dear."

"So I am told."

His mouth turned up a touch at the corners, which gave

Milena hope for him. He still existed, the happy, romantic doctor, somewhere beneath all the sadness.

He led her back to the locked door and withdrew a key from his waistcoat. Once inside, smells assaulted her, pungent herbs, spices, the blunt scent of antiseptic and soap. He opened the door at the other end of the space and lit a candle. Another small closet behind the first one contained only a bed with a girl under the blanket. Her eyes did not focus. A tear rolled down her cheek and fell to the pillow. Although heartbreaking, the tear was a good sign. Somewhere inside this shell of a young woman, Beth still lived.

"Beth." Milena sat on the bed and took the girl's hand. It felt like Cassandra's; cold, stiff, as if no blood flowed, no heart beat. "Beth."

No response. Beth's eyes focused on nothing.

"She's been like that since I found her. Someone brought her to the back door and took off."

"Had she been injured?"

"Nothing I can see."

"We can be thankful for that much."

"Anything might have happened to her. Any number of scenarios. Because she's wandered a few times I did think of locking this door from the outside, but if anyone had been locked in the Boarding House when—"

Darkness, pouring over, nothing left, nothing. Death comes to claim its own.

Milena staggered to her feet, the girl in the bed forgotten.

"Milena, what is it?"

She didn't take time to answer, but bolted out the back door.

"Milena!" the doctor called out. She did not slow, but ran toward Jasper Mountain.

A muffled explosion fills her ears. The ground trembles, and evil laughs across Jasper with a booming chuckle. She stumbles, and then a huge, invisible fist slams into her.

"Milena!" The doctor caught her when she flew back, and they both fell to the ground.

Darkness presses around her. Try as she might, she cannot breathe. She struggles to dig out, but rock folds, pulling her into a coffin's embrace. She cries against the dirt and it pours in her and through her. She is buried alive.

"Milena, what is happening to you?"

She reaches out to the cloaked stranger who will carry her to the Otherworld. He beckons with tapered, ivory fingers, and she grasps his cold hand. Quickly, she pleads. Do not let me suffer this slow death. He pulls her to him like an anxious lover.

"Milena!"

She opened her eyes to the doctor's face framed by light blue sky. Sun. Air. Milena sat up, blinking against morning light. Around her, birds sang. A breeze with a hint of cool gently teased her skin.

"Milena?" Ambrose asked. "What happened to you?"

"Did you hear that? Feel it?" The panic of the unknown edged her voice.

"Feel what?"

"The explosion. The ground shook."

"Nothing like that happened. The ground is solid, you see." Ambrose looked at her with the benevolence usually reserved for a child. "You must have imagined it."

Behind the doctor, Jasper Mountain rose, solid and constant. Yet the serene quiet hid horrors. Of this, she was sure. An avalanche of fear had come rolling down over her and across the town. And all Milena could think of was—

"Jack!" she whispered, praying for the mountain to spare him. Even as she spoke his name, she knew it was too late.

Dark. Silence. Jack couldn't move.

Then a whimper. Did it come from him? He saw nothing, not even dark. Just nothing. He didn't exist, the only thing left of him, an echo in a vast forever. Jack, the miner's ghost. What a fate, haunting Jasper Mountain for eternity. God possessed a keen sense of irony, and he was the perfect butt for this joke.

He tried to move. A lance of pain pierced through his side and stopped him.

Wait. Ghosts don't hurt. Do they?

The rich smell of dirt filled his nostrils, and he snorted it out. Yep, he hurt too damned bad to be dead. He breathed in a glimmer of hope along with a snoot of dirt and coughed. Thank the good Lord in heaven, he wasn't dead.

A realization crushed hope. He was worse than dead. He was buried alive.

Milena ran up Gooseneck Road, past the stamping mill, the steady drum shaking the ground beneath her feet. The gate to the mine proper rose ahead. A huge man came out of a building to watch her approach, a rifle held loosely in his hands. She slowed to a walk, hoping to have enough breath to talk when she reached him. She wondered how to start.

He scowled, grasping the rifle tight. "Help you?" he grunted.

"There has been an . . ." her voice trailed off. Accident?

Hardly. "Incident," she continued. "A collapse in the mountain. Men are trapped."

He grinned, several missing teeth turning his expression into a leer. "Ain't been no collapse."

"Yes, there has." She tried to move past him.

He blocked her way. "No women allowed on minin' property."

"This is a, how do you call it? Emergency. I must speak with . . ." Who? Victor Creely?

He shook his head. "Nope. You ain't steppin' foot on minin' property and you ain't speakin' with nobody."

She didn't have a plan, was a fool to think anyone here would help or care. She stared at the filthy hulk before her. She didn't know what to do.

She surveyed the area beyond the gate, searching for anything. An idea, a person. A large brick building squatted close to the gate, and several wood buildings, resembling shacks, dotted the landscape. Farther back, the headframe towered from the top of the plateau. The constant din of steam engines clouded around the complex, every so often a shout punching through. No one cared about a lone woman at the gate.

"You kin look all you want. That's it."

She returned her attention back to the huge man before her. Perhaps he possessed a conscience. "Your comrades are in trouble while we waste time speaking here. Do you want their deaths on your head?"

He laughed. Apparently, no conscience.

"Tell you what," he said to her. "Give me a free poke and I'll let you have a quick look around."

Disgusted, she turned away from him and a flash of movement behind a window in the large brick building stopped her. Someone watched.

The King of the Jackals. And this monster, his guard dog.

She turned from the mine, not sure what to do next.

The big, dirty man's laughter followed her, mocking her as she retreated down the road.

A whimper skimmed the heavy silence.

Jack figured he was buried alive. In a grave? Assumed to be dead when he wasn't?

A whimper. Again.

Was the sound faraway or close? Or inside his head?

That's right, the mine. He'd been in the mine.

"Digger?" he tried to call out, but his voice raced backward choking down his windpipe. Coughing, he clawed and pushed through a blanket of dirt and rock. He started to sit up and smacked his head on, what else, rock. Goddamned rock.

Goddamned rock? He wasn't buried in a grave. He was in the mine.

Holding his hand to the side of his head, he felt sticky wet. Blood. He rolled over and gagged, then coughed out more dirt. Grit sifted under his shirt like an army of ants skittering over him.

Well, at least he wasn't a ghost. Yet.

Again, the whimper sounded, this time, closer. Jack heard it clearly now he'd dug himself out of dirt.

"Digger?" his voice grated out. More dirt raked in his throat. Seemed he was chockful of mountain.

"Jack?" Not Digger. Pete. Jack grabbed and held to Pete's voice, reaching out to him in the dark. His mind began turning like a rusty wheel coming to life after centuries of nonuse. There'd been an explosion. Cave-in. Maybe in that order, maybe not. He was alive. With Pete. Two. There were eight in his crew. He concentrated, and the thinking made him feel real again. Six. He had six men to find.

"Pete?"

"Over here." Pete's voice wavered. Jack didn't ever think he'd hear fear come from the tough old guy, yet it shivered through the miner's voice.

Jack crawled to where he thought Pete's voice came from. Rock scraped his knees and elbows, ripping through his clothing. Pain shot through his side and stopped him after he'd only crawled a few feet.

He rolled on his good side and gasped in air, wanting to curse, to cry. No sound came. Nothing in him but a hot poker in his side and bands of ache closing around his chest. Not to mention, the throbbing through his skull. His eyes stung. He swiped gritty blood away.

Goddamn it anyway. What a mess.

He wondered if they had a chance of survival. How far did this thing reach? Were any of the other teams affected? Did anyone up top realize what had happened? Did anyone know someone was down here, alive?

Did anyone care?

He remembered someone dumped him in the tunnels, near his team, set it up, lit explosives. Mining accident? Hardly.

"Jack?" Pete's voice called out again.

Jack grunted in reply. Someone moaned from another direction, and again the whimper skipped through the dark. That added up to three alive other than him: Pete, the moaner, and the whimperer. Four to die slowly.

Stop feeling sorry for yourself, Buchanan, and move!

Four men with four still to find. He was supposed to be their leader. It was up to him to pull them together, find the others.

"Mmmmm . . ." rolled through the dark. "Mmmm . . . Jack. Jack." Digger's voice. Barely a whisper, yet enough. All Jack needed. Ignoring his pain, he resumed his crawling.

"Dig, hang on!" He dragged himself up a dirt mound. Or wall. Or whatever it was. All the times he'd imagined the mountain turning into a grave, and it was accommodating him. He felt like a smashed and blinded bug, attempting to make its way through an impossible maze.

"Digger!" he called, his voice trembling. "Pete!" He sounded feeble to himself, like a ninety-year-old man with consumption.

"Over here." Pete's voice ribboned through the dark like a guide rope. Panting against stabs of hurt, Jack crawled over the dirt pile, pulled himself through a small opening that scraped every part of him, then he skidded down. And down. For a second he thought he might be sliding into a hell of a pit, but he stopped after a few feet. The pain jolting through him felt familiar, like it had always been there.

"Jack?"

Pete spoke right next to him. Jack reached out and found the hand of his friend.

"Christ, Pete." Relief swam through his voice. Then he added, "We're in trouble."

"Yep."

"I heard Digger."

"He's right behind me." Pete's voice dropped down to a whisper. "He's bad off. Half-buried. I can't get him free."

Jack reached out and Digger was right there. Jack scooted closer and slid his hand along the miner's chest. He came up against rock. Digger groaned, the sound small. If there hadn't been dead silence, Jack might not have heard him at all.

"Hold on, buddy. It'll be fine," Jack lied. He needed to see. The dark was not black, it was blindness. "Pete, you got your candle? Or a lantern?"

"Nope."

"Damn." Jack slid his hand up Digger's neck to his head. God only knew how, but he still wore his hardboil, candle intact. Gently, Jack removed the hardboil. Digger moaned again.

"Hold on, Dig. I need to get your candle."

"Don't light it. I don't think I want to see what's lyin' on me," Digger said, his voice heavy with the effort it took to speak.

"We'll get you out," Jack promised.

"Weighs two tons. First I thought it was Rolf."

Digger's humor bolstered Jack's courage. God bless him. A small sound of movement came from behind them.

"Who is it?" Jack called out. For a moment he heard no sound at all. He thought he might break his ears, he listened so intently.

"Rolf." The big man coughed his name through the dark.

"Are you hurt?"

Only silence answered.

"Hell, Rolf, you baby. Answer us. Hey, Rolf, I'm fit as a fiddle," Digger said, although the pain stabbing through his voice didn't quite agree with his words.

Jack dug in his pocket and grabbed a match. "Hold on. I'm gonna light this candle."

"Jack," Pete's voice came softly through the dark. "What if there's powder in the air? You might ignite this whole . . . whatever it is we're in. Chamber."

Jack froze. Pete was right. Someone set this up to kill them. Someone? Who was he kidding? Luke. Who wasn't smart enough to pack in extra powder to be sure no one survived. Or was he?

One thing Jack did know for sure, next chance he got, he'd pound the sardonic grin right off the bastard's face. He wondered how much Victor paid the man to kill his friends.

"I'll crawl back far as I can from you. You're right, I might finish the job Luke and Victor began."

"We need to see what we're into," Pete answered, then his voice turned angry. "Jesus, Jack, I did hear the explosion first. You really think Luke did this on purpose? Luke?"

"I know he did. If we don't blow ourselves to Hell, we'll have plenty of time to discuss everything."

"Light it," Digger said. "I'm gonna die anyhow. Sooner'd be better than later."

"No, you aren't going to die," Jack answered. "We're all getting out. Together. Pete?"

"I say go ahead and light it."

"Rolf?"

Emptiness answered.

"Rolf?"

Silence.

"Go ahead, Jack," Pete said, "Digger and I just outvoted you. Do it."

"All right." Truthfully, he did want light, but now their lives were bound together in the mountain. Jack lifted himself to his hands and knees again. He gasped.

"What?" Pete asked.

"Sorry, nothing. Having trouble breathing."

"Just don't start pukin' again. I hate puke," Pete answered.

Jack crawled. He touched a soft mound that wasn't dirt. A man. He put his hand on whomever it was. No rise and fall of the chest. No heartbeat. But the body still felt warm.

"God have mercy on your soul, Rolf," Jack said. What a shame.

Scooting around Rolf's body, he made his way until rock stopped him. He pulled himself to his feet, and stars shot through the dark. His legs shook, and he grasped rock to steady himself. God, it was nearly impossible to tell which way was up. He figured the opposite way his body wanted to go.

Time to light the candle. He pulled matches out of his pocket.

"Ready?"

"I reckon," answered Pete's voice.

"Here goes."

At least, if he was about to get blasted into Death's waiting grip, he'd die on his feet.

He saw Milena's face. He reached out in the darkness, touched her soft hair, drank in her luminous eyes. Tasted her lips. At least he'd had sense enough to tell her he loved her. At least she knew that much.

Holding her close, in his heart, Jack Buchanan lit the match.

Chapter 27

"Milena, are you sure?" The doctor's eyes snapped to life. The man could rise to a disaster, that much was certain.

"I am. Jack Buchanan is in terrible trouble. And others."

"You get this from a feeling?"

"A knowing. He is buried alive."

Lines of pondering etched Ambrose's face, and he rubbed his chin. "Quite honestly, I've never seen anything like you flying back in the air. I'd swear on my mother's grave something actually threw you into me." He glanced over to Cassandra, his eyes growing weary. "You knew I loved her before I did. Or before I'd admit it to myself." He returned his attention to Milena. "If I listened to you and had told her, at least she'd know it, too."

"Doctor." She gently touched his arm. "Cassandra is at peace. At rest. She does not wander, does not follow you in a shroud of sadness. She has moved on. She knows."

"By God, Milena, I'm not going to let another tragedy go unanswered." A bit of the old fire of adventure jumped into his eyes. "To the mine!"

They turned. Isabella St. Claire leaned against the door

frame and crossed her arms. How long she'd been listening was anyone's guess.

The proprietress lifted her eyebrow in amusement. "And how do you think one well-meaning but, forgive me, slightly melodramatic doctor and an eccentric Gypsy are going to make any difference? Who will even listen, let alone believe what either of you have to say?"

The doctor and Milena exchanged looks.

"Well, I didn't think ahead that far," Ambrose answered. "I suppose we'll need to gather up the sheriff."

"You are a fine doctor, but a miserable tactician. The sheriff is not the most brilliant of men. Most likely, he is on Victor's payroll." She pushed away from the door and strolled over to them. "No, our best hope comes in numbers. Miners' families will be interested in what you have to say, Milena. That is, if you are correct and this isn't a bad dream or a way to garner attention."

Milena studied the proprietress, wondering what manipulations the madame practiced now. No matter, Jack was in trouble, and any help was acceptable. Although the proprietress made a dangerous ally. Milena would not soon forget Beth, locked away in a dark room, unable to do anything except cry. Still, Isabella was, as always, correct.

"No one will believe me," Milena admitted.

"Beg your pardon, Isabella, if people won't pay heed to Milena and myself, why do you think they will listen to a madame?"

"Because, Doctor," the proprietress smiled with a knowing expression, "the madame is me." She turned back to the main room and clapped her hands. "Ladies, ladies! We have a very important job at hand. Please, if you are not seriously hurt, ready yourself to follow me." She whirled back to Milena and Ambrose. "Who needs facts? Emotion and fear are the most effective way to convince ignorant masses. You two, watch how it's done. Joan of Arc has nothing on me."

Candlelight flickered, enough to turn the chamber into a murky netherworld of shadows. Jack didn't know how long they'd been buried underground, but even such a small flame burned his eyes. Silence roared in his ears while he took stock.

The space was smallest where Digger lay, his legs pinned. The rock wall had collapsed and reformed, right on top of him, the mountain half-swallowing him.

Pete sat next to Digger, his eyes sunk into dark hollows, the candle in his hardboil long gone. About five feet away and down a jagged slope, Rolf rocked back and forth, curled into a ball. The dead man Jack mistook for Rolf in the dark was actually Zebulon, one of the original prospectors and a miner who'd worked the mine since the first shovel of ore was removed. He'd been killed instantly, the side of his head and his entire left shoulder and arm torn off. Jack finally recognized the smell over dirt, the one making him nauseous. The rich metallic stench of blood.

Five out of eight accounted for, the mountain claiming one victim. So far. No sign of Mouse, Gentleman Bill, or Josef.

Jack tried not to think about the little boy.

Face it, Buchanan. Your little boy.

Jack vowed that if God got them out of this mess, he'd take Mouse in. For good. Raise him as his own son. Although, knowing Mouse, the boy would be the one to teach Jack how to get along in this miserable world.

Jack refused to consider that a deal with the Almighty might be too late.

In the murk he couldn't tell much of anything. The ground was too chopped up to see if any supplies or tools remained. They'd have to feel their way in the black.

"This is the only candle. We've got to save it. Take a good look. I'm snuffing it out."

"No!" Rolf suddenly unfurled into a sitting position. "No!"

"Rolf, goddamn it, get a hold," Pete said.

"Here goes." Jack extinguished the candle. Darkness once again closed in. "This isn't so bad. Wasn't really much light."

At least Jack knew there were no pits or holes to fall through, not an entirely good situation. They were hemmed into a small pocket. There might be feet of rock between them and a way out. He wished that thought hadn't just darted through his mind and decided to keep it to himself.

And what about the others? Jack shuddered at the thought of Mouse and Bill, buried alive. And Josef, the final member of his team. A quiet man who reminded Jack of Duke; Josef had a sort of hound-dog face and sad eyes. He was father to five children, but no wife, not since last year. She'd died giving birth to their youngest.

Jesus, this was all so unfair. Nothing new in that sentiment, especially in Jasper. Jack needed to hear Pete's voice cut through the pressing dark and help him hold to his sanity.

"Pete, what do you think?"

"'Bout what? Our chances? I'm guessin' none."

"We'll get out of here." Jack tried to lighten the heaviness of his voice.

"How? We both know this was on purpose. Creely means to kill us. Just wish it'd been a shot in the back of the head when I didn't see nothin' comin'."

"Naw, Creely wants us to suffer good afore we die," Digger

said. "What this mine is. A whole load of sufferin'."

"He's not getting the best of any of us. And this damned mountain isn't eating me for breakfast," Jack answered when inspiration struck. The mountain, latticed with delicate tunnels just waiting for a chance to collapse and break.

Insane and unreasonable danger. And their only hope.

"Collapse in the mine" slithered through the town with ungodly speed, spoken by every mouth, reaching every street, building, corner, every dark and closed place.

With each step, the crowd grew, swelling with fear and anger. Men trapped. The mine officers denying a problem. Husbands, fathers, brothers, sons discarded by the cruel and callous officers of the mine and the supreme indifference of Victor Creely.

Isabella St. Claire marched in front, between the doctor and Milena, and followed by her ladies calling the citizens to arms. She appeared even more beautifully tragic given her smudged and torn finery and the bruise on her cheek. Despite her own personal loss, the people needed her. A heroine of note. Heavens, this was almost too easy. Even the pinched nose bitch in the bonnet—the woman who'd spouted sludge about Jesus and divine retribution during the Boarding House fire—even she became part of the crowd marching behind Isabella St. Claire.

Whores and wives. Sisters and mothers. Daughters and paramours. For today, the women of Jasper marched side by side. Isabella relished the moment of women standing united. Surely Victor Creely would know, the moment he saw her leading the mob to his doorstep, he'd made a serious mistake by burning down her world.

She could not wait to see the look on his face.

No one bothered to ask how they knew about the collapse or if anyone actually saw or heard it.

"Milena, dear," Isabella said, leaning in to be sure no one else might hear, "do keep your mouth shut. If you say anything, make it some of that mysterious mumbo jumbo you spout. Leave all the lying to me."

Milena narrowed her eyes.

"Well, I am the expert," Isabella said.

The Gypsy still did not look certain.

"And men's lives depend on how we present ourselves."

Alarm flashed across Milena's face. There. That convinced her.

The good Reverend McShane, in all his sensual beauty, emerged from the rectory. The fat woman in charge of all the orphans ran after the little rats as they poured from the orphanage. The doctor scurried up the church walk, jabbering at Reverend McShane while the tide of Jasper's ordinary and underprivileged swept by, Isabella leading them all. She turned her attention to the road ahead. It simply wouldn't do to have someone catch her gawking at the preacher.

The mob began the climb up Gooseneck Road. Isabella had actually never been up this far. She looked down at the gathering of shacks and buildings making up Jasper, and below the town a smoldering hole that used to be her beautiful Boarding House. Her stomach cringed at the sight. At the thought of Victor, so smug. Amused. Sure he ran this town. No matter. The tide was about to change and, with any luck, it would sweep him away, and he'd see her smile while he drowned.

Above them and behind the main gate of the Jasper Mining Company, men spewed onto the wide porch of a brick building. She didn't recognize many of them; it was too far to see clearly.

One thing she did notice. Rifles.

Oh, dear. This march might get ugly. And, unfortunately, she walked in the front line.

"Do you see them?" the doctor asked, puffing out of breath from catching up. Isabella wanted to turn and search for the minster, see if he'd joined them. Pride required she continue to look straight ahead.

"See what? The men? Or the guns?" she answered. "Yes, they are ready to defend their miserable piece of the mountain. Why is it men always resort to instruments of violence when faced with anything they can't handle or control?"

"I've never fired one, myself," the doctor answered.

"Really? You are a rarity, dear doctor. Especially in the West."

"I am a healer. I do no harm."

"Pity. I have no such compunction," Isabella answered, and thought of the derringer strapped to her thigh. In the mêlée, she might not have time to retrieve it. How she despised overt action. She much preferred subtlety behind closed doors, not an option as of the moment.

"God help us," the preacher said, joining the front line. "All of us."

Isabella's heart skipped faster. She hid her bothersome emotion deep within. "Why, Reverend McShane. How good of you to join us."

"Nothing good about this, any of it, Miss St. Claire. I pray I'm not needed, but I sincerely doubt the outcome of this day. God only knows what you've started."

Oh, he had no idea.

The officers moved off the porch and formed a line stretching across the gate. Isabella made out faces now, Edmund, Charles, George, twenty or so men standing with rifles, including the hideous troll called, what was it? Oh, yes, Bear. It professed to be a man. Rumors circulating claimed he came from a line of ancient cavemen lost in the Rockies for generations. Seeing him now, his sloped forehead and mean, beady eyes, Isabella found the rumors absolutely believable.

But no Victor. At least, not yet. She wondered when he might decide to show. He probably began scheming and planning the moment he glimpsed the crowd coming his way.

Isabella cast a sidelong glance at the minister, walking at her side. This had really turned into the most interesting day. Originally, she'd planned to gather the ladies and start going through Boarding House rubble, even though the mess still smoldered. This mob, particularly the minister beside her, made for a far more fascinating afternoon.

She sensed the crowd losing momentum behind her as they approached the gate. The officers and men stood, shoulder to shoulder, several of them obviously nervous.

"We demand entrance," Isabella said proudly, mostly for the crowd. She had no illusions about actually gaining access to the mine.

"Doctor, Reverend, we ask that you and your, um, *friends*, all stay back or we will be forced to do something we'd really rather not," George Barger said, ignoring Isabella. Naturally, he would address the men and not her. She made a note not to indulge his fantasies in the future. He'd worn his last set of lacy drawers and corset in her establishment.

"What about the collapse?" a voice shot out.

"My man's in there!" a woman howled.

"There is no collapse," George Barger shouted, but a growing swell of shouts and jeers swallowed his words.

"Everyone!" Taryn McShane pushed to the front of the crowd.

to stand between pointed rifles and angry townsfolk. Seeing him in his black suit, his chiseled features set in determination, and his eyes pleading for understanding, Isabella almost swooned. "Calm down, all of you. We are friends and neighbors."

A male voice erupted from the crowd. "Ain't no friend of mine stands with a rifle pointed at me!" Escalated anger shivered through the group of people. Just when Isabella thought the mob might charge, screaming and shouting started from behind. Isabella looked back to see Sheriff Cain ride a horse right through the center of the crowd. People dove to the side of the road to get out of his path. The mob fell apart, disrupted. Cain leapt from his horse at the front of the gate and drew his gun. He looked straight at Isabella. Apparently, he at least had the intelligence to know whom he was dealing with.

"What's going on?"

"Sheriff, we are all terribly concerned. There's been a mine collapse and no one is addressing the situation."

Sheriff Cain grimaced in disbelief. "Collapse? How do you know?"

Ah, that bothersome question she hoped wouldn't come up. Before she managed an answer, the door to the huge brick building opened. Victor Creely himself stepped out into daylight.

Things were about to get interesting.

The mob's angry energy dissipated as Victor made his way to them. He pushed forward without any hesitation in long, sure strides, playing his part, a man forged of steel. Isabella noted Milena's body stiffen, her eyes widening with alert. Victor scanned the crowd with no expression on his face, but when his attention lit on the Gypsy, something slithered behind his eyes.

"What do we have here?" he asked, his voice calm.

Milena stepped forward. "There is a collapse in the mine."

He offered a smile, although an annoyed one. "My dear, this is no place for your mystical theatrics. We are running a business operation, something I'm sure you don't understand. You are costing me time and, therefore, money. Other than you and your friends, everything is business as usual."

"Surely, Mr. Creely," Isabella interjected, "you might allow us to come in while you at least check? Put the families' minds at ease?"

"No wimmin' allowed! 'Specially no whores," the troll growled. Really, a most distasteful specimen of man. No matter what Stone Age he came from.

"Now, Bear, that is no way to speak to our guests," Victor Creely said. "These people are concerned for their loved ones, but they are all seriously misled. Rest assured, there is no trouble here."

Milena spoke, her eyes burning, her voice level. "You lie."

Stunned silence fell. He stared at her, his expression unreadable. Isabella could only imagine what plots spun inside that head of his. She admired the boldness of the Gypsy.

"My dear, I'm not sure what you think you'll gain from this fiction of yours, but you are seriously disrupting mining business." He looked at Cain. "Sheriff, I want her arrested and removed immediately. She trespassed earlier, and our patience for dealing with a whore's shenanigans is way past."

"My pleasure, Mr. Creely."

Milena scooted back when the sheriff grabbed for her. Victor's thin lips rose on one side. Isabella recognized his expression of triumph.

Thunder sounded in the distance.

Victor's look changed into one of confusion. Frantically, people looked around and up to the sky. A cloudless day. The rumble drew nearer and, suddenly, a tremor shook the ground beneath their feet, so small it was barely noticeable. Alarm shot through Victor's expression.

Screams and prayers erupted.

"Speak no more, Victor Creely," Milena proclaimed, and she raised her hand, palm up, to stop the mine president from saying a word. "The mountain itself reveals you for the liar you are."

Really, Isabella couldn't have planned the scenario better herself.

Jack slid helplessly along with chunks of rock. The image of the mountain laughing and tossing him around in its rocky guts raced through his head. He prepared himself, for the second time, for Death to take him. The slide stopped after a moment.

Stillness. Silence. He patted his chest. Yep, still alive. Death must be mad he played so hard to get.

Who was he fooling? He still lived due to pure, dumb luck. Not sure what happened, or where he was, Jack thought another chamber might have opened up. The last collapse sounded much worse than the first one. More violent, more devastating to the network within the mountain. His fears were coming true; the entire tunnel system was compromised. Collapsing.

He opened his mouth to call out to the others when a small gasp shot through the dark. A very small gasp. A very small and welcome gasp.

He reached out and the boy filled his arms, almost knocking him over. Jack held on for all he was worth. For his life. Tears fell, and he didn't try to stop them. Mouse.

"Jack?" Pete's voice swooped down from somewhere above.

"Jack? Pete? Glory be." Gentleman Bill's voice, and from close.

"Pete," Jack called, trying to keep his voice even and the tears out, but failing miserably. "I've got Mouse and Bill down here."

He held on to both of them. He didn't even mind the pain in his side so much. Two more men. Alive. They wrapped their arms around each other in the silence of the dark, holding tight.

"Where's Josef?" Jack asked.

"We don't know. It's just us two here," Bill said.

"Okay," Jack said, trying to keep disappointment from his voice. "Pete, Dig and Rolf are above us. Zeb is, too," Jack continued. "He didn't survive." There was only the sound of breathing when Jack added, "It's a wonder any of us did."

"I can't remember much at all past coming up to work this mornin'." Small tremors shook through Bill's voice. "I think Mouse broke his leg. I'm good."

"I know you are," Jack said, grasping Gentleman Bill's shoulder and holding onto Mouse, careful not to squeeze too hard. He didn't want to let go. In this empty dark, human touch was the only comfort they had.

Chapter 28

Milena watched the rumble galvanize workers on the other side of the gate into action. Men ran to the headframe; shouting rose. The line of officers held steady, their rifles pointing directly into the gathering of townsfolk at the gate. Any moment someone might panic and pull a trigger.

The sheriff had effectively fractured the mob, and the rumble blanketed everyone with fear and shock, snuffing the growing anger of the crowd. Confusion bubbled through the group. No one knew what to do. On the other side, the so-called business side, everything shifted. Orders sliced through the air and the steam engine snorted with renewed purpose.

Reverend McShane broke through the crowd's uncertainty. "Surely now you will let us in?" The minister spoke evenly and aimed his question at Victor. Milena admired the reverend's gentle determination and took a place by his side, offering silent support.

Victor's eyes darted, and she imagined his mind whirling to figure out how to turn the new situation to his advantage.

"Do your job, Reverend. You, too, Sheriff. Keep everyone calm," Victor answered. He gestured for Cain to come closer. "We need time to assess what happened, and you have two choices. Manpower remains to hold the gate or I use some of these men to start a rescue if need be. I'm not convinced we have an emergency."

Anger shot through Milena. "What more proof do you need?"

"Shut up," Cain said, turning to face her. He cocked his gun. "The last thing we need is a hysterical whore."

Victor rolled up his shirtsleeves and spoke graciously, but his eyes stayed cold as ice. "As you can see, we really don't have the time to entertain, ladies. We have our hands full." He addressed the line of armed men. "Gentlemen, keep the crowd back and allow us to do our job. All of you are to remain at the gate."

From the men bunched around the main shaft, a miner broke through, limping in their direction, dust falling with every step. He loped like a wounded animal and wore one of the miner's hats, the candle broken. His face reminded Milena of Jack's hound dog, and his sad eyes focused on nothing. Dirt continued to fall from him, piles and piles of dirt. Yet he left no trail. And Milena knew she did not look upon a man.

The dusty miner stopped a few feet from Victor to stare silently at the mine president. Only one reason a spirit miner wandered here.

"Men are dying," Milena said.

Victor's arm darted out like a snake and wrapped around her tightly. He pulled her close, his cold breath carrying the stench of a decayed soul. "I do wonder how you foresaw this problem. Why are you insistent there's been a cave-in? Perhaps Jack Buchanan planned some sabotage?"

"No one will believe any such thing," Milena said, although in Victor Creely's tangled web, it was difficult to foresee any event. With Victor, the future shifted constantly. Though calm on the outside, the King of the Jackals was more than greed, more than evil. This man was continuous turmoil. Chaos. Like a demon, he thrived on the emotional upset of others.

"I have not forgotten we have unfinished business to attend, my dear," he whispered in her ear. "And I can hardly wait for our next tryst." He released her, almost flinging her from him. She stumbled back, cold burning where he had touched her.

"Keep out of my way." He raised his voice and looked right at the minister. "Keep everyone out of our way. We have real work to do."

"Men go blind from cave dark," Pete said. "I'm not sure how long it takes. Couple of days. Maybe."

"In a couple of days we'll be dead," Gentleman Bill answered.

"No one else is dying," Jack said, much more positive than he felt. "We're all together. That counts for something. Hell, that counts for a lot."

They could still move, after a fashion. The men huddled together, like wounded animals in a storm. Except this storm battered them with dark. And quiet. Dead quiet.

Bill and Pete were in pretty good shape. Mouse clung to Jack, his hands fisted in Jack's coat material. The boy's leg was broken. Like Rolf's mind. Digger was hurt the worst of all of them. Jack held his friend's hand. It grew colder by the minute.

"You doing okay, Dig?"

"Never better." The miner's voice faded a little more each time he spoke. He didn't have much time. If Jack was honest with himself, none of them did.

The dark grew heavier, pressing in on them with each passing minute. Or was it hour? Or days? It didn't seem like time moved at all. In the dark—actually not so much dark as an absence of everything—something watching. Waited. A presence. A creature. Not the benevolent mountain spirit Milena spoke of, but something else. Something evil.

Jack shook his head. If he wasn't careful, he'd go as crazy as Rolf. His men were counting on him to hold on. He tried to keep Milena to the forefront of his mind, her awe of the mountain, her love of spirits and creatures otherworldly. The only feelings he managed were dread and the crush of hopelessness. He needed to do something before he jumped right out of his skin or, worse, gave up. "I'm going to work my way around the edge, see how big a space we're in."

"Nothin' 'cept more rock and dark," Bill answered. "'Best to stay put and wait."

"I want to see what our options are."

"We got two. Die slow or die quick," Bill mumbled.

"I'll take quick ifin I can figure out how," Pete answered.

"I got my penknife," Bill offered. "That'll be quick. And my preferred way when I can't take no more."

"I'll take it," Jack jumped in, keeping his voice light when he spoke his next words. "I've got the candle. Best thing is to keep the supplies together. My hand's out. Give it to me."

Silence answered.

"Bill, give it to me," Jack repeated.

"It's mine."

"Bill—" Jack started, but Pete cut him off.

"Give it to him, Bill. He's the boss."

"Much as I wish things was different, we're each on our own now."

"You listen to me, Bill. We got to hold to something, or we'll all curl in a ball like Rolf. I'm holdin' to Jack. He's done right by us so far, and I trust him."

"You was callin' him 'Creely's pup' not two weeks ago."

"And I was wrong," Pete said. "Turn over the damned knife."

"No."

From a distance, Rolf's voice joined in. "No . . . no . . . no . . ."

"Now see what you done?" Pete asked. "Rolf's riled up again."

"Bill," Jack said, "I agree with you. We do have two options." He steeled his voice. "Get out, or die trying. If I do die, I'll be working to free all of us. I don't plan to cower and wait for the mountain to take me. Now, are you with me?"

". . . no . . . no . . . no . . ." Rolf's chant continued.

"Or will you give up and let this damned mine crush everything you are?"

". . . no . . . no . . . no . . ."

"All right. Here," Bill said. Cool metal plopped into Jack's waiting, open palm and Gentleman Bill's hand covered his. They gripped, just for a moment, a handshake, a promise. The warmth of Bill's hand withdrew.

"You won't be sorry," Jack promised. He gently pulled Mouse from him. He grasped at first, then he must have understood what Jack wanted, and let go.

Brave little boy. He must be terrified; no sight and no sound. How did the kid keep from going crazy? Mouse obviously possessed the courage of all of them combined. Jack felt a glimmer of pride.

". . . no . . . no . . . no . . ."

"We are going to get out. Pete, while I'm exploring, you take stock of any supplies we might have. Bill, you crawl around and see if you can't find anything else, anything at all," Jack said, ordering them to action more for their sanity than any real purpose.

"Be careful. Don't go too far."

"Yeah, don't wander off and git rescued," Pete said.

"Jack, I'd come with you," Digger whispered, "but I'm feelin' a mite flat."

"Thanks anyway, Dig. You rest."

Trying to forget the lance embedded in his side and the bands squeezing his chest, Jack set out to find something in the dark. He didn't care what. He considered lighting his candle, but it was the only one. They might need a glimmer or two down the road. He made his way on his hands and knees, looking for . . . what? Anything. He bumped into a rock wall and rose up on his knees, hands scraping up. How far did it go? He decided to crawl along, following the edge, if that's what it was.

A fool's errand, sure. But what better sport for a fool to engage in?

Rock stung Jack's palm. Pain actually became a friend, reminding him he was alive.

A ribbon of air wafted across his face. He froze. Had he dreamed it?

Please. Come again. Please. God, please.

Nothing.

"Aw, cripes, it's just a rock," Gentleman Bill's voice echoed. "I'm starting to imagine things. I thought I had me the end of a pickaxe."

". . . no . . . no . . . no . . ."

"That'll happen, Bill. No need to git upset. It's only a mistake," Pete said.

". . . no . . . no . . . no . . ."

Dejected, Jack inched along the base of the wall. There must be a way out of this hell. They couldn't die. Not Pete, Gentleman Bill. Such good men.

Please, God, save Digger. At least save Mouse. He's just a kid, God. Just a little boy.

Rolf's litany stopped. A wet thud sounded. Then a moan.

"Pete?" Jack asked.

"Wasn't me," Pete's voice answered.

Another wet thud. Like the sound of an animal carcass smacking against a wall.

"Everyone say your name," Jack ordered over the sinking feeling in his stomach.

"Digger, ornery as ever." Despite the cheerful words, Digger spoke barely above a whisper.

"Pete."

"Most folks call me Gentleman Bill." Forced geniality in Bill's words struggled against the despair in his voice. "And a little fella known as Mouse is with me."

Another thud. This time it didn't sound so much like a carcass. It sounded like a head.

"Rolf?" Jack asked.

Another thud.

"Oh, God. Leave him be," Pete said, his voice breaking. "Jesus, just leave him be."

Thud. This time, wetter. Like something finally broke.

Jack's stomach rolled. "Rolf," he said, crawling toward the sound. Another thud reverberated through the dark. "Rolf?"

Silence. Jack inched closer. "Rolf, I'm coming to you. Take my hand, buddy. Take my—"

A piston slammed into him. A sickening thud ripped through the dark, but this time it tore through him.

Victor approached the gate. The apparition continued to follow him, a tear rolling down the spirit's dusty cheek, leaving a trail. The tear, glowing with an inner light like a smooth gemstone, dropped from his face, falling into nothing.

"We've confirmed an accident," Victor said. "Cave-in. We need to keep the families back and away. This is no place for hysterics."

"Men trapped?" Cain asked.

Victor nodded. "The west side of Tunnel Fifteen collapsed; the whole thing's gone, along with the ones above and below. It's bad, Sheriff. Quite extensive. I doubt anyone is alive down there." Victor looked straight at Milena, a gleam of triumph flitting across his expression. "Jack Buchanan was overseeing a blast that must have gone wrong. I had no idea he'd prove so inept. I never should have promoted him so quickly, but he seemed sure of himself."

Revulsion swirled through Milena. And anger. She knew in her soul Victor was responsible for all of this. He remained smug and deadly as a viper. One who squeezed the mountain until it gave in.

"Jack Buchanan is alive," she said.

"Certainly it's what you want to believe. Milena. It's not possible anyone from his team survived. From what we can tell, they were at the center of the collapse. We can't even lower the platform deep enough to get anywhere near where his team worked. The shaft is partially destroyed."

"You will not even try," she said, a statement instead of a question.

"Milena, trust me. If anyone wants to believe Jack is alive, it's me. The boy was like a son to me. We'll reach them at some point. But hold no hope, my dear."

Another tear-gem slid down the ghost-miner's face.

"We're pulling Rory's men out now," Victor continued, speaking directly to Cain. "We were able to get to them right away. We've got some injuries, bad ones."

"Any dead?" Cain asked.

"One man so far." Victor raised his voice. "Doctor? We need you to come in and set up."

"I'll gather my supplies," Ambrose answered.

Another miner wandered toward them, this one missing his right shoulder and arm, his head partially collapsed.

"I'll take care of keeping things under control," Cain said. "You concentrate on the rescue, Mr. Creely."

"Thank you, Sheriff," Victor said, and the second spirit-miner stopped to stand with the first. They both stared at the mine president. "Madame Shabanov, prepare yourself. If we do find any of Jack's team, what we will bring up are bodies."

Frustration lumped in her chest. "How can you be sure? What do you know we do not?"

Noise from the gathering crowd and the rescue effort broke the silence that fell between Victor and Milena.

"Sheriff," Victor said, turning from her, "the men really are quite superstitious over women on mining territory. Be sure to keep all the ladies off the property." He shoved Milena into Cain. "Starting with this one."

Cain's body was hard as a tree, and he grabbed Milena and pulled her close. She tried to wriggle away, but he gripped her tightly.

"Let me go," she said, "or you will lose that arm."

The sheriff laughed. "You sure are a hellcat, aren't you?" he murmured into her ear. "Much as I'd like to experience you firsthand, I don't got the time right now." He drew a line in the dirt with his toe, and pushed her to the other side of it. "Now this here's the line. You stay on that side."

Milena spun to face him.

"What's happened?" a woman called out from behind.

"Don't worry, we got everything under control," Cain lied. Behind him, Victor headed for the mine shaft, the two spirit miners trailing behind him.

"A cave-in is confirmed," Milena said. "Men are dead. Men are trapped."

Cain glared at her as the crowd grew agitated. A garbled name shrieked through the air. Cain drew his gun, and behind him the officers stood ready.

"Everybody calm down. Nobody crosses past the gate. We'll let you know what we can."

"Do you plan to shoot us, Sheriff?" Milena asked.

"You need to shut your mouth," the sheriff answered, pointing his gun at Milena's forehead. "Ifin I have to make an example, I will."

"Really, Sheriff, is that necessary?" Isabella's cool voice rose above the panic of the crowd as she pushed her way through. "These people are families, loved ones. They only want to help."

"You can all help by staying back. There is a rescue operation underway." He did not lower his gun, but kept it pointed at the center of Milena's forehead. His eyes dared her to say another word.

She did not flinch. "Why do you not welcome all the help available?" Milena asked. "We are far from useless." Many voices rose in agreement.

"I told you to shut your mouth." He cocked the gun.

Isabella pulled her back. "For heaven's sake, Milena, the last thing we need is you with a hole through your head."

"Jack is alive," Milena said, a touch of desperation in her voice. "I am certain."

"If he's alive, I bet others are, too," a female voice called out.

"I'm sure Mr. Creely is doing everything possible to rescue everyone," Cain said.

"We have seen proof. He is not," Milena answered.

Cain fired, the gun's explosion followed by screams.

Chapter 29

The sheriff's expression twisted with satisfaction, his gun aimed into the sky. He fired again. More screams and people ran away from the gathering near the gate. Milena covered her ears with her hands. Cain fired yet again.

Ambrose pushed to the front of the churning crowd. "Good Lord, man, are you insane?"

"Gotta do somethin' to shut that whore's flappin' mouth." He nodded to Milena. "Next time I'm aimin' right at that empty head of yours when I pull the trigger."

"Enough!" George Barger waved his rifle. "We have injured coming up! Doctor, you may come in and set up near the head-frame." He spoke like he bestowed a great gift. "We must keep order, especially in this crisis situation. Please, Doctor, come forward. We'll stand aside and let you through."

"And my supply wagon?"

Barger nodded. "Of course."

Ambrose hooked his arm through Isabella's and Milena's. "Ladies. Come with me."

"Hold up," Barger said. "I believe we've made it abundantly clear. No women are allowed on mining property."

"Ah! Easy enough difficulty to overcome." The doctor grinned. "Don't think of these ladies as women. They're nurses."

The comment urged several hoots and whistles from the people nearest them.

"They're whores!" George Barger didn't bother to hide his disdain. Quite different from the sniveling man whose flattering words fell from his thick lips as he groveled for female attention at the Boarding House.

The doctor drew himself up to his full height. "I repeat. These ladies are my nurses. All of them." The other Boarding House women pushed through the crowd to gather around Ambrose. "I need every one. I don't have time to argue the finer points of nursing versus whoring with you. Injured men await. Ladies, please do forgive Mr. Barger his unseemly indiscretion. I am sure, in retrospect, he will be appalled by his behavior." The doctor lowered his voice. "Will you order the men to stand aside or not?"

Barger drew his lips into a pout and scurried away. At first, Milena thought he left to cry, but he headed straight for his master. The doctor let out a prolonged, theatrical sigh. Despite the intensity of the moment, Milena allowed herself a vague smile. She enjoyed seeing the doctor in his shining armor once again.

Creely stood apart, observing the rescue operation from several yards away. Around the Jackal, the group of spirit miners grew. Now five watched his every move. Five dead. She wondered if Victor felt them watching. Did he sense anything at all, perhaps a chill of unease? His solid stance indicated complete assurance. Milena marveled at his ability to keep the demon on the inside, no crack in his façade of a confident, intelligent man made of strength and passion.

"I hope you don't mind my hiring all of you." The doctor

brought Milena's attention back to the task at hand. "I will need all of your help."

"Absolutely, we are at your service, Ambrose," Isabella answered.

"Why, Dr. Kline, we'll do anything y'all desire," Suzanne chimed in. Regret bolted through the doctor's eyes, but he reclaimed his mood. Milena knew he thought of the one woman missing, the one he'd do anything to have by his side.

"We will do all we can." Milena returned to watching the King of the Jackals. As Victor spoke with George Barger, his attention shifted to her. The predator locked eyes with his prey. His glare bored into her. She refused to drop her gaze. She would not cower before the man. At least, not on the outside, she thought as a warning shivered down her spine.

He did this. This cave-in. Somehow. This entire disaster, delivering death to innocents, came courtesy of Victor Creely.

George Barger continued to speak vehemently, his fists clenching and unclenching. The mine president held up his hand, presumably to stop George's deluge of words, then he nodded. George trotted back to the crowd, his face smug with satisfaction.

"As stated previously, Doctor, only you are allowed through."

"In that case, I will set up out here," he replied cheerfully. "And you may bring the injured to me. Come, ladies." He turned his back on George Barger.

"That's not what Mr. Creely wants."

The doctor smiled over his shoulder. "Well, Mr. Creely can't always get everything he wants, can he?" Ambrose stalked away.

"Are you sure this is wise, Doctor?" Milena asked hurrying after him.

"I have no desire to be under the orders of Victor Creely. Next he'll tell me who to treat, decide to whom I turn my attention." Ambrose's voice darkened. "Which man deserves to live and which does not. I'll be damned if he controls any such thing. Not as long as I'm the doctor in this town." He clapped his hands together. "All right, ladies! To work! We have a hospital to set up."

Jack didn't know if he was awake or not. Someone called his name, over and over, in whispers. Different voices. Why couldn't he wake up? Why was he so cold, but his belly on fire? And damn it, nausea again.

"Jack?"

That's right. The mine. Buried in the mine. A hand touched him.

"Pete?" he asked.

"Jesus, Jack, we thought you was dead."

"Nearly. I think Rolf kicked me."

Another thump came from the dark. This time, Jack heard bone crunch. He gagged. The soft, moist sound of a head against rock broke the silence.

Jack heard Gentleman Bill crying, a soft shush of air and tears.

Thud.

"Rolfie." Just a whisper from Digger.

Thud.

A sob erupted. Jack thought that maybe it came from Pete. Or maybe him.

Thud.

The dark grew heavier, a smothering shroud. Jack couldn't move. He didn't want to.

Thud.

Something slid down his face, and he didn't bother to swipe it away. No one could see him. Besides, they'd earned their place, these tears in the cavern.

They'd earned their place.

The sun provided a glorious setting, intense bloodred slashing the sky. A backdrop to misery. Isabella watched while men lifted one more body from the shaft and carried it to the tarp on the other side of the road. The simple tarp made a poor morgue, but it was the only option available outside the gate. Apparently there was some idiotic superstition regarding dead bodies on mining property, too.

A woman stumbled across the road to crumple beside the new body. Reverend McShane knelt beside her, speaking in low tones of comfort. The man never ceased to melt Isabella's heart. She felt a tear and decided she must be exhausted, at the least; she grew way too sentimental around all this misery and suffering.

Suzanne came near, lighting the lanterns around the makeshift tent the doctor kept referring to as a hospital. Hospital indeed. The doctor was obviously an optimist. And a bit blind, as well.

Isabella returned her attention to the reverend until he finished with the woman, neighbors and others crowding around in support. Taryn visited each person in the morgue, living or dead. He prayed. He comforted. He caused Isabella's heart to race and break, all at once.

Finally, he headed back to the hospital. He constantly moved from one to the other in his flock, never resting, never taking even the briefest moment for himself. Isabella couldn't imagine. He caught her gaze and rewarded her with his gentle smile.

"I don't think this is the safest place for you," Taryn said.

"How kind of you to care, Reverend," she answered, clinging to the small bit of pleasure in this awful situation. The minister thought of her safety. Isabella agreed with his sentiments. She didn't enjoy commoners surrounding her. Many times when she looked up, one face or another glared at her, expressions filled with anger or distrust. Occasionally, a glance of pure hatred.

Then again, many spoke with her, welcomed her like she belonged among them. Some were even kind. Still, her options were limited, and she kept to the edge of the tent.

"Ben looks better," Taryn observed with hope.

Six miners lay on cots, the doctor scurrying from one to the other, flinging orders to the ladies. Two of the miners didn't look as if they'd live to see the next hour. Ben, the young man Taryn had just commented on, leaned over and vomited dark liquid. Isabella thought it looked quite a bit like blood. She turned away, her own nausea rising. She didn't have the constitution for this. Not surprisingly, the Gypsy did. Milena bustled from cot to cot, caring for the filthy men, performing the most distasteful tasks without hesitation.

For a brief flash, Isabella felt a bit of guilt that she didn't do more to help. Thankfully, the feeling disappeared as fast as it came. Such common work did not suit her at all. She'd done her job. They were all here, the rescue taking place, thanks to her and her magnificent powers of persuasion.

Really, she'd performed a miraculous task.

Taryn nodded to the latest casualty across the road. "It's been a while since they found anyone. That man is Donny O'Toole. The first man they've found from Quinn's team. They are that much closer to Jack."

Milena headed in their direction, her black eyes locked on the preacher. "Reverend McShane." She inclined her head slightly.

"Milena," he answered and clasped her outstretched hand. "I'm pleased to finally officially meet you, though sorry about the circumstances. I've been meaning to speak with you, but so much is happening."

"No apology is necessary, Minister."

"Jack has told me much about you."

"And he's spoken of you, too. I am privileged to meet a man of God." The Gypsy looked like she measured her words carefully, then forged ahead. "Minister, I cannot bother the doctor, but I need help."

"Please. What can I do?"

"The rescuers do not search in the right place."

"They are digging as close as they can to the collapse," Isabella said, deciding she'd remained silent long enough.

"No, they are not," Milena said, shaking her head. "Miles of tunnel web throughout the mountain. Jack Buchanan and his men are trapped deep within."

"Rory and Quinn's groups were close to the entrance when the explosion occurred," Taryn said, realization creeping into his voice. "Jack's team is deeper? How do you know this?"

"I know. Victor Creely admits it. If the rescuers continue this way," Milena said, "it will be weeks before they reach Jack and the others with him. If at all." She looked at Taryn with a helpless female expression. A familiar one Isabella used often herself. "I can feel his spirit, Reverend," the Gypsy said. "He is alive."

"I pray it is so," Taryn replied, his voice quivering with the intensity of hope. *How very interesting. The Gypsy was learning to use manipulation.*

"I hate to point out bad news," Isabella said. "If you can feel his spirit, doesn't it mean Jack is dead?"

Taryn's eyes snapped to her with shock.

"He is alive!" Milena said vehemently. "With others. And I can find them."

Taryn smiled sadly. "Your intuition astounded Jack. He told me you knew things that seemed impossible to know."

"Minister, I know of a back entrance to the mountain. Caverns and caves. Jack found me there, and he'd come from the mine tunnels. The way to help these men is not by blasting through more of the mountain, but by searching."

Isabella felt a tether of silent understanding reach from Milena to the minister. Most disagreeable, actually.

"Then we must find a way," Taryn said.

A knot twisted inside Isabella. Jealousy. She didn't recall ever experiencing such a feeling before. She found she didn't really care for it.

"There are scores of men," Milena continued, "and all in the space where only a few can work. Many stand by and watch." Milena turned her huge, dark, needful eyes to Taryn. Isabella had to admit, a neat trick. "Victor Creely will never listen to me. Will you suggest another search to him? One through the caverns on the other side of the mountain?"

"Absolutely."

"Approach the King of the Jackals with care, Minister," Milena warned.

Without another word, Taryn headed for the mine president. An eager puppy going to call out the coyote. Isabella took off after him, not sure why. She'd be stopped once she reached the gate. Sure enough, the wall of armed imbeciles led by George Barger barred her.

"Welcome, Reverend," Barger announced with a flourish. "You may come through." He looked pointedly at Isabella. "You may not."

Damned if she'd ever let the little turd near one of her ladies again. It took everything in her not to scream. Unable to do anything else, she watched Taryn continue on, heading for the snarl of men.

And Victor Creely.

Lanterns dotted the mountain, some moving pools of light, some stationary. Milena watched miners disappear and reappear in and out of splashes of illumination. The entire landscape had turned eerie with the fall of dark. The stamping mill had stopped production, the huge last thrum echoing to silence. The sound had been a part of Jasper, and the peace the mountains offered felt strange.

The night wore on, the atmosphere of the Otherworld cloaking Jasper Mountain. Sometimes voices sounded close, yet men way beyond the gate spoke. Whispers fluttered, and apparitions wandered. Death walked, inside and out. Milena shivered.

The minister returned to the pool of light surrounding the hospital tent, his face as grim as the news he carried. "Mr. Creely insists the search is going exactly as planned," he said to Milena, guilt clinging to his expression. "I tried my best to convince him of your idea. But he reports they are having great success, and ah . . ." He searched as though the words might be hanging in the air for him to pluck.

"Please, tell me," Milena encouraged. "I realize they are not your sentiments."

"He says he has more important things to do than reassure hysterical women on the fate of their men. He's too busy making life-and-death decisions."

"This is true," Milena answered. "I fear more for the side of death. Thank you, Minister, for trying."

"I'm sorry to disappoint you."

"You are a man who listens and respects. Disappointment does not dwell anywhere near you, Minister."

She inclined her head and left the tent, the privacy of night wrapping around her. She must think. Pray for a miracle. How could she convince men to come with her to the other side of the mountain?

Voices dropped into murmurs when she moved farther from activity. Even the doctor's barked orders faded into distance.

"*Shuv'hani*, help me. Please."

Nothing.

What was she to do? Look herself? What could one woman do inside a mountain? She alone would not be enough. Jack needed these men, their tools, and know-how.

Milena prayed for an answer as people came up the road continually, some without an emotional stake but simply curious. Some left to be sure children had care, some brought food, and others left to retrieve blankets. Supplies for a siege. The lanterns they held twisted their faces into ghoulish expressions by casting moving angles of light.

Milena kept watch and prayed through the night. In the dark of predawn, a short, grizzled man came up the road and changed course, headed for her, and swiped his hat off his head. "'Scuse me, ma'am. You been up here awhile?"

Milena nodded. "Since the start."

"What's the word? Have they found Jack Buchanan's team yet?"

Her heart gave a jump at the mention of Jack's name. A sign. Did this man come here to help her? Was he a friend of Jack's?

"No. They have not. He has been trapped for almost twenty-four hours, and they will not do what is needed to find him."

The man drew back, curiosity shifting his face. "What do you mean?"

"There is a way in, through the other side of the mountain. A network of caverns exists, and somewhere they connect to the mine. I do not know precisely where, but this is the way to Jack and his team. No one will listen. I am, after all, only a woman."

"Well, ma'am, if there's one thing my mama taught me, is to always listen when a woman speaks." He held out his hand. "I'm Harley Quade."

She took his hand, hoping he was as he appeared, an honest and decent man. "I am Milena Shabanov."

"Ah, I thought so. The Gypsy. Well, little lady, I happen to be the boss of the night crew. I been rounding up every able-bodied man to hustle up here, and I can see there's plenty of us at the headframe." He pulled out a handkerchief and turned away to cough into it. "Pardon me. I'd enjoy a bit of adventure, and I'll admit I'm intrigued to see these caverns."

"You believe me? You will search?"

"Ma'am, before I left my home and job in Chicago, I sought the council of a fortune-teller. A Gypsy, purty as you, in fact."

Heat rushed into Milena's cheeks, and she was grateful for the dark.

"She told me not to come; called my quest for gold a fool's dream. Being headstrong and young, I ignored her advice. Been stuck in Jasper penniless ever since."

Relief tumbled through her. "I do not have words enough to thank you."

"No need, ma'am." He tucked her arm through his and led her toward the hospital tent. "Getting Jack and his men out will be thanks enough, don't you think? Then again, the look on Creely's face when we bring him up will be a pure pleasure."

When they got to the hospital tent, Harley continued up to the mine. She watched the light of his lantern until he stopped to speak with a few miners. Finally, some hope.

One of the miners in his group turned to her. He broke from the crowd in the pool of light and walked toward her, fading into the dark. She recognized the familiar face. Rolf.

Startled, Milena took a few steps back. Panic surged through her as she watched the flame of his hat candle come closer. He reappeared on the edge of the light at the hospital tent and stopped, standing so still she did not even see him breathe.

He did not breathe.

"Oh, Rolf."

He did not answer. Spirits never did. He stared, expressionless.

She wanted to hate him, this man who'd most likely killed Baba. A brute who tried to take her and, when she escaped, followed her, threatened her. But he was completely alone. And in death even more so.

"Let go of me, of Jasper. What you seek is not here. Travel where you must. Go, Rolf, follow the light that pulls you."

He observed her for a moment. Then he turned away, disappearing into the dark. He reappeared at the edge of the crowd, passed through them, and kept walking to join the gathering around Victor. Then she realized. He wore a hardboil, the candle burning a cold, colorless flame. Dirt covered him; fell from him in puffs.

Rolf's corporeal body, devoid of spirit, was down in the mine, most likely with Jack Buchanan. They had worked together. And now Rolf was dead. Time slipped away from them all, and Victor moved slowly enough to insure none of Jack's group had a chance to survive.

On the surface of this rescue, men worked diligently and Victor led with passion, making decisions. She knew his actions reflected an agenda that was his and his alone.

Victor's spirit chorus grew.

Jack lay beside Digger, close, hoping some of his body heat would warm his friend. At least, make Digger's passing a little easier. Mouse curled on Jack's other side. Although Jack was sure he'd felt a small bit of air cross his face, he didn't find anything close to a way out. There was no way out and nothing left for any of them to do but die.

Death finally silenced Rolf. And hopelessness, the rest of them. How long had they been buried? No way of telling. Why couldn't he get them out? Digger, Mouse, Pete, Gentleman Bill. He should have done more to stop the mining mogul and his greed. There was no justice in this town. Never justice for men like Victor. Jack's friends had counted on him, and he'd let them all down. And Buck, back home. The boys. Jo.

All of them had made the mistake of trusting him. He'd failed.

"Jack?" A whisper.

"Yeah, Dig."

"Remember that night? When we was lookin' for Laney, and Rolf made a joke?" Digger's voice came out so weak, Jack strained to hear him.

"I do remember, Dig."

"I told you then you was my good friend. You are, Jack. Always. I wish I coulda been a better one for you."

Jack recognized the ripe tone of a man speaking his last words.

"You've been the best friend a man could have, Dig. You stood up for me when no one else did."

"I wish I coulda been better for Bethie, too. I hurt her bad. God, I loved her so much. Can you tell her for me?"

"Sure, Dig."

Beth? Victor's mistress? Jack felt way too weary to register much shock. One thing was certain. Creely had managed to rid himself of all his problems with one explosion. Bastard.

"Tell her I'm sorry I lost all our money. All our dreams." Digger's voice took on a weak edge of panic. "Jack, I can't feel nothin'."

He moved as close as possible and placed his hand on Digger's chest. He barely felt a rise and fall, Digger's breathing had diminished so much. "I'm right here, buddy. You're gonna be fine. They're looking for us right now, Beth and Milena and Harley and everyone. They won't let us die."

"You're . . . awful . . . liar." Digger managed to grasp Jack's hand, his touch featherlight.

"I know." Jack held his friend's hand gently.

"Tell . . . Bethie."

"I will. She knows, Dig. She knows."

"I just . . . I just . . ."

Jack's face warmed with tears. He squeezed them back, but they sprung out anyway. He spoke, trying to keep the tremble from his voice. "It's okay, Dig. Just go to sleep. It's all gonna be all right."

Digger's hand loosened. The slight rise and fall of his chest stopped. So easy. So peaceful. So gentle.

Jack went ahead and let out his sob. Mouse curled closer.

Chapter 30

Morning glow crept up behind the headframe, casting a long shadow over the mine proper and the camp at the gate. As Milena returned, she approached the hospital tent. Half a day to the other side, half a day back. Every step Milena took was an effort. Exhaustion set in and her feet dragged as if encased in rock, but she fought to keep going. She could not afford the luxury of collapse.

The hospital tent sat amidst smaller ones, as well as chairs, wagons, bedrolls, horses, dogs, and people sprawled around the temporary housing. The small, densely populated camp had hunkered down, this side of the armed and guarded gate.

Under the hospital awning, the doctor snored, slumped upright in a chair. He stirred when she came near, opened his eyes, and bolted to his feet. "Milena! What are you doing back here?" He rushed to her, taking her hands. "Oh, dear God, don't tell me—"

She shook her head. "No, no. I left the group to their work." Her connection with Jack grew steadily weaker, like a candle burned down to almost nothing, the flame sputtering as it refused to give up its hold on life.

"You left the search party? Why?"

"Why else? The blind superstition of men." She'd guided Harley and his group to the entrance to the caverns, but some refused to enter with a woman along. Many didn't like her anywhere near, saying she cursed their search. Harley convinced her she'd become a distraction and would slow the rescue.

"Blind superstition? From Harley? I don't understand."

She shrugged. "The miners refused to venture in the cave while I was there. Harley gave me his promise he'd find Jack."

"This is an outrage! Come along, we'll—"

"No, Doctor. They will find him. My presence was wasting time better spent searching." Every minute was more precious than the purest nugget of gold, and Jack couldn't afford for them to squander even one. She finally gave responsibility over to Harley and his band of rough, ignorant, yet earnest, well-meaning men. For Jack. The most difficult thing she'd ever done.

The doctor looked at her closely and squeezed her hand. "Come along. I'm relieved you've returned. You're needed."

She knew this was the place for her, tending Jack's friends, and she threw herself into helping the doctor with the injured. Hours passed, and she wondered if she'd made the right decision. Should she have waited at the entrance of the cave, helpless, wringing her hands?

No, she was right to return. Wasn't she? At least at the hospital she could make a difference. Fear constantly blocked her now; she didn't trust her feelings. Panic squirmed in her, and she struggled to keep tears from bursting through the outwardly calm demeanor she kept tightly in place. She wanted to scream, cry, rip the sanctimonious Victor Creely and his pack of jackals to shreds. The gate remained closed, the officers and their rifles taking shifts to keep out . . . whom? Women tending the injured.

Frustration exhausted Milena. Victor and the mountain

had worn them all down, and with each passing moment hope slipped away.

Joe Anderson, an injured miner barely out of his teens, coughed and wheezed. Milena and the doctor rushed to his bedside, Victor and his henchmen forgotten. Joe gripped her hand but only managed a featherlight touch.

Ambrose sat, draped his arm around her, and his hand joined hers and Joe's. They sat together, listening to his breathing become shallow. Joe suddenly reared up. Panic bolted through his expression. He settled back, his eyes staring, lifeless. His hand grew slack in hers.

"His chest was crushed. He didn't have a chance." When the doctor spoke, his voice was as lifeless as the young man.

Milena thought about summoning a curse, calling the darkest and purest demons from hell to destroy the King of the Jackals. She stood and walked away as the doctor called for men to carry Joe to the tarp.

She fought to keep rage from taking over. Victor Creely wasn't worth giving over her soul to the dark. At least not yet. Besides, these miners needed her. Jack needed her. She would not let any of them down.

"God, no."

Milena whirled around at the doctor's voice. He leaned over the bed next to Joe's and pulled a sheet over Rory's head. The miner's red hair peeked out, refusing the defeat of death.

Ambrose shook his head. "Damn. I thought he'd make it." He raised his voice. "Another one here!" He looked at Milena, immense pain creasing his face. "He probably died while I slept."

Isabella came up behind him, putting a hand on his shoulder. "Ambrose, you are doing everything you can."

"I don't need to hear meaningless platitudes."

"Don't be ridiculous. Of course you do."

Some of the anguish drained out of the doctor's face. "Well, then," he said softly.

Thank heaven for the proprietress. Her wry and somehow humorous outlook never faltered, and they all clung to her, a buoyant plank of wood in a sea of endless sorrow. Truly, Milena wanted nothing more than to fall in Isabella's arms and lean on her strength.

Well, no, something she wished more than that. Jack.

Suddenly Milena stiffened when she realized the last thread of Jack had slipped away. She'd lost their connection; she didn't know when. Desperate, she whirled around, trying to recapture the feel of him. Nothing. Behind them, the mountain stood unchanging, holding its secrets close.

Voices rose in excitement and broke through her panic.

"Lord, have mercy on all our souls, they're comin'!"

A wagon clacked around the bend, Harley Quade driving the mules. The rescue party trudged beside, exhausted, filthy. A sick feeling lurched through Milena. A funeral procession. And only one wagon? There had been two. Harley's face sagged heavily with burden. Something heaped up in the back, covered with blankets.

The dead.

Not even the gently bright colors of day lightened the somber scene. Milena did not think, but drifted toward Harley and his charge, her feet somehow knowing what to do.

No life came their way. Nothing but death, thick and heavy. A hush fell over the camp at the sight of men lying prone in the back of the wagon, stacked like cords of wood. The smell of blood thickened. She did not know if the scent came from behind or ahead. The stench of death wafted everywhere. She tried to keep panic down as she felt a kinship with the women who had collapsed and screamed, ranting when their men were pulled to the surface, lifeless.

The second wagon rounded the corner. Milena steeled herself. Whatever came, she would face it. She had no choice. Isabella stood beside her on one side, and Taryn on the other. Milena held on to them both.

"They found them." No sarcasm threaded through the proprietress's voice, and also no lift, none of her usual sparkle or fire. The mine took all. From everyone. Even the indomitable proprietress.

The wagon lumbered closer and Isabella put her arm around Milena, stopping her from bolting forward. She wanted to run, dig through the blankets, and find him. Instead, she followed the proprietress's lead, grateful to have help. Taryn rushed forward as the wagon slowed. Two men began to unload, and the minister helped lift a body down. Milena recognized him. The sad, long-faced spirit-miner with gossamer tears whose spirit first followed Victor.

They lifted another. Men carried their friends in the direction of the tarp morgue. People gathered silently to watch, accepting death with heavy silence.

The men unloaded Rolf. Milena staggered back, and the proprietress tightened her grip. It took four miners to lift the big man. Blood and gray matter spattered down Rolf's misshapen head and neck. One of the ladies, Aimee, dropped to her knees beside the road, her retching fading into background noise. No one took note or rushed to her aid. Throwing up was nothing unusual anymore.

Then they unloaded a man, his lower half crushed. More turned away, sick.

"Bring a blanket. We need to cover him. For God's sake, cover him." Taryn's voice broke and tears ran down his cheeks.

Then Milena saw blond hair and the crooked nose of Digger before Taryn wrapped him gently and carried him over to the tarp.

She wasn't aware she'd sunk to her knees. Isabella pulled on her arm. "Milena, to your feet. This is no time to waver." The proprietress lifted, helping her to stand again. The landscape grew bright, then faded, again bright, and dark. Then bright.

"Oh, for heaven's sake, bend over and let blood flow back into your head. I never took you for a swooning lady." Despite her commands, kindness ran through Isabella's voice and her arms held Milena, firm but gentle.

"I am fine, Proprietress." Her voice broke.

"Hold to me, Milena. We will get through this."

The second wagon slowed to a stop behind the first. One of the bodies sat up and coughed. Men helped him down. The body stumbled, weak. He squinted as if he could barely stand the light.

Milena didn't understand, then began to realize, slowly, like her mind churned through mud. Not a body. Not dead. One of the miners. Alive. A man from Jack's team.

Another man rose from the back of the wagon, and a roar rushed through Milena's ears.

"Pete!" A woman's cry of joy as she ran past, then the two were in each other's arms.

Hope rose, fragile, panic-laden bubbles inside Milena. One word tumbled through her mind, again and again. *Please.* She took a step forward. *Please . . . please . . . please.*

The doctor lifted Mouse off the wagon, holding the boy gently in his arms. Mouse's arms circled the doctor's neck and Ambrose hugged the child close.

"Please." Milena pushed Isabella's arms from her and ran. "God, please, please!"

Ambrose handed Mouse to the man standing behind him and

climbed into the wagon. He helped another man sit up.

Jack gasped and flinched, paused. Pale as moonlight, he nodded and the doctor and Taryn helped him down, their eyes glistening. Jack's feet touched the ground. He stood, bent and unsteady, but he stood.

The bubbles of hope burst into joy and a cry flew out, Milena realized, from her. She did not attempt to stop her tears.

He searched the crowd and found her. His eyes pooled with everything, from the sorrow of death to the hope of life. Pain unbearable, joy unbound. And loss beyond imagining.

He scooped her into his embrace. She held to him with all the strength in her, physical and of the spirit. She would never let him go again. He clung to her and trembled, shaking her to the core. Or did she shake, too? She held him tighter.

"You are safe. You are safe," she whispered, needing to say the words, making sure he was real, and there, and whole. He was. "Jack, I love you," she whispered.

He pulled her away from him and looked at her as if he, too, needed proof she was real. She swiped tears from his filthy, wonderful, handsome face.

A thin smile surfaced, and he ran his hands up and down her arms. "Just when I thought I'd never see anything more beautiful than the sun and fresh air." His voice scraped, raw, just above a whisper. "And here you are, telling me . . ." He cocked his head to one side. "What did you say again? I don't think I quite heard. Rock dust in my ears."

"I love you, Jack Buchanan. And I will tell you this whenever you like."

He hugged her to him. "Then one more time. Please."

Strange, this sensation, Isabella thought. Doing good. Helping. Especially miners, even the few with wives. Their women weren't really bad, once they stopped scowling at her and her ladies. All her work, attention, and there was no benefit, not really. How odd. The last few days must have changed her. She wasn't sure if it was for the better.

Thankfully, Isabella didn't have to do much of the actual work. She left that to the doctor and the others. The doctor assigned her the job of keeping the men's spirits up. Such a simple thing, to charm these men. Much easier than the surly officers who insisted the world owed them everything. The miners took a small kindness and cherished it, along with the person who gave it. Most amazing of all, not one untoward suggestion ruined her benevolent mood. She'd always assumed manual laborers were crude and mean, yet found the opposite to be true.

How utterly incredible. She'd been wrong.

"You sure you ain't an angel?" a miner, Gentleman Bill, croaked out as she brought him a glass of water. His windpipes were raw; he could barely speak. Although in a bed in the clinic, bandaged from injuries, weak from his ordeal, he had insisted on wearing a cravat. Rather endearing, actually.

"I've been told I'm anything but," she replied, handing the water to him.

"I'll shoot the mouth off anyone who dares to show you disrespect. Ever. You just let me know, ma'am. I'll take care of it." He sipped and swallowed like it was liquid fire. These men hurt, inside and out. They reminded her of children who had had something dear taken from them but couldn't figure out why. Yes, pain, but more, disbelief. The men who'd survived seemed so innocent, yet at the same time something in their eyes revealed they'd seen evil and horror beyond imagining.

Their faces sent shivers down Isabella's spine at first, but she became used to their haunted expressions. Some, like Gentleman Bill, tried to bury the entire episode deep. He refused to speak of the experience, keeping such awfulness away from decent folks, he claimed. He made it abundantly clear he considered Isabella a decent woman. Bless him.

Outside the clinic, rain threatened as the air grew dark and heavy. At least the downpour held off until they'd rescued those still living, but rain would make a mess of the funeral services. She'd heard volunteers were digging the graves right now, trying to beat the gathering storm. Strange how Jasper Mountain erased society's lines and leveled them all into people needing and helping each other. The mountain's price for such a lesson was high.

Fourteen dead. Ten alive. They'd turned the newspaper office into a temporary morgue, where the victims of the collapse waited for their burial, and also one woman who perished in a fire. When Isabella promised Cassandra a fine funeral, she never imagined the event would turn huge and involve so many.

The Boarding House ladies worked tirelessly, focusing on the effort of care, gentle and kind. There was no monetary compensation for it. Not even for Isabella. Just the undying gratitude of a polite, kind man named Gentleman Bill. She rewarded him with a smile and he sank back into his pillows, the light in his eyes brighter, a little of what he'd suffered fading away.

Isabella found, for the moment, such payment was enough. Of course, she would never let on. No need to allow anyone to see she'd entered the ranks of mundane goodness.

Chapter 31

Mouse was safe. Jack clung to that.

He sat in his rocking chair by the fire Milena built for them. Mouse slept in his bed, his leg healing quite nicely, according to Ambrose. His crutch leaned against the wall. The boy needed rest, easy enough for Jack to provide. He hadn't forgotten his promise, and Mouse was in his care now, for him to protect. Forever. Duke slept, curled around Jack's feet. All in all, a warm family scene.

Except for the anger, the burn in his chest, each death a fist slamming into him. Tom. Stoop. Cassandra. Rolf. Josef. Zeb. Digger. The others who'd died on Rory and Quinn's teams. Fatalities during the last year. Hell, since the mine opened its gates.

Jack knew in his heart who was responsible, although Victor declared Jack and his men the cause of the collapse, claiming their blast went bad. Victor produced a signed work order from mining records to prove everything. He kept his story steady and the officers backed him. Especially Barger, the sniveling, lying jackass. Only problem: Jack hadn't signed a work order. In fact, the mine didn't even have work orders. Yet documentation miraculously appeared.

Some chose to believe Creely. People turning away from truth because of its inconvenience, or because they didn't dare question a rich, powerful man of authority. Jack's friends knew better. The miners knew better. The town split in half thanks to Victor Creely and his unending quest for money and power.

Milena checked on Mouse and tucked a quilt around the boy. She glanced over and smiled. Jack almost trembled at how beautiful she looked, how kind she was, how incredible for her to be here, with him. Everything felt right.

Then anguish intruded. Pain smashed the cozy comfort of his home. Loss emptied him and distanced him from the ones he loved. And it wasn't over.

Jack knew it was only a matter of time before he was killed, or perhaps he might simply vanish like Stoop and Tom. Next, Victor would silence Pete and Gentleman Bill. Probably even Mouse, although the kid hadn't spoken a word since he'd gone deaf. And Victor wouldn't stop; there were plenty of people around to raise a ruckus. Milena, Taryn. Ambrose. Even Isabella. Jack's stomach knotted. Surely it wasn't possible for Victor to execute half the entire town?

Surely it was. Victor Creely's gluttony for money consumed anything and everything in its way. Jack had barely survived the man's greed. Many didn't.

He leaned his head back against the chair as Milena pulled one up to change his bandages.

"I have to stop him."

"Hush." Milena put a finger to his cracked lips. "Now is not the time for retribution."

He took her hand and kissed her fingers, relaxing as she rolled up his shirtsleeves.

"Not retribution," he said. "Survival. And not only mine."

"Allow your soul to heal along with your body. You need time, Jack."

"It's the one thing I don't have." Jack shook his head. "He won't stop, Milena."

She met his gaze. "I know."

"The only reason I'm still alive is the suspicion it would cause if I up and killed myself. He'll probably hang me; make it look like I did it. Which is one of the possible scenarios I'm sure he's planning. Distraught after my horrendous mistake."

"No one would believe it."

"Won't matter. I'll be dead." *Me and everyone I love.*

He fisted his hand and slammed the arm of the chair. Duke jumped to his feet and trotted a few feet away, glancing over his shoulder, eyes widened with worry.

"Goddamn it, and those sniveling bastards are backing him up. They all know the truth. Hell, they probably helped Victor forge hundreds of work orders. Signed work orders, one of the suggestions in my proposal." He shook out his throbbing hand. "I handed it to him, Milena, gave my ideas over like he is some sort of human being who might actually use them to do some good. He turned them into more ammunition for his sick, twisted arsenal. George Barger is blatantly lying! Right to my face!"

She watched, her eyes huge and infinitely patient. Her gentle composure was beyond calm, a steadiness to hold to, yet it did nothing to soothe him.

"They take what they want, say what they want. Everyone knows they are lying and they act like we are the ones who are wrong! Like we are too stupid to understand the situation." He jumped to his feet, and pain rolled through him. He didn't care. If he sat another second, he'd explode out of his skin. He wanted to pound something into bits.

Then her arms wrapped around him, and she settled her head against his chest. Holding her to him, he took in the scent of her hair. He'd never felt so downright furious and blessed at the same time.

She raised her face to look him in the eye. "You are not calming down." She reached up and smoothed his cheek, her touch cool and gentle. She kissed him.

He fell into the kiss; let her serene love wash through him. Then he demanded more, deepening his kiss, tasting her, feeling her. She responded; opened to him. His body took over, need driving him to take what she offered, pain decreasing to a small nuisance. A soft groan escaped from her lips, and she shivered, nearly driving him mad.

He pulled back before he lost the last bit of control he still possessed. "I guess calm is about the last thing I have on my mind." He glanced over at the bed. Duke hopped up to join Mouse, stretching himself out along the sleeping boy. Jack turned back to her amused expression. He let her go and, much as it pained him, returned to his seat. "Mouse isn't going to work another day in that mine," Jack said.

"No, he will not. Nor will you." She knelt down. "I need to change your bandages before the funeral," she said, unwrapping the gauze from his burns. His pain was fresh, but the fire seemed like it happened a hundred years ago.

"Luke," he said. "He's mixed up in all this. And Sam. He's vouching for Luke, saying I left the bar alone while Luke stayed behind. I think Sam spiked the whiskey he served me. Jesus, does Victor own this whole town?"

"Much of it, I think." Milena sighed. "I thought I had effectively distracted you."

"Oh, you did. Ouch!"

"I'm sorry," she said, her expressing changing into worry.

He hated that he'd put something other than happiness in her eyes. "Never mind me. I'm being difficult to get more attention."

He noticed, with a small pang of regret, that she continued a bit more carefully. This place had turned him into a jackass. His thoughts whirled back to the unending churn of Jasper. The mess was driving him to distraction, and he'd be damned if it mired him down another day. He'd leave. Positive the ranch was gone, he figured he had nowhere to go, but even the middle of the desert with no food, shelter, or water was safer than Jasper. He had no home, no guarantees of anything. He didn't care. All he cared about was a boy, a dog, and the most beautiful, intriguing woman in the world.

"Milena, I need to ask you a question."

She stopped her work and sat back to consider him. Her contemplation folded around him and stirred up desire. Again. Lord God Almighty, how could he be so damned angry, in such pain, and want a woman, all at the same time?

He wrapped himself in his courage and forged ahead. "If I leave, might you consider coming with me? I have nothing to my name at this point," he admitted. "I am, however, a fairly able man. I will take care of you and Mouse, and I want to head back to Texas. I'm sure Victor has foreclosed on the ranch by now, and I need to find out what happened to Buck and the boys. I've had enough of Jasper."

She nodded. "This is the way my people survived for hundreds of years. There is no disgrace in running."

Her words stopped the whirl in his brain.

"Running? I'm moving on with my life, taking you and Mouse to safety. Not running, exactly."

"Call it what you will, there is no shame."

Running. Shame. Damn.

He couldn't let Victor Creely hurt her. If they left, she'd be safer. He wasn't sure what to do about the others: Taryn, Pete, Bill, Ambrose.

A knock at the door blasted through the room. Jack jumped to his feet and ripped the door open before another knock sounded.

Sam stood outside. "Pardon me, Jack. Can I get a word?"

Jack glanced back to Milena. "I'll be right back." He closed the door behind him. "What the hell are you doing here?"

"I don't blame you for bein' sore. I swear I didn't have no inklin' of what Luke was doin'. I'm scared, Jack." Sam's words rushed out, over each other, panic pushing his voice close to tears.

"What? Slow down. Start over. Luke?"

"He paid me, Jack. A hunnert dollars. Just like he paid Rolf to help him with the Boarding House. Luke's gone and I'm next. I'm good as dead."

"Luke paid you? To what? Spike my whiskey?"

Sam nodded, his eyes watery. Jack wanted to feel sorry for the man. He just couldn't.

"What do you mean, Luke's gone?"

"Been missing since before you came up. Disappeared. I'm next. I swear I thought he just wanted you passed out for a time. I din't never think he'd hurt you, or Pete, or Dig or anyone like that."

"And Luke paid Rolf?"

"The night the Boarding House burned down. I swear, I didn't realize nothin'. Luke paid Rolf, drunked him up, and the two of them took off. Then the Boarding House burned down. I din't know what I got myself into." Sam looked down at the ground and then up into Jack's face. "I don't deserve nothin' from you, in fact, I owe you more than I'll ever be able to make up, but you gotta help me. I din't know. I swear."

Jack slammed his fist into Sam's face and the man crumpled at his feet. Blood ran down his face, along with tears. Jack grabbed Sam by the collar and pulled him up.

"You dare, you dare come to me for help? I held Digger in my arms. He died, Sam. Died." He shook the barkeep. "I'd just as soon kill you, but I don't think I'll need to. You're on your own." Jack tossed Sam off the porch, and he rolled in dirt. "You're right. You are a dead man. My best advice is to get out of town." Jack opened his door.

"I got nowheres to go," Sam wailed.

"Guess you should have thought about that sooner." He slammed the door behind him and stared into the fireplace. Watched the flames. Felt Victor's squeeze, like a snake around a rabbit, tighter and tighter.

"Jack?" Milena asked from Mouse's bedside. "Are you planning on leaving him out there?"

"I suppose not." He opened the door, stepped outside, and watched Sam cringe when he approached. He leaned over and pulled the crying man to his feet. "Come on in, let's get you cleaned up."

"You forgive me?"

"I wouldn't go that far," Jack said, helping him into the cabin. Milena was waiting at the door, and she helped Sam to the rocker and then scooted her chair up to him. Milena dabbed at the blood on his face while Jack talked.

"We're leaving right after the funeral," he told Sam, "and you should, too. You're right about being a dead man. So am I."

"Can I go with you?"

Jack shook his head. "Nope. I don't trust you, Sam. Digger died lying right next to me, thanks to you."

"I didn't—"

"Save it, Sam. I've been through too much. I might turn human again, but it's going to take some time. Until then, I don't trust myself not to thrash the bejesus out of you. It's a side of me I'd just as soon not let out."

Sam's face crumpled and a sound erupted. A sob. Jack realized he did feel sorry for the idiot. Milena finished up, and Jack walked Sam out to the porch.

"You were used. So was I. So were we all. I understand that, Sam, but please, do us both a favor. Stay out of my way."

Sam nodded. "Jack, I'm sorry."

"I know."

He went back into his house. Milena sat at Mouse's bedside, watching him. It hit Jack. This magical, caring, precious woman was as good as dead, too. And most likely Mouse.

Christ, he was going to explode into fury.

"You are a kind man, Jack Buchanan."

"Not sure it's for my own good."

"It is for good, your kindness. Do you need another distraction?"

"Always." He focused on her face, needing her now beyond anything, beyond reason. "When I came up from the mine, I remember you said something to me. I can't quite remember what it was. Memory's a mite feeble."

"I believe I told you I loved you." She rose and came to him to kiss him. "And feeble is not a word to describe you."

"Oh, I'm feeble all right." He held her, every muscle in him still brittle with tension. "What was that again? I didn't quite understand."

"I love you. I will say this as often as you like. You need no tricks with me, Jack Buchanan." She paused. "There is one other thing we must have clear between us."

"Oh?"

"Your offer earlier to take care of me and Mouse."

"Yes?"

"I will agree to this under one condition. You allow me to take care of you, as well. I am capable to stand on my own."

"You don't have to tell me that. I guess taking care of you and Mouse is what I want." Duke whimpered and they laughed softly. "Yeah, buddy, you, too. Duke and Milena and Mouse. And me."

"Together we will survive anything."

He bent down and kissed her. God, he'd waited his whole life to have this, a woman he loved in his arms to hold. A little boy. And not to forget the dog.

A family, a whole family. His.

He planned to keep them all safe. No matter the price.

People dotted the hillside, the number of open graves staggering. The worst disaster in Jasper's short history, and the man responsible stood on the west side of the graveyard, his officers closing ranks around him like an army of dandily dressed protectors. Some astonished Jack, folks like Constance Brown the schoolteacher; or Augustus Pritt the newspaper editor. An entire score of people he thought had more sense. Perhaps they'd given in to their fear despite what they knew in their hearts to be true, taking the safest and easiest way through the storm in Jasper.

On the opposite side of the freshly dug graves, Jack stood with the miners and their families. The Boarding House ladies congregated on the edge of the graveyard, their fine dresses ragged and worn. Strangely, their bedraggled state made the women even more appealing.

Between the two sides of the town, Reverend Taryn McShane stood with the dead.

Jack glared, shooting daggers of fury at Victor. The mine president returned his usual cool appraisal. Jack felt Milena's touch on the small of his back. She leaned into him, and her familiarity distracted him, along with how damned good she felt. He didn't drop his glare, in fact, he hoped Victor saw how much he enjoyed Milena's intimate touch. Victor's countenance did sour, just a bit.

"This is not the time for anger, Jack," she murmured under her breath.

"So you've said. What more appropriate opportunity than at the graves of these people?"

"Honor them. Mourn them. Hate has no place here."

He broke his stare down with Victor and looked at her. She smiled sadly, her face filled with compassion. Understanding. He put his arm around her shoulders and brushed his lips against her forehead.

"I hate it when you're right."

"You will become used to it." The teasing glint in her eyes diffused some of his outrage, for which he was grateful. It was hell keeping all this fury locked inside. Milena was correct, there would be a time and place to let it loose, just not now.

"Jack!" Gentleman Bill limped toward him, along with the other men from the clinic, quite a motley bunch. Two of the miners' wives helped their husbands. As Gentleman Bill passed he bowed slightly at Isabella, and offered her his arm. She took it, and Gentleman Bill escorted the madame of Jasper into the graveyard. Jack clenched his jaw to keep his mouth from dropping open in amazement. Isabella St. Claire on the arm of a miner? Her ladies followed suit, and even the unmarried miners found help as they gathered around the graves.

Bill hugged Jack. "You're lookin' pretty damned good. Guess you're getting 'bout the best care around. Other than us, of course." He stepped back and tipped his bowler hat. "Miss Milena, pleasure."

"I'm sure happy to convalesce at home. I've had plenty of the clinic for a while." Jack said. "I didn't realize you were out yet."

"Well, I'm not. We're not. Officially, that is."

"I can't keep a one of them away from this," Ambrose said as he approached. "I don't have the heart to try."

"Always said the doc knew what he was doing," Gentleman Bill answered.

"Jack, you do look very well. Milena, I see you are doing your job, of which I had no doubt. Where is Mouse?" Ambrose asked.

"Where you told us he should stay," Jack said. "In bed. With a big old hound dog for a nursemaid. Kid's pretty much slept since we brought him home. I didn't have the heart to wake him." Jack glanced over at Victor. "I intend to keep him as far from harm's way as I can."

Taryn stepped up and Jack's attention returned to the open graves, wood caskets lining each one. Fifteen coffins: fourteen miners, and one young woman.

Taryn began by flipping open his Bible. Jack saw markers, passages the minister intended to read. Taryn's voice rose, clear and strong, over the graves and crowd. "I will begin with some words from the holy Scripture. 'So will it be with the resurrection of the dead. The body that is sown is perishable, it is raised imperishable; it is sown in dishonor, it is raised in glory; it is sown in weakness, it is raised in power; it is sown a natural body, it is raised a spiritual body. If there is a natural body, there is also a spiritual body.'"

"And how many spirit bodies are here?" Jack whispered to Milena.

"I have no wish to upset you further," she said. "This day of grief and acknowledgment will help to release them."

Taryn raised his eyes and surveyed the gathering crowd. "Lord, we ask you to take these men and this woman into thy love and forgiveness, opening the gates to the Kingdom of Heaven, for these are thy servants, kind and true. Please join me, everyone, for the Lord's Prayer."

Voices skimmed through the graveyard, praying together. They rose and entwined from both sides, east and west, men and women, rich and poor. Fifteen men, not one an officer, moved forward with spades to shovel dirt over each casket.

From Victor's side, Cain smirked, probably contemplating Jack in one of the caskets. Thunder rumbled overhead, accompanied by the sound of dirt falling on wood. The prayer finished and the entire town paused, the quiet broken by an occasional ragged sob.

Taryn looked around both sides. "We, the people of Jasper, bury our fathers, husbands, friends, neighbors, and loved ones, and we give them over to you, dear Lord. Thank you for blessing us and granting us time on this earth in their company. We thank you for our lives, enriched by their love."

Thunder boomed and the sky flashed and split, pelting ice and cold rain over them all. Some people ducked and ran. Umbrellas popped open, black blooms speckling a field of mourners. The men who were shoveling kept to their task. Jack removed his hat and pulled it down over Milena's head. Ice stung his unprotected face, but he didn't move. The west side of the graveyard cleared, leaving only Victor, his officers, and Cain. The group around Jack held fast. Something here was more important than earthly comfort, the spirits of their friends, and the bodies they gave to the mountain.

Taryn raised his voice over the torrent of showering ice and rain, reading again from his book. "'The Lord is for me; I will not fear.'" The minister looked to Victor, his meaning unmistaken. "'What can man do to me? Blessed is the man who perseveres under trial, because when he is tried, he shall receive the crown of life God has promised to those who love him.'"

The mine president returned Taryn's glance with a glare of deadly intimidation.

"'Though a mighty army surrounds me, my heart shall not fear. Even if I am attacked, in this I will be confident.'" The minister didn't waver, but continued, solid and sure. "'The Lord hath delivered us from the dominion of darkness and hath brought us into the kingdom of the Son he loves, in whom we have redemption through his blood, even the forgiveness of sins.'"

Taryn closed his Bible. Victor's deadly attention never left the minister. And Jack knew Taryn had about as much chance of surviving Jasper as he did.

Chapter 32

Milena woke in the dark and knew immediately. She rose from the bedroll on the floor and lit the lantern. Mouse slept in the bed, Duke snoring beside him. But no Jack.

How did he get by without waking her? She ripped her shawl from the rocker, slung it around her shoulders, and headed outside, shutting the door with care. No sign of Jack outside either. Rain splattered, slow and steady, a constant pulse of falling drops.

The world wept.

Shuv'hani, *where is he?*

No answer, although it didn't surprise her. Her grandmother had moved on, as she was destined to do when Milena became Shuv'hani in her own right. The silences were confirmation Milena possessed her own awareness now. Apparently, the time to stand on her own was here.

She looked up in the direction of the mountain, now wrapped in nothing but the whisper of gently falling rain. Victor had been smart enough to agree to a pause in mining production, playing the bereaved mine president. Yet another of his façades.

When the sun rose, the deserted mine would again surge to

life as if nothing had happened. As if men hadn't lost their lives. The quest for precious metal would begin anew.

Where was Jack? Up at the mine? Or down at the graveyard? She did not sense any warning of danger, yet somewhere a sense of dread built. Foreboding. With a last glance through the window at the boy sleeping safely with Jack's huge dog, she grabbed the porch lantern and headed for the clinic, unable to stay in his house, worrying and waiting.

Perhaps sleep did not come to him, and he went to the clinic to check on his friends. Even as she hoped for this explanation to be true, she knew it was not. He would not up and vanish without telling her, not in a town struggling under the King of the Jackals.

As possibilities and fears whirled through her mind, she tried to run, only managing a quick, slippery pace. Rain soaked through her shawl. She shivered and tried to keep panic at bay; she grew tired of feeling it. She wanted some time where the fate of Jasper did not rest with her or Jack, where she could simply love him. Hold him. He needed time to rebuild his strength and life. He needed her. An air of melancholy had wrapped around him since he'd come out of the mountain, drained, his spirit crushed. The only real emotion left in him was the anger he constantly struggled to hold inside.

She reached the edge of town, her breath puffing out in a frosted mist against the cold, wet night. Spirits clumped, thicker than flesh-and-blood beings. They did not roam but watched her from every dark corner. Lurking in the shadows of the mercantile building, the Golden Guard glared, a spirit now, tied to Jasper forever by his anger. He frightened her, his fury a heavy cape whipping around him.

She spun around, not sure where to search. She didn't feel Jack was anywhere in town. Then where did he go? The nameless dread bloomed into a wave of anticipation. Something was about to happen. She looked up. From the night, the Church of God kept watch above the town of Jasper.

The minister. Taryn McShane would help her.

Jack saw a lantern spring to life in the dark of the Creely mansion. Perhaps the man's soul was rotted through with evil and mean, or maybe, as Milena had insisted, Victor really was a demon. But after everything that had happened, as sure as the sunrise would come in a few hours, Jack watched as Victor Creely kept to his schedule.

This was it. The moment to define Jack forever, one way or another. He'd either find the courage to do what was needed, stop the murderous evil from continuing in Jasper, or shrink and run.

He listened for footsteps while he breathed in chilly, predawn air. The death of winter crept near, closer than people thought.

Lantern light moved through the house and finally to the outside. Boots crunched on gravel. Jack imagined what was going through Victor's head. Three a.m. and this was a workday, after all. Never mind the dead. Open the mine. Start rebuilding. As every second passed, money ticked away. There was gold to mine, rules to instate, dignity to crush, people to kill.

Unless someone stopped Victor. Now.

Jack positioned himself on the path. The footsteps stopped. Silence. He knew Victor was too far off to see any more than a dark form. The lamplight molded the mine president's face into a semblance of a skull. When he'd first seen Victor, Jack mistook him for a portent of death. Now he knew the truth. Victor Creely was death.

"I have my gun trained on you, Victor. Even if you throw the lantern, I'll get you. Put your hands, palms out, in the air."

Victor's shadowed face grinned. Milena had dubbed him the "King of the Jackals," and never did he look more like a predator than now. "Oh, please, Jack. Shoot me where I stand?"

"I'm serious as a judge. Get your hands up," Jack said. Victor complied, the lantern dangling. It worried Jack, how damned good it felt to hold a gun on Victor Creely.

"Jack, I really don't have time for this. I need to start the operation up again. Without you." He paused. "Let me see, a desperate, bumbling shift boss, one about to be fired. I wonder who will hang for my murder? That is, if you ever find the nerve to pull the trigger."

"You think I care? I have Milena and Mouse packed and ready to go. We'll be long gone before anyone realizes and starts celebrating your demise." Jack hoped Victor didn't see the gun shaking.

The Jackal chuckled. "If you are hoping for a confession backing up your delusions, you have quite a long wait."

"Save it, Victor. We both know what happened. You paid to have the Boarding House burned down. You paid Luke to knock me out and stuff me in the mine. You sent my team, innocent men, including a child, to the area, away from everyone else. Then Luke or . . . Christ, you own half the people in this town. You paid someone to set blasts to kill us. Only we didn't die so good."

"And did Luke tell you all this? Has he surfaced to accuse me?"

"You killed him. No one in your employ seems to live very long."

"I've foreclosed on the ranch, you know. Buck is probably sitting on a pile of dirt by the side of the road as we speak."

"You think I care about Tumbling Creek anymore? After all this? Friends died in my arms."

"So you are going to shoot me? Somehow I can't see it."

Shooting Victor. The thought caused Jack's heart to thunder in his chest. Damn. This was no time for panic.

Victor continued, his voice smooth and easy, "After you kill me, you could put the gun in my hand; make it look like suicide. You should have thought this scheme through a tad better and ambushed me in my office. Much more effective and believable."

"You are one sick son of a bitch."

Victor laughed, an easy, amused sound. "Me? You're the one holding a gun on an unarmed man."

Jack lowered the weapon a bit. His arms trembled from the weight of the weapon, just as his body trembled from the weight of what he was about to do. "I'll give you a fighting chance."

Victor chuckled. "Oh, how very exciting."

"You're lucky I'm giving you a chance at all. You didn't give us one. Digger? He grew up in the orphanage. Worked for you since the age of thirteen."

"Mundane man, as I recall."

"Josef. His wife died, leaving his children with no mother. Now no father, thanks to you. Zebulon. One of the original prospectors. You must remember him. You tricked him, bought his land right out from under him."

"Is there a point to all this? Or are you attempting to work up your nerve to fire your gun? I must admit, I really preferred the silent, cowed Jack Buchanan."

Jack brought the gun level again. "Cassandra. Mild, gentle girl."

Victor sneered. "The whore? She died in the Boarding House fire."

"You were behind it."

Victor shrugged, the lantern swaying. "Really, Jack. Why bother to destroy such an inconsequential place?"

"To get to Milena. Beth. Because you are a sick excuse of a man. When Digger was dying, he told me he and Beth were in love. Your mistress preferred a miner to the great Victor Creely."

No response.

"You didn't realize Beth and Milena were gone from the Boarding House. You were too late, Victor. You're slowing down, like the old man you are."

Victor's expression soured. Jack knew he'd hit a mark.

"Tom Gallagher. Sent his check back to his family in Nebraska every month. Five beautiful girls. God only knows what will happen to them now."

"I didn't realize verbal torture was part of our deal."

"Tom. Stoop. Cassandra. Rolf. Josef. Zebulon. Digger."

"It's drizzling. You are causing me to ruin one of my best suits."

"Miles, Donny, Eddie, Rory, Joe, Riley, Ben, Gil, Limpy, Franklin. And all the others who have died since I got here."

"My arms grow weary from holding this ridiculous position."

"And the men who died before I ever came to Jasper." Jack's voice trembled with anger. "You have been mining copper and gold from innocent men's blood for years. And I won't even go through your list of deceased henchmen. As soon as you use people up, you kill them. God only knows how many people you've murdered. How many more you will. I can't let you go on, Victor. I just can't."

Now Jack did see a crack in Victor's façade. Uncertainty.

"I'm going to give you one chance. One chance, Victor."

Silence.

"Quit. Ask the New York investors to send someone else to run the mine. I'll be damned if I let you keep on like this."

Victor looked confused, even in the sketchy lamplight. "I'm a major shareholder. Even if I step down, I'll still receive my cut."

"Exactly, and you can do whatever you want with your filthy money. I don't give a damn about anything else other than getting you out of the equation. Sit back and collect your gold. But you can't have a hand in making it. Or running the mine. Or destroying people's lives. Your reign is over."

"You could have had everything, Jack. I loved you like a son."

"You don't have it in you to care about anyone or anything except yourself and your money. Hole up in your ugly mansion with your piles of gold, for all I care."

Victor sighed. "We could have built Jasper together. You turned away from all of it. From me."

"You thrive on causing pain. You trap and trick and torture. I swear, if you don't step down and quit, I'll stop you."

The demonic smile resurfaced on Victor's face. "The work orders prove you were responsible for the mine collapse. I planned to fire you today. I foreclosed on your ranch. It will be obvious who shot me in the dark. Like a coward."

"The mine doesn't have work orders. It was an idea in my proposal."

Victor's grin grew. "Oh, yes, we do. We have since the day the mine opened. I have the documentation to prove it."

"You are unbelievable." Jack started shaking again, and this time it was more than his hand and arm holding the gun. He shook to his core.

"Face it, Jack. You aren't man enough to forge your future. You let it happen to you and plodded along feeling sorry for your friends, drinking whiskey, and most pathetic of all, falling in love with a whore."

"Don't call her that again."

"Go ahead and shoot me. However, I believe Cain is right. You aren't a man. Of any kind."

Jack clenched his teeth to keep the shakes from reaching his voice. "Don't go to the mine, ever again. Turn around. Go home. Your time is finished."

"If anything happens to me, you'll be hanging from the gallows at dawn."

"Sit on your ass, and I'll let you live. We'll go right this moment and telegraph New York to tender your resignation."

Victor pressed forward, the light swinging. "I don't quit."

"Then I'll quit for you." Jack cocked his gun. The sound ricocheted through the dark night. "Don't go up there, Victor. This is your last warning. Turn around, go back home, and live. Or keep going and die. Your choice."

Victor didn't slow his step. "And I will enjoy consoling the Gypsy whore once you swing from the gallows."

"I warned you not to call her that again." He tried to suppress his anger but it came shaking right out of him. His throat closed.

Victor stopped, right in front of Jack, the gun almost touching his face. "Why, Jack, your gun is shaking." He brushed past. Jack swung around, still pointing the pistol. Victor stopped and turned. "Oh, one other thing I need to mention. I actually do know who burned down the Boarding House. Mr. Barger witnessed Reverend McShane set fire to the place. Seems our minister decided to clean up Jasper, take matters into his own hands. Barger's entire statement is in my safe, along with the work orders." He shrugged. "Look at it this way. At least you'll have company swinging from the gallows." Victor turned his back and chuckled. "Try shooting me in the back. You might be able to do it the coward's way. Although from what I see, I sincerely doubt you'll manage even that."

Jack held the gun at Victor's retreating back. "Stop now. This is your last warning."

Victor laughed. Jack watched the light climb up and disappear beyond the gate. Then boot heels, a hollow clack against wood. The office door slammed shut.

Jack lowered his gun and holstered it. Steeled himself against the hammering of his heart. Damned gun never did him much good, in his top dresser drawer or out. He wasn't sure if he even remembered how to fire it. But one thing he did know how to do.

Set a blast.

The office exploded, orange fingers of fire spitting out from windows. A fireball formed around the building as it collapsed. For a second, Jack saw the other buildings against the orange glow, the stamping mill, the headframe. Then all hell burst open, another explosion blossomed, and surrounding buildings smashed to the ground. Debris flew, twirling through the air and the dirt beneath his feet shook. A huge gust of pressure rolled over him, and two invisible thumbs pushed into his ears. He dove to the ground, covering his head.

Charred pieces of grit, dirt, wood, and probably Victor Creely rained down on him.

Chapter 33

"You will leave this behind." Milena pulled the pipe from Mouse as he tried to light it. "Little boys do not smoke pipes."

Mouse grimaced, leaned on his crutch, and glared at Jack.

"You wanted to come with us," Jack said, facing Mouse for the boy to read his lips. After hours of sound coming to him through muffled, rounded tones, Jack held a new appreciation for Mouse's world. But Jack's hearing had cleared by morning.

Milena never said a word, not even when he'd staggered home covered in dirt and ashes. She helped him clean up, her eyes not judging. He wished his heart could do the same.

"Don't worry, Mouse. A pipe is a small enough thing to give up. I hear her cooking's worth putting up with her bossiness."

"I do not cook," Milena said.

Jack piled the last box on their wagon. What Mouse owned he fit into a pack, and Milena's possessions were in a small, velvet sack she tied to her waist. Jack was the one with all the baggage.

"We leave so fast. Are you sure this is what you want?" Milena asked.

"If I stay another day, Cain will find a way to hang me."

"He is one of the few who hasn't turned on the King of the Jackals."

Jack shook his head. "The man had no friends. Only people he paid. All the officers care about is clawing over each other to get the promotion to president."

He helped Milena climb up to the seat as Mouse limped on his crutch, heading to the back. Jack lifted him up to sit with the furniture and Duke. Jack looked up at the mine. Only smoldering rubble was left. The blasts and fires had leveled the buildings, the stamping mill burned to leave a partial skeleton. The headframe had collapsed, the gallows finally gone. Jesus, he couldn't believe the chain reaction the explosion had started. "I warned Victor not to keep explosives so close to everything. Bound to happen someday."

What a waste. So much misery up there. Jasper taught him nothing was worth selling his soul, but something was worth throwing it away. He couldn't shake the heaviness weighing him down. Maybe he shouldn't try. Maybe he'd always feel this, the knot in his chest that wouldn't leave. The sick feeling he woke with in the morning.

Their wagon clacked down the road, Willow not at all pleased with the demotion to wagon horse. He promised her he'd never do this to her again, but he needed her, just this once.

Before they left town, they had one stop to make.

Taryn waited in the cemetery, Ambrose, too, and a pleasant surprise. Beth. She sat beside Digger's grave, a fresh bouquet of flowers lying on the muddy mound. The flowers' colors were faded, and some of the dirt splashed up on their delicate petals, yet they were still pretty. Although not quite as innocent and fresh, they survived despite their harsh surroundings.

Jack lifted Milena down and she headed straight for Beth,

kneeling beside the girl. Milena hugged her. Beth didn't respond, but continued to stare at the grave.

Taryn grabbed Jack and clapped him on the back. Ambrose shook his hand.

"She ever break from that?" Jack asked.

"Not so far," Ambrose answered. "I do have the highest of hopes. If you gentlemen will excuse me for a moment." He walked down the hill to Cassy's grave, kneeling beside it and bowing his head. Mouse hobbled over, grasping his crutch with one hand, swiping off his hat with his other.

Taryn turned to Jack. "Milena came to me last night, frantic. She couldn't find you," he said low for only Jack to hear.

He leveled a look straight into the minister's eyes. "I know."

It seemed Taryn waited for more. Jack refused to lie to him. He'd make no apologies, but he did have regrets. And guilt. More than he'd ever imagined. Although the world was much better off without Victor Creely, and Milena and Mouse were as safe as he could keep them, Jack didn't think he'd sleep in a long, long time.

Taryn finally broke the silence between them. "I can't believe you're leaving."

"Neither can I. I thought I'd be stuck in Jasper forever, and I didn't even make it a year. Now I have no home to return to."

"Any word from Buck?" Taryn asked.

"Nope. I have no idea where he and the boys are. I figure we'll head to the ranch and go from there. Someone will have heard or might have information. Besides, I travel with my own personal seer."

Taryn smiled although his expression remained sad. Jack knew how he felt. Empty. Used up. Old.

"What a damned waste. All this, nothing but a waste."

Taryn shrugged. "Life, Jack. Just life. Sometimes it calls on you to do things you'd never imagine." His eyes looked sharply beyond Jack, concern wrinkling his face. Jack turned.

Pete and Gentleman Bill were coming in his direction.

"Jesus, Mary, and Joseph, glad we caught you," Gentleman Bill said. Taryn winced. "Oh, sorry, Reverend," Bill added. "Jack, you ain't gonna believe this. Those blowhards from New York City are sending a gaggle of dandies to come and rebuild the company. They've named Barger interim president."

Victor had always been adamant that the miners were replaceable. Apparently, mining presidents were, too. Jack knew Barger came with his own danger. He might not be smart, or strong, but he loved money and control as much as Victor ever did.

Jack sighed. "I guess I shouldn't be surprised."

"Well," Pete said, "all in all not such a bad thing. We need jobs, Jack."

"Just not those ones we had," Gentleman Bill added.

Jack didn't believe what he heard. And from Bill and Pete, of all men. "It will start all over again, don't you see? The oppression, abuse, greed driving every decision."

Pete shook his head. "No, it won't. Not if you help us."

Milena rose and came to stand by his side.

Pete continued, "We have them right where we want 'em. They need workers to rebuild. We can negotiate going in. Just like you talked about. All of us. Together."

"We can fight for everything, Jack: your proposal, the petition, all of it," Gentleman Bill added. "We're starting from scratch and you have to help us."

"Oh, no," Jack answered. "I'm sick and tired of fighting. I'm leaving. Now."

"You have to stay." Pete grabbed his arm and Jack almost

flinched at the naked desperation in Pete's eyes. "No one can talk like you, is smart as you, can lead like you. You're the reason any of us came out of that mess alive. We need you with us, to start things right."

"There isn't a chance I will work at the mine again." Jack looked from Pete to Gentleman Bill. "My choice as well as theirs."

"We know you don't want to stay, so we're gonna collect money and pay you. You'll be the one to speak for us," Gentleman Bill said. Pete dropped his hand from Jack's arm and followed his every move, watching him intently. Jack decided to put words to it.

"You're talking about organized labor. A union." Jack glanced over at Taryn, who looked very concerned. "Are you aware of what happens when that starts? All this," he said, gesturing around him, "all this came from just a hint of us organizing. We aren't talking negotiation. It's confrontation, and it gets bad."

"Yep, well, we've heard tell. All this hasn't scairt us off," Bill said. "Tom, God rest his soul, the whole thing was his idea. Said over the water, workers fight for their rights, and we should, too. He's gone, Jack, and we need you. You started up where Tom left off, and you know we got lots farther to go."

Tom, not really a sheep, as it turned out. A leader. Just a gentle, unassuming one. God, he missed Tom and Dig. All of them.

"I don't have the heart for it anymore," Jack almost whispered.

"Thing is, Jack, you do. You got everything," Pete said. "All a man needs to face what's comin'. You'll do what a man's gotta do. No matter what." He looked straight at Jack. Pete's eyes didn't waver into judgment. "Look, we're takin' you by surprise. Why don't you talk to the missus and we'll wait at Sam's for you."

"Sam's?"

Bill shrugged. "Only saloon in town. And I need a whiskey. Besides, Sam's been awful generous with us and drinks since the cave-in. Only charges me half."

Pete jumped in. "Another settler party came in and they say another one is comin' soon after. This town is booming and we want to get Jasper Mine started out right this time. We can do it, if you help us."

Gentleman Bill nodded. "We need you, Jack"

Taryn rested his hand on Jack's shoulder. "You know where to find me if you want to discuss anything. Anything at all. But Jack, you'll know the right thing. You always do."

He supposed it was the closest he'd ever get to a statement of forgiveness from the minister. Now if he'd only forgive himself. He watched their backs as they left and then hugged Milena to him.

"What am I going to do?"

Milena looked up. "Whatever you decide, I will agree. You travel a sure path, Jack Buchanan. A strong one."

"You said your people survived by running. Will I end mine by staying?"

She shook her head. "I cannot answer this for you."

"Buck. The boys."

"They will find you. Your father knows you are in Jasper."

"And you and Mouse. I want the two of you to be happy. Safe. Always."

"Mouse is home here. He will not work at the mine, and perhaps never play as a little boy, but he has us now. And Duke. And Willow. He has everything in Jasper. As long as you are here, I do, as well."

Jack looked up at the mountain. Maybe not so much Hell as Purgatory. He wondered if he'd ever make it out.

Isabella St. Claire handed a pamphlet to Jack, Pete, and Gentleman Bill when they came through the swinging doors and stepped off the porch saloon. The three were in the bar for several hours and in the middle of the day. Shameful.

The trio's collective bewildered expression begged her to take it upon herself to enlighten them, as it seemed all men needed. Insight from the superior of the species.

"I'm running for mayor. The elections are in two weeks."

"Isabella, I hate to break the news to you, but women don't have any vote in the Colorado Territory," Jack said.

"Minor detail. We'll be a state any day now. The mayor we have is pathetic, in many, many ways, some of which I won't mention." She smiled. "Jasper needs me."

"I completely agree, however, women don't vote in the States, either," Jack said with his usual, boring Jack-earnestness.

"Another minor detail. And only a matter of time. Since when did Jasper follow any laws anyway?"

"I take exception to that," Cain said, pushing himself from his leaning position under the eaves of the saloon. "Plenty of law here."

"Besides," Isabella continued, "I've never had any problem with the male population of Jasper, which outnumbers women, oh, around a hundred to one." She winked at Bill. "I've become especially popular with the rough-living, hard-working men of the town."

She looked up to the church, the setting sun causing it to glow in a glorious, heavenly way. Wouldn't it be fun, the first time the minister of Jasper interacted with her as the mayor? They'd both sit on the town council. Perhaps she'd finally walk into the church, accepted. Mayor St. Claire. Her list of goals also included getting the handsome and forthright Reverend McShane exactly where she wanted him. She always aimed for the best. When he stood up to Victor Creely at the funeral in the rain, citing Scripture with such intense, unleashed passion, she'd almost swooned.

"You'll be a wondrous mayor, Miss St. Claire." Gentleman Bill swept off his hat. She granted a smile to him and him alone. The man was sweet, no argument there, and quite besotted, as well. Like a love-blinded pet. The perfect place for a man to be, in her opinion. The most important part: she knew she could trust him. Quite the important point to her, after everything she'd seen. And a surprise. Trustworthy men did exist. Not many, but even one was more than she would have ever believed.

"I do thank you, Gentleman Bill. By the by, I need a campaign manager."

"At your service, ma'am. Although, I'm not really the persuadin' type. You might as well want Jack."

"Trust me, I have my hands full for the next few decades," Jack answered cryptically with none of the usual, boring Jack-earnestness. How very interesting.

"You'll be rotting in jail, Junior."

"Really? For what, exactly?"

Dead silence blanketed the group. Cain finally broke it. "All them work orders and such were destroyed in the explosion. It wasn't no accident. The safe had to be packed with powder for it to blow to pieces like it did. You were behind it, and everybody knows it."

"Prove it," Jack said.

"Oh, I will. Somewhere, somehow, you slipped up, Junior."

"Gentlemen, a vote for me is a vote for Jasper's future," Isabella said quickly. "People are pouring in; the Jasper Mining Company has made a commitment to rebuild; we are becoming, quite honestly, the premier town of the territory. I will lead us into prosperity tempered with plenty of old-fashioned humility."

"You will," Bill said, as if on cue, "and this town will have an angel for a mayor."

Even the now-ever-serious Jack Buchanan groaned at Bill's words and chuckled, and Isabella was glad to see a bit of the old Jack come out.

Jack climbed the last part of the town walk and headed up Gooseneck Road. He'd talked Taryn into performing his and Milena's wedding ceremony in the heart of the mountain. Now he just needed to convince Milena to marry him. And before he took that step, he had to ask for her hand.

He laughed. He needed a wagon-load of courage now more than ever. Courage like, well, like Isabella St. Claire's. He had no doubt she would be the next mayor of Jasper. And he would be more than a handful for the New York investors.

Skeletal remains of mining buildings still smoldered. He wondered what the mine might see in the next year. Rebuilding, a new set of officers, men from New York coming to the frontier for the first time, yes. But what else? He smiled to himself, thinking he'd have to ask his seer.

Pete, Gentleman Bill, and the other miners had decided to call their group "Diggers Labor" in memory of their fallen friend. Jack wasn't sure exactly what was starting, but it was important. Bigger than the people beginning it. Jack saw every emotion at their first organized meeting, from hope and pride to anger and fear. Frustration and dreams. He knew enough to prepare for anything, no matter what his seer might reveal to him.

A chill brushed across his face, and he wondered who else might be watching. Behind him lay the town, the cemetery, the mine. Ahead of him rose Jasper Mountain, unforgiving and unchanging.

More than rock and trees and brush and gold, Jasper Mountain was an ancient force, one that lived, breathed. Watched. He had seen firsthand what swirled beneath the surface: the horrors and wonders, magic and realities, fears and hopes, promises and dreams, and not just of the ordinary. Dreams fragile and strong. Crystal dreams.

Jack knew the heart of Jasper Mountain. Just as he finally knew his own.

First, there is a River
Kathy Steffen

A family conceals a cruel secret.

Emma Perkins' life appears idyllic. Her husband, Jared, is a hardworking farmer and a dependable neighbor. But Emma knows intimately the brutality prowling beneath her husband's façade. When he sends their children away, Emma's life unravels.

A woman seeks her spirit.

Deep in despair, Emma seeks refuge aboard her uncle's riverboat, the Spirit of the River. She travels through a new world filled with colorful characters: captains, mates, the rich, the working class, moonshiners, prostitutes, and Gage-the Spirit's reclusive engineer. Scarred for life from a riverboat explosion, Gage's insight into heartache draws him to Emma, and as they heal together, they form a deep and unbreakable bond. Emma learns to trust that anything is possible, including reclaiming her children and facing her husband.

A man seeks revenge.

Jared Perkins makes a journey of his own. Determined to bring his wife home and teach her the lesson of her life, Jared secretly follows the Spirit. His rage burns cold as he plans his revenge for everyone on board.

Against the immense power of the river, the journey of the Spirit will change the course of their lives forever.

ISBN# 9781932815931
Trade Paperback
US $14.95 / CDN $18.95
Available Now
www.kathysteffen.com

Flight to Freedom
D.J. Wilson

I killed my husband, a town hero, and then called the police and turned myself in. "He's dead as a doornail," I said to the officer and then spit on Harland Jeffers' bloody, dead body.

With my head held high, I allowed myself to be escorted to a squad car outside my house. A house which had been more of a prison than the cell I was headed for.

Cameras flashed.

"Why did you kill Harland?"

Because he needed killing. And I, Montana Ines Parsons-Jeffers did just that.

So begins the rest of what's left of Montana's life. Not that she ever really had one.

Now she's headed for prison. There's no escaping it. It was the ultimate destination in her Flight to Freedom.

But one man might be able to help . . .

ISBN# 9781933836379
Trade Paperback
US $15.95 / CDN $17.95
Available Now
www.doloresjwilson.com

THE STRANGELY WONDERFUL

KAREN MERCURY

IT'S 1828, AND LIFE IS GOOD FOR THE
PIRATES OF MADAGASCAR . . .

Their Captain is the Hungarian Count Tomaj Balashazy, a refugee from the United States Navy. Count Balashazy rules the coast from his tropical plantation, a fortress built against enemies he's made cruising the Indian Ocean. Tomaj feels guilt at the loss of his family in New Orleans, and he wallows in clouds of opium, soothed by courtesans. When the American naturalist Dagny Ravenhurst, seeking the dreaded and mystical aye-aye lemur, falls into Tomaj's lagoon, it's the beginning of the end of arcadian bliss on the island.

In the central highlands, the French industrialist Paul Boneaux commands his empire of factories. As the special pet of psychotic Malagasy Queen Ranavalona, Boneaux enjoys a monopoly over all manufacturing, commerce, and his mistress. Beholden to Boneaux, Dagny and her two brothers need his patronage to survive. Dagny's joyless scientific heart melts for the Count's poetic nature, pitting the two adversaries against each other. Boneaux yearns for progress and industry, Tomaj for liberty and peace.

When the King dies—or is he murdered?—the Queen gives free reign to her merciless anti-European impulses. The island boils with blood, and only one world can emerge triumphant.

In Madagascar's utopian paradise, all is . . .
STRANGELY WONDERFUL

ISBN# 9781933836027
Trade Paperback / Historical Fiction
US $15.95 / CDN $19.95
www.karenmercury.com

BROKEN WING

Judith James

Abandoned as a child and raised in a brothel, Gabriel St. Croix has never known tenderness, friendship, or affection. Although fluent in sex, he knows nothing of love. Lost and alone inside a nightmare world, all he's ever wanted was companionship and a place to belong. Hiding physical and emotional scars behind an icy façade, his only relationship is with a young boy he has spent the last five years protecting from the brutal reality of their environment. But all that is about to change. The boy's family has found him, and they are coming to take him home.

Sarah Munroe blames herself for her brother's disappearance. When he's located, safe and unharmed despite where he has been living, Sarah vows to help the man who rescued and protected him in any way she can. With loving patience she helps Gabriel face his demons and teaches him to trust in friendship and love. But when the past catches up with him, Gabriel must face it on his own.

Becoming a mercenary, pirate and a professional gambler, Gabriel travels to London, France, and the Barbary Coast in a desperate attempt to find Sarah again and all he knows of love. On the way, however, he will discover the most dangerous journey, and the greatest gamble of all, is within the darkest reaches of his own heart.

ISBN# 9781933836447
US $7.95 / CDN $8.95
Mass Market Paperback / Historical Romance
www.judithjamesauthor.com

For more information
about other great titles from
Medallion Press, visit
www.medallionpress.com